NIGHT FANCIES

"The Pathways of Desire" by Ursula K. Le Guin—When an alien world seems to echo your own is it coincidence, illusion . . . or all too frighteningly true?

"Dream Done Green" by Alan Dean Foster—To humans Earth was a barely remembered legend but to another of the planet's star-faring descendants it was a dream to be reclaimed at any cost. . . .

"All On A Golden Afternoon" by Robert Bloch—As a film star she had made fantasy seem real for her many devoted fans. Now had she found someone who could work the same magic for her?

"Dreaming Is A Private Thing" by Isaac Asimov—First there were the movies, then there were the dreamies. . . .

These are but some of the dream realms you'll explore in—

THE NIGHT FANTASTIC

THE NIGHT FANTASTIC

edited by

POUL & KAREN ANDERSON

DAW BOOKS, INC.

DONALD A. WOLLHEIM, FOUNDER

375 Hudson Street, New York, NY 10014

ELIZABETH R. WOLLHEIM
SHEILA E. GILBERT
PUBLISHERS

Cover art by Peter Goodfellow.

DAW Book Collectors No. 848.

First Printing, April 1991

1 2 3 4 5 6 7 8 9

DAW TRADEMARK REGISTERED
U.S. PAT. OFF. AND FOREIGN COUNTRIES
—MARCA REGISTRADA.
HECHO EN U.S.A.

PRINTED IN THE U.S.A.

ACKNOWLEDGMENTS

CONTENTS

INTRODUCTION

by Poul and Karen Anderson

O passerby, pause and hear a tale!

In a faraway land there lived a king whose wife's beauty was the wonder of the age. It happened that a poor man dreamed that he kissed her, and afterward foolishly boasted of this. The king, hearing of it, summoned him and sentenced him to pay a fine of one hundred cows.

"Where am I to get a hundred cows?" cried the unhappy offender. And he went to a wise man for advice.

Said the wise man, "Borrow them, drive them to the bank of a lake, and let the king take their reflections; for a dream is only a reflection, and the reflection of a crime can be paid for with the reflection of a fine."

This old Oriental story comes as a surprise. Such a pragmatic attitude toward dreams was otherwise almost unheard of until quite recent times. Even today, these events in our heads can have obscure power; and science has yet to fathom their nature.

To primitive humans they were often not subjective at all, but of the same order of reality as everything else. (So they still often are to small children.) The dead came back; animals, trees, the wind spoke words; one flew, or one fell into endless depths; horror, joy, dread, comfort radiated from beings half seen. It may have been the origin of belief in an afterlife, demons, and gods. Surely it had much to do with the forms that belief took.

What courage there must have been in those individuals who first sought to understand and actually use their dreams! Disciplines and institutions evolved, whole ways of life. A shaman's training prepared him to enter the dream state at will and get instruction from its dwellers. In a number of societies it was thought that, while his body lay quietly in sleep, his soul roved widely through this world and the next.

Also, for the ordinary tribesman, dreaming could be an important part of life. Thus, the young Plains Indian brave, during his initiation into manhood, fasted alone until his spirit protector came to him in his sleep. Among certain Pacific islanders, the relating of dreams to each other in the morning was a daily ritual. Everywhere, anyone might have a dream that warned, counseled, or foretold the future. In our own high-tech civilization, millions of people continue to suppose that this happens.

Jacob's ladder and Pharaoh's dream that Joseph interpreted are just the most familiar examples from the Bible. God promised Joel that "your sons and your daughters shall prophesy, your old men shall dream dreams, your young men shall see visions."

Not all were to be trusted, of course. The Greeks distinguished between the false, which came through the gates of ivory, and the true, which came through the gates of horn.

The Far East philosophized about them. It is said that Chuang Tzu once dreamed that he was a butterfly that dreamed it was a sage. On awakening, he asked, "Am I, even now, only a butterfly's dream?" Many Hindus hold that the entire universe is a dream that Brahm is having. This will remind English-speaking readers of the White King in *Alice Through the Looking Glass*.

After the scientific method conditioned Western awareness, the search for a rational theory of dreams was inevitable. Sigmund Freud's idea, that they express memories and desires the conscious mind would fain hold down, became a foundation stone of whole schools of psychology and psychotherapy. Later research, especially in the laboratory, seems to disconfirm this as a general explanation, though it may keep some limited validity.

Experiments have shown that normal sleep alternates between periods of dreaming, indicated by rapid movements of the closed eyes, and dreamlessness. Dreaming is evidently essential to health; subjects consistently roused when they begin to dream soon become nervous, irritable, less and less rational, and at last well-nigh psychotic. In everyday life, too, prolonged sleep deprivation is apt to bring on hallucinations, as though the organism is trying desperately to provide itself with dreams. The reason for this need remains unknown. The late Christopher Evans compared the brain to a computer and suggested that it, like its analogue, requires intervals of "down time," and that dreaming represents its revision of its selfprogramming. Francis Crick, of DNA fame, feels that dreams are, roughly speaking, garbage of which the brain is ridding itself, and that the sooner we forget ours afterward, the better.

Maybe. Yet most of us recall several that were wonderful. We think of August Kekulé, who first envisioned the benzene ring in a dream, or of writers, composers, and other artists to whom great ideas came in that fashion. Lately, a few persons have been undertaking lucid dreaming, the course of which they choose and control. They report nothing but good of it.

So humankind remains far from understanding this thing that it spends so much of its earthly span doing. Perhaps it never quite will.

We do know that the fact of dreaming has inspired many stories. Some of them are almost as rich and strange as their source. We offer a sample here, for the pleasure of your waking hours—and your sleeping ones?

THE PATHWAYS OF DESIRE

by Ursula K. Le Guin

Tamara had thought he was off taping, but he was in his hut, lying on the cot, looking thin and cold. "Sorry, Ram! I'm after those photographs of the kids."

"That box." His gesture pointing out which box was so uncharacteristically languid that she asked guardedly, "You all right?"

"Could be better." From him, the admission was a catalogue of misery; but still she did not drop her guard. She waited, and he said, "Diarrhea."

"You should have said something."

"Humiliation."

Bob was wrong, then. He did have a sense of humor.

"I'll ask Kara," she said. "They must have something for the trots."

"Anything but hotdogs and milkshakes," Ramchandra said, and she laughed, for the description was apt; the staple foods of the Ndif were boneless poro meat and the mushy sweet fruit of the lamaba tree.

"Keep drinking plenty. I'll refill that. Lomox doesn't help?"

"Nothing left for it to work on." He looked up at her; his eyes were large, black, and clear. "I wish that I throve here," he said, "like Bob."

That took her off guard. Rebuff and aloofness she expected, trust and candor she did not. She was unready, and her response inadequate. "Oh, he's happy here."

12

"Are you?"

"I hate it." She dangled the crude clay water jug and sought exactness. "Not really. It's beautiful. But I . . . get impatient."

"Nothing to chew," Ramchandra said bitterly. She laughed again, and went to fill his water jug at the spring a few meters away. The brightness of the sunshine, the perfumes of the air, the gorgeous colors of the lamaba trees, purple trunks, blue and green leaves, red and yellow fruits, all were delightful; the little spring welled up holy and innocent in its bed of clean brown sand. But she returned with gratitude to the hut containing one sullen linguist with diarrhea. "Take it easy, Ram," she said, "and I'll try and get something useful out of Kara and the others."

"Thank you," he said.

Lovely words, she thought as she went down the path through perfumed light and shadows toward the river; lovely in the man's soft, precise accent. When their team of three had first been put together, at the Base on Ankara, she had been drawn to Ramchandra, a direct, powerful, unmistakable attraction of sex. She had suppressed it, with self-mockery and some shame, for the man was cold, holding himself ostentatiously apart and untouched. And then there was Bob, big beautiful blond Bob, lean tanned tough Bob, perfect hero of male wish fulfillment, irresistible. Why resist? Easier to give the easy pleasure he expected; easy, pleasant, a little depressing, but never mind that. Don't look down into depressions. You might fall in. Live life as it comes, etc. She and Bob would come together inevitably. But they hadn't; for the three of them had come to Yirdo, and met Yirdo's inhabitants, the Ndif.

The Young Women of the Ndif—all females between age twelve and age twenty-two or -three—were sexually available, eager, and adept. They had bright wavy hair of gold or russet, long tilted eyes of green or violet, slender waists and ankles. They wore soft garments of slit pandsu leaves, clinging, modestly parting to reveal the merest glimpse of buttock or nipple. The under-fourteens danced the hypnotic saweya dance in long lines, chanting in their soft, light voices, their round faces mischievously serious. From fourteen to eighteen they danced the baliya, leaping naked, one at a time, into the circle of swaying, clapping men, twisting their sinuous bodies into all the postures of practiced eroticism, while the girls waiting their turn to dance sang the pulsing chorus, "Ah-weh, weh, ah-weh, weh . . ." After they were eighteen they no longer danced in public. Tamara left it to Bob to find out what they did in private. After forty-one days on Yirdo he was indubitably an expert in that.

She saw now that though she hadn't wanted him the promptness, the flatness of his loss of interest in her had hurt. Even last night she had been flirting at him; competing, with short wiry hair, shitbrindle eyes that tilted the wrong way, muscular wrists. . . . Stupid, stupid her self-mockery, her self-abasement, her self, self, self swept away now like veils of cobweb as she followed the forest path downward to the washing place at the river thinking, how beautiful the bridge of Ram's nose is. He can't weigh much more than I do, maybe less; fine-boned. Thank you, he said. "Askiös, Muna! How's the baby? Askiös, Vanna! Askiös, Kara!" How beautiful thy nose, my beloved, like unto a promontory between two wells of water, and the water thereof is exceeding black and cold. Thank you, thank you. "Hot today, no?"

"Hot today, hot today," all the Middle-Aged Women agreed enthusiastically as they trampled out the village laundry in the shallow laughing water. "Put your feet in the river, you'll get cool," Vanna encouraged her. Brella patted her shoulder affectionately, murmuring, "Askiös!" as she went by to lay out her portion of the village laundry on a rock to dry.

The Middle-Aged Women were between twenty-three and (forty? data still uncertain), and some of them, in Tamara's opinion, were more beautiful than the Young Women, a beauty which included missing teeth, sagging breasts, and stretchy bellies. The gapped smiles were blithe, the drooping tits held the milk of human kindness, the pregnancy-streaked bellies were full of belly-laughs. The Young Women giggled; the Middle-Aged Women laughed. They laughed, Tamara thought watching them now, as if they had been set free.

The Young Men were off hunting poro (the pursuit of the fanged hotdog, she thought, and she too, being a Middle-Aged Woman of twenty-eight, laughed); or they were sitting goggling at the saweya and baliya dancers; or they were sleeping. There were no Middle-Aged Men. Males were Young till about forty, when they stopped hunting, stopped watching the dancers, and became Old. And died.

"Kara," she said to her best informant, while she took off her sandals to put her feet in the cool water as Vanna had suggested, "my friend Ram is sick in the belly."

"Oh me, oh dear, askiös, askiös," the nearby women murmured. Kara, who looked to be pretty nearly an Old Woman, her knotted hair thin and graying, demanded practically, "Is it gwullaggh or kafa-faka?"

Tamara had never heard either word before, but translation was superfluous. "Kafa-faka," she said.

"Puti berries, he needs," said Kara, slapping a loin-cloth on a wet boulder.

"The food we eat here, he says it's very good, too good."

"Too much fried poro," said Kara, nodding. "When children eat too much and spend all night shitting in the bushes, you feed them puti berries and boiled guo for a week. It tastes all right, with honey. I'll boil Uvana Ram a pot of guo as soon as the washing's done."

"Kara is a beautiful noble person," Tamara said. It was a stock phrase, the usual Ndif way of saying thank you.

"Askiös!" said Kara, grinning. That was a much commoner, and more difficult, expression. Ramchandra had arrived at no set translation for it. Bob had suggested the German *bitte*, but it covered even more ground than *bitte*. Please, you're welcome, sorry, wait a minute, never mind, hello, goodbye, yes, no, and maybe all seemed to fall within the connotations of askiös.

With her questions about kafa-faka and how to wean babies and when you had to stay in the Unclean Huts and what was the best kind of cooking pot, Tamara was always a welcome excuse for a conversation break. They sat around on hot boulders in the cool water and let the river wash the laundry and the sun dry and bleach it while they talked. With a part of her mind Tamara listened to Heraclitus telling her that you shall not step twice into the same river, with the rest of it she sought information concerning birth control among the Ndif. The subject once opened, the women discussed it leisurely and frankly, but there wasn't much to discuss. There were no devices or systems of birth control at all. Nature provided for the Young Women: for all their single-minded devotion to erotic practice, they did not become fertile till they were over twenty. Tamara was incredulous, but the women were perfectly certain: the dividing line between the Young and the Middle-Aged was, in fact, fertility. Once the line was crossed, their only protection against perpetual pregnancy was abstinence, which they admitted was boring. Abortion and infanticide were not mentioned. When Tamara cautiously suggested them, heads were shaken. "*Women* can't kill *babies*," Brella said with horror. Kara observed more dryly, "If they get caught at it, the Men pull out all their hair and send them to the Unclean Huts to stay." "Nobody in our village would do such a thing," Brella said. "Nobody got caught at it," Kara said.

A group of Juvenile Males (nine to twelve) came whooping down to the river to swim and fish. They ran right over the drying laundry; the laundresses scolded, unauthoritatively; and the conversation ceased, because the ears of Males were not to be polluted with Unclean talk. The women rescued the laundry and set off back to the village. Tamara looked in on Ramchandra, who was asleep, and went on to take some photographs of Juvenile Males playing bhasto. After supper—communal, cooked and served by the Middle-Aged Women—she saw Kara, Vanna, and old Binira go into Ramchandra's hut, and followed them.

They woke him up and fed him boiled guo, pinkish cereal like sticky tapioca; they rubbed his legs, sat on his shoulders, put heated stones on his stomach, rearranged his cot so that he lay with his head to the north, made him drink a sip of something hot, black, and minty-smelling; Binira sang at him for a while; they left him at last with a fresh hot stone and went off. He accepted all this with ethnological aplomb or with the satisfaction of the invalid being fussed over. When they had gone he looked comfortable, curled up around the large rock and half asleep. Tamara was going out when he asked in a remote, tranquil voice, "Did you tape the old lady's song?"

"No. Sorry."

"Askiös, askiös," he whispered. Then, propping himself on his elbow, "I am better. Too bad we didn't tape that. I missed most of the words."

"Is Old Ndif a different language?"

"No. Only much fuller. Complete."

"The Middle-Aged Women seem to have a much bigger vocabulary than the Youngs."

"At Buvuna, the Young Women averaged seven hundred words and the Young Men eleven hundred, since they have the hunting vocabulary; I estimate the Middle-Aged Women here to know at least twenty-five hundred words. I can make no estimate of the Old Men and Women yet. These are odd people." Ramchandra lay back and cautiously rearranged himself around the hot stone. His tone also was cautious. There was a slight pause.

"Do you want to sleep?"

"To talk," he said.

Tamara sat down on the woven cane stool. Beyond the open doorway the night was growing bright as day had been; Uper, the big gas-planet of which Yirdo was a moon, was rising over the forest like a vast striped balloon. Its silver-gilt light pierced every crack in the mud and wattle walls of the hut and pooled incandescent on the ground outside the doorway. The dusk inside the hut was shot through with gleams, shafts, arrows dazzling the eye, a light that revealed nothing, that dissolved bodies and faces into radiant darkness.

"Nothing is real," Tamara said.

"Of course not," said the other shadow, amused, precise.

"They're like actors."

"No."

"Yes. I don't mean consciously acting, deceiving. I mean artificial. Too simple. Beautiful simple people in ever-bountiful paradise."

"Ha," Ramchandra said, and a patch of planetlight blazed in his hair as he sat up.

"Why shouldn't there be a South Sea Island world?" she argued with herself. "Why does it seem too simple—phony? Am I a puritan, am I looking for original sin?"

"No, no, of course not. Rubbish," he said. "All that is theories. But listen." For a minute he said nothing to listen to, then he said some Ndif words: "Vini. Pandsu. Askiös. Askiös-bhis iyava oe is-bhassa. . . . What is that in English?"

"Well . . . 'Please let me get by.' "

"Literal translation!"

"The great teaching tradition of the Brahmin Caste," Tamara said. "I don't know, the words have so many uses. 'Sorry, I want to go this way'?"

"You don't hear it."

"Hear what?"

"People cannot hear their native language. All right, listen carefully, please!" He was charming when he got excited; the hauteur fell off him like dried mud from a water buffalo. "I'm going to say a sentence in English the way my uncle, who didn't attend World Government School, spoke English. Now. 'Excuse please I have to go by this path.' Repeat!"

"Excuse please I have to go by this path."

"Askiös-bhis iyava oe is-bhassa."

A chill, like a touch of that cold dazzling planetlight, proceeded slowly up Tamara's backbone and prickled in the roots of her hair.

"Funny," she said.

"Saweya: sway. Baliya: belly-dance, Bali. Fini: ravine, vines. Bhasto: bat, baseball. Bhani: cabin, cabana. Shuwushu: ocean, sea—"

"Onomatopoeia."

"Oe: go. Tunu: return. Itunu: I return, utunu: you return, tunusi: he returns. Padu, to hit, strike. Fatu, to build, make—facere, factus—factory. Say a word in Ndif!"

"Sikka."

"Fishing lines. Wait. No, I can't get that one. Another please."

"Fillisa."

"The Unclean Huts—filth, filthy."

"Uvanai."

"Strangers. Visitors. Foreigners . . . singular uvana. You—foreigner."

"Ram, you don't have diarrhea. You have paranoia."

"No," he said, so harsh and loud that she started. He cleared his throat. She could see his eyes but she knew him to be looking at her. "I am serious, Tamara," he said. "I am frightened."

"Of what?" she jeered.

"Frightened sick," he said. "Scared shitless. You must take words seriously. They are all we have."

"*What* are you frightened of?"

"We are thirty-one light-years from Earth. No one from Earth ever came to this solar system before us. These people speak English."

"They don't!"

"The structure and vocabulary of Young Ndif is based at least sixty percent upon the structure and vocabulary of Modern English."

His voice shook, as if with fear, or with relief.

Tamara sat stolidly, clasping her knees, and held

fast to incredulity. A Ndif word went through her
mind, and another, and another, each one followed by
its English root or shadow, shadows that had been
waiting for the light to show them; but it was absurd.
She should not have said the word "paranoia." It was
true. The man was ill. Weeks of touch-me-not rude-
ness and now this sudden change to talk, excitement,
warmth. A manic change; and paranoid. The Ndif
speaking an English-based code, for mysterious purposes, understood by the expert alone. . . . ono, one.
Te, two. Ti, three . . .

"All female names," Ramchandra said morosely,
"end in 'a.' That is a cosmic constant established
by H. Rider Haggard. Male names never end in 'a.'
Never."

His voice, light-timbred, still a little uneven, confused her thoughts. "Listen, Ram."

"Yes."

He was listening, all right. She could not ask him, as
she had intended, whether he was playing an elaborate
and disagreeable joke on her. His trust must be met in
kind. She did not know how to go on; and he broke
urgently into her pause: "I saw this within a week,
Tamara. First the syntax—then I wouldn't see it. Meaningless coincidence, et cetera, et cetera. I said no. But
it says yes. It is so. It is English."

"Even the Old Language?"

"No, no, that's different," he said, hurried, grateful, "that's not English, that's itself, wherever it's not
based on the babytalk. But the—"

"All right, then. The Old Language *is* old, the original language, and the Youngs have been influenced,
corrupted, by some contact with Space Service people
we don't know about, weren't told about."

"How? When? They say we are the first. Why would
they lie?"

"The Space Service?" she asked.

"Or the Ndif. They both say we are the first!"

"Well, if we are the first, then it's us. *We*'re influencing the Ndif. They talk the way we unconsciously expect people to talk. Telepathy. They're telepaths."

"Telepaths," he said, seizing the idea eagerly; and during the pause that followed he was evidently wrestling with it, trying to make it fit the circumstances, for he said at last, with frustration, "If only we knew anything about telepathy!" Tamara meanwhile had been going around the problem in another direction, and asked, "Why didn't you say anything about this till now?"

"I thought I was insane," he said in the controlled precise tone that sounded arrogant because his honesty would not permit him to evade. "I have been insane. Six years ago, after my wife died. There were two episodes. Linguists are often unstable."

After a little while Tamara said almost in a whisper, "Ramchandra is a beautiful noble person." She spoke in Ndif.

Ah-weh, weh, ah-weh, weh, went the chanting of the baliya dancers off on the dancing grounds at the edge of the village. A baby cried in a nearby hut. The dark-dazzling air was rich with the scent of the night-blooming flowers.

"Look," she said. "Doesn't a telepath know what you're thinking? The Ndif don't. I've known people who do. My grandfather, he was Russian, he always knew what people were thinking. It was maddening. I don't know if it was telepathy, or being old, or being Russian, or what. But anyhow, they'd get the *thoughts*, not the *words*—wouldn't they?"

"Who knows? Maybe—You said it's like a stage play, a movie, the island paradise. Maybe they sense what we expect or desire, and act it, perform it."

"What for?"

"Adaptation," he said, triumphant. "So that we like them and therefore don't harm them."

"But I *don't* like them! They're boring! No kinship systems, no social structure except stupid age-grading and detestable male dominance, no real skills, no arts—lousy carved spoons, all right, like a Hawaiian tourist trap—no ideas. Once they grow up, *they're* bored.

Kara told me yesterday, 'Life's much too long.' If they're trying to produce a facsimile of somebody's heart's desire, it isn't mine!"

"Nor mine," Ramchandra said. "But Bob?"

There was a harshness, a homing-in quality, to the question. Tamara hesitated. "I don't know. At first, sure. But he's been restless lately. After all he's a myths man. And they don't even tell stories. All they ever talk about is who they slept with last night and how many poro they shot. He says they all talk like Hemingway characters."

"He doesn't talk with the Old Ones." Again that harshness, and Tamara, defensive of Bob, said, "Neither do I much; do you? They don't participate, they seem so shadowy . . . unimportant."

"That was a healing song old Binira sang."

"Maybe."

"I think so. A ritual song, in the more complex language. If there is high culture, the Old Ones have it. Maybe they lose the telepathic power as they grow older; so then they can withdraw; they're no longer influenced, forced to adapt—"

"Forced by whom to adapt to what? They're the only intelligent species on the planet."

"Other villages, other tribes."

"But then they'd all talk each other's language, all their customs would melt together—"

"Exactly! That explains the homogeneity of the culture! A solution to Babel!"

He sounded so pleased, and it sounded so plausible, that Tamara did her best to accept the hypothesis. The best she could do was admit finally, "The idea makes me queasy, for some reason."

"The Old Ones have developed true language, nontelepathic language. They are the ones to talk with. I will request admission to the Old Men's House tomorrow."

"You'll have to grow some gray hair."

"Easily! Is it still black?"

"You'd better get some sleep."

He was silent awhile, but did not lie down. "Tamara," he said, "you are not humoring me, are you?"

"No," she said gruffly, shocked that he was so vulnerable.

"It is so very like a delusional system."

"Then it's *folie à deux*. All this about the language just brings the rest into focus. All six villages we've visited, all the same, the same things missing, the same . . . improbability. Only it's like overprobability—"

"*Projected* telepathy," he said, brooding. "*They* are influencing *us*. Confusing our perceptions, forcing us into subjectivity—"

"Driving us away from the Reality Principle?" she said, defensive now of him. "Rubbish." She recognized the quotation and laughed. "We're talking much too cleverly to be gaga."

"I talked brilliantly in the mental institution," he said. "In several languages. Even Sanskrit." He sounded reassured, however; and she stood up. "I'm going to bed," she said. "A fine night's sleep I'll have now! Do you need a fresh hot rock?"

"No, no. Listen. I'm sorry—"

"Askiös, askiös."

No rest for the wicked. She had just lit her oil lamp and was spitting on her fingers and pinching the wick to keep it from smoking, which it continued to do, when Bob appeared in the doorway of her hut. The light of Uper haloed his thick fair hair; the importance of his return filled the entire biosphere as the bulk of his body filled the doorway. "I just got back," he announced.

"From where?"

"Gunda." The next village downriver. He came in and sat down on the cane stool while she swore at the burned poro fat on her fingers. An even more world-shaking announcement than that of his return loomed imminent in his scowl. She beat him to the draw. "Ram's sick," she said.

"What with?"

"Delhi belly, you could call it."

"How could anybody get sick here?"

"They have a cure. You sleep with a hot boulder."

"Christ! Sounds like a cure for potency!" Bob said, and they both broke into laughter. While laughing she almost began to tell Bob about Ram's peculiar linguistic discovery, which for a moment seemed equally ridiculous; but she should let Ram do it, even if it was just a joke. Bob had gone serious again, and now emitted his announcement. "I have to fight a duel. Single combat."

"Oh, Lord. When? Why?"

"Well, that girl. Potita, you know, the redhead. One of the Young Men in Gunda has his eye on her. So he challenged me."

"An exogamy arrangement? Has he a claim on her?"

"No, you know they don't have any affiliation patterns. Stop hunting for them. All she is is an excuse for a combat."

"I thought you'd get into trouble," Tamara said priggishly, though she had thought no such thing. "You can't sleep with all the native girls and not expect the assegai of a maddened savage in your back. Half the native girls, OK, but not all of them— "

"Shit," Bob said with discouragement "I know. Look, I never got mixed up like this before. Sleeping with informants and stuff. I can't seem to keep anything straight here. But they *expect* it. We talked it all out, way back in Buvuna, remember? Ram said he wouldn't. That's OK. He's forty, he's an old man to them. Anyhow, he looks alien. But I look just like them, and if I refuse I'm offending local custom. It's practically the only custom they've got. I have no choice—"

A laugh, a deep Middle-Aged Woman belly-laugh, welled up from Tamara. He looked at her a little startled. "All right, all right," he said, and laughed too. "But God damn it! They always talked like these combats were voluntary!"

"They're not?"

Bob shook his head. "I represent Hamo village

against Gunda. It's the only kind of war they have. All the Young Men are really worked up. They haven't won a combat with Gunda for half a year, or some such huge historical timespan. It's the World Cup. Tomorrow I get purified."

"A ceremony?" Tamara found Bob's predicament funny but trivial; she leapt from it to the hope of a ceremony, a ritual, anything that would prove some sense and structure in the rudimentary social life of the Ndif.

"Dances. Saweya and baliya. All day."

"Bah."

"Look, I know you'd like some patterns to study, being a configurationist and all, but I have an even more urgent problem. I have to fight a man day after tomorrow. With knives. In front of the entire population of two villages."

"With knives?"

"Right. Hunters wrestle. Sallenzii fight with knives."

"Sallenzii?"—As Bob translated, "Competitors for a girl," she transliterated: "Challengers . . ."

After a short silence she suggested, "Could you just give him the girl?"

"No. Honor, local pride, all that."

"And she . . . she's content just to be the prize pig?"

Bob nodded.

"The pattern is familiar," she said, and then abruptly, "Nothing—there is nothing alien about these people. Nothing!"

"What?"

"Never mind. Let me work it out. Ram has an idea. . . . Listen, Bob, I think you ought to get out of this, even if you lose face. We can always move on. It would be better than you killing the fellow! Or getting killed."

"Thanks for the afterthought," Bob said kindly. "Don't worry. I'll cheat."

"Hypodermic?"

"Karate ought to do. I don't mind. It's just that I

feel so damned foolish. Public knife fights for a girl. Like a lot of stupid teen-agers."

"It's a teen-age society, Bob."

"Locker-room aliens!" He scratched his lion's-mane hair and stood up stretching. He was very beautiful; no wonder the villagers had picked him for their champion. The fact that his physical splendor was informed and animated by an intellectual spirit of no less splendor, a passionate trained mind that sought the stuff of poetry for its own sake—this fact would mean nothing much to the Ndif, or to many people on Earth, for that matter. But Tamara, in that moment, saw the young man as what he was, a king.

"Bob," she said, "say no. Beg off. We can just move on."

"No sweat!" he said and, grateful for her concern, gave her an affectionate bear hug. "I'll clobber the poor bastard before he knows what hit him. And then give a lecture. Freshman Hygiene: Murder Is Hazardous to Your Health. It'll wow 'em."

"Do you want me there, or not there?"

"There," he said. "Just in case he's a black belt too."

She was down at the laundry beach next afternoon having an interesting discussion of menopause with Kara and Libisa when Ramchandra came out onto the beach from the peacock-colored forest. Watching him from her rock amid the swirling waters, she thought how foreign he looked, how alien, as Bob had said, like the shadow of somebody standing up in the front row against the marvelous flowing colors of a jungle epic on a movie screen: too small, too black, too solid. Kara saw him too and shouted, "How's the belly, Uvana Ram?"

When he was close enough not to have to shout, he replied, "Askiös, Kara, much better. I finished the guo this morning."

"Good, good. Another potful tonight. You're all skin," Kara said, not inaccurately.

"Maybe if he eats enough guo he'll turn people-colored," said Brella, studying him. Kara's mention of skin seemed to have brought Ramchandra's swarthy, dusky complexion to her notice for the first time. The Ndif were remarkably inattentive to details. Brella now compared the two foreigners and said, "You too, Tamara. If you only ate people-colored food, maybe you wouldn't be so ugly and brown."

"I never thought of that," said Tamara.

"Tamara, we are invited to the Old Men's House."

"Both of us? When?"

"Both. Now."

"How did you swing that?" Tamara asked in English, splashing ashore from the boulder she had been sharing with Kara, Libisa, and a lot of freshly washed loincloths.

"I asked."

"I'll come too," Kara announced, splashing after Tamara. "Askiös!"

"Is it right for women to do, Kara?"

"Of course. It's the *Old* Men's House, isn't it?" Kara dusted off her flat little breasts and brought the fold of her sari-like garment neatly across them. "Go on ahead. I'll stop by and pick up Binira. She told me it's worth listening to sometimes in there. I'll see you there."

Tamara, her wet feet rimmed with the silvery river sand, joined Ramchandra and entered the peacock forest with him on the narrow path.

She was intensely aware of his brown shoulder beside hers, his dark, well-knit, and fragile body, the excellent nose in the stern profile. She was aware that she was aware of this, but it was not the important thing just now. "Are they holding a ceremony for us?"

"I don't know. I haven't got some of the key words yet. My request to go there appears to be sufficient reason for a gathering there."

"Is it all right to bring that?" He was carrying a tape recorder.

"Anything goes in Cloud-Cuckoo-Land," he said, and the stern profile softened with a laugh.

Two of the withered, shadowy, scarce Old Men of the Ndif preceded them into the House, a large decrepit dugout; six or seven more were sitting around inside. There was much muttering of "askiös" and a strong reek of poro fat. The two foreigners joined the ill-defined circle, sitting on the dirt. No fire was lit. No apparatus or atmosphere of ritual was apparent. Presently Kara and Binira came in and sat down muttering "askiös" and cracking mild jokes with the Old Men. From across the circle—the place was lit only by the smokehole, and it was hard to see faces clearly— somebody asked something of Kara. Tamara did not understand the question. Kara's response was "I'm getting old enough, aren't I?" There was a general laugh. One more came in, Bro-Kap, said once to have been a famous hunter, still a big man but stooped, wrinkled, and turtle-mouthed from the loss of his teeth. Instead of sitting down he went to the empty firepit under the smokehole and stood there, arms at his sides. Silence grew around him.

He turned slowly till he faced Ramchandra.

"Have you come to learn to dance?"

"If I may," Ramchandra answered clearly.

"Are you old?"

"I am no longer young."

My God, Tamara thought, it's an initiation. Can Ram keep it up? And the next question, sure enough, she did not understand at all; there were no Young or Middle Ndif words in it. Ram, however, appeared to understand, and replied promptly, "Not often."

"When did you last bring home the kill?"

"I have never killed an animal."

That brought a hoot, laughs, and some critical discussion. "He must have been born fifty years old!" Binira said, sniggering. "Or else he is terribly lazy," said a youngish Old Man with a simple look, very earnestly.

Two more questions and answers Tamara could not follow, and then Bro-Kap demanded, harshly she thought, "What do you hunt?"

"I hunt peremensoe."

Whatever it was, it was right. Audible and tangible approval, backslaps, relaxation. Bro-Kap nodded once, shortly, wiped his nose with the back of his hand, and sat down in the circle beside Ramchandra. "What do you want to know?" he inquired in a thoroughly unritualistic and offhand manner.

"I should like to know," Ramchandra said, "how the world began."

"Oh ho ho!" went a couple of geezers across the circle. "Too old for his years, this one! A hundred years old, this fellow!"

"We say," Bro-Kap replied, "Man made the world."

"I should like to know how he did it."

"In his head, between his ears, how else? Everything is in the head. Nothing is wood, nothing is stone, nothing is water, nothing is blood, nothing is bone; all things are sanisukiarad."

In her frustration at never knowing the key word, Tamara watched Ram's face as if she could interpret from it; and indeed he understood. His eyes shone; he smiled, so that his features rounded out and grew gentle.

"He dances," he said. "He dances."

"Maybe so," Bro-Kap replied. "Maybe Man dances in his head, and that makes sanisukiarad."

Only with this repetition did Tamara hear the name "Man" as a name, a Ndif name or word which happened to coincide in sound with the English word "man"—but she had taken it to coincide in meaning.

Did it?

For a minute everything fell apart into two levels, two overlapping screens or veils, one of them sounds, one of them meanings, neither of them real. Their overlap and interplay, their shift and movement, confused everything, concealed or revealed everything; in that flow there was nothing to take hold of, not even once can you step into the river unless you are the river. The world began and nothing was happening, some wizened old men and women talking nonsense with Lord Shiva in a smelly hut. Talking, merely talking, words, words that meant nothing twice.

The parted veils closed again.

She checked that the tape was running in the recorder and turned up the gain a little. Replaying all this later, with Ram to interpret and explain, maybe it would make sense.

They did dance, at last. After much talk Binira announced, "That's enough peremenkiarad without music," and Bro-Kap rather ungraciously said, "All right, askiös, go ahead." At which Binira began to sing in a small unearthly creaking voice; and presently one old man, and then another, got up and danced, a slow dance, the feet close to the ground, the torso still and poised, intensity concentrated in the hands, arms, and face. It brought tears to Tamara's eyes, the dance of the shadowy old men. Others joined; now they were all dancing, all but Kara and herself. Sometimes they touched one another, lightly and solemnly, or bowed like cranes. All of them? Yes, Ram was dancing with them. The golden dusty light from the smokehole flowed along his arms; lightly and softly he lifted and set down his bare feet. An old man faced him. "O komeya, O komeya, ama, O, O," sang the creaking cricket-trill, and Kara's hands, Tamara's hands patted time on the brown dirt. The old man's hands were lifted as in supplication. Ramchandra reached to him, the flowing arm, the poised and separated fingers; smiling, he touched, and turned, still dancing, and the old man smiled and began to sing, "O komeya, ama, ama, O . . ."

"Do we have a session on tape for you to listen to!" Tamara said, but she said it mainly to distract Bob from his hangdog mood as they went together down the path toward the clearing where the duel was to be fought. The path was littered with lamaba-fruit rinds, as most of the village had preceded them.

"More love songs?"

"No. Well, yes. Love songs to God. . . . You know what God's name is?"

"Yes," Bob said indifferently. "Old man at Gunda told me. Bik-Kop-Man."

The duel went nearly, but not quite, as planned by both parties. Since it was the one group action by the Young Ndif besides saweya and baliya dancing which seemed to be a genuine ritual or meaning-focused act, Tamara diligently taped, filmed, and note-took the whole thing, including the redheaded Potita's expression (and here she is, Miss America); the infliction of a knife stab in Bob's thigh by Pit-Wat, the Gunda Challenger; Bob's fine gesture throwing away his long-bladed knife (a glittering arc into the pink-flowered puti bushes); and the karate throw that stretched Pit-Wat flat and apparently lifeless on the ground.

Bob did not stay to deliver his lecture on the unhygienic aspects of murder. His wound was bleeding hard, and Tamara cut off the movie camera and got to work with the first aid kit. Thus the jubilation of Hamo village and the discomfiture of Gunda were recorded only on sound tape; and the tape recorder was off when Pit-Wat revived, to the discomfiture of both Hamo and Gunda. Slain sallenzii were not supposed to come alive and get up, staggering but undamaged. By this time, however, Bob was on the homeward path to Hamo, white-faced and not unwilling to hold on to Tamara's arm. "Where's Ram?" he asked for the first time, and she explained that she had not even told Ram a duel was to take place.

"Good," Bob said. "I know what he'd say."

"I don't."

"Irresponsible involvement in native lifeways—"

She shook her head. "I didn't tell him because I didn't even see him today, and I thought . . ." She had in fact forgotten about the duel, it had seemed so silly, so unreal, compared to that dancing in the Old Men's House; it had all been a stupid annoying joke, right up to the moment when she saw the color, the splendid and terrible color, of blood in the sunlight; but she could not tell Bob that. "He's made a kind of breakthrough. By getting involved himself— He spent all day in the Old Men's House. I want him to talk with you tonight. Once we get your leg looked after. And he'll want to know what the people in Gunda said about Man. About God, I mean. Look out for that vine. Oh, Lord, here come the football fans." A troupe of Young Women were pursuing them, halfheartedly pelting Bob with puti flowers.

"Where's Potita?" Bob muttered, setting his teeth.

"Not in this lot. Are you really fond of her, Bob?"

"No. It's that my leg hurts. No, it was just fun and games. I just wondered if Pit-Wat got her or I did."

It turned out that Pit-Wat got her, since he stayed on the field of combat and performed the Victory Dance, rather shakily to be sure. Bob was relieved, since Pit-Wat was certainly better suited to Potita by temperament and circumstance; and as for the Victory Dance, a two-minute fit of stomping and posing, they had already got several films of champion wrestlers performing it. "All we needed was a movie of *me* beating my chest," Bob said. "Christ! With my leg spouting. And feeling like a prize ass all round anyhow."

"Ass all round, curious image," Ramchandra said. They had got a fire going in Bob's hut. It was raining—it rained only at night on Yirdo—and Bob had lost enough blood that a little extra warmth and cheer might do him good. The air got smoky, but the ruddy light was pleasant; it made Tamara think of winter, of rain and firelight in winter, a season unknown to Yirdo. Bob lay stretched out on his cot, and the other two sat by the hearth feeding the fire with dried lamaba rinds, which burned with a clear flame and a scent of pineapple.

"Ram, what does peremensoe mean?"

"Thinking. Ideas. Understanding. Talk."

"And peremenkiarad, is that right?"

"About the same. Plus a connotation of . . . illusion, deception, trickery—play."

"Is this Old Ndif?" Bob inquired. "If you're making dictionaries, let me see 'em, Ram. I couldn't understand anything the old boys were telling me in Gunda."

"Except God's name," Tamara said.

Ramchandra raised his eyebrows.

"Bik-Kop-Man made the world with his ears," Bob said. "And that is the Ndif equivalent of Genesis, Book One."

"Between his ears," Ramchandra corrected coldly.

"With them or between them, it's a pretty poor excuse for a Creation myth."

"How do you know, if your vocabulary is inadequate?"

Why did he take that tone with Bob? Supercilious, pedantic, offensive, even the voice high and schoolmarmish. Bob's solid good nature shone by contrast in his reply: "It's taken me weeks to realize that if I'm after myth or history the only people here who may have them are the Old Ones. I should have been checking in with you much earlier."

Ramchandra stared into the fire and said nothing.

"Ram," Tamara said, profoundly irritated with him, "Bob should know about this thing we talked about the other night. The derivation of Young Ndif."

He went on staring into the fire, mute.

"You can explain it better than I can."

After a moment he merely shook his head.

"You've decided it was a mistake?" she demanded, more exasperated than ever, but also with a flash of hope.

"No," he said. "The documentation is in that notebook I gave you."

She fetched the notebook from her hut, lighted the oil lamp, and sat down on the floor by Bob's cot so he could read over her shoulder. For half an hour they went over Ramchandra's orderly and exhaustive proofs of the direct derivation of Young Ndif from Modern Standard English. Bob laughed at first, taking the whole thing as a grand scholarly joke; then he laughed at the sheer lunacy of it. It did not seem to disturb him as it disturbed Tamara.

"If it's not your hoax, Ram, it's still a hoax—a terrific one."

"By whom? How? Why?" Tamara asked, hopeful again. A mistake made sense; a hoax made sense.

"All right. This language"—and he tapped the notebook—"isn't authentic. It's a fake, a construct—invented. Right?"

Ramchandra, who had not said a word all this while, agreed in a remote, unwilling tone: "Invented. By an amateur. The correspondences with English are naïve, unconscious, as in 'speaking in tongues.' But Old Ndif is an authentic language."

"An older one, an archaic survival—"

"No." Ramchandra said no often, flatly, and with satisfaction, Tamara thought. "Old Ndif is alive. It is based upon Young Ndif, has grown out of it, or over it, like ivy on a telephone pole."

"Spontaneously?"

"As spontaneously as any language, or as deliberately. When words are wanted, needed, people have to make them. It 'happens,' like a bird singing, but it's also 'work,' like Mozart writing music."

"Then you'd say the Old Ones are gradually making a real language out of this fake one?"

"I cannot define the word 'real' and therefore would not use it." Ramchandra shifted his position, reclasping his arms around his knees, but did not look up from the fire. "I would say that the Old Ndif seem to be engaged in creating the world. Human beings do this primarily by means of language, music, and the dance."

Bob stared at him, then at Tamara. "Come again?"

Ramchandra was silent.

"So far," Tamara said, "working in three widely separate localities, we've found the same language, without major dialectical variations, and the same set of very rudimentary social and cultural patterns. Bob hasn't found any legends, any expressions of the archetypes, any developed symbology. I haven't found much more social structure than I'd find in a herd of cattle, about what I might find in a primate troop. Sex and age determine all roles. The Ndif are culturally subhuman; they don't exist fully as human beings. The Old Ndif are beginning to. Is that it, Ram?"

"I don't know," the linguist said, withdrawn.

"That's missionary talk!" Bob said. "Subhuman? Come on. Stagnant, sure. Maybe because there's no environmental challenge. Food falls out of the trees, game's plentiful, and they don't have sexual hang-ups—"

"That's *in*human," Tamara interjected; Bob ignored her.

"There's no stimulus. OK. But the Old Ones get shoved out of the fun and games. They get bored; that's the stimulus. They start playing around with words and ideas. So what rudiments of mythopoetics and ritual they've got are their creation. That's not an unusual situation—the young busy with sex and physical competitions, the old as culture transmitters. The only weird thing is this English-Ndif business. That needs explaining. I just don't buy telepathy; you can't build a scientific explanation on an occultist theory. The only rational explanation is that these people— the whole society—are a plant. A quite recent one."

"Correct," Ramchandra said.

"But listen," Tamara said with fury, "how can a quarter of a million people be 'planted'? What about the ones over thirty? We've only had FTL spaceflight for thirty years! The Exploratory Survey to this system was unmanned, and it was only eight years ago! Your rational explanation is pure nonsense!"

"Correct," Ramchandra said again, his clear, dark, sorrowful gaze on the flickering fire.

"Evidently there's been a manned mission, a colonizing mission, to this planet, which the World Government doesn't know about. We have stumbled into something, and it begins to scare me. The So-Hem faction—"

Bob was interrupted by the sudden entrance (the Ndif never knocked) of Bro-Kap, two other Old Men, and two baliya dancers, beautiful half-naked sixteen-year-olds with flowers in their tawny hair. They knelt by Bob's cot and made soft lamenting sounds. Bro-Kap stood as majestically as he could in the now very crowded hut and gazed down at Bob. He was clearly waiting for the girls to be quiet, but one of them was now chattering cheerfully and the other was drawing circles around Bob's nipples with her long fingernails. "Uvana Bob!" Bro-Kap said at last. "Are you Bik-Kop-Man?"

"Am I—? Askiös, Wana!—No. Askiös, Bro-Kap, I don't understand."

"Sometimes Man comes," the old Ndif said. "He has come to Hamo, and to Farwe. Never to Gunda or to Akko. He is strong and tall, golden-haired and golden-skinned, a great hunter, a great fighter, a great lover. He comes from far away and goes away again. We have thought that you were He. You are not He?"

"No, I am not," Bob said decisively.

Bro-Kap took a breath that heaved his wrinkled chest. "Then you will die," he said.

"Die?" Bob repeated without comprehension.

"Die how? Of what?" Tamara demanded, standing up so that in the press of people in the little hut she was brought face to face with the old man. "What do you mean, Bro-Kap?"

"Gunda challengers use poisoned knives," the old man said. "To find out which ones from Hamo are Bik-Kop-Man. Poison doesn't kill Bik-Kop-Man."

"What poison?"

"That's their secret," Bro-Kap said. "Gunda is full of wicked people. We of Hamo use no poisons."

"For Christ's sake," Bob said in English; and in Ndif, "Why didn't you tell me?"

"The Young Men thought you knew. They thought you were Man. Then when you let Pit-Wat wound you, when you threw away your knife, when you killed him but he came back to life, they weren't sure. They came to the Old Men's House to ask. Because we in the Old Men's House have peremensoe about Man." There was pride in the old man's voice. "Thus I came to you. Askiös, Uvana Bob." Bro-Kap turned and pushed his way out; the other Old Men followed him.

"Go away," Bob said to the smiling, caressing girls. "Go on now." They left, reluctant, swaying, their pretty faces troubled.

"I'll go to Gunda," Ramchandra said, "see if there's an antidote." And he was off at a run.

Bob's face was dead white.

"Another damned hoax," he said, smiling.

"You bled a lot, Bob. Probably bled out the poison right away, if there really was any. Let me have a look at it. . . . It looks absolutely clean. No inflammation."

"My breath's been coming short," the young man said. "Most likely shock."

"Yes. Let me get the medical handbook."

The handbook had no recommendations, and Gunda had no antidote. The poison acted on the central nervous system. Paroxysms began two hours after Bro-Kap's visit. They increased quickly in severity and frequency. Sometime after midnight, long before dawn, Bob died.

Ramchandra struck the tenth useless blow over the stopped heart, raised his arm to strike again, and did not strike. The dancer's raised arm: creator, destroyer. The clenched dark fist relaxed; the poised and separated fingers hovered above the white face and the unbreathing chest. "Ah!" Ramchandra cried aloud and, dropping down beside the cot, broke into tears, a passion of tears.

Wind gusted the rain against the roof. Time passed and Ramchandra was silent, as silent as Bob, beside whom he crouched, his arms stretched across Bob's body and his head sunk between them; exhausted, he had fallen asleep. The rain thinned and weakened and then beat hard again. Tamara put out the oil lamp, her movements slow and certain, full of the knowledge of what they meant. She added the last of the fuel to the fire and sat down at the little hearth. One must watch with the newly dead, and the sleeping should not sleep unprotected. She sat awake and watched the fire die out and, long afterward, the gray light reborn.

Ndif funerals were, as she had expected, graceless. There was a burying ground not far off in the forest, which nobody talked about or ever visited except for burials. Grave digging was the Old Men's task. They had dug a shallow pit. Two of them, plus Kara and Binira, helped carry Bob's body to the grave. The Ndif used no coffins; dumped their dead naked in the earth. It was too cold that way, too cold, Tamara thought with rage, and she had put Bob's white shirt and trousers on him, left his gold Swiss watch strapped on his wrist, since he owned no other treasure, and wrapped the long silky bluish leaves of the pandsu carefully about him. She lined the shallow grave with leaves before they laid him in it; the four Old Men and Women watched, expressionless. They laid him on his side, his knees a little bent. Tamara turned for a flower to put by his hand, but the pink and purple blossoms sickened her; she broke the chain around her neck, on which hung a little turquoise her mother had given her, a fragment of the Earth, and put that in the dead man's hand. She had to be quick; the Old Men were already scraping the dirt back over the grave with their crude wooden shovels. As soon as that was done, all four Ndif turned without a word and went off, not looking back.

Ramchandra knelt down by the grave. "I am sorry I was jealous of you," he said. "If we meet reborn, you will be a king again, but I will be the dog at your heel." He bowed down, touching the raw damp clods of the grave, then slowly stood up. He looked at Tamara. She knew his look, the dark, clear, grieving eyes, but she could not meet them, or speak. It was her turn to cry. He came to her across the grave, as if it was any bit of ground, and put his arms around her, holding her so she could weep. When the first hardest sobbing was done and she could walk, they set off slowly down the narrow half-overgrown path through the peacock splendors of the forest, back to the village.

"Burning is better," Ramchandra said. "The spirit is freed sooner to go on."

"Earth is best," Tamara said, very low and hoarse.

"Tamara. Do you want to radio Ankara Base to send the launch to us?"

"I don't know."

"There's no hurry to decide."

The gorgeous colors of the lamabas blurred and cleared and blurred again. She stumbled, though Ramchandra's hand was kind and firm on her arm.

"We might as well go on and finish what we came for."

"The ethnology of dreams."

"Dreams? Oh no. This is real . . . much realer than I wish it were."

"So are all dreams."

In three days they put in their regular call to Ankara, the inner planet where the central base for the various research groups in Yirdo's solar system was established; they reported Bob's death, "by misunderstanding—no blame," in the Ethnographic Corps code. They did not request relief.

Life in Hamo village went on as before. The Middle-Aged Women said nothing about Bob's death to Tamara, but several evenings old Binira sat just outside her hut and sang to her, a quiet cricket-trill. Once she saw two of the little saweya dancers leaving a flowering branch at the door of Bob's empty hut; she went toward them, but they trotted off giggling. Soon after, the Young Men set fire to the hut, deliberately or by accident, there was no telling; it burned to ashes and all trace of it was gone within a week. Ramchandra spent his days and nights with the Old Ones of Hamo and Gunda, gathering an increasingly solid bulk of linguistic and mythic data. The long lines of saweya dancers undulated, the baliya dancers thrust their high breasts left and right, the singers chanted, "Ah-weh, weh, ah-weh, weh," and the forest glades around the dancing ground at dusk swarmed with coupled bodies. Hunters returned proudly with dead poro, like suckling pigs with blunt curved fangs, slung on carrying poles. On the twelfth night after Bob's death Ramchandra came to Tamara's hut. She had been trying to read over some notes, but the pages might as well have been empty; her head ached and nothing made sense, nothing meant anything. He came to the doorway, dark, slight, shadowy, and she looked up at him with dull eyes. He said something that meant nothing about loneliness, and then he said, with the darkness around him and behind him, "It's like fire. Like burning in a fire. But the spirit caught too, burning—"

"Come in," she said.

A few nights later they lay talking in the dark, the soft windy rain sighing in the forest and on the thatch of the hut above them.

"Since I first saw you," he said. "Truly, since the day we met, in the canteen at Ankara Base."

With a laugh, Tamara said, "You scarcely behaved as if—"

"I didn't like it! I refused. I said, No, no, no!—my wife was enough, this doesn't come twice to a man in one life, I will remember her."

"You do," Tamara murmured.

"Of course. To her in me now I can say Yes, and to you with me, Yes, yes. . . . Listen, Tamara, you set me free, your hands free me. And bind me. Tighter to the wheel, never in this life now will I get free, never cease to desire you. I don't *want* to cease. . . ."

"It's so simple now. What was in our way?"

"My fear. My jealousy."

"Jealousy?—Of Bob?"

"Oh, yes," he said, shivering.

"Oh, Ram, never. Right from the beginning, you—"

"Confusion," he whispered. "Illusion."

His warmth against her the length of her body; and cold Bob, cold in the ground. Fire is better than earth.

She woke; he was stroking her hair and cheek, soothing her, whispering, "Sleep again, it's all right, Tamara," his voice heavy with sleep and tenderness.

"What—did I . . ."

"A bad dream."

"Dream. Oh, no. It wasn't bad—just queer."

The rain had ceased and the light of the giant planet,

grayed and filtered by clouds, was like a faint mist in the hut. She could just make out the hook of his nose, the darkness of his hair, in that gray dust of light.

"What was the dream?"

"A boy—a young man—no, a boy, about fifteen. Standing in front of me. Sort of filling everything, taking up all the room, so that I couldn't possibly get past him or around him. But just an ordinary boy, with glasses, I think. And he was staring at me, not threatening, not really seeing me, but he kept staring and saying, 'Bill me, bill me.' And I didn't think he owed me anything, so I said, 'What for?' But he just kept saying, 'Bill me!' Then I woke up."

"Bill me, how funny," Ramchandra said sleepily. "Bill me . . . Me Bill . . ."

"Yes. That's it. I'm Bill, that's what he meant."

"Oh," Ramchandra said, a deep exhalation, and she felt his relaxed body go tense. Since Bob's death she had not trusted the Ndif, or rather without distrusting any one of them she had lost trust in their world; she feared harm. She raised her head quickly to see if someone had entered the hut. "What's wrong?"

"Nothing is wrong."

"What is it?"

"Nothing. Go back to sleep. You talked to God."

"The dream?"

"Yes. He told you his name."

"Bill?" she said, and because the alarm was past and she was still sleepy and Ramchandra was laughing, she laughed. "God's name is Bill?"

"Yes, yes. Bill Kopman, or Kopfman, or Cupman."

"Bik-Kop-Man?"

"The 'l' assimilates to the 'k', as in sikka, the fiber they make fishing lines of—silk."

"What are you babbling about?"

"Bill Kopman, who made this world."

"Who what? Who?"

"Who made this world. *This* world—Yirdo, the poro, the puti bushes, the Ndif. You saw him in your dream. A fifteen-year-old boy with glasses, probably also acne and weak ankles. You saw him, and so my eyes see for a moment too. A skinny boy, lazy, shy. He reads stories, he daydreams, about the great blond hero who can hunt and fight and make love all day and night. His head is full of the hero, himself, and so it all comes to be."

"Ram, stop it."

"But you talked to him, not I! You asked him, 'What for?' But he couldn't tell you. He doesn't know. He doesn't understand desire. He is entirely caught in it, bound by it; he sees and knows nothing but his own immense desire. And so he makes the world. Only one free of desire is free of the worlds, you know."

Tamara looked, as if over her shoulder, back into her dream. "He speaks English," she said unwillingly.

Ramchandra nodded. His tranquility, his acceptant playful tone, reassured her; it was interesting to lie looking together at the same silly dream. "He writes it all down," she said, "his fantasies about the Ndif. Maps and everything. A lot of kids do that. And some adults."

"Perhaps he has a notebook of his invented language. It would be interesting to compare with my notebooks."

"Much easier just to go find him and borrow his."

"Yes, but he doesn't know Old Ndif."

"Ramchandra."

"Beloved."

"You are saying that because a boy writes nonsense in a notebook in—in Topeka, a planet thirty-one light-years away comes into existence, with all its plants and animals and people. And always has been in existence. Because of the boy and the notebook. And what about the boy with a notebook in Schenectady? or New Delhi?"

"Evidently!"

"Your nonsense is much worse than Bill Kopman's."

"Why?"

"Time. And there isn't room—"

"There is room. There is time. All the galaxies. All

the universes. That is infinity. The worlds are infinite, the cycles are endless. There is room. Room for all the dreams, all the desires. No end to it. Worlds without end."

His voice now was remote.

"Bill Kopman dreams," he said, "and the God dances. And Bob dies, and we make love."

She saw the boy's blind yearning face before her, filling the world, no way around it, no path.

"You're only joking, Ramchandra," she said; she was shivering now.

"I'm only joking, Tamara," he said.

"If it weren't a joke I couldn't bear it. Being caught here, stuck in somebody else's dream, dreamworld, alternate world, whatever it is."

"Why caught? We call Ankara; they send the launch for us; next passage out we can go back to Earth if we like. Nothing has changed."

"But this idea that it's somebody else's world. What if—what if—while we're still here—Bill Kopman woke up?"

"Once in a thousand thousand years does a soul wake up," Ramchandra said, and his voice was sad.

She wondered why that made him sad; she found it comforting. Brooding, she found further comfort. "It wouldn't all depend on him, even if he started it," she said. "All the uninhabited places, they'd just be blanks on his maps, but they're full of life—animals and trees and ferns and little flies. . . . Reality is what works, isn't it? And the Old Men and Women. They aren't, they wouldn't be, part of . . . of Bill's wet dreams. He probably doesn't even know any old people; he isn't interested. So they get free."

"Yes—they begin to imagine their world for themselves. To think, to dance, to make up words and stories."

"I wonder if he ever thinks of death."

"Can anyone think of death?" Ramchandra asked. "One can only do it. As Bob did it. . . . Can one dream of sleep?"

The soft dust-gray light was more intense as the clouds thinned, drifting silent to the east.

"He looked anxious, in the dream," Tamara murmured. "Frightened. As if . . . 'Bill me.' As if Bob paid . . . the debt."

"Tamara, Tamara, you go before me, always before me." His forehead was against her breasts; she touched his hair lightly. "Ramchandra," she said, "I want to go home, I think. Away from this place. Back to the real world."

"You go before, I follow you."

"Oh, humble you are, liar, hoaxer, dancer, you're so humble, but you don't really care, do you? You're not frightened."

"Not any more," he said, in a breath, barely audible.

"How long have you understood about this place? Since you danced with Bro-Kap and the others, that first time?"

"No, no. Only now, since your dream, this night, now. You saw. All I can do is say. But yes, if you like, I can say it because I have always known it. I speak my native tongue, because you have brought me home. The house under the trees behind the temple of Shiva in a suburb of Calcutta, is that my home? Is this? The world, the real world, which one? What does it matter? Who dreamed the Earth? A greater dreamer than you or I, but we are the dreamer, Shakti, and the worlds will endure as long as our desire."

DREAM DONE GREEN

by Alan Dean Foster

The life of the woman Casperdan is documented in the finest detail, from birth to death, from head to toe, from likes to dislikes to indifferences.

Humans are like that.

The stallion Pericles we know only by his work.

Horses are like that.

We know it all began the year 1360 Imperial, 1822 After the Breakthrough, 2305 after the human Micah Schell found the hormone that broke the lock on rudimentary animal intelligence and enabled the higher mammals to attain at least the mental abilities of a human ten-year-old.

The quadrant was the Stone Crescent, the system Burr, the planet Calder, and the city Lalokindar.

Lalokindar was a wealthy city on a wealthy world. It ran away from the ocean in little bumps and curlicues. Behind it was virgin forest; in front, the Beach of Snow. The homes were magnificent and sat on spacious grounds, and that of the industrialist Dandavid was one of the most spacious and magnificent of all.

His daughter Casperdan was quite short, very brilliant, and by the standards of any age an extraordinary beauty. She had the looks and temperament of a Titania and the mind of a Baron Sachet. Tomorrow she came of legal age, which on Calder at that time was seventeen.

Under Calderian law she could then, as the oldest (and only) child, assume control of the family business or elect not to. Were one inclined to wager on the former course he would have found plenty of takers. It was only a formality. Girls of seventeen did not normally assume responsibility and control for multimillion-credit industrial complexes.

Besides, following her birthday Casperdan was to be wed to Comore du Sable, who was handsome and intelligent (though not so rich as she).

Casperdan was dressed in a blue nothing and sat on the balustrade of the wide balcony overlooking Snow Beach and a bay of the Greengreen Sea. The aged German shepherd trotted over to her, his claws clicking softly on the purple porphyry.

The dog was old and grayed and had been with the family for many years. He panted briefly, then spoke.

"Mistress, a strange mal is at the entrance."

Casperdan looked idly down at the dog.

"Who's its master?"

"He comes alone," the dog replied wonderingly.

"Well, tell him my father and mother are not at home and to come back tomorrow."

"Mistress"—the dog flattened his ears and lowered his head apologetically—"he says he comes to see *you*."

The girl laughed, and silver flute notes skittered off the polished stone floor.

"To see me? Stranger and stranger. And really alone?" She swung perfect legs off the balustrade. "What kind of mal is this?"

"A horse, mistress."

The flawless brow wrinkled. "Horse? Well, let's see this strange mal that travels alone."

They walked toward the foyer, past cages of force filled with rainbow-colored tropical birds.

"Tell me, Patch . . . what is a 'horse'?"

"A large four-legged vegetarian." The dog's brow twisted with the pain of remembering. Patch was extremely bright for a dog. "There are none on Calder. I do not think there are any in the entire system."

"Off-planet, too?" Her curiosity was definitely piqued, now. "Why come to see me?"

"I do not know, mistress."

"And without even a human over h—"

Voice and feet stopped together.

The mal standing in the foyer was not as large as some. La Moure's elephants were much bigger. But it was extraordinary in other ways. Particularly the head. Why . . . it was exquisite! Truly breathtaking. Not an anthropomorphic beauty, but something uniquely its own.

Patch slipped away quietly.

The horse was black as the Pit, with tiny exceptions. The right front forelock was silver, as was the diamond on its forehead. And there was a single streak of silver partway through the long mane, and another in the black tail. Most mal wore only a lifepouch, and this one's was strapped to its neck. But it also wore an incongruous, utterly absurd hat of green felt, with a long feather, protruding out and back.

With a start she realized she'd been staring . . . very undignified. She started toward it again. Now the head swung to watch her. She slowed and stopped involuntarily, somehow constrained from moving too close.

This is ridiculous! she thought, *It's only a mere mal, and not even very big. Why, it's even herbivorous!*

Then whence this strange fluttering deep in her tummy?

"You are Casperdan," said the horse suddenly. The voice was exceptional, too: a mellow tenor that tended to rise on concluding syllables, only to break and drop like a whitecap on the sea before the next word.

She started to stammer a reply, angrily composed herself.

"I am. I regret that I'm not familiar with your species, but I'll accept whatever the standard horse-man greeting is."

"I give no subservient greeting to any man," replied the horse. It shifted a hoof on the floor, which here was deep foam.

A stranger and insolent to boot, thought Casperdan furiously. She would call Patch and the household guards and . . . Her anger dissolved in confusion and uncertainty.

"How did you get past Row and Cuff?" Surely this harmless-looking, handless quadruped could not have overpowered the two lions. The horse smiled, showing white incisors.

"Cats, fortunately, are more subject to reason than many mal. And now I think I'll answer the rest of your questions.

"My name is Pericles. I come from Quaestor."

Quaestor! Magic, distant, Imperial capital! Her anger at this mal's insolence was subsumed in excitement.

"You mean you've actually traveled all the way from the capital . . . to meet me?"

"There is no need to repeat," the horse murmured, "only to confirm. It took a great deal of time and searching to find someone like you. I need someone young . . . you are that. Only a young human would be responsive to what I have to offer. I needed someone bored, and you are wealthy as well as young."

"I'm not bored," Casperdan began defiantly, but he ignored her.

"I needed someone very rich, but without a multitude of ravenous relatives hanging about. Your father is a self-made tycoon, your mother an orphan. You have no other relatives. And I needed someone with the intelligence and sensitivity to take orders from a mere mal."

This last was uttered with a disdain alien to Casperdan. Servants were not sarcastic.

"In sum," he concluded, "I need you."

"Indeed?" she mused, too overwhelmed by the outrageousness of this animal's words to compose a suitable rejoinder.

"Indeed," the horse echoed dryly.

"And what, pray tell, do you need me for?"

The horse dropped its head and seemed to consider how best to continue. It looked oddly at her.

"Laugh now if you will. I have a dream that needs fulfilling."

"Do you, now? Really, this is becoming quite amusing." What a story she'd have to tell at the preparty tomorrow!

"Yes, I do. Hopefully it will not take too many years."

She couldn't help blurting, "Years!"

"I cannot tell for certain. You see, I am a genius and a poet. For me it's the dream part that's solid. The reality is what lacks certitude. That's one reason why I need human help. Need you."

This time she just stared at him.

"Tomorrow," continued the horse easily, "you will not marry the man du Sable. Instead, you will sign the formal Control Contract and assume directorship of the Dan family business. You have the ability and brains to handle it. With my assistance the firm will prosper beyond the wildest dreams of your sire or any of the investors.

"In return, I will deed you a part of my dream, some of my poetry, and something few humans have had for millennia. I would not know of this last thing myself had I not chanced across it in the Imperial archives."

She was silent for a brief moment, then spoke brightly.

"I have a few questions."

"Of course."

"First, I'd like to know if horses as a species are insane, or if you are merely an isolated case."

He sighed, tossing his mane. "I didn't expect words to convince you." The long black hair made sailor's knots with sunbeams. "Do you know the Meadows of Blood?"

"Only by name." She was fascinated by the mention of the forbidden place. "They're in the Ravaged Mountains. It's rumored to be rather a pretty place. But no one goes there. The winds above the canyon make it fatal to aircars."

"I have a car outside," the horse whispered. "The driver is mal and knows of a winding route by which, from to time, it is possible to reach the Meadows. The winds war only above them. They are named, by the way, for the color of the flora there and not for a bit of human history . . . unusual.

"When the sun rises up in the mouth of a certain canyon and engulfs the crimson grasses and flowers in light . . . well, it's more than 'rather pretty.' "

"You've already been there," she said.

"Yes, I've already been." He took several steps and that powerful, strange face was close to hers. One eye, she noticed offhandedly, was red, the other blue.

"Come with me now to the Meadows of Blood and I'll give you that piece of dream, that something few have had for thousands of years. I'll bring you back tonight and you can give me your answer on the way.

"If it's 'no,' then I'll depart quietly and you'll never see me again."

Now, in addition to being both beautiful and intelligent, Casperdan also had her sire's recklessness.

"All right . . . I'll come."

When her parents returned home that night from the party and found their daughter gone, they were not distressed. After all, she was quite independent and, heavens, to be married tomorrow! When they learned from Patch that she'd gone off, not with a man, but with a strange mal, they were only mildly concerned. Casperdan was quite capable of taking care of herself. Had they known where she'd gone, things would have been different.

So nothing happened till the morrow.

"Good morning, Cas," said her father.

"Good morning, dear," her mother added. They were eating breakfast on the balcony. "Did you sleep well last night, and where did you go?"

"I didn't sleep at all, and I went into the Ravaged Mountains. And there's no need to get excited, Father"—the old man sat back in his chair—"because as you see, I'm back safely and in one piece."

"But not unaffected," her mother stated, noticing the strangeness in her daughter's eyes.

"No, Mother, not unaffected. There will be no wedding." Before that lovely woman could reply, Casperdan turned to her father. "Dad, I want the contract of Control. I intend to begin as director of the firm eight o'clock tomorrow morning. No, better make it noon . . . I'll need some sleep." She was smiling faintly. "And I don't think I'm going to get any right now."

On that she was right. Dandavid, that usually even-tempered but mercurial gentleman, got very, very excited. Between his bellows and her sobs, her mother leveled questions and then accusations at her.

When they found out about the incipient change-over, the investors immediately threatened to challenge it in court—law or no law, they weren't going to be guided by the decisions of an inexperienced snippet. In fact, of all those affected, the intended bride-groom took it best. After all, he was handsome and intelligent (if not as rich), and could damn well find himself another spouse. He wished Casperdan well and consoled himself with his cello.

Her father (for her own good, of course) joined with the investors to challenge his daughter in the courts. He protested most strongly. The investors ranted and pounded their checkbooks.

But the judge was honest, the law machines incorruptible, and the precedents clear. Casperdan got her Contract and a year in which to prove herself.

Her first official action was to rename the firm Dream Enterprises. A strange name, many thought, for an industrial concern. But it was more distinctive than the old one. The investors grumbled, while the advertising men were delighted.

Then began a program of industrial expansion and acquisition unseen on somnolent Calder since the days of settlement. Dream Enterprises was suddenly everywhere and into everything. Mining, manufacturing, raw materials. These new divisions sprouted tentacles of their own and sucked in additional businesses.

Paper and plastics, electronics, nucleonics, hydrologics and parafoiling, insurance and banking, tridee stations and liquid tanking, entertainments and hydroponics and velosheeting.

Dream Enterprises became the wealthiest firm on Calder, then in the entire Stone Crescent.

The investors and Dandavid clipped their coupons and kept their mouths shut, even to ignoring Casperdan's odd relationship with an outsystem mal.

Eventually there came a morning when Pericles looked up from his huge lounge in the executive suite and stared across the room at Casperdan in a manner different from before.

The stallion had another line of silver in his mane. The girl had blossomed figuratively and figurewise. Otherwise the years had left them unchanged.

"I've booked passage for us. Put Rollins in charge. He's a good man."

"Where are we going?" asked Casperdan. Not why nor for how long, but where. She'd learned a great deal about the horse in the past few years.

"Quaestor."

Sudden sparkle in beautiful green eyes. "And then will you give me back what I once had?"

The horse smiled and nodded. "If everything goes smoothly."

In the Crescent, Dream Enterprises was powerful and respected and kowtowed to. In the Imperial sector it was different. There were companies on the capital planet that would classify it as a modest little family business. Bureaucratic trip-wires here ran not for kilometers, but for light-years.

However, Pericles had threaded this maze many times before, and knew both men and mal who worked within the bowels of Imperial Government.

So it was that they eventually found themselves in the offices of Sim-sem Alround, subminister for Unincorporated Imperial Territories.

Physically, Alround wasn't quite that. But he did

have a comfortable bureaucratic belly, a rectangular face framed by long bushy sideburns and curly red hair tinged with white. He wore the current fashion, a monocle. For all that, and his dry occupation, he proved charming and affable.

A small stream ran through his office, filled with trout and tadpoles and cattails. Casperdan reclined on a long couch made to resemble solid granite. Pericles preferred to stand.

"You want to buy some land, then?" queried Alround after drinks and pleasantries had been exchanged.

"My associate will give you the details," Casperdan informed him. Alround shifted his attention from human to horse without a pause. Naturally he'd assumed . . .

"Yes sir?"

"We wish to purchase a planet," said Pericles. "A small planet . . . not very important."

Alround waited. Visitors interested in small transactions didn't get in to see the subminister himself.

"Just one?"

"One will be quite sufficient."

Alround depressed a switch on his desk. A red light flashed on, indicated that all details of the conversation to follow were now being taken down for the Imperial records.

"Purpose of purchase?"

"Development."

"Name of world?"

"Earth."

"All right . . . fine," said the subminister. Abruptly, he looked confused. Then he smiled. "Many planets are called Earth by their inhabitants or discoverers. Which particular Earth is this?"

"*The* Earth. Birthplace of mankind and malkind. Old Earth. Also known variously as Terra and Sol III."

The subminister shook his head. "Never heard of it."

"It is available, though?"

"We'll know in a second." Alround studied the screen in his desk.

Actually it took several minutes before the gargantuan complex of metal and plastic and liquid buried deep in the soil beneath them could come up with a reply.

"Here it is, finally," said Alround. "Yes, it's available . . . by default, it seems. The price will be . . ." He named a figure which seemed astronomical to Casperdan and insanely low to the horse.

"Excellent!" husked Pericles. "Let us conclude the formalities now."

"Per," Casperdan began, looking at him uncertainly. "I don't know if we have enough . . ."

"Some liquidation will surely be necessary, Casperdan, but we will manage."

The subminister interrupted: "Excuse me . . . there's something you should know before we go any further. I *can* sell you Old Earth, but there is an attendant difficulty."

"Problems can be solved, difficulties overcome, obstructions removed," said the horse irritably. "Please get on with it."

Alround sighed. "As you wish." He drummed the required buttons. "But you'll need more than your determination to get around this one.

"You see, it seems no one knows how to get to Old Earth anymore . . . or even where it is."

Later, strolling among the teeming mobs of Imperial City, Casperdan ventured a hesitant question.

"I take it this means it's not time for me to receive my part of the dream again?"

"Sadly, no, my friend."

Her tone turned sharp. "Well, what do you intend to do now? We've just paid quite an enormous number of credits for a world located in obscurity, around the corner from no place."

"We shall return to Calder," said the horse with finality, "and continue to expand and develop the company." He pulled back thick lips in an equine smile.

"In all the research I did, in all my careful planning and preparation, never once did I consider that the location of the home world might have been lost.

"So now we must go back and hire researchers to research, historians to historize, and ships to search and scour the skies in sanguine directions. And wait."

A year passed, and another, and then they came in small multiples. Dream Enterprises burgeoned and grew, grew and thrived. It moved out of the Stone Crescent and extended its influence into other quadrants. It went into power generation and multiple metallurgy, into core mining and high fashion.

And finally, of necessity, into interstellar shipping.

There came the day when the captain with the stripped-down scoutship was presented to Casperdan and the horse Pericles in their executive office on the two hundred and twentieth floor of the Dream building.

Despite a long, long, lonely journey the captain was alert and smiling. Smiling because the endless trips of dull searching were over. Smiling because he knew the company reward for whoever found a certain aged planet.

Yes, he'd found Old Earth. Yes, it was a long way off, and in a direction only recently suspected. Not in toward the galactic center, but out on the Arm. And yes, he could take them there right away.

The shuttleboat settled down into the atmosphere of the planet. In the distance, a small yellow sun burned smooth and even.

Pericles stood at the observation port of the shuttle as it drifted planetward. He wore a special protective suit, as did Casperdan. She spared a glance at the disconsolate mal. Then she did something she did very rarely. She patted his neck.

"You mustn't be too disappointed if it's not what you expected, Per." She was trying to be comforting. "History and reality have a way of not coinciding."

It was quiet for a long time. Then the magnificent

head, lowered now, turned to face her, Pericles snorted bleakly.

"My dear, dear Casperdan, I can speak eighteen languages fluently and get by in several more, and there are no words in any of them for what I feel. 'Disappointment'? Consider a nova and call it warm. Regard Quaestor and label it well-off. Then look at me and call me disappointed."

"Perhaps," she continued, not knowing what else to say, "it will be better on the surface."

It was worse.

They came down in the midst of what the captain called a mild local storm. To Casperdan it was a neat slice of the mythical hell.

Stale yellow-brown air whipped and sliced its way over high dunes of dark sand. The uncaring mounds marched in endless waves to the shoreline. A dirty, dead beach melted into brackish water and a noisome green scum covered it as far as the eye could see. A few low scrubs and hearty weeds eked out a perilous existence among the marching dunes, needing only a chance change in the wind to be entombed alive.

In the distance, stark, bare mountains gave promise only of a higher desolation.

Pericles watched the stagnant sea for a long time. Over the intercom his voice was shrunken, the husk of a whisper, those compelling tones beaten down by the moaning wind.

"Is it like this everywhere, Captain?"

The spacer replied unemotionally. "Mostly. I've seen far worse worlds, sir . . . but this one is sure no prize. If I may be permitted an opinion, I'm damned if I can figure out why you want it."

"Can't you feel it, Captain?"

"Sir?" The spacer's expression under his faceglass was puzzled.

"No, no. I guess you cannot. But I do, Captain. Even though this is not the Earth I believed in, I still feel it. I fell in love with a dream. The dream seems to have departed long ago, but the memory of it is still here, still here . . ." Another long pause, then, "You said 'mostly'?"

"Well, yes." The spacer turned and gestured at the distant range. "Being the discovering vessel, we ran a pretty thorough survey, according to the general directives. There are places—near the poles, in the higher elevations, out in the middle of the three great oceans—where a certain amount of native life still survives. The cycle of life here has been shattered, but a few of the pieces are still around.

"But mostly, it's like this." He kicked at the sterile sand. "Hot or cold desert—take your pick. The soil's barren and infertile, the air unfit for man or mal.

"We did find some ruins . . . God, they were old! You saw the artifacts we brought back. But except for its historical value, this world strikes me as particularly worthless."

He threw another kick at the sand, sending flying shards of mica and feldspar and quartz onto the highways of the wind.

Pericles had been thinking. "We won't spend much more time here, Captain." The proud head lifted for a last look at the dead ocean. "There's not much to see."

They'd been back in the offices on Calder only a half-month when Pericles announced his decision.

Dream-partner or no dream-partner, Casperdan exploded.

"You quadrupedal cretin! Warm-blooded sack of fatuous platitudes! Terraforming is only a theory, a hypothesis in the minds of sick romantics. It's impossible!"

"No one has ever attempted it," countered the horse, unruffled by her outburst.

"But . . . my God!" Casperdan ran delicate fingers through her flowing blond hair. "There are no facilities for doing such a thing . . . no company, no special firms to consult. Why, half the industries that would be needed for such a task don't even exist."

"They will," Pericles declared.

"Oh, yes? And just *where* will they spring from?"

"You and I are going to create them."

She pleaded with him. "Have you gone absolutely mad? We're not in the miracle business, you know."

The horse walked to the window and stared down at the Greengreen Sea. His reply was distant. "No . . . we're in the dream business . . . remember?"

A cloud of remembrance came over Casperdan's exquisite face. For a moment, she did—but it wasn't enough to stem the tide of objection. Though she stopped shouting.

"Please, Per . . . take a long, logical look at this before you commit yourself to something that can only hurt you worse in the end."

He turned and stared evenly at her. "Casperdan, for many, many years now I've done nothing but observe things with a reasoned eye, done nothing without thinking it through beginning, middle, and end and all possible ramifications, done nothing I wasn't absolutely sure of completing.

"Now I'm going to take a chance. Not because I want to do it this way, but because I've run out of options. I'm not mad, no . . . but I *am* obsessed." He looked away from her.

"But I can't do it without you, damn it, and you know why . . . no mal can head a private concern that employs humans."

She threw up her hands and stalked back to her desk. It was silent in the office for many minutes. Then she spoke softly.

"Pericles, I don't share your obsession . . . I've matured, you know . . . now I think I can survive with just the memory of my dream-share. But you rescued me from my own narcissism. And you've given me . . . other things. If you can't shake this psychotic notion of yours, I'll stay around till you can."

Horses and geniuses don't cry . . . ah, but poets. . .!

And that is how the irony came about—that the first world where terraforming was attempted was not some sterile alien globe, but Old Earth itself. Or as the horse Pericles is reputed to have said, "Remade in its own image."

The oceans were cleared . . . the laborious, incredibly costly first step. That done, and with a little help from two thousand chemists and bioengineers, the atmosphere began to cleanse itself. That first new air was neither sweet nor fresh—but neither was it toxic.

Grasses are the shock troops of nature. Moved in first, the special tough strains took hold in the raped soil. Bacteria and nutrients were added, fast-multiplying strains that spread rapidly. From the beachheads near the Arctic and in the high mountains flora and fauna were reintroduced.

Then came the major reseeding of the superfast trees: spruce and white pine, juniper and birch, cypress and mori and teak, fir and ash. And from a tiny museum on Duntroon, long preserved sequoia and citrus.

Eventually there was a day when the first flowers were replanted. The hand-planting of the first bush—a green rose—was watched by the heads of the agricultural staffs, a black horse, and a ravishing woman in the postbloom of her first rejuvenation.

That's when Pericles registered the Articles. They aroused only minor interest within the sleepy, vast Empire. The subject was good for a few days' conversation before the multitudes returned to more important news.

But among the mal, there was something in the Articles and accompanying pictures that tugged at nerves long since sealed off in men and mankind by time and by choice. Something that pulled each rough soul toward an unspectacular planet circling an unremarkable star in a distant corner of space.

So the mal went back to Old Earth. Not all, but many. They left the trappings of Imperial civilization and confusing intelligence and went to the first mal planet.

More simply, they went home.

There they labored not for man, but for themselves. And when a few interested humans applied for permission to emigrate there, they were turned back by the private patrol. For the Articles composed by the horse Pericles forbade the introduction of man to Old Earth. Those Articles were written in endurasteel, framed in paragraphs of molten duralloy. Neither human curiosity nor money could make a chip in them.

It was clear to judges and law machines that while the Articles (especially the phrase about "the meek finally inheriting the Earth") might not have been good manners or good taste, they were very good law.

It was finished.

It was secured.

It was given unto the mal till the end of time.

Casperdan and Pericles left the maze that was now Dream Enterprises and went to Old Earth. They came to stand on the same place where they'd stood decades before.

Now clean low surf grumbled and subsided on a beach of polished sand that was home to shellfish and worms and brittle stars. They stood on a field of low, waving green grass. In the distance a family of giraffe moved like sentient signal towers toward the horizon. The male saw them, swung its long neck in greeting. Pericles responded with a long, high whinny.

To their left, in the distance, the first mountains began. Not bare and empty now, but covered with a mat of thick evergreen crowned with new snow.

They breathed in the heady scent of fresh clover and distant honeysuckle.

"It's done," he said.

Casperdan nodded and began to remove her clothes. Someday she would bring a husband down here. She was the sole exception in the Articles. Her golden hair fell in waves to her waist. Someday, yes . . . But for now . . .

"You know, Pericles, it really wasn't necessary. All this, I mean."

The stallion pawed at the thick loam underfoot.

"What percentage of dreams are necessary, Casperdan? You know, for many mal intelligence was not a gift but a curse. It was always that way for man, too, but he had more time to grow into it. For the mal it came like lightning, as a shock. The mal are still tied to their past—to this world. As I am still tied. Have you ever seen mal as happy as they are here?

"Certainly sentience came too quickly for the horse. According to the ancient texts we once had a special relationship with man that rivaled the dog's. That vanished millennia ago. The dog kept it, though, and so did the cat, and certain others. Other mal never missed it because they never had it. But the horse did, and couldn't cope with the knowledge of that loss that intelligence brought. There weren't many of us left, Casperdan.

"But we'll do well here. This is home. Man would feel it too, if he came here now. Feel it . . . and ruin this world all over again. That's why I wrote the Articles."

She was clad only in shorts now and to her great surprise found she was trembling slightly. She hadn't done that since she was fifteen. How long ago was that? Good God, had she ever been fifteen? But her face and figure were those of a girl of twenty. Rejuvenation.

"Pericles, I want back what you promised. I want back what I had in the Meadows of Blood in the Ravaged Mountains."

"Of course," he replied, as though it had happened yesterday. A mal's sense of time is different from man's, and Pericles' was different from that of most mal.

"You know, I have a confession to make."

She was startled to see the relentless dreamer was embarrassed!

"It was done only to bribe you, you know. But in truth . . . in truth, I think I enjoyed it as much as you. And I'm ashamed, because I still don't understand *why*."

He kicked at the dirt.

She smiled understandingly. "It's the old bonds you talk about, Per. I think they must work both ways."

She walked up to him and entwined her left hand in his mane, threw the other over his back. A pull and she was up. Her movement was done smoothly . . . she'd practiced it ten thousand times in her mind.

Both hands dug tightly into the silver-black mane. Leaning forward, she pressed her cheek against the cool neck and felt ropes of muscle taut beneath the skin. The anticipation was so painful it hurt to speak.

"I'm ready," she whispered breathlessly.

"So am I," he replied.

Then the horse Pericles gave her what few humans had had for millennia, what had been outlawed in the Declaration of Animal's Rights, what they'd shared in the Meadows of Blood a billion years ago.

Gave her back the small part of the dream that was hers.

Tail flying, hooves digging dirt, magnificent body moving effortlessly over the rolling hills and grass, the horse became brother to the wind as he and his rider thundered off toward the waiting mountains . . .

And that's why there's confusion in the old records. Because they knew all about Casperdan in the finest detail, but all they knew about the horse Pericles was that he was a genius and a poet. Now, there's ample evidence as to his genius. But the inquisitive are puzzled when they search and find no record of his poetry.

Even if they knew, they wouldn't understand.

The poetry, you see, was when he moved.

MIDNIGHT BY THE MORPHY WATCH

by Fritz Leiber

Being World's Chess Champion (crowned or un-crowned), puts a more deadly and maddening strain on a man even than being President of the United States. We have a prime example enthroned right now. For more than ten years the present champion was clearly the greatest chess player in the world, but during that time he exhibited such willful and seem-ingly self-destructive behavior—refusing to enter cru-cial tournaments, quitting them for crankish reasons while holding a commanding lead, entertaining what many called a paranoid delusion that the whole world was plotting to keep him from reaching the top—that many informed experts wrote him off as a contender for the highest honors. Even his staunchest supporters experienced agonizing doubts—until he finally silenced his foes and supremely satisfied his friends by deci-sively winning the crucial and ultimate match on a fantastic polar island.

Even minor players bitten by the world's-championship bug—or the fantasy of it—experience a bit of that terrible strain, occasionally in very strange and even eerie fashion. . . .

Stirf Ritter-Rebil was indulging in one of his numer-ous creative avocations—wandering at random through his beloved downtown San Francisco with its some-times dizzily slanting sidewalks, its elusive narrow courts and alleys, and its kaleidescope of ever-changing store and restaurant-fronts amongst the ones that persist as landmarks. To divert his gaze there were interesting almond and black faces among the paler ones. There was the dangerous surge of traffic threatening to invade the humpy sidewalks.

The sky was a careless silvery gray, like an expensive whore's mink coat covering bizarre garb or nakedness. There were even wisps of fog, that Bay Area benison. There were bankers and hippies, con men and corporation men, queers of all varieties, beggars, and sports, murderers and saints (at least in Ritter's freewheeling imagination). And there were certainly alluring girls aplenty in an astounding variety of packages—and pretty girls are the essential spice in any really tasty ragout of people. In fact there may well have been Martians and time travelers.

Ritter's ramble had taken on an even more dreamlike, whimsical and unpredictable quality than usual—with an unflagging anticipation of mystery, surprise, and erotic or diamond-studded adventure around the very next corner.

He frequently thought of himself by his middle name, Ritter, because he was a sporadically ardent chess player now in the midst of a sporad. In German "Ritter" means "knight," yet Germans do not call a knight a Ritter, but a springer, or jumper (for its crookedly hopping move), a matter for inexhaustible philological, historical, and socioracial speculation. Ritter was also a deeply devoted student of the history of chess, both in its serious and anecdotal aspects.

He was a tall, white-haired man, rather thin, saved from the look of mere age by ravaged handsomeness, an altogether youthful though worldly and sympathetically cynical curiosity in his gaze (when he wasn't daydreaming), and a definitely though unobtrusively theatrical carriage.

He was more daydreamingly lost than usual on this particular ramble, though vividly aware of all sorts of floating, freakish, beautiful and grotesque novelties about him. Later he recollected that he must have been fairly near Portsmouth Square and not terribly far from the intersection of California and Montgomery. At all events, he was fascinated looking into the display window of a secondhand store he'd never recalled seeing before. It must be a new place, for he knew all the stores in the area, yet it had the dust and dinginess of an *old* place—its owner must have moved in without refurbishing the premises or even cleaning them up. And it had a delightful range of items for sale, from genuine antiques to mod facsimiles of same. He noted in his first scanning glance, and with growing delight, a Civil War saber, a standard promotional replica of the starship *Enterprise*, a brand-new deck of tarots, an authentic shrunken head like a black globule of detritus from a giant's nostril, some fancy roach-clips, a silver lusterware creamer, a Sony tape recorder, a last year's whiskey jug in the form of a cable car, a scatter of Gene McCarthy and Nixon buttons, a single brass Lucas "King of the Road" headlamp from a Silver Ghost Rolls Royce, an electric toothbrush, a 1920's radio, a last month's copy of the *Phoenix*, and three dime-a-dozen plastic chess sets.

And then, suddenly, all these were wiped from his mind. Unnoticed were the distant foghorns, the complaining prowl of slowed traffic, the shards of human speech behind him mosaicked with the singsong chatter of Chinatown, the reflection in the plate glass of a girl in a grandmother dress selling flowers, and of opening umbrellas as drops of rain began to sprinkle from the mist. For every atom of Stirf Ritter-Rebil's awareness was burningly concentrated on a small figure seeking anonymity among the randomly set-out chessmen of one of the plastic sets. It was a squat, tarnished silver chess pawn in the form of a barbarian warrior. Ritter knew it was a chess pawn—and what's more, he knew to what fabulous historic set it belonged, because he had seen one of its mates in a rare police photograph given him by a Portuguese chess-playing acquaintance. He knew that he had quite without warning arrived at a once-in-a-lifetime experience.

Heart pounding but face a suave mask, he drifted into the store's interior. In situations like this it was all-essential not to let the seller know what you were interested in or even that you were interested at all.

The shadowy interior of the place lived up to its display window. There was the same piquant clutter of dusty memorables and among them several glass cases housing presumably choicer items, behind one of which stood a gaunt yet stocky elderly man whom Ritter sensed was the proprietor, but pretended not even to notice.

But his mind was so concentrated on the tarnished silver pawn he *must* possess that it was a stupefying surprise when his automatically flitting gaze stopped at a second even greater once-in-a-lifetime item in the glass case behind which the proprietor stood. It was a dingy, old-fashioned gold pocket watch with the hours not in Roman numerals as they should have been in so venerable a timepiece, but in the form of dull gold and silver chess pieces as depicted in game-diagrams. Attached to the watch by a bit of thread was a slim, hexagonal gold key.

Ritter's mind almost froze with excitement. Here was the big brother of the skulking barbarian pawn. Here, its true value almost certainly unknown to its owner, was one of the supreme rarities of the world of chess-memorabilia. Here was no less than the gold watch Paul Morphy, meteorically short-reigned King of American chess, had been given by an adoring public in New York City on May 25, 1859, after the triumphal tour of London and Paris which had proven him to be perhaps the greatest chess genius of all time.

Ritter veered as if by lazy chance toward the case, his eyes resolutely fixed on a dull silver ankh at the opposite end from the chess watch.

He paused like a sleepwalker across from the proprietor after what seemed like a suitable interval and— hoping the pounding of his heart wasn't audible—made a desultory inquiry about the ankh. The proprietor replied in as casual a fashion, though getting the item out for his inspection.

Ritter brooded over the silver love-cross for a bit, then shook his head and idly asked about another item and still another, working his insidious way toward the Morphy watch.

The proprietor responded to his queries in a low, bored voice, though in each case dutifully getting the item out to show Ritter. He was a very old and completely bald man with a craggy Baltic cast to his features. He vaguely reminded Ritter of someone.

Finally Ritter was asking about an old silver railroad watch next to the one he still refused to look at directly.

Then he shifted to another old watch with a complicated face with tiny windows showing the month and the phases of the moon, on the other side of the one that was keeping his heart a-pound.

His gambit worked. The proprietor at last dragged out the Morphy watch, saying softly, "Here is an odd old piece that might interest you. The case is solid gold. It threatens to catch your interest, does it not?"

Ritter at last permitted himself a second devouring glance. It confirmed the first. Beyond shadow of a doubt this was the genuine relic that had haunted his thoughts for two thirds of a lifetime.

What he said was "It's odd, all right. What are those funny little figures it has in place of hours?"

"Chessmen," the other explained. "See, that's a King at six o'clock, a pawn at five, a Bishop at four, a Knight at three, a Rook at two, a Queen at one, another King at midnight, and then repeat, eleven to seven, around the dial."

"Why midnight rather than noon?" Ritter asked stupidly. He knew why.

The proprietor's wrinkled fingernail indicated a small window just above the center of the face. In it showed the letters P.M. "That's another rare feature," he explained. "I've handled very few watches that knew the difference between night and day."

"Oh, and I suppose those squares on which the chessmen are placed and which go around the dial in two and half circles make a sort of checkerboard!"

"Chessboard," the other corrected. "Incidentally, there are exactly 64 squares, the right number."

Ritter nodded. "I suppose you're asking a fortune for it," he remarked, as if making conversation.

The other shrugged. "Only a thousand dollars."

Ritter's heart skipped a beat. He had more than ten times that in his bank account. A trifle, considering the stake.

But he bargained for the sake of appearances. At one point he argued, "'But the watch doesn't run, I suppose."

"But it still has its hands," the old Balt with the hauntingly familiar face countered. "And it still has its works, as you can tell by the weight. They could be repaired, I imagine. A French movement. See, there's the hexagonal winding-key still with it."

A price of seven hundred dollars was finally agreed on. He paid out the fifty dollars he always carried with him and wrote a check for the remainder. After a call to his bank, it was accepted.

The watch was packed in a small box in a nest of fluffy cotton. Ritter put it in a pocket of his jacket and buttoned the flap.

He felt dazed. The Morphy watch, the watch Paul Morphy had kept his whole short life, despite his growing hatred of chess, the watch he had willed to his French admirer and favorite opponent Jules Arnous de Riviere, the watch that had then mysteriously disappeared, the watch of watches—was his!

He felt both weightless and dizzy as he moved toward the street, which blurred a little.

As he was leaving he noticed in the window something he'd forgotten—he wrote a check for fifty dollars for the silver barbarian pawn without bargaining.

He was in the street, feeling glorious and very tired. Faces and umbrellas were alike blurs. Rain pattered on his face unnoticed, but there came a stab of anxiety.

He held still and very carefully used his left hand to transfer the heavy little box—and the pawn in a twist of paper—to his trouser pocket, where he kept his left hand closed around them. Then he felt secure.

He flagged down a cab and gave his home address.

The passing scene began to come unblurred. He recognized Rimini's Italian Restaurant where his own chess game was now having a little renaissance after five years of foregoing tournament chess because he knew he was too old for it. A chess-smitten young cook there, indulged by the owner, had organized a tourney. The entrants were mostly young people. A tall, moody girl he thought of as the Czarina, who played a remarkable game, and a likeable, loudmouthed young Jewish lawyer he thought of as Rasputin, who played almost as good a game and talked a better one, both stood out. On impulse Ritter had entered the tournament because it was such a trifling one that it didn't really break his rule against playing serious chess. And, his old skills reviving nicely, he had done well enough to have a firm grip on third place, right behind Rasputin and the Czarina.

But now that he had the Morphy watch. . . .

Why the devil should he think that having the Morphy watch should improve his chess game? he asked himself sharply. It was as silly as faith in the power of the relics of saints.

In his hand inside his left pocket the watch box vibrated eagerly, as if it contained a big live insect, a golden bee or beetle. But that, of course, was his imagination.

Stirf Ritter-Rebil (a proper name, he always felt, for a chess player, since they specialize in weird ones, from Euwe to Znosko-Borovsky, from Noteboom to Dus-Chotimirski) lived in a one-room and bath, five blocks west of Union Square and packed with files, books and also paintings wherever the wall space allowed, of his dead wife and parents, and of his son. Now that he was older, he liked living with clues to all of his life in view. There was a fine view of the Pacific and the Golden Gate and their fogs to the west, over a sea of roofs. On the orderly cluttered tables were two fine chess sets with positions set up.

Ritter cleared a space beside one of them and set in its center the box and packet. After a brief pause—as if for propitiatory prayer, he told himself sardonically —he gingerly took out the Morphy watch and centered it for inspection with the unwrapped silver pawn behind it.

Then, wiping and adjusting his glasses and from time to time employing a large magnifying glass, he examined both treasures exhaustively.

The outer edge of the dial was circled with a ring or wheel of 24 squares, 12 pale and 12 dark alternating. On the pale squares were the figures of chessmen indicating the hours, placed in the order the old Balt had described. The Black pieces went from midnight to five and were of silver set with tiny emeralds or bright jade, as his magnifying glass confirmed. The White pieces went from six to eleven and were of gold set with minute rubies or amythysts. He recalled that descriptions of the watch always mentioned the figures as being colored.

Inside that came a second circle of 24 pale and dark squares.

Finally, inside *that*, there was a two-thirds circle of 16 squares below the center of the dial.

In the corresponding space above the center was the little window showing PM.

The hands on the dial were stopped at 11:57—three minutes to midnight.

With a paperknife he carefully pried open the hinged back of the watch, on which were floridly engraved the initials PM—which he suddenly realized also stood for Paul Morphy.

On the inner golden back covering the works was engraved "France H&H"—the old Balt was right again—while scratched in very tiny—he used his magnifier once more—were a half dozen sets of numbers, most of the sevens having the French slash. Pawnbrokers' marks. Had Arnous de Riviere pawned the treasure? Or later European owners? Oh well, chess players were an impecunious lot. There was also a hole by which the watch could be wound with its hexagonal key. He carefully wound it but of course nothing happened.

He closed the back and brooded on the dial. The 64 squares—24 plus 24 plus 16—made a fantastic circular board. One of the many variants of chess he had played once or twice was cylindrical.

"*Les echecs fantasques*," he quoted. "It's a cynical madman's allegory with its doddering monarch, vampire queen, gangster knights, double-faced bishops, ramming rooks and inane pawns, whose supreme ambition is to change their sex and share the dodderer's bed."

With a sigh of regret he tore his gaze away from the watch and took up the pawn behind it. Here was a grim little fighter, he thought, bringing the tarnished silver figure close to his glasses. Naked long-sword clasped against his chest, point down, iron skullcap low on forehead, face merciless as Death's. What did the golden legionaires look like?

Then Ritter's expression grew grim too, as he decided to do something he'd had in mind ever since glimpsing the barbarian pawn in the window. Making a long arm, he slid out a file drawer and after flipping a few tabs drew out a folder marked "Death of Alekhine." The light was getting bad. He switched on a big desk lamp against the night.

Soon he was studying a singularly empty photograph. It was of an unoccupied old armchair with a peg-in chess set open on one of the flat wooden arms. Behind the chess set stood a tiny figure. Bringing the magnifying glass once more into play, he confirmed what he had expected: that it was a precise mate to the barbarian pawn he had bought today.

He glanced through another item from the folder—an old letter on onionskin paper in a foreign script with cedillas under half the "C's" and tildes over half the "A's."

It was from his Portuguese friend, explaining that the photo was a reproduction of one in the Lisbon police files.

The photo was of the chair in which Alexander Alekhine had been found dead of a heart attack on the top floor of a cheap Lisbon rooming house in 1946.

Alekhine had won the World's Chess Championship from Capablanca in 1927. He had held the world's record for the greatest number of games played simultaneously and blindfolded—32. In 1946 he was preparing for an official match with the Russian champion Botvinnik, although he had played chess for the Axis in World War II. Though at times close to psychosis, he was considered the profoundest and most brilliant attacking player who had ever lived.

Had he also, Ritter asked himself, been one of the players to own the Morphy silver-and-gold chess set and the Morphy watch?

He reached for another file folder labeled "Death of Steinitz." This time he found a brownish daguerreotype showing an empty, narrow, old-fashioned hospital bed with a chessboard and set on a small table beside it. Among the chess pieces, Ritter's magnifier located another one of the unmistakable barbarian pawns.

Wilhelm Steinitz, called the Father of Modern Chess, who had held the world's championship for 28 years, until his defeat by Emmanuel Lasker in 1894. Steinitz, who had had two psychotic episodes and been hospitalized for them in the last years of his life, during the second of which he had believed he could move the chess pieces by electricity and challenged God to a match, offering God the odds of Pawn and Move. It was after the second episode that the daguerreotype had been taken which Ritter had acquired many years ago from the aged Emmanuel Lasker.

Ritter leaned back wearily from the table, took off his glasses and knuckled his tired eyes. It was later than he'd imagined.

He thought about Paul Morphy retiring from chess at the age of 21 after beating every important player in the world and issuing a challenge, never accepted, to take on any master at the odds of Pawn and Move. After that contemptuous gesture in 1859 he had brooded for 25 years, mostly a recluse in his family home in New Orleans, emerging only fastidiously dressed and be-caped for an afternoon promenade and regular attendance at the opera. He suffered paranoid episodes during which he believed his relatives were trying to steal his fortune and, of all things, his clothes. And he never spoke of chess or played it, except for an occasional game with his friend Maurian at the odds of Knight and Move.

Twenty-five years of brooding in solitude without the solace of playing chess, but with the Morphy chess set and the Morphy watch in the same room, testimonials to his world mastery.

Ritter wondered if those circumstances—with Morphy constantly thinking of chess, he felt sure—were not ideal for the transmission of the vibrations of thought and feeling into inanimate objects, in this case the golden Morphy set and watch.

Material objects intangibly vibrating with 25 years of the greatest chess thought and then by strange chance (chance alone?) falling into the hands of two other periodically psychotic chess champions, as the photographs of the pawns hinted.

An absurd fancy, Ritter told himself. And yet one to the pursuit of which he had devoted no small part of his life.

And now the richly vibrant objects were in *his* hands. What would be the effect of that on *his* game?

But to speculate in that direction was doubly absurd.

A wave of tiredness went through him. It was close to midnight.

He heated a small supper for himself, consumed it, drew the heavy window drapes tight, and undressed.

He turned back the cover of the big couch next to

the table, switched off the light, and inserted himself into bed.

It was Ritter's trick to put himself to sleep by playing through a chess opening in his thoughts. Like any talented player, he could readily contest one blindfold game, though he could not quite visualize the entire board and often had to count moves square by square, especially with the Bishops. He selected Breyer's Gambit, an old favorite of his.

He made a half dozen moves. Then suddenly the board was brightly illuminated in his mind, as if a light had been turned on there. He had to stare around to assure himself that the room was still dark as pitch. There was only the bright board inside his head.

His sense of awe was lost in luxuriant delight. He moved the mental pieces rapidly, yet saw deep into the possibilities of each position.

Far in the background he heard a church clock on Franklin boom out the dozen strokes of midnight. After a short while he announced mate in five by White. Black studied the position for perhaps a minute, then resigned.

Lying flat on his back he took several deep breaths. Never before had he played such a brilliant blindfold game—or game with sight even. That it was a game with himself didn't seem to matter—his personality had split neatly into two players.

He studied the final position for a last time, returned the pieces to their starting positions in his head, and rested a bit before beginning another game.

It was then he heard the ticking, a nervous sound five times as fast as the distant clock had knelled. He lifted his wristwatch to his ear. Yes, it was ticking rapidly too, but this was another ticking, louder.

He sat up silently in bed, leaned over the table, switched on the light.

The Morphy watch. That was where the louder ticks were coming from. The hands stood at twelve ten and the small window showed AM.

For a long while he held that position—mute, motionless, aghast, wondering, fearing, doubting, dreaming dreams no mortal ever dared to dream before.

Let's see, Edgar Allan Poe had died when Morphy was 12 years old and beating his uncle, Ernest Morphy, then chess king of New Orleans.

It seemed impossible that a stopped watch with works well over one hundred years old should begin to run. Doubly impossible that it should begin to run at approximately the right time—his wrist watch and the Morphy watch were no more than a minute apart.

Yet the works might be in better shape than either he or the old Balt had guessed; watches did capriciously start and stop running. Coincidences were only coincidences.

Yet he felt profoundly uneasy. He pinched himself and went through the other childish tests.

He said aloud, "I am Stirf Ritter-Rebil, an old man who lives in San Francisco and plays chess, and who yesterday discovered an unusual curio. But really, everything is perfectly normal . . ."

Nevertheless, he suddenly got the feeling of "A man-eating lion is aprowl." It was the childish form terror still took for him on rare occasions. For a minute or so everything seemed *too* still, despite the ticking. The stirring of the heavy drapes at the window gave him a shiver, and the walls seemed thin, their protective power nil.

Gradually the sense of a killer lion moving outside them faded and his nerves calmed.

He switched off the light, the bright mental board returned, and the ticking became reassuring rather than otherwise. He began another game with himself, playing for Black the Classical Defense to the Ruy Lopez, another of his favorites.

This game proceeded as brilliantly and vividly as the first. There was the sense of a slim, man-shaped glow standing beside the bright board in the mental dark. After a while the shape grew amorphous and less bright, then split into three. However, it bothered him

little, and when he at last announced mate in three for
Black, he felt great satisfaction and profound fatigue.

Next day he was in exceptionally good spirits. Sunlight banished all night's terrors as he went about his
ordinary business and writing chores. From time to
time he reassured himself that he could still visualize a
mental chessboard very clearly, and he thought now
and again about the historical chess mystery he was in
the midst of solving. The ticking of the Morphy watch
carried an exciting, eager note. Toward the end of the
afternoon he realized he was keenly anticipating visiting Rimini's to show off his new-found skill.

He got out an old gold watch chain and fob, snapped
it to the Morphy watch, which he carefully wound
again, pocketed them securely in his vest, and set out
for Rimini's. It was a grand day—cool, brightly sunlit
and a little windy. His steps were brisk. He wasn't
thinking of all the strange happenings but of *chess*. It's
been said that a man can lose his wife one day and
forget her that night, playing *chess*.

Rimini's was a good, dark, garlic-smelling restaurant with an annex devoted to drinks, substantial free
pasta appetizers and, for the nonce, chess. As he
drifted into the long L-shaped room, Ritter became
pleasantly aware of the row of boards, chessmen, and
the intent, mostly young, faces bent above them.

Then Rasputin was grinning at him calculatedly and
yapping at him cheerfully. They were due to play their
tournament game. They checked out a set and were
soon at it. Beside them the Czarina also contested a
crucial game, her moody face askew almost as if her neck
were broken, her bent wrists near her chin, her long
fingers pointing rapidly at her pieces as she calculated
combinations, like a sorceress putting a spell on them.

Ritter was aware of her, but only peripherally. For
last night's bright mental board had returned, only
now it was superimposed on the actual board before
him. Complex combinations sprang to mind effortlessly. He beat Rasputin like a child. The Czarina
caught the win from the corner of her eye and growled

faintly in approval. She was winning her own game;
Ritter beating Rasputin bumped her into first place.
Rasputin was silent for once.

A youngish man with a black mustache was sharply
inspecting Ritter's win. He was the California state
champion, Martinez, who had recently played a simultaneous at Rimini's, winning fifteen games, losing none,
drawing only with the Czarina. He now suggested a
casual game to Ritter, who nodded somewhat abstract-
edly.

They contested two very hairy games—a Sicilian
Defense by Martinez in which Ritter advanced all his
pawns in front of his castled King in a wild-looking
attack, and a Ruy Lopez by Martinez that Ritter answered with the Classical Defense, going to great lengths
to preserve his powerful King's Bishop. The mental
board stayed superimposed, and it almost seemed to
Ritter that there was a small faint halo over the piece
he must next move or capture. To his mild astonish-
ment he won both games.

A small group of chess-playing onlookers had gathered around their board. Martinez was looking at him
speculatively, as if to ask, "Now just where did you
spring from, old man, with your power game? I don't
recall ever hearing of you."

Ritter's contentment would have been complete, except that among the kibitzers, toward the back, there
was a slim young man whose face was always shadowed when Ritter glimpsed it. Ritter saw him in three
different places, though never in movement and never
for more than an instant. Somehow he seemed one
onlooker too many. This disturbed Ritter obscurely,
and his face had a thoughtful, abstracted expression
when he finally quit Rimini's for the faintly drizzling
evening streets. After a block he looked around, but
so far as he could tell, he wasn't being followed. This
time he walked the whole way to his apartment, passing several landmarks of Dashiell Hammett, Sam Spade,
and *The Maltese Falcon*.

Gradually, under the benison of the foggy droplets,

his mood changed to one of exaltation. He had just now played some beautiful chess, he was in the midst of an amazing historic chess mystery he'd always yearned to penetrate, and somehow the Morphy watch was working *for* him—he could actually hear its muffled ticking in the street, coming up from his waist to his ear.

Tonight his room was a most welcome retreat, *his* place, like an extension of his mind. He fed himself. Then he reviewed, with a Sherlock Holmes smile, what he found himself calling "The Curious Case of the Morphy Timepiece." He wished he had a Dr. Watson to hear him expound. First, the appearance of the watch after Morphy returned to New York on the *Persia* in 1859. Over paranoid years Morphy had imbued it with psychic energy and vast chessic wisdom. Or else—mark this, Doctor—he had set up the conditions whereby subsequent owners of the watch would *think* he had done such, for the supernatural is not our bailiwick, Watson. Next (after de Riviere) great Steinitz had come into possession of it and challenged God and died mad. Then, after a gap, paranoid Alekhine had owned it and devised diabolically brilliant, hyper-Morphian strategies of attack, and died all alone after a thousand treacheries in a miserable Lisbon flat with a peg-in chess set and the telltale barbarian pawn next to his corpse. Finally after a hiatus of almost thirty years (where had the watch and set been then? Who'd had their custody? Who was the old Balt?) the timepiece and a pawn had come into his own possession. A unique case, Doctor. There isn't even a parallel in Prague in 1863.

The nighted fog pressed against the windowpane and now and again a little rain pattered. San Francisco was a London City and had its own resident great detective. One of Dashiell Hammett's hobbies had been chess, even though there was no record of Spade having played the game.

From time to time Ritter studied the Morphy watch as it glowed and ticked on the table space he'd cleared. PM once more, he noted. The time: White Queen, ruby glittering, past Black King, microscopically emerald studded—I mean five minutes past midnight, Doctor. The witching hour, as the superstitiously-minded would have it.

But to bed, to bed, Watson. We have much to do tomorrow—and, paradoxically, tonight.

Seriously, Ritter was glad when the golden glow winked out on the watch face, though the strident ticking kept on, and he wriggled himself into his couch-bed and arranged himself for thought. The mental board flashed on once more and he began to play. First he reviewed all the best games he'd ever played in his life—there weren't very many—discovering variations he'd never dreamed of before. Then he played through all his favorite games in the history of chess, from MacDonnell-La Bourdonnais to Fischer-Spasski, not forgetting Steinitz-Zukertort and Alekhine-Bogolyubov. They were richer masterpieces than ever before—the mental board saw very deep. Finally he split his mind again and challenged himself to an eight-game blindfold match, Black against White. Against all expectation, Black won with three wins, two losses, and three draws.

But the night was not all imaginative and ratiocinative delight. Twice there came periods of eerie silence, which the ticking of the watch in the dark made only more complete, and two spells of the man-eating lion a-prowl that raised his hair at the roots. Once again there loomed the slim, faint, man-shaped glow beside the mental board and he wouldn't go away. Worse, he was joined by two other man-shaped glows, one short and stocky, with a limp, the other fairly tall, stocky too, and restless. These inner intruders bothered Ritter increasingly—who were they? And wasn't there beginning to be a faint fourth? He recalled the slim young elusive watcher with shadowed face of his games with Martinez and wondered if there was a connection.

Disturbing stuff—and most disturbing of all, the apprehension that his mind might be racked apart and fragmented abroad with all its machine-gun thinking, that it already extended by chessic veins from one chess-playing planet to another, to the ends of the universe.

He was profoundly glad when toward the end of his self-match, his brain began to dull and slow. His last memory was of an attempt to invent a game to be played on the circular board on the watch dial. He thought he was succeeding as his mind at last went spiraling off into unconsciousness.

Next day he awoke restless, scratchy, and eager— and with the feeling that the three or four dim figures had stood around his couch all night vibrating like strobe lights to the rhythm of the Morphy watch.

Coffee heightened his alert nervousness. He rapidly dressed, snapped the Morphy watch to its chain and fob, pocketed the silver pawn, and went out to hunt down the store where he'd purchased the two items.

In a sense he never found it, though he tramped and minutely scanned Montgomery, Kearny, Grant, Stockton, Clay, Sacramento, California, Pine, Bush, and all the rest.

What he did find at long last was a store window with a grotesque pattern of dust on it that he was certain was identical with that on the window through which he had first glimpsed the barbarian Pawn day before yesterday.

Only now the display space behind the window was empty and the whole store too, except for a tall, lanky Black with a fabulous Afro hair-do, sweeping up.

Ritter struck up a conversation with the man as he worked, and slowly winning his confidence, discovered that he was one of three partners opening a store there that would be stocked solely with African imports.

Finally, after the Black had fetched a great steaming pail of soapy water and a long-handled roller mop and begun to efface forever the map of dust by which Ritter had identified the place, the man at last grew confidential.

"Yeah," he said, "there *was* a queer old character had a second-hand store here until yesterday that had every crazy thing you could dig for sale, some junk, some real fancy. Then he cleared everything out into two big trucks in a great rush, with me breathing down his neck every minute because he'd been supposed to do it the day before.

"Oh, but he was a fabulous cat, though," the Black went on with a reminiscent grin as he sloshed away the last peninsulas and archipelagos of the dust map. "One time he said to me. 'Excuse me while I rest,' and—you're not going to believe this—he went into a corner and stood on his head. I'm telling you he did, man. I'd like to bust a gut. I thought he'd have a stroke—and he did get a bit lavender in the face—but after three minutes exact—I timed him—he flipped back onto his feet neat as you could ask and went on with his work twice as fast as before, supervising his carriers out of their skulls. Wow, that was an event."

Ritter departed without comment. He had got the final clue he'd been seeking to the identity of the old Balt and likewise the fourth and most shadowy form that had begun to haunt his mental chessboard.

Casually standing on his head, saying "It threatens to catch your interest"—why, it had to be Aaron Nimzovich, most hyper-eccentric player of them all and Father of Hypermodern Chess, who had been Alekhine's most dangerous but ever-evaded challenger. Why, the old Balt had even looked exactly like an aged Nimzovich—hence Ritter's constant sense of a facial familiarity. Of course, Nimzovich had supposedly died in the 1930's in his home city of Riga in the U.S.S.R., but what were life and breath to the forces with which Ritter was now embroiled?

It seemed to him that there were four dim figures stalking him relentlessly as lions right now in the Chinatown crowds, while despite the noise he could hear and feel the ticking of the Morphy watch at his waist.

He fled to the Danish Kitchen at the St. Francis Hotel and consumed cup on cup of good coffee and two orders of Eggs Benedict, and had his mental chessboard flashing on and off in his mind like a strobe light, and wondered if he shouldn't hurl the Morphy watch into the Bay to be rid of the influence racking his mind apart and destroying his sense of reality.

But then with the approach of evening, the urge toward *chess* gripped him more and more imperiously and he headed once again for Rimini's.

Rasputin and the Czarina were there and also Martinez again, and with the last a distinguished silver-haired man whom Martinez introduced as the South American international master, Pontebello, suggesting that he and Ritter have a quick game.

The board glowed again with the superimposed mental one, the halos were there once more, and Ritter won as if against a tyro.

At that, chess fever seized him entirely and he suggested he immediately play four simultaneous blindfold games with the two masters and the Czarina and Rasputin, Pontebello acting also as referee.

There were incredulous looks aplenty at that, but he *had* won those two games from Martinez and now the one from Pontebello, so arrangements were quickly made. Ritter insisting on an actual blindfold. All the other players crowded around to observe.

The simul began. There were now four mental boards glowing in Ritter's mind. It did not matter—*now*—that there were four dim forms with them, one by each. Ritter played with a practiced brilliance, combinations bubbled, he called out his moves crisply and unerringly. And so he beat the Czarina and Rasputin quickly. Pontebello took a little longer, and he drew with Martinez by perpetual check.

There was silence as he took off the blindfold to scan a circle of astonished faces and four shadowed ones behind them. He felt the joy of absolute chess mastery. The only sound he heard was the ticking, thunderous to him, of the Morphy watch.

Pontebello was first to speak. To Ritter, "Do you realize, master, what you've just done?" To Martinez, "Have you the scores of all four games?" To Ritter again, "Excuse me, but you look pale, as if you've just seen a ghost." "Four," Ritter corrected quietly. "Those of Morphy, Steinitz, Alekhine, and Nimzovich."

"Under the circumstances, most appropriate," commented Pontebello, while Ritter sought out again the four shadowed faces in the background. They were still there, though they had shifted their positions and withdrawn a little into the varied darknesses of Rimini's.

Amid talk of scheduling another blindfold exhibition and writing a multiple-signed letter describing tonight's simul to the U.S. Chess Federation—not to mention Pontebello's searching queries as to Ritter's chess career—he tore himself away and made for home through the dark streets, certain that four shadowy figures stalked behind him. The call of the mental *chess* in his own room was not to be denied.

Ritter forgot no moment of that night, for he did not sleep at all. The glowing board in his mind was an unquenchable beacon, and all-demanding mandala. He replayed all the important games of history, finding new moves. He contested two matches with himself, then one each with Morphy, Steinitz, Alekhine and Nimzovich, winning the first two, drawing the third, and losing the last by a half point. Nimzovich was the only one to speak, saying, "I am both dead and alive, as I'm sure you know. Please don't smoke, or threaten to."

He stacked eight mental boards and played two games of three-dimensional chess, Black winning both. He traveled to the ends of the universe, finding chess everywhere he went, and contesting a long game, more complex than 3-D chess, on which the fate of the universe depended. He drew it.

And all through the long night the four were with him in the room and the man-eating lion stared in through the window with black-and-white checkered mask and silver mane. While the Morphy watch ticked like a death-march drum. All figures vanished when the dawn came creeping, though the mental board stayed bright and busy into full daylight and showed no signs of vanishing ever. Ritter felt overpoweringly tired, his mind racked to atoms, on the verge of death.

But he knew what he had to do. He got a small box and packed into it, in cotton wool, the silver barbarian Pawn, the old photograph and daguerrotype, and a piece of paper on which he scribbled only:

Morphy, 1859-1884
de Riviere, 1884-?
Steinitz, ?-1900
Alekhine, ?-1946
Nimzovich, 1946-now
Ritter-Rebil, 3 days

Then he packed the watch in the box too, it stopped ticking, its hands were still at last, and in Ritter's mind the mental board winked out.

He took one last devouring gaze at the grotesque, glittering dial. Then he shut the box, wrapped and sealed and corded it, boldly wrote on it in black ink "Chess Champion of the World" and added the proper address.

He took it to the post office on Van Ness and sent it off by registered mail. Then he went home and slept like the dead.

Ritter never received a response. But he never got the box back either. Sometimes he wonders if the subsequent strange events in the Champion's life might have had anything to do with the gift.

And on even rarer occasions he wonders what would have happened if he had faced the challenge of death and let his mind be racked to bits, if that was what was to happen.

But on the whole he is content. Questions from Martinez and the others he has put off with purposefully vague remarks.

He still plays chess at Rimini's. Once he won another game from Martinez, when the latter was contesting a simul against twenty-three players.

ALL ON A GOLDEN AFTERNOON

by Robert Bloch

1

The uniformed man at the gate was very polite, but he didn't seem at all in a hurry to open up. Neither Dr. Prager's new Cadillac nor his old goatee made much of an impression on him.

It wasn't until Dr. Prager snapped, "But I've an appointment—Mr. Dennis said it was urgent!" that the uniformed man turned and went into the little guard booth to call the big house on the hill.

Dr. Saul Prager tried not to betray his impatience, but his right foot pressed down on the accelerator and a surrogate of exhaust did his fuming for him.

Just how far he might have gone in polluting the air of Bel Air couldn't be determined, for after a moment the man came out of the booth and unlocked the gate. He touched his cap and smiled.

"Sorry to keep you waiting, Doctor," he said. "You're to go right up."

Dr. Prager nodded curtly and the car moved forward.

"I'm new on this job and you got to take precautions, you know," the man called after him, but Dr. Prager wasn't listening. His eyes were fixed on the panorama of the hillside ahead. In spite of himself he was mightily impressed.

There was reason to be—almost half a million dollars' worth of reason. The combined efforts of a dozen architects, topiarists, and landscape gardeners had served to create what was popularly known as "the Garden of Eden." Although the phrase was a complimentary reference to Eve Eden, owner of the estate, there was much to commend it, Dr. Prager decided. That is, if one can picture a Garden of Eden boasting two swimming pools, an eight-car garage, and a corps of resident angels with power mowers.

This was by no means Dr. Prager's first visit, but he never failed to be moved by the spectacle of the palace on the hill. It was a fitting residence for Eve, the First Woman. The First Woman of the Ten Box-Office Leaders, that is.

The front door was already open when he parked in the driveway, and the butler smiled and bowed. He was, Dr. Prager knew, a genuine English butler, complete with accent and sideburns. Eve Eden had insisted on that, and she'd had one devil of a time obtaining an authentic specimen from the employment agencies. Finally she'd managed to locate one—from Central Casting.

"Good afternoon," the butler greeted him. "Mr. Dennis is in the library, sir. He is expecting you."

Dr. Prager followed the manservant through the foyer and down the hall. Everything was furnished with magnificent taste—as Mickey Dennis often observed, "Why not? Didn't we hire the best inferior decorator in Beverly Hills?"

The library itself was a remarkable example of calculated decor. Replete with the traditional overstuffed chairs, custom-made by a firm of reliable overstuffers, it boasted paneled walnut walls, polished mahogany floors, and a good quarter mile of bookshelves rising to the vaulted ceiling. Dr. Prager's glance swept the shelves, which were badly in need of dusting anyway. He noted a yard of Thackeray in green, two yards of brown Thomas Hardy, complemented by a delicate blue Dostoevski. Ten feet of Balzac, five feet of Dickens, a section of Shakespeare, a mass of Molière. Complete works, of course. The booksellers would naturally want to give Eve Eden the works. There must have been two thousand volumes on the shelves.

In the midst of it all sat Mickey Dennis, the agent, reading a smudged and dog-eared copy of *Variety*.

As Dr. Prager stood, hesitant, in the doorway, the little man rose and beckoned to him. "Hey, Doc!" he called. "I been waiting for you!"

"Sorry," Dr. Prager murmured. "There were several appointments I couldn't cancel."

"Never mind the appointments. You're on retainer with us, ain'cha? Well, sweetheart, this time you're really gonna earn it."

He shook his head as he approached. "Talk about trouble," he muttered—although Dr. Prager had not even mentioned the subject. "Talk about trouble, we got it. I ain't dared call the studio yet. If I did there'd be wigs floating all over Beverly Hills. Had to see you first. And you got to see *her*."

Dr. Prager waited. A good fifty percent of his professional duties consisted of waiting. Meanwhile he indulged in a little private speculation. What would it be this time? Another overdose of sleeping pills—a return to narcotics—an attempt to prove the old maxim that absinthe makes the heart grow fonder? He'd handled Eve Eden before in all these situations and topped it off with more routine assignments, such as the time she'd wanted to run off with the Japanese chauffeur. Come to think of it, that hadn't been exactly routine. Handling Eve was bad; handling the chauffeur was worse, but handling the chauffeur's wife and seven children was a nightmare. Still, he'd smoothed things over. He always smoothed things over, and that's why he was on a fat yearly retainer.

Dr. Prager, as a physician, generally disapproved of obesity, but when it came to yearly retainers he liked them plump. And this was one of the plumpest. Because of it he was ready for any announcement Mickey Dennis wanted to make.

The agent was clutching his arm now. "Doc, you gotta put the freeze on her, fast! This time it's murder!"

Despite himself, Dr. Prager blanched. He reached up and tugged reassuringly at his goatee. It was still there, the symbol of his authority. He had mastered the constriction in his vocal chords before he started to speak. "You mean she's killed someone?"

"No!" Mickey Dennis shook his head in disgust. "*That* would be bad enough, but we could handle it. I was just using a figger of speech, like. She wants to murder herself, Doc. Murder her career, to throw away a brand-new seven-year noncancelable no-option contract with a percentage of the gross. She wants to quit the industry."

"Leave pictures?"

"Now you got it, Doc. She's gonna walk out on four hundred grand a year."

There was real anguish in the agent's voice—the anguish of a man who is well aware that ten percent of four hundred thousand can buy a lot of convertibles.

"You gotta see her," Dennis moaned. "You gotta talk her out of it, fast."

Dr. Prager nodded. "Why does she want to quit?" he asked.

Mickey Dennis raised his hands. "I don't know," he wailed. "She won't give any reasons. Last night she just up and told me. Said she was through. And when I asked her politely just what the hell's the big idea, she dummied up. Said I wouldn't understand." The little man made a sound like trousers ripping in a tragic spot. "Damned right I wouldn't understand! But I want to find out."

Dr. Prager consulted his beard again with careful fingers. "I haven't seen her for over two months," he said. "How has she been behaving lately? I mean, otherwise?"

"Like a doll," the agent declared. "Just a living doll. To look at her you wouldn't of thought there was anything in her head but sawdust. Wrapped up the last picture clean, brought it in three days ahead of schedule. No blowups, no goofs, no nothing. She hasn't been hitting the sauce or anything else. Stays home mostly and goes to bed early. Alone, yet." Mickey Dennis made the pants-ripping sound again. "I might of figgered it was too good to be true."

"No financial worries?" Dr. Prager probed.

Dennis swept his arm forward to indicate the library and the expanse beyond. "With *this*? All clear and paid for. Plus a hunk of real estate in Long Beach and two oil wells gushing like Lolly Parsons over a hot scoop. She's got more loot than Fort Knox and almost as much as Crosby."

"Er—how old is Eve, might I ask?"

"You might ask, and you might get some funny answers. But I happen to know. She's thirty-three. I can guess what you're thinking, Doc, and it don't figger. She's good for another seven years, maybe more. Hell, all you got to do is look at her."

"That's just what I intend to do," Dr. Prager replied. "Where is she?"

"Upstairs, in her room. Been there all day. Won't see me." Mickey Dennis hesitated. "She doesn't know you're here either. I said I was gonna call you and she got kinda upset."

"Didn't want to see me, eh?"

"She said if that long-eared nanny goat got within six miles of this joint she'd—" The agent paused and shifted uncomfortably. "Like I mentioned, she was upset."

"I think I can handle the situation," Dr. Prager decided.

"Want me to come along and maybe try and soften her up a little?"

"That won't be necessary." Dr. Prager left the room, walking softly.

Mickey Dennis went back to his chair and picked up the magazine once more. He didn't read, because he was waiting for the sound of the explosion.

When it came he shuddered and almost gritted his teeth until he remembered how much it would cost to buy a new upper plate. Surprisingly enough, the sound of oaths and shrieks subsided after a time, and Dennis breathed a deep sigh of relief.

The doc was a good headshrinker. He'd handle her. He was handling her. So there was nothing to do now but relax.

2

"Relax," Dr. Prager said. "You've discharged all your aggression. Now you can stretch out. That's better."

The spectacle of Eve Eden stretched out in relaxation on a chaise longue was indeed better. In the words of many eminent lupine Hollywood authorities, it was the best.

Eve Eden's legs were long and white and her hair was long and blonde; both were now displayed to perfection, together with a whole series of coming attractions screened through her semitransparent lounging pajamas. The face that launched a thousand closeups was that of a petulant child, well-versed in the more statutory phases of juvenile delinquency.

Dr. Prager could cling to his professional objectivity only by clinging to his goatee. As it was, he dislodged several loose hairs and an equal number of loose impulses before he spoke again.

"Now," he said, "tell me all about it."

"Why should I?" Eve Eden's eyes and voice were equally candid. "I didn't ask you to come here. I'm not in any jam."

"Mr. Dennis said you're thinking of leaving pictures."

"Mr. Dennis is a cockeyed liar. I'm not thinking of leaving. I've left, period. Didn't he call the lawyers? Hasn't he phoned the studio? I told him to."

"I wouldn't know," Dr. Prager soothed.

"Then he's the one who's in a jam," Eve Eden announced happily. "Sure, I know why he called you. You're supposed to talk me out of it, right? Well, it's no dice, Doc. I made up my mind."

"Why?"

"None of your business."

Dr. Prager leaned forward. "But it is my business, Wilma."

"Wilma?"

Dr. Prager nodded, his voice softening. "Wilma Kozmowski. Little Wilma Kozmowski. Have you forgotten that I know all about her? The little girl whose mother deserted her. Who ran away from home when she was twelve and lived around. I know about the waitress jobs in Pittsburgh, and the burlesque show, and the B-girl years in Calumet City. And I know about Frank, and Eddie, and Nino, and Sid, and—all the others." Dr. Prager smiled. "You told me all this yourself, Wilma. And you told me all about what happened after you became Eve Eden. When you met me you weren't Eve Eden yet, not entirely. Wilma kept interfering, didn't she? It was Wilma who drank, took the drugs, got mixed up with the men, tried to kill herself. I helped you fight Wilma, didn't I, Eve? I helped you *become* Eve Eden, the movie star. That's why it's my business now to see that you stay that way. Beautiful, admired, successful, happy—"

"You're wrong, Doc. I found that out. If you want me to be happy, forget about Eve Eden. Forget about Wilma, too. From now on I'm going to be somebody else. So please, just go away."

"Somebody else?" Dr. Prager leaped at the phrase. An instant later he leaped literally.

"What's that?" he gasped.

He stared down at the floor, the hairs in his goatee bristling as he caught sight of the small white furry object that scuttled across the carpet.

Eve Eden reached down and scooped up the creature, smiling.

"Just a white rabbit," she explained. "Cute, isn't he? I bought him the other day."

"But—but—"

Dr. Prager goggled. It was indeed a white rabbit which Eve Eden cradled in her arms, but not *just* a white rabbit. For this rabbit happened to be wearing a vest and a checkered waistcoat, and Dr. Prager could almost swear that the silver chain across the vest terminated in a concealed pocket watch.

"I bought it after the dream," Eve Eden told him.

"Dream?"

"Oh, what's the use?" She sighed. "I might as well let you hear it. All you headshrinkers are queer for dreams anyway."

"You had a dream about rabbits?" Dr. Prager began.

"Please, Doc, let's do it my way," she answered. "This time *you* relax and I'll do the talking. It all started when I fell down this rabbit hole. . . ."

3

In her dream, Eve Eden said, she was a little girl with long golden curls. She was sitting on a riverbank when she saw this white rabbit running close by. It was wearing the waistcoat and a high collar, and then it took a watch out of its pocket, muttering, "Oh dear, I shall be too late." She ran across the field after it, and when it popped down a large rabbit hole under a hedge, she followed.

"Oh no!" Dr. Prager muttered. "Not *Alice*!"

"Alice who?" Eve Eden inquired.

"*Alice in Wonderland.*"

"You mean that movie Disney made, the cartoon thing?"

Dr. Prager nodded. "You saw it?"

"No. I never waste time on cartoons."

"But you know what I'm talking about, don't you?"

"Well—" Eve Eden hesitated. Then from the depths of her professional background an answer came. "Wasn't there another movie, way back around the beginning of the Thirties? Sure, Paramount made it, with Oakie and Gallagher and Horton and Ruggles and Ned Sparks and Fields and Gary Cooper. And let's see now, who played the dame—Charlotte Henry?"

Dr. Prager smiled. *Now* he was getting somewhere. "So that's the one you saw, eh?"

Eve Eden shook her head. "Never saw that one either. Couldn't afford movies when I was a brat, remember?"

"Then how do you know the cast and—"

"Easy. Gal who used to work with Alison Skipworth told me. She was in it too. And Edna May Oliver. I got a good memory, Doc. You know that."

"Yes." Dr. Prager breathed softly. "And so you must remember reading the original book, isn't that it?"

"Was it a book?"

"Now look here, don't tell me you've never read ALICE IN WONDERLAND, by Lewis Carroll. It's a classic."

"I'm no reader, Doc. You know that too."

"But surely as child you must have come across it. Or had somebody tell you the story."

The blonde curls tossed. "Nope. I'd remember if I had. I remember everything I read. That's why I'm always up on my lines. Best sight reader in the business. I not only haven't read ALICE IN WONDERLAND, I didn't even know there was such a story, except in a screenplay."

Dr. Prager gave an irritable tug at his goatee. "All right. You *do* have a remarkable memory, I know. So let's think back now. Let's think back very carefully to your earliest childhood. Somebody must have taken you on their lap, told you stories."

The star's eyes brightened. "Why, sure!" she exclaimed. "That's right! Aunt Emma was always telling me stories."

"Excellent." Dr. Prager smiled. "And can you recall now the first story she ever told you? The very first?"

Eve Eden closed her eyes, concentrating with effort. When her voice came it was from far away. "Yes," she whispered. "I remember now. I was only four. Aunt Emma took me on her lap and she told me my first story. It was the one about the drunk who goes in this bar, and he can't find the john, see, so the bartender tells him to go upstairs and—"

"No," said Dr. Prager. "No, no! Didn't she ever tell you any fairy tales?"

"Aunt Emma?" Eve Eden laughed. "I'll say she didn't. But stories—she had a million of 'em! Did you ever hear the one about the young married couple who wanted to—"

"Never mind." The psychiatrist leaned back. "You are quite positive you have never read or heard or seen ALICE IN WONDERLAND?"

"I told you so in the first place, didn't I? Now, do you want to hear my dream or not?"

"I want to very much," Dr. Prager answered, and he did. He took out his notebook and uncapped his fountain pen. In his own mind he was quite certain that she had heard or read ALICE, and he was interested in the reasons for the mental block which prevented her from recalling the fact. He was also interested in the possible symbolism behind her account. This promised to be quite an enjoyable session. "You went down the rabbit hole," he prompted.

"Into a tunnel," Eve continued. "I was falling, falling very slowly."

Dr. Prager wrote down *tunnel—womb fixation*? And he wrote down *falling dream*.

"I fell into a well," Eve said. "Lined with cupboards and bookshelves. There were maps and pictures on pegs."

Forbidden sex knowledge, Dr. Prager wrote.

"I reached out while I was still falling and took a jar from a shelf. The jar was labeled 'Orange Marmalade.' "

Marmalade—Mama? Dr. Prager wrote.

Eve said something about "Do cats eat bats?" and "Do bats eat cats?" but Dr. Prager missed it. He was too busy writing. It was amazing, now that he thought of it, just how much Freudian symbolism was packed into ALICE IN WONDERLAND. Amazing, too, how well her subconscious recalled it.

Eve was now telling how she had landed in the long hall with the doors all around and how the rabbit disappeared, muttering, "Oh, my ears and whiskers, how late it's getting." She told about approaching the three-legged solid-glass table with the tiny golden key on it, and Dr. Prager quickly scribbled *phallic symbol*. Then she described looking through a fifteen-inch door into a garden beyond and wishing she could get through it by shutting up like a telescope. So Dr. Prager wrote *phallic envy*.

"Then," Eve continued, "I saw this little bottle on the table, labeled 'Drink Me.' And so I drank, and do you know something? I did shut up like a telescope. I got smaller and smaller, and if I hadn't stopped drinking I'd have disappeared! So of course I couldn't reach the key, but then I saw this glass box under the table labeled 'Eat Me,' and I ate and got bigger right away."

She paused. "I know it sounds silly, Doc, but it was real interesting."

"Yes indeed," Dr. Prager said. "Go on. Tell everything you remember."

"Then the rabbit came back, mumbling something about a Duchess. And it dropped a pair of white gloves and a fan."

Fetishism, the psychiatrist noted.

"After that it got real crazy." Eve giggled. Then she told about the crying and forming a pool on the floor composed of her own tears. And how she held the fan and shrank again, then swam in the pool.

Grief fantasy, Dr. Prager decided.

She went on to describe her meeting with the mouse and with the other animals, the caucus race, and the recital of the curious poem about the cur, Fury, which ended, "I'll prosecute you, I'll be judge, I'll be jury— I'll try the whole cause and condemn you to death."

Superego, wrote Dr. Prager and asked, "What are you afraid of, Eve?"

"Nothing," she answered. "And I wasn't afraid in the dream either. I liked it. But I haven't told you anything yet."

"Go on."

She went on, describing her trip to the rabbit's

house to fetch his gloves and fan and finding the bottle labeled "Drink Me" in the bedroom. Then followed the episode of growth, and being stuck inside the house (*Claustrophobia*, the notebook dutifully recorded), and her escape from the animals who pelted her with pebbles as she ran into the forest.

It was ALICE all right, word for word, image for image. *Father image* for the caterpillar, who might (Dr. Prager reasoned wisely) stand for himself as the psychiatrist, with his stern approach and enigmatic answers. The *Father William* poem which followed seemed to validate this conclusion.

Then came the episode of eating the side of the mushroom, growing and shrinking. Did this disguise her drug addiction? Perhaps. And there was a moment when she had a long serpentine neck and a pigeon mistook her for a serpent. A viper was a serpent. And weren't drug addicts called "vipers"? Of course. Dr. Prager was beginning to understand now. It was all symbolic. She was telling about her own life. Running away and finding the key to success—alternating between being very "small" and insignificant and trying every method of becoming "big" and important. Until she entered the garden—her Garden of Eden here— and became a star and consulted him and took drugs. It all made sense now.

He could understand as she told of the visit to the house of the Duchess (*mother image*) with her cruel "Chop off her head." He anticipated the baby who turned into a pig and wrote down *rejection fantasy* quickly.

Then he listened to the interview with the Cheshire cat, inwardly marveling at Eve Eden's perfect memory for dialogue.

" 'But I don't want to go among mad people,' I said. And the crazy cat came back with, " 'Oh, you can't help that. We're all mad here. I'm mad. You're mad.' And I said, 'How do you know I'm mad?' and the cat said, 'You must be—or you wouldn't have come here.' Well, I felt plenty crazy when the cat started to vanish. Believe it or not, Doc, there was nothing left but a big grin."

"I believe it," Dr. Prager assured her.

He was hot on the trail of another scent now. The talk of madness had set him off. And sure enough, now came the tea party. With the March Hare and the Mad Hatter, of course—the *Mad* Hatter. Sitting in front of their house (*asylum*, no doubt) with the sleeping dormouse between them. *Dor*mouse—*dor*mant sanity. She was afraid of going insane, Dr. Prager decided. So much so did he believe it that when she quoted the line, "Why is a raven like a writing desk?" he found himself writing down, *Why is a raving like a Rorschach test*? and had to cross it out.

Then came the sadistic treatment of the poor dormouse and another drug fantasy with mushrooms for the symbol, leading her again into a beautiful garden. Dr. Prager heard it all: the story of the playing-card people (*club* soldiers and *diamond* courtiers and *heart* children were perfectly fascinating symbols too!).

And when Eve said, "Why, they're only a pack of cards after all—I needn't be afraid of them," Dr. Prager triumphantly wrote *paranoid fantasies: people are unreal*.

"Now I must tell you about the croquet game," Eve went on, and so she told him about the croquet game and Dr. Prager filled two whole pages with notes.

He was particularly delighted with Alice-Eve's account of the conversation with the ugly Duchess, who said among other things, "Take care of the sense and the sounds will take care of themselves," and "Be what you seem to be—or more simply, never imagine yourself not to be otherwise than what it might appear to others that what you were or might have been was not otherwise than what you had been who have appeared to them to be otherwise."

Eve Eden rattled it off, apparently verbatim. "It didn't seem to make sense at the time," she admitted. "But it does now, don't you think?"

Dr. Prager refused to commit himself. It made sense

all right. A dreadful sort of sense. This poor child was struggling to retain her identity. Everything pointed to that. She was adrift in a sea of illusion, peopled with Mock Turtles—*Mock* Turtle, very significant, that—and distorted imagery.

Now the story of the Turtle and the Gryphon and the Lobster Quadrille began to take on a dreadful meaning. All the twisted words and phrases symbolized growing mental disturbance. Schools taught "reeling and writhing" and arithmetic consisted of "ambition, distraction, uglification, and derision." Obviously fantasies of inferiority. And Alice-Eve growing more and more confused with twisted, inverted logic in which "blacking" became "whiting"—it was merely an inner cry signifying she could no longer tell the difference between black and white. In other words, she was losing all contact with reality. She was going through an ordeal—a trial.

Of course it was a trial! Now Eve was telling about the trial of the Knave of Hearts, who stole the tarts (*Hadn't Eve once been a "tart" herself?*) and Alice-Eve noted all the animals on the jury (*another paranoid delusion: people are animals*) and she kept growing (*delusions of grandeur*) and then came the white rabbit reading the anonymous letter.

Dr. Prager picked up his own ears, rabbit fashion, when he heard the contents of the letter.

> "My notion was that you had been
> (before she had this fit)
> An obstacle that came between
> Him, and ourselves, and it.
> Don't let him know she liked them best
> For this must ever be
> A *secret* kept from all the rest
> Between yourself and me."

Of course. A *secret*, Dr. Prager decided. Eve Eden had been afraid of madness for a long time. That was the root of all her perverse behavior patterns, and he'd never probed sufficiently to uncover it. But the dream, welling up from the subconscious, provided the answer.

"I said I didn't believe there was an atom of meaning in it." Eve told him. "And the Queen cried, 'Off with her head,' but I said, 'Who cares for *you*? You're nothing but a pack of cards.' And they all rose up and flew at me, but I beat them off, and then I woke up fighting the covers."

She sat up. "You've been taking an awful lot of notes," she said. "Mind telling me what you think?"

Dr. Prager hesitated. It was a delicate question. Still the dream content indicated that she was perfectly well aware of her problem on the subliminal level. A plain exposition of the facts might come as a shock but not a dangerous one. Actually a shock could be just the thing now to lead her back and resolve the initial trauma, whatever it was."

"All right," Dr. Prager said. "Here's what I think it means." And in plain language he explained his interpretation of her dream, pulling no punches but, occasionally, his goatee.

"So there you have it," he concluded. "The symbolic story of your life—and the dramatized and disguised conflict over your mental status which you've always tried to hide. But the subconscious is wise, my dear. It always knows and tries to warn. No wonder you had this dream at this particular time. There's nothing accidental about it. Freud says—"

But Eve was laughing. "Freud says? What does he know about it? Come to think of it, Doc, what do you know about it either? You see, I forgot to tell you something when I started. I didn't just *have* this dream." She stared at him, and her laughter ceased. "I bought it." Eve Eden said. "I bought it for ten thousand dollars."

4

Dr. Prager wasn't getting anywhere. His fountain pen ceased to function and his goatee wouldn't respond properly to even the most severe tugging. He heard Eve Eden out and waved his arms helplessly, like a bird about to take off. He felt like taking off, but on the other hand he couldn't leave this chick in her nest. Not with a big nest egg involved. But why did it have to be so involved?

"Go over that again," he begged finally. "Just the highlights. I can't seem to get it."

"But it's really so simple," Eve answered. "Like I already told you. I was getting all restless and keyed up, you know, like I've been before. Dying for a ball, some new kind of kick. And then I ran into Wally Redmond and he told me about this Professor Laroc."

"The charlatan," Dr. Prager murmured.

"I don't know what nationality he is," Eve answered. "He's just a little old guy who goes around selling these dreams."

"Now wait a minute—"

"Sure, it sound screwy. I thought so, too, when Wally told me. He'd met him at a party somewhere and got to talking. And pretty soon he was spilling his—you'll pardon the expression—guts about the sad story of his life and how fed up he was with everything, including his sixth wife. And how he wanted to get away from it all and find a new caper.

"So this Professor Laroc asked him if he'd ever been on the stuff, and Wally said no, he had a weak heart. And he asked him if he'd tried psychiatry, and Wally said sure, but it didn't help him any."

"Your friend went to the wrong analyst," Dr. Prager snapped in some heat. "He should have come to a Freudian. How could he expect to get results from a Jungian—"

"Like you say, Doc, relax. It doesn't matter. What matters is that Professor Laroc sold him this dream. It was a real scary one, to hear him tell it, all about being a burglar over in England someplace and getting into a big estate run by a little dwarf with a head like a baboon. But he liked it; liked it fine. Said he was really relaxed after he had it: made him feel like a different person. And so he bought another, about a guy who was a pawnbroker, only a long time ago in some real gone country. And this pawnbroker ran around having himself all kinds of women who—"

"JURGEN," Dr. Prager muttered. "And if I'm not mistaken, the other one was from LUKUNDOO. I think it was called *The Snout*."

"Let's stick to the point, Doc," Eve Eden said. "Anyway, Wally was crazy about these dreams. He said the professor had a lot more to peddle, and even though the price was high, it was worth it. Because in the dream you felt like somebody else. You felt like the character you were dreaming about. And, of course, no hangover, no trouble with the law. Wally said if he ever tried some of the stuff he dreamed about on real women they'd clap him into pokey, even here in Hollywood. He planned to get out of pictures and buy more. Wanted to dream all the time. I guess the professor told him if he paid enough he could even *stay* in a dream without coming back."

"Nonsense!"

"That's what I told the man. I know how you feel, Doc. I felt that way myself before I met Professor Laroc. But after that it was different."

"You met this person?"

"He isn't a person, Doc. He's a real nice guy, a sweet character. You'd like him. I did when Wally brought him around. We had a long talk together. I opened up to him, even more than I have to you, I guess. Told him all my troubles. And he said what was wrong with me was I never had any childhood. That somewhere underneath there was a little girl trying to live her life with a full imagination. So he'd sell me a dream for that. And even though it sounded batty it made sense to me. He really seemed to understand things I didn't understand about myself.

"So I thought here goes, nothing to lose if I try it once, and I bought the dream." She smiled. "And now that I know what it's like I'm going to buy more. All he can sell me. Because he was right, you know. I don't want the movies. I don't want liquor or sex or H or gambling or anything. I don't want Eve Eden. I want to be a little girl, a little girl like the one in the dream, having adventures and never getting hurt. That's why I made up my mind. I'm quitting, getting out while the getting is good. From now on, me for dreamland."

Dr. Prager was silent for a long time. He kept staring at Eve Eden's smile. It wasn't *her* smile—he got the strangest notion that it belonged to somebody else. It was too relaxed, too innocent, too utterly seraphic for Eve. It was, he told himself, the smile of a ten-year-old girl on the face of a thirty-three-year-old woman of the world.

And he thought *hebephrenia* and he thought *schizophrenia* and he thought *incipient catatonia* and he said, "You say you met this Professor Laroc through Wally Redmond. Do you know how to reach him?"

"No, he reaches me." Eve Eden giggled. "He sends me, too, Doc."

She was really pretty far gone, Dr. Prager decided. But he had to persist. "When you bought this dream, as you say, what happened?"

"Why, nothing. Wally brought the professor here to the house. Right up to this bedroom actually. Then he went away and the professor talked to me and I wrote out the check and he gave me the dream."

"You keep saying he 'gave' you this dream. What does that mean?" Dr. Prager leaned forward. He had a sudden hunch. "Did he ask you to lie down, the way I do?"

"Yes. That's right."

"And did he talk to you?"

"Sure. How'd you guess?"

"And did he keep talking until you went to sleep?"

"I—I think so. Anyway, I did go to sleep, and when I woke up he was gone."

"Aha."

"What does that mean?"

"It means you were hypnotized, my dear. Hypnotized by a clever charlatan, who sold you a few moments of prepared patter in return for ten thousand dollars."

"But—but that's not true!" Eve Eden's childish smile became a childish pout. "It was *real*. The dream, I mean. It *happened*."

"Happened?"

"Of course. Haven't I made that clear yet? The dream *happened*. It wasn't like other dreams. I mean, I could feel and hear and see and even taste. Only it wasn't *me*. It was this little girl. Alice. I was Alice. That's what makes it worthwhile, can't you understand? That's what Wally said, too. The dream place is real. You *go* there, and you *are* somebody else."

"Hypnotism," Dr. Prager murmured.

Eve Eden put down the rabbit. "All right," she said. "I can prove it." She marched over to the big bed—the bed large enough to hold six people, according to some very catty but authenticated reports. "I didn't mean to show you this," she said, "but maybe I'd better."

She reached under her pillow and pulled out a small object which glittered beneath the light. "I found this in my hand when I woke up," she declared. "Look at it."

Dr. Prager looked at it. It was a small bottle bearing a white label. He shook it and discovered that the bottle was half-filled with a colorless transparent liquid. He studied the label and deciphered the hand-lettered inscription which read simply, "Drink Me."

"Proof, eh?" he mused. "Found in your hand when you woke up?"

"Of course. I brought it from the dream."

Dr. Prager smiled. "You were hypnotized. And before Professor Laroc stole away—and *stole* is singularly appropriate, considering that he had your check for ten thousand dollars—he simply planted this bottle in your hand as you slept. That's my interpretation of your proof." He slipped the little glass container into his pocket. "With your permission, I'd like to take this along," he said. "I'm going to ask you now to bear with me for the next twenty-four hours. Don't make any announcements about leaving the studio until I return. I think I can clear everything up to your satisfaction."

"But I am satisfied," Eve told him. "There's nothing to clear up. I don't want to—"

"Please." Dr. Prager brushed his brush with authority. "All I ask is that you be patient for twenty-four hours. I shall return tomorrow at this same time. And meanwhile, try to forget about all this. Say nothing to anyone."

"Now wait a minute, Doc—"

But Dr. Prager was gone. Eve Eden frowned for a moment, then sank back on the chaise longue. The rabbit scampered out from behind a chair and she picked it up again. She stroked its long ears gently until the creature fell asleep. Presently Eve's eyes closed and she drifted off to slumber herself. And the child's smile returned to her face.

5

There was no smile, childish or adult, on Dr. Prager's face when he presented himself again to the gate-keeper on the following day.

His face was stern and set as he drove up to the front door, accepted the butler's greeting, and went down the hall to where Mickey Dennis waited.

"What's up?" the little agent demanded, tossing his copy of *Hollywood Reporter* to the floor.

"I've been doing a bit of investigating," Dr. Prager told him. "And I'm afraid I have bad news for you."

"What is it, Doc? I tried to get something out of her after you left yesterday, but she wasn't talking. And today—"

"I know." Dr. Prager sighed. "She wouldn't be likely to tell you, under the circumstances. Apparently she realizes the truth herself but won't admit it. I have good reason to believe Miss Eden is disturbed. Seriously disturbed."

Mickey Dennis twirled his forefinger next to his ear. "You mean she's flipping?"

"I disapprove of that term on general principles," Dr. Prager replied primly. "And in this particular case the tense is wrong. *Flipped* would be much more correct."

"But I figured she was all right lately. Outside of this business about quitting, she's been extra happy—happier'n I ever seen her."

"Euphoria," Dr. Prager answered. "Cycloid manifestation."

"You don't say so."

"I just did," the psychiatrist reminded him.

"Level with me," Dennis pleaded. "What's this all about?"

"I can't until after I've talked to her," Dr. Prager told him. "I need more facts. I was hoping to get some essential information from this Wally Redmond, but I can't locate him. Neither his studio nor his home seems to have information as to his whereabouts for the past several days."

"Off on a binge," the agent suggested. "It figgers. Only just what did you want from him?"

"Information concerning Professor Laroc," Dr. Prager answered. "He's a pretty elusive character. His name isn't listed on any academic roster I've consulted, and I couldn't find it in the City Directory of this or other local communities. Nor could the police department aid me with their files. I'm almost afraid my initial theory was wrong and that Professor Laroc himself is only another figment of Eve Eden's imagination."

"Maybe I can help you out there, Doc."

"You mean you met this man, saw him when he came here with Wally Redmond that evening?"

Mickey Dennis shook his head. "No. I wasn't around then. But I been around all afternoon. And just about a half hour ago a character named Professor Laroc showed up at the door. He's with Eve in her room right now."

Dr. Prager opened his mouth and expelled a gulp. Then he turned and ran for the stairs.

The agent sought out his overstuffed chair and riffled the pages of his magazine.

More waiting. Well, he just hoped there wouldn't be any explosions this afternoon.

6

There was no explosion when Dr. Prager opened the bedroom door. Eve Eden was sitting quietly on the chaise longue, and the elderly gentleman occupied an armchair.

As Dr. Prager entered, the older man rose with a smile and extended his hand. Dr. Prager felt it wise to ignore the gesture. "Professor Laroc? " he murmured.

"That is correct." The smile was a bland blend of twinkling blue eyes behind old-fashioned steel-rimmed spectacles, wrinkled creases in white cheeks, and a rictus of a prim, thin-lipped mouth. Whatever else he might be, Professor Laroc aptly fitted Mickey Dennis's description of a "character." He appeared to be about sixty-five, and his clothing seemed of the same vintage, as though fashioned in anticipation at the time of his birth.

Eve Eden stood up now. "I'm glad you two are getting together," she said. "I asked the professor to come this afternoon so we could straighten everything out."

Dr. Prager preened his goatee. "I'm very happy that you did so," he answered. "And I'm sure that matters can be set straight in very short order now that I'm here."

"The professor has just been telling me a couple of things," Eve informed him. "I gave him your pitch about me losing my buttons and he says you're all wet."

"A slight misquotation," Professor Laroc interposed.

"I merely observed that an understanding of the true facts might dampen your enthusiasm."

"I think I have the facts," Dr. Prager snapped. "And they're dry enough. Dry, but fascinating."

"Do go on."

"I intend to." Dr. Prager wheeled to confront Eve Eden and spoke directly to the girl. "First of all," he said, "I must tell you that your friend here is masquerading under a pseudonym. I have been unable to discover a single bit of evidence substantiating the identity of anyone named Professor Laroc."

"Granted," the elderly man murmured.

"Secondly," Dr. Prager continued, "I must warn you that I have been unable to ascertain the whereabouts of your friend Wally Redmond. His wife doesn't know where his is, or his producer. Mickey Dennis thinks he's off on an alcoholic fugue. I have my own theory. But one fact is certain—he seems to have completely disappeared."

"Granted," said Professor Laroc.

"Third and last," Dr. Prager went on. "It is my considered belief that the man calling himself Professor Laroc did indeed subject you to hypnosis and that, once he had managed to place you in a deep trance, he deliberately read to you from a copy of ALICE IN WONDERLAND and suggested to you that you were experiencing the adventures of the principal character. Whereupon he placed the vial of liquid labeled 'Drink Me' in your hand and departed."

"Granted in part." Professor Laroc nodded. "It is true that I placed Miss Eden in a receptive state with the aid of what you choose to call hypnosis. And it is true that I suggested to her that she enter into the world of ALICE, as Alice. But that is all. It was not necessary to read anything to her, nor did I stoop to deception by supplying a vial of liquid, as you call it. Believe me, I was as astonished as you were to learn that she had brought back such an interesting souvenir of her little experience."

"Prepare to be astonished again then," Dr. Prager

said grimly. He pulled the small bottle from his pocket and with it a piece of paper.

"What's that, Doc?" Eve Eden asked.

"A certificate from Haddon and Haddon, industrial chemists," the psychiatrist told her. "I took this interesting souvenir, as your friend calls it, down to their laboratories for analysis." He handed her the report. "Here, read for yourself. If your knowledge of chemistry is insufficient, I can tell you that H_2O means water." He smiled. "Yes, that's right. This bottle contains nothing but half an ounce of water."

Dr. Prager turned and stared at Professor Laroc. "What have you to say now?" he demanded.

"Very little." The old man smiled. "It does not surprise me that you were unable to find my name listed in any registry or directory of activities, legal or illegal. As Miss Eden already knows, I chose to cross over many years ago. Nor was 'Laroc' my actual surname. A moment's reflection will enable you to realize that 'Laroc' is an obvious enough anagram for 'Carroll,' give or take a few letters."

"You don't mean to tell me—"

"That I am Lewis Carroll, or rather, Charles Lutwidge Dodgson? Certainly not. I hold the honor of being a fellow alumnus of his at Oxford, and we did indeed share an acquaintance—"

"But Lewis Carroll died in 1898," Dr. Prager objected.

"Ah, you *were* interested enough to look up the date." The old man smiled. "I see you're not as skeptical as you pretend to be."

Dr. Prager felt that he was giving ground and remembered that attack is the best defense. "Where is Wally Redmond?" he countered.

"With the Duchess of Towers, I would presume," Professor Laroc answered. "He chose to cross over permanently, and I selected PETER IBBETSON for him. You see, I'm restricted to literature which was directly inspired by the author's dream, and there's a rather small field available. I still have Cabell's SMIRT to sell, and *The Brushwood Boy* of Kipling, but I don't imagine I shall ever manage to dispose of any Lovecraft —too gruesome, you know." He glanced at Eve Eden. "Fortunately, as I told you, I've reserved something very special for you. And I'm glad you decided to take the step. The moment I saw you my heart went out to you. I sensed the little girl buried away beneath all the veneer, just as I sensed the small boy in Mr. Redmond. So many of you Hollywood people are frustrated children. You make dreams for others but have none of your own. I am glad to offer my modest philanthropy—"

"At ten thousand dollars a session!" Dr. Prager exploded.

"Now, now," Professor Laroc chided. "That sounds like professional jealousy, sir! And I may as well remind you that a permanent crossover requires a fee of fifty thousand. Not that I need the money, you understand. It's merely that such a fee helps to establish me as an authority. It brings about the necessary transference relationship between my clients and myself, to borrow from your own terminology. The effect is purely psychological."

Dr. Prager had heard enough. This, he decided, was definitely the time to call a halt. Even Eve Eden in her present disturbed state should be able to comprehend the utter idiocy of this man's preposterous claims.

He faced the elderly charlatan with a disarming smile. "Let me get this straight," he began quietly. "Am I to understand that you are actually selling dreams?"

"Let us say, rather, that I sell experiences. And the experiences are every bit as real as anything you know."

"Don't quibble over words." Dr. Prager was annoyed. "You come in and hypnotize patients. During their sleep you suggest they enter a dream world. And then—"

"If you don't mind, let us quibble a bit over words, please," Professor Laroc said. "You're a psychiatrist.

Very well, as a psychiatrist, please tell me one thing. Just what *is* a dream?"

"Why, that's very simple," Dr. Prager answered. "According to Freud, the dream phenomenon can be described as—"

"I didn't ask for a description, Doctor. Nor for Freud's opinion. I asked for an exact definition of the dream state, as you call it. I want to know the etiology and epistemology of dreams. And while you're at it, how about a definition of 'the hypnotic state' and of 'sleep'? And what is 'suggestion'? After you've given me precise scientific definitions of these phenomena, as you love to call them, perhaps you can go on and explain to me the nature of 'reality' and the exact meaning of the term 'imagination.' "

"But these are only figures of speech," Dr. Prager objected. "I'll be honest with you. Perhaps we can't accurately describe a dream. But we can observe it. It's like electricity: nobody knows what it *is*, but it's a measurable force which can be directed and controlled, subject to certain natural laws."

"Exactly," Professor Laroc said. "That's just what I would have said myself. And dreams are indeed like electrical force. Indeed, the human brain gives off electrical charges, and all life—matter—energy—enters into an electrical relationship. But this relationship has never been studied. Only the physical manifestations of electricity have been studied and harnessed, not the psychic. At least, not until Dodgson stumbled on certain basic mathematical principles, which he imparted to me. I developed them, found a practical use. The dream, my dear doctor, is merely an electrically charged dimension given a reality of its own beyond our own space-time continuum. The individual dream is weak. Set it down on paper, as some dreams have been set down, share it with others, and watch the charge build up. The combined electrical properties tend to create a *permanent* plane—a dream dimension, if you please."

"I don't please," answered Dr. Prager.

"That's because you're not receptive," Professor

Laroc observed smugly. "Yours is a negative charge rather than a positive one. Dodgson—Lewis Carroll—was positive. So was Lovecraft and Poe and Edward Lucas White and a handful of others. Their dreams live. Other positive charges can live in them, granted the proper method of entry. It's not magic. There's nothing supernatural about it at all, unless you consider mathematics as magic. Dodgson did. He was a professor of mathematics, remember. And so was I. I took his principles and extended them, created a practical methodology. Now I can enter dream worlds at will, cause others to enter. It's not hypnosis as you understand it. A few words of non-Euclidean formula will be sufficient—"

"I've heard enough," Dr. Prager broke in. "Much as I hate to employ the phrase, this is sheer lunacy."

The professor shrugged. "Call it what you wish," he said. "You psychiatrists are good at pinning labels on things. But Miss Eden here has had sufficient proof through her own experience. Isn't that so?"

Eve Eden nodded, then broke her silence. "I believe you," she said. "Even if Doc here thinks we're both batty. And I'm willing to give you the fifty grand for a permanent trip."

Dr. Prager grabbed for his goatee. He was clutching at straws now. "But you can't," he cried. "This doesn't make sense."

"Maybe not your kind of sense," Eve answered. "But that's just the trouble. You don't seem to understand there's more than *one* kind. That crazy dream I had, the one you say Lewis Carroll had first and wrote up into a book—it makes sense to you if you really *live* it. More sense than Hollywood, than this. More sense than a little kid named Wilma Kozmowski growing up to live in a half-million-dollar palace and trying to kill herself because she can't be a little kid any more and never had a chance to be one when she was small. The professor here, he understands. He knows everybody has a right to dream. For the first time in my life I know what it is to be happy."

"That's right," Professor Laroc added. "I recognized her as a kindred spirit. I saw the child beneath, the child of pure unclouded brow, as Lewis Carroll put it. She deserved this dream."

"Don't try and stop me," Eve cut in. "You can't, you know. You'll never drag me back to your world, and you've got no reason to try—except that you like the idea of making a steady living off me. And so does Dennis, with his lousy ten percent, and so does the studio with its big profits. I never met anyone who really liked me as a person except Professor Laroc here. He's the only one who ever gave me anything worth having. The dream. So quit trying to argue me into it, Doc. I'm not going to be Eve any more or Wilma either. I'm going to be Alice."

Dr. Prager scowled, then smiled. What was the matter with him? Why was he bothering to argue like this? After all, it was so unnecessary. Let the poor child write out a check for fifty thousand dollars—payment could always be stopped. Just as this charlatan could be stopped if he actually attempted hypnosis. There were laws and regulations. Really, Dr. Prager reminded himself, he was behaving like a child himself: taking part in this silly argument as if there actually was something to it besides nonsense words.

What was really at stake, he realized was professional pride. To think that this old mountebank could actually carry more authority with Eve Eden than he did himself!

And what was the imposter saying now, with that sickening, condescending smile on his face?

"I'm sorry you cannot subscribe to my theories, Doctor. But at least I am grateful for one thing, and that is that you didn't see fit to put them to the test."

"Test? What do you mean?"

Professor Laroc pointed his finger at the little bottle labeled "Drink Me" which now rested on the table before him. "I'm happy you merely analyzed the contents of that vial without attempting to drink them."

"But it's nothing but water."

"Perhaps. What you forget is that water may have very different properties in other worlds. And this water came from the world of Alice."

"You planted that," Dr. Prager snapped. "Don't deny it."

"I do deny it. Miss Eden knows the truth."

"Oh, does she?" Dr. Prager suddenly found his solution. He raised the bottle, turning to Eve with a commanding gesture. "Listen to me now. Professor Laroc claims, and you believe, that this liquid was somehow transported from the dream world of AL-ICE IN WONDERLAND. If that is the case, then a drink out of this bottle would cause me either to grow or to shrink. Correct?"

"Yes," Eve murmured.

"Now wait—" the professor began, but Dr. Prager shook his head impatiently.

"Let me finish," he insisted. "All right. By the same token, if I took a drink from this bottle and nothing happened, wouldn't it prove that the dream-world story is a fake?"

"Yes, but—"

"No 'buts.' I'm asking you a direct question. Would it or wouldn't it?"

"Y-yes. I guess so. Yes."

"Very well, then." Dramatically, Dr. Prager un-corked the little bottle and raised it to his lips. "Watch me," he said.

Professor Laroc stepped forward. "Please!" he shouted. "I implore you—don't—"

He made a grab for the bottle, but he was too late.

Dr. Prager downed the half ounce of colorless fluid.

7

Mickey Dennis waited and waited until he couldn't stand it any longer. There hadn't been any loud sounds from upstairs at all, and this only made it worse.

Finally he got the old urge so bad he just had to go on up there and see for himself what was going on.

As he walked down the hall he could hear them talking inside the bedroom. At least he recognized Professor Laroc's voice. He was saying something about, "There, there, I know it's quite a shock. Perhaps you'd feel better if you didn't wait—do you want to go now?"

That didn't make too much sense to Mickey, and neither did Eve's reply. She said, "Yes, but don't I have to go to sleep first?"

And then the professor answered, "No, as I explained to him, it's just a question of the proper formulae. If I recite them we can go together. Er—you might bring your checkbook along."

Eve seemed to be giggling. "You too?" she asked.

"Yes. I've always loved this dream, my dear. It's a sequel to the first one, as you'll discover. Now if you'll just face the mirror with me—"

And then the professor mumbled something in a very low voice, and Mickey bent down with his head close to the door but he couldn't quite catch it. Instead his shoulder pushed the door open.

The bedroom was empty.

That's right, empty.

THE HELMET

by Barry N. Malzberg

Wearing the helmet, I am just like everyone else and the world makes sense. The war is not an endless war, but a necessary defensive action in the interest of peace and will end shortly. The Masters are not creatures who lie to us and keep us in bondage, but lords of great wisdom and justice who, in the rooms of this great building, prepare us kindly for the world which we will in turn someday ourselves rule. The others who accompany me through these corridors and classrooms are not fellow victims but fellow students, and in the long or short run, everything is for the best. That is why I have been assigned to wear the helmet, and it is why I like to have it, because I cannot stand the way the world looks without it, but for certain reasons having to do with medical science, and which I do not understand—

Well, the Masters say that for one or two hours every day I must remove it to rest. It is related to sensors, they tell me, or nerve sheath exhaustion, but the explanation mystifies and I go through my periods without the helmet closing my eyes as much as possible, counting the moments until I can don it and make the world sensible again. It is important that I wear the helmet, and necessary that I wear the helmet, and the Masters promise that in not too much longer a time the nerve sheaths or sensors will have corrected themselves and I will be able to use it for weeks at a time.

How I hope so!

Now it is one of my hours without the helmet. Standing by the window, looking from this great height at the buildings of the city, I know fear of the machinery hanging in the distance, fear in the very smell of the heavy air which hangs within this enclosure. Listening to Serafino as he talks about the wonders of our age, I close my eyes. Serafino is my closest friend, perhaps my only friend at this time, but the fact is that I like him no better than any of the others; with the helmet I find him engaging and friendly but without it he strikes me as dull and stupid. How I envy him for not needing the helmet as I do to enjoy the life we have been given! "Isn't it beautiful, Jonno?" Serafino asks, playing idly with his fingers. We are in a free time period between instructions and have come to this window to look upon the city. "Mankind has striven for ten thousand years to create a civilization like this, and we are the ones to inherit it. Isn't that wonderful? The city gives us everything and we will never have to leave it."

I do not think that it is wonderful and without the helmet the thought that we will never be able to leave the city fills me with disgust, but I do not want to discourage Serafino or have him leave me; in these periods without the helmet I am very lonely and easily frightened. "I suppose so," I say, "I suppose it's a great thing," and then turn to find that unexpectedly one of the Masters has come upon us. They move so silently in the halls and with so much grace that it is almost impossible to be prepared for their entrance, and therefore it is best to make sure one is following the laws of obedience at all times. "Hello, Serafino," the Master says, "hello, Jonno."

They know all of our names, although we do not know theirs. They are simply *Masters* indivisible. Some of them are tall, others are short, some are older and some younger, but we have been advised that each may fulfill the function of all and that it would be a serious mistake to personalize any of them. This is advice which is worth being taken seriously because the Masters never make idle statements. Everything they say is always filled with significance, and the one true path of difficulty lies in not heeding them.

"Hello, Master," my friend says and bows slightly, as is the approved procedure. He smiles comfortably and turns back to the window then, for it is a rule that if the Masters do not wish to prolong a conversation, students will not call unnecessary attention to themselves but will merely continue their regular activities. "Hello, Jonno," the Master says again to me, somewhat more sharply.

"Hello, Master," I say and then turn from him. Without the helmet, I see the Master as an ugly alien creature with green skin and scales, large, staring eyes and claws, an ugly excrescence on those scales, but I remind myself that this is merely an illusion caused by my failure to adapt and that I must in no way show my loathing, fear or disgust. In the past while not wearing the helmet I have once or twice let the hallucinations get the better of me and have been taken into small rooms for education, something which I do not want to discuss.

"How are you?" the Master says, seeking conversation.

"Fine. I am fine."

"I note that you do not wear the helmet. Why is this so?"

This must be a new Master, one not acquainted with the special rules and procedures of my case. "I can't wear it all the time yet," I say. "For one or two hours a day it must come off."

"I have heard no word of this in your case," the creature says. "Malcontents are instructed to wear the helmet at all times. I am displeased."

"But it's true!" says Serafino, taking my part. "He

can't wear it all the time yet. That's why I'm keeping him company, so that the fear does not affect him."

"No one asked you to speak," the Master says angrily. "You will speak only when contact is indicated and you will be dealt with for this. I want you to go at once and place yourself in quarters."

Pale, shaking, Serafino detaches himself from the balcony and walks quickly through the hall. It is pointless to argue with these Masters for any reason, and as this can only deepen his problem, Serafino leaves without a word. Watching him I can see from the slump of his shoulders, the faint tremors in his legs, that he is very frightened. I am very frightened also, then. I turn from the city and try to look past the creature, but he catches my gaze and I cannot break past. I want to dive past him and run but know that leaving without excuse is the most serious offense, possibly, of all, and therefore I stay. The Master looks at me, scales fluttering in the breeze. "Come here, Jonno," it says and beckons to me. I move there, and then with a gap of inches, am halted. The eyes are very large and round in the creature's empty face. "You know the rules," it says, "the helmet at all times."

"Yes," I say. It is pointless to argue with them. Either truly or untruly he does not know my case, but there is no use in arguing with them, because things only become far worse. "Yes."

"You have broken those rules."

"Yes. Yes, I have."

"Therefore you must accept punishment."

"I will. I do."

"And the punishment is—" The Master pauses, flutters scales again, seems to be pondering. "The only fair punishment," it says, "is this. You will never wear the helmet again. You must go through the rest of your life without the helmet. For failing to take the terms of your salvation you are therefore not saved."

And it walks quickly from me then, leaving me rooted in place, sickened. The corridor sifts toward gray, the breeze through the balcony makes me shiver. I feel a chill unlike any I have known before and know then, know well, the cruelty and cunning of the Master's punishment: the first touch of the realization then that I will have to go through the rest of my life seeing and knowing it exactly as it is.

DREAMS ARE SACRED

by Peter Phillips

When I was seven, I read a ghost story and babbled of the consequent nightmare to my father.

"They were coming for me, Pop," I sobbed. "I couldn't run, and I couldn't stop 'em, great big things with teeth and claws like the pictures in the book, and I couldn't wake myself up, Pop, I couldn't come awake."

Pop had a few quiet cuss words for folks who left such things around for a kid to pick up and read; then he took my hand gently in his own great paw and led me into the six-acre pasture.

He was wise, with the canny insight into human motives that the soil gives to a man. He was close to Nature and the hearts and minds of men, for all men ultimately depend on the good earth for sustenance and life.

He sat down on a stump and showed me a big gun. I know now it was a heavy Service Colt .45. To my child eyes, it was enormous. I had seen shotguns and sporting rifles before, but this was to be held in one hand and fired. Gosh, it was heavy. It dragged my thin arm down with its sheer, grim weight when Pop showed me how to hold it.

Pop said: "It's a killer, Pete. There's nothing in the whole wide world or out of it that a slug from Billy here won't stop. It's killed lions and tigers and men. Why, if you aim right, it'll stop a charging elephant.

Believe me, son, there's nothing you can meet in dreams that Billy here won't stop. And he'll come into your dreams with you from now on, so there's no call to be scared of anything."

He drove that deep into my receptive subconscious. At the end of half an hour, my wrist ached abominably from the kick of that Colt. But I'd seen heavy slugs tear through two-inch teakwood and mild steel plating. I'd looked along that barrel, pulled the trigger, felt the recoil rip up my arm and seen the fist-size hole blasted through a sack of wheat.

And that night, I slept with Billy under my pillow. Before I slipped into dreamland, I'd felt again the cool, reassuring butt.

When the Dark Things came again, I was almost glad. I was ready for them. Billy was there, lighter than in my waking hours—or maybe my dream-hand was bigger—but just as powerful. Two of the Dark Things crumpled and fell as Billy roared and kicked, then the others turned and fled.

Then I was chasing them, laughing, and firing from the hip.

Pop was no psychiatrist, but he'd found the perfect antidote to fear—the projection into the subconscious mind of a common-sense concept based on experience.

Twenty years later, the same principle was put into operation scientifically to save the sanity—and perhaps the life—of Marsham Craswell.

"Surely you've heard of him?" said Stephen Blakiston, a college friend of mine who'd majored in psychiatry.

"Vaguely," I said. "Science-fiction, fantasy . . . I've read a little. Screwy."

"Not so. Some good stuff." Steve waved a hand round the bookshelves of his private office in the new Pentagon Mental Therapy Hospital, New York State. I saw multicolored magazine backs, row on row of them. "I'm a fan," he said simply. "Would you call me screwy?"

I backed out of that one. I'm just a sports columnist, but I knew Blakiston was tops in two fields—the psycho stuff and electronic therapy.

Steve said: "Some of it's the old 'peroo, of course, but the level of writing is generally high and the ideas thought-provoking. For ten years, Marsham has been one of the most prolific and best-loved writers in the game.

"Two years ago, he had a serious illness, didn't give himself time to convalesce properly before he waded into writing again. He tried to reach his previous output, tending more and more toward pure fantasy. Beautiful in parts, sheer rubbish sometimes.

"He forced his imagination to work, set himself a wordage routine. The tension became too great. Something snapped. Now he's here."

Steve got up, ushered me out of his office. "I'll take you to see him. He won't see you. Because the thing that snapped was his conscious control over his imagination. It went into high gear, and now instead of writing his stories, he's living them—quite literally, for him.

"Far-off worlds, strange creatures, weird adventures—the detailed phantasmagoria of a brilliant mind driving itself into insanity through the sheer complexity of its own invention. He's escaped from the harsh reality of his strained existence into a dream world. But he may make it real enough to kill himself.

"He's the hero of course," Steve continued, opening the door into a private world. "But even heroes sometimes die. My fear is that his morbidly overactive imagination working through his subconscious mind will evoke in this dream world in which he is living a situation wherein the hero must die.

"You probably know that the sympathetic magic of witchcraft acts largely through the imagination. A person imagines he is being hexed to death—and dies. If Marsham Craswell imagines that one of his fantastic creations kills the hero—himself—then he just won't wake up again.

"Drugs won't touch him. Listen."

Steve looked at me across Marsham's bed. I leaned down to hear the mutterings from the writer's bloodless lips.

". . . We must search the Plains of Istak for the Diamond. I, Multan, who now have the Sword, will lead thee; for the Snake must die and only in virtue of the Diamond can his death be encompassed. Come."

Craswell's right hand, lying limp on the coverlet, twitched. He was beckoning his followers.

"Still the Snake and the Diamond?" asked Steve. "He's been living that dream for two days. We only know what's happening when he speaks in his role of hero. Often it's quite unintelligible. Sometimes a spark of consciousness filters through, and he fights to wake up. It's pretty horrible to watch him squirming and trying to pull himself back into reality. Have you ever tried to pull yourself out of a nightmare and failed?"

It was then that I remembered Billy, the Colt .45. I told Steve about it, back in his office.

He said: "Sure. Your Pop had the right idea. In fact, I'm hoping to save Marsham by an application of the same principle. To do it, I need the cooperation of someone who combines a lively imagination with a severely practical streak, hoss-sense—and a sense of humor. Yes—you."

"Uh? How can I help? I don't even know the guy."

"You will," said Steve, and the significant way he said it sent a trickle of ice water down my back. "You're going to get closer to Marsham Craswell than one man has ever been to another.

"I'm going to project you—the essential you, that is, your mind and personality—into Craswell's tortured brain."

I made pop-eyes, then thumbed at the magazine-lined wall. "Too much of yonder, brother Steve," I said. "What you need is a drink."

Steve lit his pipe, draped his long legs over the arm of his chair. "Miracles and witchcraft are out. What I propose to do is basically no more miraculous than the way your Pop put that gun into your dreams so you weren't afraid anymore. It's merely more complex scientifically.

"You've heard of the encephalograph? You know it picks up the surface neural currents of the brain, amplifies and records them, showing the degree—or absence—of mental activity. It can't indicate the kind or quality of such activity save in very general terms. By using comparison-graphs and other statistical methods to analyze its data, we can sometimes diagnose incipient insanity, for instance. But that's all—until we started work on it, here at the Pentagon.

"We improved the penetration and induction pickup and needled the selectivity until we could probe any known portion of the brain. What we were looking for was a recognizable pattern among the millions of tiny electric currents that go to make up the imagery of thought, so that if the subject thought of something—a number, maybe—the instruments would react accordingly, give a pattern for it that would be repeated every time he thought of that number.

"We failed, of course. The major part of the brain acts as a unity, no one part being responsible for either simple or complex imagery, but the activity of one portion inducing activity in other portions—with the exception of those parts dealing with automatic impulses. So if we were to get a pattern we should need thousands of pickups—a practical impossibility. It was as if we were trying to divine the pattern of a colored sweater by putting one tiny stitch of it under a microscope.

"Paradoxically, our machine was too selective. We needed, not a probe, but an all-encompassing field, receptive simultaneously to the multitudinous currents that made up a thought pattern.

"We found such a field. But we were no further forward. In a sense, we were back where we started from—because to analyze what the field picked up would have entailed the use of thousands of complex instruments. We had amplified thought, but we could not analyze it.

"There was only one single instrument sufficiently sensitive and complex to do that—another human brain."

I waved for a pause. "I'm home," I said. "You've got a thought-reading machine."

"Much more than that. When we tested it the other day, one of my assistants stepped up the polarity-reversal of the field—that is, the frequency—by accident. I was acting as analyst and the subject was under narcosis.

"Instead of 'hearing' the dull incoherencies of his thoughts, I became part of them. I was inside that man's brain. It was a nightmare world. He wasn't a clear thinker. I was aware of my own individuality. . . . When he came round, he went for me bald-headed. Said I'd been trespassing inside his head.

"With Marsham, it'll be a different matter. The dream world of his coma is detailed, as real as he used to make dream worlds to his readers."

"Hold it," I said. "Why don't you take a peek?"

Steve Blakiston smiled and gave me a high-voltage shot from his big gray eyes. "Three good reasons: I've soaked in the sort of stuff he dreams up, and there's a danger that I would become identified too closely with him. What he needs is a salutary dose of common sense. You're the man for that, you cynical old whisky-hound.

"Secondly, if my mind gave way under the impress of his imagination, I wouldn't be around to treat myself; and thirdly, when—and if—he comes round, he'll want to kill the man who's been heterodyning his dreams. You can scram. But I want to stay and see the results."

"Sorting that out, I gather there's a possibility that I shall wake up as a candidate for a bed in the next ward?"

"Not unless you let your mind go under. And you won't. You've got a cast-iron non-gullibility complex. Just fool around in your usual iconoclastic manner. Your own imagination's pretty good, judging by some of your fight reports lately."

I got up, bowed politely, said: "Thank you, my friend. That reminds me—I'm covering the big fight at the Garden tomorrow night. And I need sleep. It's late. So long."

Steve unfolded and reached the door ahead of me.

"Please," he said, and argued. He can argue. And I couldn't duck those big eyes of his. And he is—or was—my pal. He said it wouldn't take long—(just like a dentist)—and he smacked down every "if" I thought up.

Ten minutes later, I was lying on a twin bed next to that occupied by a silent, white-faced Marsham Craswell. Steve was leaning over the writer adjusting a chrome-steel bowl like a hair-drier over the man's head. An assistant was fixing me up the same way.

Cables ran from the bowls to a movable arm overhead and thence to a wheeled machine that looked like something from the Whacky Science Section of the World's Fair, A.D. 2000.

I was bursting with questions, but the only ones that would come out seemed crazily irrelevant.

"What do I say to this guy? 'Good morning, and how are all your little complexes today?' Do I introduce myself?"

"Just say you're Pete Parnell, and play it off the cuff," said Steve. "You'll see what I mean when you get there."

Get there. That hit me—the idea of making a journey into some nut's nut. My stomach drew itself up to a softball size.

"What's the proper dress for a visit like this? Formal?" I asked. At least, I think I said that. It didn't sound like my voice.

"Wear what you like."

"Uh-huh. And how do I know when to draw my visit to a close?"

Steve came round to my side. "If you haven't snapped Craswell out of it within an hour, I'll turn off the current."

He stepped back to the machine. "Happy dreams."

I groaned.

It was hot. Two high summers rolled into one. No, two suns, blood-red, stark in a brazen sky. Should be cool underfoot—soft green turf, pool table smooth to the far horizon. But it wasn't grass. Dust. Burning green dust—

The gladiator stood ten feet away, eyes glaring in disbelief. All of six-four high, great bronzed arms and legs, knotted muscles, a long shining sword in his right hand.

But his face was unmistakable.

This was where I took a good hold of myself. I wanted to giggle.

"Boy!" I said. "Do you tan quickly! Couple of minutes ago, you were as white as the bed sheet."

The gladiator shaded his eyes from the twin suns. "Is this yet another guise of the magician Garor to drive me insane—an Earthman here, on the Plains of Istak? Or am I already—mad?" His voice was deep, smoothly modulated.

My own was perfectly normal. Indeed, after the initial effort, I felt perfectly normal, except for the heat.

I said: "That's the growing idea where I've just come from—that you're going nuts."

You know those half-dreams, just on the verge of sleep, in which you can control your own imagery to some extent? That's how I felt. I knew intuitively what Steve was getting at when he said I could play it off the cuff. I looked down. Tweed suit, brogues—naturally. That's what I was wearing when I last looked at myself. I had no reason to think I was wearing—and therefore to be wearing—anything else. But something cooler was indicated in this heat, generated by Marsham Craswell's imagination.

Something like his own gladiator costume, perhaps.

Sandals—fine. There were my feet—in sandals.

Then I laughed. I had nearly fallen into the error of accepting his imagination.

"Do you mind if I switch off one of those suns?" I asked politely. "It's a little hot."

I gave one of the suns a very dirty look. It disappeared.

The gladiator raised his sword. "You are—Garor!" he cried. "But your witchery shall not avail you against the Sword!"

He rushed forward. The shining blade cleaved the air toward my skull.

I thought very, very fast.

The sword clanged, and streaked off at a sharp tangent from my G.I. brain-pan protector. I'd last worn that homely piece of hardware in the Argonne, and I knew it would stop a mere sword. I took it off.

"Now listen to me, Marsham Craswell," I said. "My name's Pete Parnell, of the Sunday *Star*, and—"

Craswell looked up from his sword, chest heaving, startled eyes bright as if with recognition. "Wait! I know now who you are—Nelpar Retrep, Man of the Seven Moons, come to fight with me against the Snake and his ungodly disciple, magician and sorceress, Garor. Welcome, my friend!"

He held out a huge bronzed hand. I shook it.

It was obvious that, unable to rationalize—or irrationalize—me, he was writing me into the plot of his dream! Right. It had been amusing so far. I'd string along for a while. My imagination hadn't taken a licking—yet.

Craswell said: "My followers, the great-hearted Dokmen of the Blue Hills, have just been slain in a gory battle. We are about to brave the many perils of the Plains of Istak in our quest for the Diamond—but all this, of course, you know."

"Sure," I said. "What now?"

Craswell turned suddenly, pointed. "There," he muttered. "A sight that strikes terror even into my heart— Garor returns to the battle, at the head of her dread Legion of Lakros, beasts of the Overworld, drawn into evil symbiosis with alien intelligences—invulnerable to men, but not to the Sword, or to the mighty weapons of Nelpar of the Seven Moons. We shall fight them alone!"

Racing across the vast plain of green dust toward us was a horde of . . . er . . . creatures. My vocabulary can't cope fully with Craswell's imagination. Gigantic, shimmering things, drooling thick ichor, half-flying, half-lolloping. Enough to say I looked around for a washbasin to spit in. I found one, with soap and towels complete, but I pushed it over, looked at a patch of green dust and thought hard.

The outline of the phone booth wavered a little before I could fix it. I dashed inside, dialed "Police H.Q.? Riot squad here—and quick!"

I stepped outside the booth. Craswell was whirling the Sword round his head, yelling war cries as he faced the onrushing monsters.

From the other direction came the swelling scream of a police siren. Half a dozen good, solid patrol cars screeched to a dust-spurting stop outside the phone booth. I don't have to think hard to get a New York cop car fixed in my mind. These were just right. And the first man out, running to my side and patting his cap on firmly, was just right, too.

Michael O'Faolin, the biggest, toughest, nicest cop I know.

"Mike," I said, pointing. "Fix 'em."

"Shure, an' it's an aisy job f'the bhoys I've brought along," said Mike, hitching his belt.

He deployed his men.

Craswell looked at them fanning out to take the charge, then staggered back toward me, hand over his eyes. "Madness!" he shouted. "What madness is this? What are you doing?"

For a moment, the whole scene wavered. The lone red sun blinked out, the green desert became a murky transparency through which I caught a split-second glimpse of white beds with two figures lying on them. Then Craswell uncovered his eyes.

The monsters began to diminish some twenty yards from the riot squad. By the time they got to the cops, they were man-size, and very amenable to discipline— enforced by raps over their horny noggins with nightsticks. They were bundled into the squad cars, which set off again over the plains.

Michael O'Faolin remained. I said: "Thanks, Mike. I may have a couple of spare tickets for the big fight tomorrow night. See you later."

"Just what I was wantin', Pete. 'Tis me day off. Now, how do I get home?"

I opened the door of the phone booth. "Right inside." He stepped in. I turned to Craswell.

"Mighty magic, O Nelpar!" he exclaimed. "To creatures of Garor's mind you opposed creatures of your own!"

He'd woven the whole incident into his plot already.

"We must go forward now, Nelpar of the Seven Moons—forward to the Citadel of the Snake, a thousand lokspans over the burning Plains of Istak."

"How about the Diamond?"

"The Diamond—?"

Evidently, he'd run so far ahead of himself getting me fixed into the landscape that he'd forgotten all about the Diamond that could kill the Snake. I didn't remind him.

However, a thousand lokspans over the burning plains sounded a little too far for walking, whatever a lokspan might be.

I said: "Why do you make things tough for yourself, Craswell?"

"The name," he said with tremendous dignity, "is Multan."

"Multan, Sultan, Shashlik, Dikkidam, Hammaneggs or whatever polysyllabic pooh-bah you wish to call yourself—I still ask, why make things tough for yourself when there's plenty of cabs around? Just whistle."

I whistled. The Purple Cab swung in, perfect to the last detail, including a hulking-backed, unshaven driver, dead ringer for the impolite gorilla who'd brought me out to Pentagon that evening.

There is nothing on earth quite so unutterably prosaic as a New York Purple Cab with that sort of driver. The sight upset Craswell, and the green plains wavered again while he struggled to fit the cab into his dream.

"What new magic is this! You are indeed mighty, Nelpar!"

He got in. But he was trembling with the effort to maintain the structure of this world into which he had escaped, against my deliberate attempts to bring it crashing round his ears and restore him to colorless—but sane—normality.

At this stage, I felt curiously sorry for him; but I realized that it might only be by permitting him to reach the heights of creative imagery before dousing him with the sponge from the cold bucket that I could jerk his drifting ego back out of the dreamland.

It was dangerous thinking. Dangerous—for me.

Craswell's thousand lokspans appeared to be the equivalent of ten blocks. Or perhaps he wanted to gloss over the mundane near-reality of a cab ride. He pointed forward, past the driver's shoulder: "The Citadel of the Snake!"

To me, it looked remarkably like a wedding cake designed by Dali in red plastic: ten stories high, each story a platter half a mile thick, each platter diminishing in size and offset to the one beneath so that the edifice spiraled toward the glossy sky.

The cab rolled into its vast shadow, stopped beneath the sheer, blank precipice of the base platter, which might have been two miles in diameter. Or three. Or four. What's a mile or two among dreamers?

Craswell hopped out quickly. I got out on the driver's side.

The driver said: "Dollar-fifty."

Square, unshaven jaw, low forehead, dirty-red hair straggling under his cap. I said: "Comes high for a short trip."

"Lookit the clock," he growled, squirming his shoulders. "Do I come out and get it?"

I said sweetly: "Go to hell."

Cab and driver shot downward through the green

sand with the speed of an express elevator. The hole closed up. The times I've wanted to do just that—

Craswell was regarding me open-mouthed. I said: "Sorry. Now I'm being escapist, too. Get on with the plot."

He muttered something I didn't catch, strode across to the red wall in which a crack, meeting place of mighty gates, had appeared, and raised his sword.

"Open, Garor! Your doom is nigh. Multan and Nelpar are here to brave the terrors of this Citadel and free the world from the tyranny of the Snake!" He hammered at the crack with the sword-hilt.

"Not so loud," I murmured. "You'll wake the neighbors. Why not use the bell-push?" I put my thumb on the button and pressed. The towering gates swung slowly open.

"You . . . you have been here before—"

"Yes—after my last lobster supper." I bowed. "After you."

I followed him into a great, echoing tunnel with fluorescent walls. The gates closed behind us. He paused and looked at me with an odd gleam in his eyes. A gleam of—sanity. And there was anger in the set of his lips. Anger for me, not Garor or the Snake.

It's not nice to have someone trampling all over your ego. Pride is a tiger—even in dreams. The subconscious, as Steve had explained to me, is a function or state of the brain, not a small part of it. In thwarting Craswell, I was disparaging not merely his dream, but his very brain, sneering at his intellectual integrity, at his abilities as an imaginative writer.

In a brief moment of rationality, I believe he was strangely aware of this.

He said quietly: "You have limitations, Nelpar. Your outward-turning eyes are blind to the pain of creation; to you the crystal stars are spangles on the dress of a scarlet woman, and you mock the God-blessed unreason that would make life more than the crawling of an animal from womb to grave. In tearing the veil from mystery, you destroy not mystery—for there are many mysteries, a million veils, worlds within and beyond worlds—but beauty. And in destroying beauty, you destroy your soul."

These last words, quiet as they sounded, were caught up by the curving walls of the huge tunnel, amplified then diminished in pulsing repetition, loud then soft, a surging hypnotic echo: "Destroy your SOUL, DE-STROY your soul. SOUL—"

Craswell pointed with his sword. His voice was exul-tant. "There is a Veil, Nelpar—and you must tear it lest it become your shroud! The Mist—the Sentient Mist of the Citadel!"

I'll admit that, for a few seconds, he'd had me a little groggy. I felt—subdued. And I understood for the first time his power as a word-spinner.

I knew that it was vital for me to reassert myself.

A thick, gray mist was rolling, wreathing slowly toward us, filling the tunnel to roof-height, puffing out thick, groping tentacles.

"It lives on Life itself," Craswell shouted. "It feeds, not on flesh, but on the vital principle that animates all flesh. I am safe, Nelpar, for I have the Sword. Can your magic save you?"

"Magic!" I said. "There's no gas invented yet that'll get through a Mark 8 mask."

Gas-drill—face-piece first, straps behind the ears. No, I hadn't forgotten the old routine.

I adjusted the mask comfortably. "And if it's not gas," I added, "this will fix it." I felt over my shoul-der, unclipped a nozzle, brought it round into the "ready" position.

I had only used a one-man flame-thrower once—in training—but the experience was etched on my memory.

This was a de luxe model. At the first thirty-foot oily, searing blast, the Mist curled in on itself and rolled back the way it had come. Only quicker.

I shucked off the trappings. "You were in the Army for a while, Craswell. Remember?"

The shining translucency of the walls dimmed sud-denly, and beyond them I glimpsed, as in a movie close-up through an unfocused projector, the square, intense face of Steve Blakiston.

Then the walls re-formed, and Craswell, still the bronzed, naked-limbed giant of his imagination, was looking at me again, frowning, worried. "Your words are strange, O Nelpar. It seems you are master of mysteries beyond even my knowing."

I put on the sort of face I use when the sports editor queries my expenses, aggrieved, pleading. "Your trouble, Craswell, is that you don't want to know. You just won't remember. That's why you're here. But life isn't bad if you oil it a little. Why not snap out of this and come with me for a drink?"

"I do not understand," he muttered. "But we have a mission to perform. Follow." And he strode off.

Mention of drink reminded me. There was nothing wrong with my memory. And that tunnel was as hot as the green desert. I remembered a very small pub just off the streetcar depot end of Sauchiehall Street, Glasgow, Scotland. A ginger-whiskered ancient, an exile from the Highlands, who'd listened to me enthusing over a certain brand of Scotch. "If ye think that's guid, mon, ye'll no' tasted the brew from ma own private deestillery. Smack yer lips ower this, laddie—" And he'd produced an antique silver flask and poured a generous measure of golden whisky into my glass. I had never tasted such mellow nectar before or since. Until I was walking down the tunnel behind Craswell.

I nearly envisaged the glass, but changed my mind in time to make it the antique flask. I raised it to my lips. Imagination's a wonderful thing.

Craswell was talking. I'd nearly forgotten him.

". . . near the Hall of Madness, where strange music assaults the brain, weird harmonies that enchant, then kill, rupturing the very cells by a mixture of subsonic and supersonic frequencies. Listen!"

We had reached the end of the tunnel and stood at the top of a slope which, broadening, ran gently downward, veiled by a blue haze, like the smoke from fifty million cigarettes, filling a vast circular hall. The haze eddied, moved by vagrant, sluggish currents of air, and revealed on the farther side, dwarfed by distance but obviously enormous, a complex structure of pipes and consoles.

A dozen Mighty Wurlitzers rolled into one would have appeared as a miniature piano at the foot of this towering music-machine.

At its many consoles which, even at that distance, I could see consisted of at least half a dozen manuals each, were multilimbed creatures—spiders or octopuses or Polilollipops—I didn't ask what Craswell called them—I was listening.

The opening bars were strange enough, but innocuous. Then the multiple tones and harmonies began to swell in volume. I picked out the curious, sweet harshness of oboes and bassoons, the eldritch, rising ululation of a thousand violins, the keen shrilling of a hundred demonic flutes, the sobbing of many cellos. That's enough. Music's my hobby, and I don't want to get carried away in describing how that crazy symphony nearly carried me away.

But if Craswell ever reads this, I'd like him to know that he missed his vocation. He should have been a musician. His dream-music showed an amazing intuitive grasp of orchestration and harmonic theory. If he could do anything like it consciously, he would be a great modern composer.

Yet not too much like it. Because it began to have the effects he had warned about. The insidious rhythm and wild melodies seemed to throb inside my head, setting up a vibration, a burning, in the brain tissue.

Imagine Puccini's "Recondita Armonia" re-orchestrated by Stravinsky then re-arranged by Honegger, played by fifty symphony orchestras in the Hollywood Bowl, and you might begin to get the idea.

I was getting too much of it. Did I say music was my hobby? Certainly—but the only instrument I play is the harmonica. Quite well, too. And with a microphone, I can make lots of nice noise.

A microphone—and plenty of amplifiers. I pulled

the harmonica from my pocket, took a deep breath, and whooped into "Tiger Rag," my favorite party-piece.

The stunning blast-wave of jubilant jazz, riffs, tiger-growls and tremolo discords from the tiny mouth organ, crashed into the vast hall from the amplifiers, completely swamping Craswell's mad music.

I heard his agonized shout even above the din. His tastes in music were evidently not as catholic as mine. He didn't like jazz.

The music-machine quavered, the multi-limbed organists, ludicrous in their haste to escape from an unreal doom, shrank, withered to scuttling black beetles; the lighting effects that had sprayed a rich, unearthly effulgence over the consoles died away into pastel, blue gloom; then the great machine itself, caught in swirl upon wave of augmented chords complemented and reinforced by its own outpourings, shivered into fragments, poured in a chaotic stream over the floor of the hall.

I heard Craswell shout again, then the scene changed abruptly. I assumed that, in his desire to blot out the triumphant paean of jazz from his mind, and perhaps in an unconscious attempt to confuse me, he had skipped a part of his plot and, in the opposite of the flashback beloved of screen writers, shot himself forward. We were—somewhere else.

Perhaps it was the inferiority complex I was inducing, or in the transition he had forgotten how tall he was supposed to be, but he was now a mere six feet, nearer my own height.

He was so hoarse, I nearly suggested a gargle. "I . . . I left you in the Hall of Madness. Your magic caused the roof to collapse. I thought you were—killed."

So the flash-forward wasn't just an attempt to confuse me. He'd tried to lose me, write me out of the script altogether.

I shook my head. "Wishful thinking, Craswell, old man," I said reproachfully. "You can't kill me off between chapters. You see, I'm not one of your characters at all. Haven't you grasped that yet? The only way you can get rid of me is by waking up."

"Again you speak in riddles," he said, but there was little confidence in his voice.

The place in which we stood was a great, high-vaulted chamber. The lighting effects—as I was coming to expect—were unusual and admirable—many colored shafts of radiance from unseen sources, slowly moving, meeting and merging at the farther end of the chamber in a white, circular blaze which seemed to be suspended over a thronelike structure.

Craswell's size-concepts were stupendous. He'd either studied the biggest cathedrals in Europe, or he was reared inside Grand Central Station. The throne was apparently a good half-mile away, over a completely bare but softly resilient floor. Yet it was coming nearer. We were not walking. I looked at the walls, realized that the floor itself, a gigantic endless belt, was carrying us along.

The slow, inexorable movement was impressive. I was aware that Craswell was covertly glancing at me. He was anxious that I should be impressed. I replied by speeding up the belt a trifle. He didn't appear to notice.

He said: "We approach the Throne of the Snake, before which, his protector and disciple, stands the female magician and sorceress, Garor. Against her, we shall need all your strange skills, Nelpar, for she stands invulnerable within an invisible shield of pure force.

"You must destroy that barrier, that I may slay her with the Sword. Without her, the Snake, though her master and self-proclaimed master of this world, is powerless, and he will be at our mercy."

The belt came to a halt. We were at the foot of a broad stairway leading to the throne itself, a massive metal platform on which the Snake reposed beneath a brilliant ball of light.

The Snake was—a snake. Coil on coil of overgrown python, with an evil head the size of a football swaying slowly from side to side.

I spent little time looking at it. I've seen snakes before. And there was something worth much more prolonged study standing just below and slightly to one side of the throne.

Craswell's taste in feminine pulchritude was unimpeachable. I had half-expected an ancient, withered horror, but if Flo Ziegfeld had seen this baby, he'd have been scrambling up those steps waving a contract, force-shield or no force-shield, before you could get out the first glissando of a wolf-whistle.

She was a tall, oval-faced, green-eyed brunette, with everything just so, and nothing much in the way of covering—a scanty metal chest-protector and a knee-length, filmy green skirt. She had a tiny, delightful mole on her left cheek.

There was a curious touch of pride in Craswell's voice as he said, rather unnecessarily: "We are here, Garor," and looked at me expectantly.

The girl said: "Insolent fools—you are here to die."

Mm-m-m—that voice, as smooth and rich as a Piatigorski cello note. I was ready to give quite a lot of credit to Craswell's imagination, but I couldn't believe that he'd dreamed up this baby just like that. I guessed that she was modeled on life; someone he knew; someone I'd like to know—someone pulled out of the grab bag of memory in the same way as I had produced Mike O'Faolin and that grubby-chinned cab driver.

"A luscious dish," I said. "Remind me to ask you later for a phone number of the original, Craswell."

Then I said and did something that I have since regretted. It was not the behavior of a gentleman. I said: "But didn't you know they were wearing skirts longer, this season?"

I looked at the skirt. The hem line shot down to her ankles, evening-gown length.

Outraged, Craswell glared at his girlfriend. The skirt became knee-length. I made it fashionable again.

Then that skirt hem was bobbing up and down between her ankles and her knees like a crazy window blind. It was a contest of wills and imaginations, with a very pretty pair of well-covered tibiae as battleground. A fascinating sight, Garor's beautiful eyes blazed with fury. She seemed to be strangely aware of the misbecoming nature of the conflict.

Craswell suddenly uttered a ringing, petulant howl of anger and frustration—a score of lusty-lunged infants whose rattles had been simultaneously snatched from them couldn't have made more noise—and the intriguing scene was erased from view in an eruption of jet-black smoke.

When it cleared, Craswell was still in the same relative position but his sword was gone, his gladiator rig was torn and scorched, and thin trickles of blood streaked his muscular arms.

I didn't like the way he was looking at me. I'd booted his super-ego pretty hard that time.

I said: "So you couldn't take it. You've skipped a chapter again. Wise me up on what I've missed, will you?" Somehow it didn't sound as flippant as I intended.

He spoke incisively. "We have been captured and condemned to die, Nelpar. We are in the Pit of the Beast, and nothing can save us, for I have been deprived of the Sword and you of your magic.

"The ravening jaws of the Beast cannot be stayed. It is the end, Nelpar. The End—"

His eyes, large, faintly luminous, looked into mine. I tried to glance away, failed.

Irritated beyond bearing by my importunate clowning, his affronted ego had assumed the whole power of his brain, to assert itself through his will—to dominate me.

The volition may have been unconscious—he could not know why he hated me—but the effect was damnable.

And for the first time since my brash intrusion into the most private recesses of his mind, I began to doubt whether the whole business was quite—decent.

Sure, I was trying to help the guy, but . . . but dreams are sacred.

Doubt negates confidence. With confidence gone, the gateway is open to fear.

*Another voice, sibilant. Steve Blakiston saying,
". . . unless you let your mind go under."* My own
voice, *". . . wake up as a candidate for a bed in the
next ward—"* No, not— *". . . not unless you let your
mind go under—"* And Steve had been scared to do it
himself, hadn't he? I'd have something to say to that
guy when I got out. If I got out . . . if—

The whole thing just wasn't amusing any more.

"Quit it, Craswell," I said harshly. "Quit making
goo-goo eyes, or I'll bat you one—and you'll feel it,
coma or no coma."

He said: "What foolish words are these, when we
are both so near to death?"

*Steve's voice: ". . . sympathetic magic . . . imagina-
tion. If he imagines that one of his fantastic creations
kills the hero—himself—he just won't wake up again."*

That was it. A situation in which the hero must die.
And he wanted to envisage my death, too. But he
couldn't kill me. Or could he? How could Blakiston
know what powers might be unleashed by the concept
of death during this ultramundane communion of minds?

Didn't psychiatrists say that the death-urge, the will
to die, was buried deep, but potent, in the subconscious minds of men? It was not buried deep here. It
was glaring, exultant, starkly displayed in the eyes of
Marsham Craswell.

He had escaped from reality into a dream, but it
was not far enough. Death was the only full escape—

Perhaps Craswell sensed the confusion of thought
and speculation that laid my mind wide open to the
suggestions of his rioting, perfervid, death-intent imagination. He waved an arm with the grandiloquent gesture of a Shakespearean Chorus introducing a last act,
and brought on his monster.

In detail and vividness it excelled everything that he
had dreamed up previously. It was his swan-song as a
creator of fantastic forms, and he had wrought well.

I saw, briefly, that we were in the center of an
enormous, steep-banked amphitheater. There were no
spectators. No crowd scenes for Craswell. He pre-

ferred that strange, timeless emptiness which comes from using a minimum number of characters.

Just the two of us, under the blazing rays of great, red suns swinging in a molten sky. I couldn't count them.

I became visually aware only of the Beast.

An ant in the bottom of a washbowl with a dog snuffling at it might feel the same way. If the Beast had been anything like a dog. If it had been anything like *anything*.

It was a mass the size of several elephants. An obscene hulking gob of animated, semi-transparent purple flesh, with a gaping, circular mouth or vent, ringed inside with pointed beslimed tusks, and outside with—eyes.

As a static thing, it would have been a filthy envenomed horror, a thing of surpassing dread in its mere aspect; but the most fearsome thing was its nightmarish mode of progression.

Limbless, it jerked its prodigious bulk forward in a series of heaves—and lubricated its path with a glaucous, viscid fluid which slopped from its mouth with every jerk.

It was heading for us at an incredible pace. Thirty yards—Twenty—

The rigidity of utter fear gripped my limbs. This was true nightmare. I tried desperately to think . . . . flamethrower . . . how . . . I couldn't remember . . . my mind was slipping away from me in face of the onward surging of that protoplasmic juggernaut . . . the slime first, then the mouth, closing . . . my thoughts were a screaming turmoil—

Another voice, a deep, drawling, kindly voice, from an unforgettable hour in childhood—"There's nothing in the whole wide world or out of it that a slug from Billy here won't stop. There's nothing you can meet in dreams that Billy here won't stop. He'll come into your dreams with you from now on. There's no call to be scared of anything." *Then the cool, hard butt in my hand, the recoil, the whining irresistible chunk of hot, heavy metal—deep in my subconscious.*

"Pop!" I gasped. "Thanks, Pop."

The Beast was looming over me. But Billy was in my hand, pointing into the mouth. I fired.

The Beast jerked back on its slimy trail, began to dwindle, fold in on itself. I fired again and again.

I became aware once more of Craswell beside me. He looked at the dying Beast, still huge, but rapidly diminishing, then at the dull metal of the old Colt in my hand, the wisp of blue smoke from its uptilted barrel.

And then he began to laugh.

Great, gusty laughter, but with a touch of hysteria.

And as he laughed, he began to fade from view. The red suns sped away into the sky, became pin points; and the sky was white and clean and blank—like a ceiling.

In fact—what beautiful words are "In fact"—In fact, in sweet reality, it *was* a ceiling.

Then Steve Blakiston was peering down, easing the chromium bowl off the rubber pads round my head.

"Thanks, Pete," he said. "Half an hour to the minute. You worked on him quicker than an insulin shock."

I sat up, adjusting myself mentally. He pinched my arm. "Sure—you're awake. I'd like you to tell me just what you did—but not now. I'll ring you at your office."

I saw an assistant taking the bowl off Craswell's head.

Craswell blinked, turned his head, saw me. Half a dozen expressions, none of them pleasant, chased over his face.

He heaved upright, pushed aside the assistant.

"You lousy bum," he shouted. "I'll murder you!"

I just got clear before Steve and one of the others grabbed his arms.

"Let me get at him—I'll tear him open!"

"I warned you," Steve panted. "Get out, quick."

I was on my way. Marsham Craswell in a nightshirt may not have been quite so impressive physically as the bronzed gladiator of his dreams, but he was still passably muscular.

* * *

That was last night. Steve rang this morning.

"Cured," he said triumphantly. "Sane as you are. Said he realized he'd been overworking, and he's going to take things easier—give himself a rest from fantasy and write something else. He doesn't remember a thing about his dream-coma—but he had a curious feeling that he'd still like to do something unpleasant to a certain guy who was in the next bed to him when he woke up. He doesn't know why, and I haven't told him. But better keep clear."

"The feeling is mutual," I said. "I don't like his line in monsters. What's he going to write now—love stories?"

Steve laughed. "No. He's got a sudden craze for Westerns. Started talking this morning about the sociological and historical significance of the Colt revolver. He jotted down the title of his first yarn—'Six-Gun Rule.' Hey—is that based on something you pulled on him in his dream?"

I told him.

So Marsham Craswell's as sane as me, huh? I wouldn't take bets.

Three hours ago, I was on my way to the latest heavyweight match at Madison Square Garden when I was buttonholed by an off-duty policeman.

Michael O'Faolin, the biggest, toughest, nicest cop I know.

"Pete, m'boy," he said. "I had the strangest dream last night. I was helpin' yez out of a bit of a hole, and when it was all over, you said, in gratitude it may have been, that yez might have a couple of spare tickets f'the fight this very night, and I was wondering whether it could have been a sort of tellypathy like, and—"

I grabbed the corner of the bar doorway to steady myself. Mike was still jabbering on when I fumbled for my own tickets and said: "I'm not feeling too well, Mike. You go. I'll pick my stuff up from the other sheets. Don't think about it, Mike. Just put it down to the luck of the Irish."

I went back to the bar and thought hard into a large whisky, which is the next best thing to a crystal ball for providing a focus of concentration.

"Tellypathy, huh?"

No, said the whisky. Coincidence. Forget it.

Yet there's something in telepathy. Subconscious telepathy—two dreaming minds in rapport. But I wasn't dreaming. I was just tagging along in someone else's dream. Minds are particularly receptive in sleep. Premonitions and what-have-you. But I wasn't sleeping either. Six and four makes minus ten, strike three— you're out. You're nuts, said the whisky.

I decided to find myself a better quality crystal ball. A Scotch in a crystal glass at Cevali's club.

So I hailed a Purple Cab. There was something reminiscent about the back of the driver's head. I refused to think about it. Until the payoff.

"Dollar-fifty," he growled, then leaned out. "Say— ain't I seen you some place?"

"I'm around," I said, in a voice that squeezed with reluctance past my larynx. "Didn't you drive me out to Pentagon yesterday?"

"Yeah, that's it," he said. Square unshaven jaw, low forehead, dirty red hair straggling under his cap. "Yeah—but there's something else about your pan. I took a sleep between cruises last night and had a daffy dream. You seemed to come into it. And I got the screwiest idea you already owe me a dollar-fifty."

For a moment, I toyed with the idea of telling him to go to hell. But the roadway wasn't green sand. It looked too solid to open up. So I said, "Here's five," and staggered into Cevali's.

I looked into a whisky glass until my brain began to clear, then I phoned Steve Blakiston and talked. "It's the implications," I said finally. "I'm driving myself bats trying to figure out what would have happened if I'd conjured up a few score of my acquaintants. Would they all have dreamed the same dream if they'd been asleep?"

"Too diffuse," said Steve, apparently through a mouthful of sandwich. "That would be like trying to broadcast on dozens of wavelengths simultaneously with the same transmitter. Your brain was an integral part of that machine, occupying the same position in the circuit as a complexus of recording instruments, keyed in place with Craswell's brain—until the pick-up frequency was raised. What happened then I imagined purely as an induction process. It was—as far as the Craswell hook-up was concerned, but—"

I couldn't stand the juicy champing noises any longer, and said: "Swallow it before you choke." The guy lives on sandwiches.

His voice cleared. "Don't you see what we've got? During the amplification of the cerebral currents, there was a backsurge through the tubes and the machine became a transmitter. These two guys were sleeping, their unconscious minds wide open and acting as receivers; you'd seen them during the day, envisaged them vividly—and got tuned in, disturbing their minds and giving them dreams. Ever heard of sympathetic dreams? Ever dreamed of someone you haven't seen for years, and the next day he looks you up? Now we can do it deliberately—mechanically assisted dream telepathy, the waves reinforced and transmitted electronically! Come on over. We've got to experiment some more."

"Sometimes," I said, "I sleep. That's what I intend to do now—without mechanical assistance. So long."

A nightcap was indicated. I wandered back to the club bar. I should have gone home.

She hipped her way to the microphone in front of the band, five-foot ten of dream wrapped up in a white, glove-tight gown. An oval-faced, green-eyed brunette with a tiny, delightful mole on her left cheek. The gown was a little exiguous about the upper regions, perhaps, but not as whistle-worthy as the outfit Craswell had dreamed on her.

Backstage, I got a double shot of ice from those green eyes. Yes, she knew Mr. Craswell slightly. No, she wasn't asleep around midnight last night. And would I be so good as to inform her what business it was of mine? College type, ultra. How they do drift into the entertainment business. Not that I mind.

When I asked about the refrigeration, she said: "It's merely that I have no particular desire to know you, Mr. Parnell."

"Why?"

"I'm hardly accountable to you for my preferences." She frowned as if trying to recall something, added: "In any case—I don't know. I just don't like you. Now if you'll pardon me, I have another number to sing—"

"But, please . . . let me explain—"

"Explain what?"

She had me there. I stumble-tongued, and got a back view of the gown.

How can you apologize to a girl when she doesn't even know that you owe her an apology? She hadn't been asleep, so she couldn't have dreamed about the skirt incident. And if she had—she was Craswell's dream, not mine. But through some aberration a trickle of thought waves from Blakiston's machine had planted an unreasonable antipathy to me in her subconscious mind. And it would need a psychiatrist to dig it out. Or—

I phoned Steve from the club office. He was still chewing. I said: "I've got some intensive thinking to do—into that machine of yours. I'll be right over."

She was leaving the microphone as I passed the band on my way out. I looked at her as she came up, getting every detail fixed.

"What time do you go to bed?" I asked.

I saw the slap coming and ducked.

I said: "I can wait. I'll be seeing you. Happy dreams."

DREAMING IS A PRIVATE THING

by Isaac Asimov

Jesse Weill looked up from his desk. His old, spare body, his sharp, high-bridged nose, deep-set, shadowy eyes and amazing shock of white hair had trademarked his appearance during the years that Dreams, Inc., had become world-famous.

He said, "Is the boy here already, Joe?"

Joe Dooley was short and heavy-set. A cigar caressed his moist lower lip. He took it away for a moment and nodded. "His folks are with him. They're all scared."

"You're sure this is not a false alarm, Joe? I haven't got much time." He looked at his watch. "Government business at two."

"This is a sure thing, Mr. Weill." Dooley's face was a study in earnestness. His jowls quivered with persuasive intensity. "Like I told you, I picked him up playing some kind of basketball game in the schoolyard. You should've seen the kid. He stunk. When he had his hands on the ball, his own team had to take it away, and fast, but just the same he had all the stance of a star player. Know what I mean? To me it was a giveaway."

"Did you talk to him?"

"Well, sure. I stopped him at lunch. You know me." Dooley gestured expansively with his cigar and caught the severed ash with his other hand. "Kid, I said—"

"And he's dream material?"

"I said, 'Kid, I just came from Africa and—' "

"All right." Weill held up the palm of his hand. "Your word I'll always take. How you do it I don't know, but when you say a boy is a potential dreamer, I'll gamble. Bring him in."

The youngster came in between his parents. Dooley pushed chairs forward and Weill rose to shake hands. He smiled at the youngster in a way that turned the wrinkles of his face into benevolent creases.

"You're Tommy Slutsky?"

Tommy nodded wordlessly. He was about ten and a little small for that. His dark hair was plastered down unconvincingly and his face was unrealistically clean.

Weill said, "You're a good boy?"

The boy's mother smiled at once and patted Tommy's head maternally (a gesture which did not soften the anxious expression on the youngster's face). She said, "He's always a very good boy."

Weill let this dubious statement pass. "Tell me, Tommy," he said, and held out a lollipop which was first hesitated over, then accepted, "do you ever listen to dreamies?"

"Sometimes," said Tommy trebly.

Mr. Slutsky cleared his throat. He was broad-shouldered and thick-fingered, the type of laboring man who, every once in a while, to the confusion of eugenics, sired a dreamer. "We rented one or two for the boy. Real old ones."

Weill nodded. He said, "Did you like them, Tommy?"

"They were sort of silly."

"You think up better ones for yourself, do you?"

The grin that spread over the ten-year-old face had the effect of taking away some of the unreality of the slicked hair and washed face.

Weill went on gently, "Would you like to make up a dream for me?"

Tommy was instantly embarrassed. "I guess not."

"It won't be hard. It's very easy. . . . Joe."

Dooley moved a screen out of the way and rolled forward a dream recorder.

The youngster looked owlishly at it.

Weill lifted the helmet and brought it close to the boy. "Do you know what this is?"

Tommy shrank away. "No."

"It's a thinker. That's what we call it because people think into it. You put it on your head and think anything you want."

"Then what happens?"

"Nothing at all. It feels nice."

"No," said Tommy, "I guess I'd rather not."

His mother bent hurriedly toward him. "It won't hurt, Tommy. You do what the man says." There was an unmistakable edge to her voice.

Tommy stiffened, and looked as though he might cry but he didn't. Weill put the thinker on him.

He did it gently and slowly and let it remain there for some thirty seconds before speaking again, to let the boy assure himself it would do no harm, to let him get used to the insinuating touch of the fibrils against the sutures of his skull (penetrating the skin so finely as to be insensible almost), and finally to let him get used to the faint hum of the alternating field vortices.

Then he said, "Now would you think for us?"

"About what?" Only the boy's nose and mouth showed.

"About anything you want. What's the best thing you would like to do when school is out?"

The boy thought a moment and said, with rising inflection, "Go on a stratojet?"

"Why not? Sure thing. You go on a jet. It's taking off right now." He gestured lightly to Dooley, who threw the freezer into circuit.

Weill kept the boy only five minutes and then let him and his mother be escorted from the office by Dooley. Tommy looked bewildered but undamaged by the ordeal.

Weill said to the father, "Now, Mr. Slutsky, if your boy does well on this test, we'll be glad to pay you five hundred dollars each year until he finishes high school. In that time, all we'll ask is that he spend an hour a week some afternoon at our special school."

"Do I have to sign a paper?" Slutsky's voice was a bit hoarse.

"Certainly. This is business, Mr. Slutsky."

"Well, I don't know. Dreamers are hard to come by, I hear."

"They are. They are. But your son, Mr. Slutsky, is not a dreamer yet. He might never be. Five hundred dollars a year is a gamble for us. It's not a gamble for you. When he's finished high school, it may turn out he's not a dreamer, yet you've lost nothing. You've gained maybe four thousand dollars altogether. If he *is* a dreamer, he'll make a nice living and you certainly haven't lost then."

"He'll need special training, won't he?"

"Oh, yes, most intensive. But we don't have to worry about that till after he's finished high school. Then, after two years with us, he'll be developed. Rely on me, Mr. Slutsky."

"Will you guarantee that special training?"

Weill, who had been shoving a paper across the desk at Slutsky, and punching a pen wrong-end-to at him, put the pen down and chuckled. "A guarantee? No. How can we when we don't know for sure yet if he's a real talent? Still, the five hundred a year will stay yours."

Slutsky pondered and shook his head. "I tell you straight out, Mr. Weill . . . after your man arranged to have us come here, I called Luster-Think. They said they'll guarantee training."

Weill sighed. "Mr. Slutsky, I don't like to talk against a competitor. If they say they'll guarantee schooling, they'll do as they say, but they can't make a boy a dreamer if he hasn't got it in him, schooling or not. If they take a plain boy without the proper talent and put him through a development course, they'll ruin him. A dreamer he won't be, I guarantee you. And a normal human being he won't be, either. Don't take the chance of doing it to your son.

"Now Dreams, Inc., will be perfectly honest with you. If he can be a dreamer, we'll make him one. If not, we'll give him back to you without having tampered with him and say, 'Let him learn a trade.' He'll be better and healthier that way. I tell you, Mr. Slutsky—I have sons and daughters and grandchildren so I know what I say—I would not allow a child of mine to be pushed into dreaming if he's not ready for it. Not for a million dollars."

Slutsky wiped his mouth with the back of his hand and reached for the pen. "What does this say?"

"This is just an option. We pay you a hundred dollars in cash right now. No strings attached. We'll study the boy's reverie. If we feel it's worth following up, we'll call you in again and make the five-hundred-dollar-a-year deal. Leave yourself in my hands, Mr. Slutsky, and don't worry. You won't be sorry."

Slutsky signed.

Weill passed the document through the file slot and handed an envelope to Slutsky.

Five minutes later, alone in the office, he placed the unfreezer over his own head and absorbed the boy's reverie intently. It was a typically childish daydream. First Person was at the controls of the plane, which looked like a compound of illustrations out of the filmed thrillers that still circulated among those who lacked the time, desire or money for dream cylinders.

When he removed the unfreezer, he found Dooley looking at him.

"Well, Mr. Weill, what do you think?" said Dooley, with an eager and proprietary air.

"Could be, Joe. Could be. He has the overtones and, for a ten-year-old boy without a scrap of training, it's hopeful. When the plane went through a cloud, there was a distinct sensation of pillows. Also the smell of clean sheets, which was an amusing touch. We can go with him a ways, Joe."

"Good."

"But I tell you, Joe, what we really need is to catch them still sooner. And why not? Someday, Joe, every child will be tested at birth. A difference in the brain there positively must be and it should be found. Then we could separate the dreamers at the very beginning."

"Hell, Mr. Weill," said Dooley, looking hurt. "What would happen to my job, then?"

Weill laughed. "No cause to worry yet, Joe. It won't happen in our lifetimes. In mine, certainly not. We'll be depending on good talent scouts like you for many years. You just watch the playgrounds and the streets"—Weill's gnarled hand dropped to Dooley's shoulder with a gentle, approving pressure—"and find us a few more Hillarys and Janows and Luster-Think won't ever catch us. . . . Now get out. I want lunch and then I'll be ready for my two o'clock appointment. The government, Joe, the government." And he winked portentously.

Jesse Weill's two o'clock appointment was with a young man, apple-cheeked, spectacled, sandy-haired and glowing with the intensity of a man with a mission. He presented his credentials across Weill's desk and revealed himself to be John J. Byrne, an agent of the Department of Arts and Sciences.

"Good afternoon, Mr. Byrne," said Weill. "In what way can I be of service?"

"Are we private here?" asked the agent. He had an unexpected baritone.

"Quite private."

"Then, if you don't mind, I'll ask you to absorb this." Byrne produced a small and battered cylinder and held it out between thumb and forefinger.

Weill took it, hefted it, turned it this way and that and said with a denture-revealing smile, "Not the product of Dreams, Inc., Mr. Byrne."

"I didn't think it was," said the agent. "I'd still like you to absorb it. I'd set the automatic cutoff for about a minute, though."

"That's all that can be endured?" Weill pulled the receiver to his desk and placed the cylinder into the unfreeze compartment. He removed it, polished either end of the cylinder with his handkerchief and tried again. "It doesn't make good contact," he said. "An amateurish job."

He placed the cushioned unfreeze helmet over his skull and adjusted the temple contacts, then set the automatic cutoff. He leaned back and clasped his hands over his chest and began absorbing.

His fingers grew rigid and clutched at his jacket. After the cutoff had brought absorption to an end, he removed the unfreezer and looked faintly angry. "A raw piece," he said. "It's lucky I'm an old man so that such things no longer bother me."

Byrne said stiffly, "It's not the worst we've found. And the fad is increasing."

Weill shrugged. "Pornographic dreamies. It's a logical development, I suppose."

The government man said, "Logical or not, it represents a deadly danger for the moral fiber of the nation."

"The moral fiber," said Weill, "can take a lot of beating. Erotica of one form or another have been circulated all through history."

"Not like this, sir. A direct mind-to-mind stimulation is much more effective than smoking room stories or filthy pictures. Those must be filtered through the senses and lose some of their effect in that way."

Weill could scarcely argue that point. He said, "What would you have me do?"

"Can you suggest a possible source for this cylinder?"

"Mr. Byrne, I'm not a policeman."

"No, no, I'm not asking you to do our work for us. The Department is quite capable of conducting its own investigations. Can you help us, I mean, from your own specialized knowledge? You say your company did not put out that filth. Who did?"

"No reputable dream distributor. I'm sure of that. It's too cheaply made."

"That could have been done on purpose."

"And no professional dreamer originated it."

"Are you sure, Mr. Weill? Couldn't dreamers do this sort of thing for some small, illegitimate concern for money—or for fun?"

"They could, but not this particular one. No overtones. It's two-dimensional. Of course, a thing like this doesn't need overtones."

"What do you mean, overtones?"

Weill laughed gently. "You are not a dreamie fan?"

Byrne tried not to look virtuous and did not entirely succeed. "I prefer music."

"Well, that's all right, too," said Weill tolerantly, "but it makes it a little harder to explain overtones. Even people who absorb dreamies would not be able to explain if you asked them. Still they'd know a dreamie was no good if the overtones were missing, even if they couldn't tell you why. Look, when an experienced dreamer goes into reverie, he doesn't think a story like in the old-fashioned television or book films. It's a series of little visions. Each one has several meanings. If you studied them carefully, you'd find maybe five or six. While absorbing in the ordinary way, you would never notice, but careful study shows it. Believe me, my psychological staff puts in long hours on just that point. All the overtones, the different meanings, blend together into a mass of guided emotion. Without them, everything would be flat, tasteless.

"Now, this morning, I tested a young boy. A ten-year-old with possibilities. A cloud to him isn't a cloud, it's a pillow, too. Having the sensations of both, it was more than either. Of course, the boy's very primitive. But when he's through with his schooling, he'll be trained and disciplined. He'll be subjected to all sorts of sensations. He'll store up experience. He'll study and analyze classic dreamies of the past. He'll learn how to control and direct his thoughts, though, mind you, I have always said that when a good dreamer improvises—"

Weill halted abruptly, then proceeded in less impassioned tones, "I shouldn't get excited. All I try to bring out now is that every professional dreamer has his own type of overtones which he can't mask. To an expert it's like signing his name on the dreamie. And I, Mr. Byrne, know all the signatures. Now that piece of dirt you brought me has no overtones at all. It was done by an ordinary person. A little talent, maybe, but like you and me, he really can't think."

Byrne reddened a trifle. "A lot of people can think, Mr. Weill, even if they don't make dreamies."

"Oh, tush," and Weill wagged his hand in the air. "Don't be angry with what an old man says. I don't mean think as in reason. I mean think as in dream. We all can dream after a fashion, just like we all can run. But can you and I run a mile in four minutes? You and I can talk, but are we Daniel Websters? Now when I think of a steak, I think of the word. Maybe I have a quick picture of a brown steak on a platter. Maybe you have a better pictorialization of it and you can see the crisp fat and the onions and the baked potato. I don't know. But a *dreamer* . . . he sees it and smells it and tastes it and everything about it, with the charcoal and the satisfied feeling in the stomach and the way the knife cuts through it and a hundred other things all at once. Very sensual. Very sensual. You and I can't do it."

"Well, then," said Byrne, "no professional dreamer has done this. That's something anyway." He put the cylinder in his inner jacket pocket. "I hope we'll have your full co-operation in squelching this sort of thing."

"Positively, Mr. Byrne. With a whole heart."

"I hope so." Byrne spoke with a consciousness of power. "It's not up to me, Mr. Weill, to say what will be done and what won't be done, but this sort of thing"—he tapped the cylinder he had brought—"will make it awfully tempting to impose a really strict censorship on dreamies."

He rose. "Good day, Mr. Weill."

"Good day, Mr. Byrne. I'll hope always for the best."

Francis Belanger burst into Jesse Weill's office in his usual steaming tizzy, his reddish hair disordered and his face aglow with worry and a mild perspiration. He was brought up sharply by the sight of Weill's head cradled in the crook of his elbow and bent on the desk until only the glimmer of white hair was visible.

Belanger swallowed. "Boss?"

Weill's head lifted. "It's you, Frank?"

"What's the matter, boss? Are you sick?"

"I'm old enough to be sick, but I'm on my feet. Staggering, but on my feet. A government man was here."

"What did he want?"

"He threatens censorship. He brought a sample of what's going round. Cheap dreamies for bottle parties."

"God damn!" said Belanger feelingly.

"The only trouble is that morality makes for good campaign fodder. They'll be hitting out everywhere. And, to tell the truth, we're vulnerable, Frank."

"*We* are? Our stuff is clean. We play up straight adventure and romance."

Weill thrust out his lower lip and wrinkled his forehead. "Between us, Frank, we don't have to make believe. Clean? It depends on how you look at it. It's not for publication, maybe, but you know and I know that every dreamie has its Freudian connotations. You can't deny it."

"Sure, if you *look* for it. If you're a psychiatrist—"

"If you're an ordinary person, too. The ordinary observer doesn't know it's there and maybe he couldn't tell a phallic symbol from a mother image even if you pointed it out. Still, his subconscious knows. And it's the connotations that make many a dreamie click."

"All right, what's the government going to do? Clean up the subconscious?"

"It's a problem. I don't know what they're going to do. What we have on our side, and what I'm mainly depending on, is the fact that the public loves its dreamies and won't give them up. . . . Meanwhile, what did you come in for? You want to see me about something, I suppose?"

Belanger tossed an object onto Weill's desk and shoved his shirttail deeper into his trousers.

Weill broke open the glistening plastic cover and took out the enclosed cylinder. At one end was engraved in a too fancy script in pastel blue "Along the Himalayan Trail." It bore the mark of Luster-Think.

"The Competitor's Product." Weill said it with capitals, and his lips twitched. "It hasn't been published yet. Where did you get it, Frank?"

"Never mind. I just want you to absorb it."

Weill sighed. "Today, everyone wants me to absorb dreams. Frank, it's not dirty?"

Belanger said testily, "It has your Freudian symbols. Narrow crevasses between the mountain peaks. I hope that won't bother you."

"I'm an old man. It stopped bothering me years ago, but that other thing was so poorly done, it hurt. . . . All right, let's see what you've got here."

Again the recorder. Again the unfreezer over his skull and at the temples. This time, Weill rested back in his chair for fifteen minutes or more, while Francis Belanger went hurriedly through two cigarettes.

When Weill removed the headpiece and blinked dream out of his eyes, Belanger said, "Well, what's your reaction, boss?"

Weill corrugated his forehead. "It's not for me. It was repetitious. With competition like this, Dreams, Inc., doesn't have to worry for a while."

"That's your mistake, boss. Luster-Think's going to win with stuff like this. We've got to do something."

"Now, Frank—"

"No, you listen. This is the coming thing."

"This!" Weill stared with half-humorous dubiety at the cylinder. "It's amateurish, it's repetitious. Its overtones are very unsubtle. The snow had a distinct lemon sherbet taste. Who tastes lemon sherbet in snow these days, Frank? In the old days, yes. Twenty years ago, maybe. When Lyman Harrison first made his Snow Symphonies for sale down south, it was a big thing. Sherbet and candy-striped mountaintops and sliding down chocolate-covered cliffs. It's slapstick, Frank. These days it doesn't go."

"Because," said Belanger, "you're not up with the times, boss. I've got to talk to you straight. When you started the dreamie business, when you bought up the basic patents and began putting them out, dreamies were luxury stuff. The market was small and individual. You could afford to turn out specialized dreamies and sell them to people at high prices."

"I know," said Weill, "and we've kept that up. But also we've opened a rental business for the masses."

"Yes, we have and it's not enough. Our dreamies have subtlety, yes. They can be used over and over again. The tenth time you're still finding new things, still getting new enjoyment. But how many people are connoisseurs? And another thing. Our stuff is strongly individualized. They're First Person."

"Well?"

"Well, Luster-Think is opening dream palaces. They've opened one with three hundred booths in Nashville. You walk in, take your seat, put on your unfreezer and get your dream. Everyone in the audience gets the same one."

"I've heard of it, Frank, and it's been done before. It didn't work the first time and it won't work now. You want to know why it won't work? Because, in the first place, dreaming is a private thing. Do you like your neighbor to know what you're dreaming? In the second place, in a dream palace, the dreams have to start on schedule, don't they? So the dreamer has to dream not when he wants to but when some palace manager says he should. Finally, a dream one person likes another person doesn't like. In those three hundred booths, I guarantee you, a hundred fifty people are dissatisfied. And if they're dissatisfied, they won't come back."

Slowly, Belanger rolled up his sleeves and opened his collar. "Boss," he said, "you're talking through your hat. What's the use of proving they won't work? They *are* working. The word came through today that Luster-Think is breaking ground for a thousand-booth palace in St. Louis. People can get used to public dreaming, if everyone else in the same room is having the same dream. And they can adjust themselves to having it at a given time, as long as it's cheap and convenient.

"Damn it, boss, it's a social affair. A boy and a girl go to a dream palace and absorb some cheap romantic thing with stereotyped overtones and commonplace situations, but still they come out with stars sprinkling their hair. They've had the same dream together. They've gone through identical sloppy emotions. They're *in tune*, boss. You bet they go back to the dream palace, and all their friends go, too."

"And if they don't like the dream?"

"That's the point. That's the nub of the whole thing. They're bound to like it. If you prepare Hillary specials with wheels within wheels within wheels, with surprise twists on the third-level undertones, with clever shifts of significance and all the other things we're so proud of, why, naturally, it won't appeal to everyone. Specialized dreamies are for specialized tastes. But Luster-Think is turning out simple jobs in Third Person so both sexes can be hit at once. Like what you've just absorbed. Simple, repetitious, commonplace. They're aiming at the lowest common denominator. No one will love it, maybe, but no one will hate it."

Weill sat silent for a long time and Belanger watched him. Then Weill said, "Frank, I started on quality and I'm staying there. Maybe you're right. Maybe dream palaces are the coming thing. If so we'll open them, but we'll use good stuff. Maybe Luster-Think underestimates ordinary people. Let's go slowly and not panic. I have based all my policies on the theory that there's always a market for quality. Sometimes, my boy, it would surprise you how big a market."

"Boss—"

The sounding of the intercom interrupted Belanger. "What is it, Ruth?" said Weill.

The voice of his secretary said, "It's Mr. Hillary, sir. He wants to see you right away. He says it's important."

"Hillary?" Weill's voice registered shock. Then, "Wait five minutes, Ruth, then send him in."

Weill turned to Belanger. "Today, Frank, is definitely not one of my good days. A dreamer's place is in his home with his thinker. And Hillary's our best dreamer so he especially should be at home. What do you suppose is wrong with him?"

Belanger, still brooding over Luster-Think and dream palaces, said shortly, "Call him in and find out."

"In one minute. Tell me, how was his last dream? I haven't tried the one that came in last week."

Belanger came down to earth. He wrinkled his nose. "Not so good."

"Why not?"

"It was ragged. Too jumpy. I don't mind sharp transitions for the liveliness, you know, but there's got to be some connection, even if only on a deep level."

"Is it a total loss?"

"No Hillary dream is a *total* loss. It took a lot of editing, though. We cut it down quite a bit and spliced in some odd pieces he'd sent us now and then. You know, detached scenes. It's still not Grade A, but it will pass."

"You told him about this, Frank?"

"Think I'm crazy, boss? Think I'm going to say a harsh word to a dreamer?"

And at that point the door opened and Weill's comely young secretary smiled Sherman Hillary into the office.

Sherman Hillary, at the age of thirty-one, could have been recognized as a dreamer by anyone. His eyes, unspectacled, had nevertheless the misty look of one who either needs glasses or who rarely focuses on anything mundane. He was of average height but underweight, with black hair that needed cutting, a narrow chin, a pale skin and a troubled look.

He muttered, "Hello, Mr. Weill," and half-nodded in hangdog fashion in the direction of Belanger.

Weill said heartily, "Sherman, my boy, you look fine. What's the matter? A dream is cooking only so-so at home? You're worried about it? . . . Sit down, sit down."

The dreamer did, sitting at the edge of the chair and holding his thighs stiffly together as though to be ready for instant obedience to a possible order to stand up once more.

He said, "I've come to tell you, Mr. Weill, I'm quitting."

"Quitting?"

"I don't want to dream any more, Mr. Weill."

Weill's old face looked older now than at any time in the day. "Why, Sherman?"

The dreamer's lips twisted. He blurted out, "Because I'm not *living*, Mr. Weill. Everything passes me by. It wasn't so bad at first. It was even relaxing. I'd dream evenings, weekends when I felt like, or any other time. And when I felt like I wouldn't. But now, Mr. Weill, I'm an old pro. You tell me I'm one of the best in the business and the industry looks to me to think up new subtleties and new changes on the old reliables like the flying reveries, and the worm-turning skits."

Weill said, "And is anyone better than you, Sherman? Your little sequence on leading an orchestra is selling steadily after ten years."

"All right, Mr. Weill. I've done my part. It's gotten so I don't go out any more. I neglect my wife. My little girl doesn't know me. Last week, we went to a dinner party—Sarah made me—and I don't remember a bit of it. Sarah says I was sitting on the couch all evening just staring at nothing and humming. She said everyone kept looking at me. She cried all night. I'm tired of things like that, Mr. Weill. I want to be a normal person and live in this world. I promised her I'd quit and I will, so it's good-by, Mr. Weill." Hillary stood up and held out his hand awkwardly.

Weill waved it gently away. "If you want to quit, Sherman, it's all right. But do an old man a favor and let me explain something to you."

"I'm not going to change my mind," said Hillary.

"I'm not going to try to make you. I just want to explain something. I'm an old man and even before you were born I was in this business so I like to talk about it. Humor me, Sherman? Please?"

Hillary sat down. His teeth clamped down on his lower lip and he stared sullenly at his fingernails.

Weill said, "Do you know what a dreamer is, Sherman? Do you know what he means to ordinary people? Do you know what it is to be like me, like Frank Belanger, like your wife, Sarah? To have crippled minds that can't imagine, that can't build up thoughts? People like myself, ordinary people, would like to escape just once in a while this life of ours. We can't. We need help.

"In olden times it was books, plays, radio, movies, television. They gave us make-believe, but that wasn't important. What was important was that for a little while our own imaginations were stimulated. We could think of handsome lovers and beautiful princesses. We could be beautiful, witty, strong, capable, everything we weren't.

"But, always, the passing of the dream from dreamer to absorber was not perfect. It had to be translated into words in one way or another. The best dreamer in the world might not be able to get any of it into words. And the best writer in the world could put only the smallest part of his dreams into words. You understand?

"But now, with dream recording, any man can dream. You, Sherman, and a handful of men like you, supply those dreams directly and exactly. It's straight from your head into ours, full strength. You dream for a hundred million people every time you dream. You dream a hundred million dreams at once. This is a great thing, my boy. You give all those people a glimpse of something they could not have by themselves."

Hillary mumbled, "I've done my share." He rose desperately to his feet. "I'm through. I don't care what you say. And if you want to sue me for breaking our contract, go ahead and sue. I don't care."

Weill stood up, too. "Would I sue you? . . . Ruth," he spoke into the intercom, "bring in our copy of Mr. Hillary's contract."

He waited. So did Hillary and so did Belanger. Weill smiled faintly and his yellowed fingers drummed softly on his desk.

His secretary brought in the contract. Weill took it,

showed its face to Hillary and said, "Sherman, my boy, unless you want to be with me, it's not right you should stay."

Then, before Belanger could make more than the beginning of a horrified gesture to stop him, he tore the contract into four pieces and tossed them down the waste chute. "That's all."

Hillary's hand shot out to seize Weill's. "Thanks, Mr. Weill," he said earnestly, his voice husky. "You've always treated me very well, and I'm grateful. I'm sorry it had to be like this."

"It's all right, my boy. It's all right."

Half in tears, still muttering thanks, Sherman Hillary left.

"For the love of Pete, boss, why did you let him go?" demanded Belanger distractedly. "Don't you see the game? He'll be going straight to Luster-Think. They've bought him off."

Weill raised his hand. "You're wrong. You're quite wrong. I know the boy and this would not be his style. Besides," he added dryly, "Ruth is a good secretary and she knows what to bring me when I ask for a dreamer's contract. What I had was a fake. The real contract is still in the safe, believe me.

"Meanwhile, a fine day I've had. I had to argue with a father to give me a chance at new talent, with a government man to avoid censorship, with you to keep from adopting fatal policies and now with my best dreamer to keep him from leaving. The father I probably won out over. The government man and you, I don't know. Maybe yes, maybe no. But about Sherman Hillary, at least, there is no question. The dreamer will be back."

"How do you know?"

Weill smiled at Belanger and crinkled his cheeks into a network of fine lines. "Frank, my boy, you know how to edit dreamies so you think you know all the tools and machines of the trade. But let me tell you something. The most important tool in the dreamie business is the dreamer himself. He is the one you have to understand most of all, and I understand them.

"Listen. When I was a youngster—there were no dreamies then—I knew a fellow who wrote television scripts. He would complain to me bitterly that when someone met him for the first time and found out who he was, they would say: Where do you get those crazy ideas?

"They honestly didn't know. To them it was an impossibility to even think of one of them. So what could my friend say? He used to talk to me about it and tell me: Could I say, I don't know? When I go to bed, I can't sleep for ideas dancing in my head. When I shave, I cut myself; when I talk, I lose track of what I'm saying; when I drive, I take my life in my hands. And always because ideas, situations, dialogues are spinning and twisting in my mind. I can't tell you where I get my ideas. Can you tell me, maybe, your trick of *not* getting ideas, so I, too, can have a little peace.

"You see, Frank, how it is. *You* can stop work here anytime. So can I. This is our job, not our life. But not Sherman Hillary. Wherever he goes, whatever he does, he'll dream. While he lives, he must think; while he thinks, he must dream. We don't hold him prisoner, our contract isn't an iron wall for him. His own skull is his prisoner, Frank. So he'll be back. What can he do?"

Belanger shrugged. "If what you say is right, I'm sort of sorry for the guy."

Weill nodded sadly. "I'm sorry for all of them. Through the years, I've found out one thing. It's their business; making people happy. *Other* people."

THE MONARCH OF DREAMS

by *Thomas Wentworth Higginson*

φάσμα δόξει δόμων ἀνάσσειν.
Aeschylus, Agamemnon, 391.

He who forsakes the railways and goes wandering through the hill-country of New England must adopt one rule as invariable. When he comes to a fork in the road, and is told that both ways lead to the desired point, he must simply ask which road is the better; and, on its being pointed out, must at once take the other. The explanation is easy. The passers-by will always recommend the new road, which keeps to the valley and avoids the hills; but the old road, now deserted by the general public, ascends the steeper grades, and thus offers the more desirable views.

Turning to the old road, you soon feel that both houses and men are, in a manner, stranded. They see very little of the world, and are under no stimulus to keep themselves in repair. You are wholly beyond the dreary sway of French roofs; and the caricatures of good Queen Anne's day are far from you. If any farmhouse on the hill-road was really built within the reign of that much-abused potentate, it is probably a solid, square mansion of brick, three stories high, blackened with time, and frowning rather gloomily from some hilltop,—as essentially a part of the past as an Irish round tower or a Scotch border fortress. A branching elm-tree or two may droop above it. It is partly screened from the road by a lilac hedge, and by what seems an unnecessarily large wood-pile. A low stone wall surrounds the ample barns and sheds, made of

165

unpainted wood, and now gray with age; and near these is a neglected garden, where phlox and pinks and tiger-lilies are intersected with irregular hedges of treebox. The house looks upon gorgeous sunsets and distant mountain ranges, and lakes surrounded by pine and chestnut woods. Against a lurid sky, or in a brooding fog, it is as impressive in the landscape as a feudal castle; and like that, it is almost deserted: human life has slipped away from it into the manufacturing village, swarming with French Canadians, in the valley below.

It was in such a house that Francis Ayrault had finally taken up his abode, leaving behind him the old family homestead in a Rhode Island seaside town. A series of domestic cares and watchings had almost broken him down: nothing debilitates a man of strong nature like the too prolonged and exclusive exercise of the habit of sympathy. At last, when the very spot where he was born had been chosen as a site for a new railway station, there seemed nothing more to retain him. He needed utter rest and change; and there was no one left on earth whom he profoundly loved, except a little sunbeam of a sister, the child of his father's second marriage. This little five-year-old girl, of whom he was sole guardian, had been christened by the quaint name of Hart, after an ancestor, Hart Ayrault, whose moss-covered tombstone the child had often explored with her little fingers, to trace the vanishing letters of her own name.

The two had arrived one morning from the nearest railway station to take possession of the old brick farmhouse. Ayrault had spent the day in unpacking and in consultations with Cyrus Gerry,—the farmer from whom he had bought the place, and who was still to conduct all outdoor operations. The child, for her part, had compelled her old nurse to follow her through every corner of the buildings. They were at last seated at an early supper, during which little Hart was too much absorbed in the novelty of wild red raspberries to notice, even in the most casual way, her brother's worn and exhausted look.

"Brother Frank," she incidentally remarked, as she began upon her second saucerful of berries, "I love you!"

"Thank you, darling," was his mechanical reply to the customary ebullition. She was silent for a time, absorbed in her pleasing pursuit, and then continued more specifically, "Brother Frank, you are the kindest person in the whole world! I am so glad we came here! May we stay here all winter? It must be lovely in the winter; and in the barn there is a little sled with only one runner gone. Brother Frank, I love you so much, I don't know what I shall do! I love you a thousand pounds, and fifteen, and eleven and a half, and more than tongue can tell besides! And there are three gray kittens—only one of them is almost all white,—and Susan says I may bring them for you to see in the morning."

Half an hour later, the brilliant eyes were closed in slumber; the vigorous limbs lay in perfect repose; and the child slept that night in the little room beside her brother's, on the same bed that she had occupied ever since she had been left motherless. But her brother lay awake, absorbed in a project too fantastic to be talked about, yet which had really done more than anything else to bring him to that lonely house.

There has belonged to Rhode Islanders, ever since the days of Roger Williams, a certain taste for the ideal side of existence. It is the only State in the American Union where chief justices habitually write poetry, and prosperous manufacturers print essays on the Freedom of the Will. Perhaps, moreover, Francis Ayrault held something of these tendencies from a Huguenot ancestry, crossed with a strain of Quaker blood. At any rate it was there, and asserted itself at this crisis of his life. Being in a manner detached from almost all ties, he resolved to use his opportunity in a direction yet almost unexplored by man. His earthly joys being prostrate, he had resolved to make a mighty effort at self-concentration, and to render himself what no human being had ever yet been,—the ruler of his own dreams.

Coming from a race of day-dreamers, Ayrault had inherited an unusual faculty of dreaming also by night; and, like all persons having an especial gift, he perhaps overestimated its importance. He easily convinced himself that no exertion of the intellect during wakeful hours can for an instant be compared with that we employ in dreams. The finest brain-structures of Shakespeare or Dante, he reasoned, are yet but such stuff as dreams are made of; and the stupidest rustic, the most untrained mind, will sometimes have, could they be but written out, visions that surpass those of these masters. From the dog that hunts in dreams, up to Coleridge dreaming "Kubla Khan" and interrupted by the man on business from Porlock, every sentient, or even half-sentient, being reaches its height of imaginative action in dreams. In these alone, Ayrault reasoned, do we grasp something beyond ourselves; every other function is self-limited, but who can set a limit to his visions? Of all forms of the Inner Light, they afford the very inmost; in these is fulfilled the early maxim of Friends,—that a man never rises so high as when he knows not where he is going. On awaking, indeed, we cannot even tell where we have just been. Probably the very utmost wealth of our remembered dreams is but a shred and fragment of those whose memory we cannot grasp.

But Ayrault had been vexed, like all others, by the utter incongruity of successive dreams. This sublime navigation still waited, like that of balloon voyages, for a rudder. Dreams, he reasoned, plainly try to connect themselves. We all have the frequent experience of half-recognizing new situations or even whole trains of ideas. We have seen this view before; reached this point; struck in some way the exquisite chord of memory. When half-aroused, or sometimes even long after clear consciousness, we seem to draw a half-drowned image of association from the deep waters of the mind; then another, then another, until dreaming seems inseparably entangled with waking. Again, over nightly dreams we have at least a certain amount of negative control, sufficient to bring them to an end. Ayrault had long since discovered and proved to himself the fact, insisted upon by Currie and by Macnish, that a nightmare can be banished by compelling one's self to remember that it is unreal. Again and again, during sleep, had he cast himself from towers, dropped from balloons, fallen into the sea,—and all unscathed. This way of ending an unpleasant dream was but a negative power indeed; but it was a substantial one: it implied the existence of some completer authority. If we can stop motion, we can surely originate it. He had already searched the books, therefore, for recorded instances of more positive control.

There was opium of course; but he was one of those on whom opium has little exciting influence, and so far as it had any, it only made his visions more incoherent. Haschish was in this respect still worse. It was not to be thought of, that one should resort, for the sake of dreams, to raw meat, like Dryden and Fuseli; or to other indigestible food, like Mrs. Radcliffe. The experiments of Giron de Buzareingues promised a little more; for he actually obtained recurrent dreams. He used to sleep with his knees uncovered on cool nights, and fancied during his sleep that he was riding in a stage-coach, where the lower extremities are apt to grow cold. Again, by wearing a nightcap over the front part of his head only, he seemed, when asleep, to be uncovering before a religious procession, and feeling chilly in the nape of the neck; this same result being obtained on several different occasions. It was recorded of some one else, that, by letting his feet hang over the bedside, he repeatedly imagined himself tottering on the brink of a precipice. Even these crude and superficial experiments had a value, Ayrault thought. If coarse physical processes could affect the mind's action, could not the will by some more powerful levers control the silent reveries of the night?

He derived some encouragement, too, from such instances as that recorded of Alderman Clay of Newark, England, during the siege of that town by Cromwell. He dreamed on three successive nights that his house had taken fire. Because of this supposed warning, he removed his family from the dwelling; and, when it was afterwards really burned by Cromwell's troops, left a bequest of a hundred pounds to supply penny loaves to the town poor, in acknowledgement of his marvellous escape. It is true that the three dreams were apparently mere repetitions of one another, and in no way continuous; it is true that they were not the result of any conscious will. So much the better: they were produced by the continuous working of some powerful mental influence; and this again was the result of external conditions. The experiment could not be reproduced. One could not be always dreaming under pressure of a cannonade by Cromwell, any more than Charles Lamb's Chinese people could be always burning down their houses in order to taste the flavor of roast pig. But the point was, that if dreams could be made to recur by accidental circumstances, the same thing might perhaps be effected by conscious thought.

Now that he was in a position for free experiment, he hoped to accomplish something more substantial than any casual or vague results; and he therefore so arranged his methods as to avoid interruption. Instead of exciting himself by day, he adopted a course of strict moderation; took his food regularly with the little girl, amused by her prattle; began systematic exercise on horseback and on foot; avoided society and the newspapers; and went to bed at an early hour, locking himself into a wing of the large farmhouse, the little Hart sleeping in a room within his. Once retired, he did not permit himself to be called on any pretext. Hart always slept profoundly; and with her first call of waking in the morning, he rang the bell for old Susan, who took the child away. It would have left him more free, of course, to intrust her altogether to the nurse's charge, but to this he could not bring himself. She was his one sacred trust, and not even his beloved projects could wholly displace her.

The thought had occurred to him, long since, at what point to apply his efforts for the control of his dreams. He had been quite fascinated, some time before, by a large photograph in a shop window, of the well-known fortress known as Mont Saint Michel, in Normandy. Its steepness, its airy height, its winding and returning stairways, its overhanging towers and machicolations, had struck him as appealing powerfully to that sense of the vertical which is, for some reason or other, so peculiarly strong in dreams. We are rarely haunted by visions of plains; often of mountains. The sensation of uplifting or downlooking is one of our commonest nightly experiences. It seemed to Ayrault that by going to sleep with the vivid mental image in his brain of a sharp and superb altitude like that of Mont Saint Michel, he could avail himself of this magic, whatever it was, that lay in the vertical line. Casting himself off into the vast sphere of dreams, with the thread of his fancy attached to this fine image, he might risk what would next come to him; as a spider anchors his web and then floats away on it. In the silence of the first night at the farmhouse,—a stillness broken only by the answering cadence of two whip-poor-wills in the neighboring pinewood,—Ayrault pondered long over the beautiful details of the photograph, and then he went to sleep.

That night he was held, with the greatest vividness and mastery, in the grasp of a dream such as he had never before experienced. He found himself on the side of a green hill, so precipitous that he could only keep his position by lying at full length, clinging to the short, soft grass, and imbedding his feet in the turf. There were clouds about him: he could see but a short distance in any direction, nor was any sign of a human being within sight. He was absolutely alone upon the dizzy slope, where he hardly dared to look up or down, and where it took all his concentration of effort to keep a position at all. Yet there was a kind of friendliness in the warm earth; a comfort and fragrance in the crushed herbage. The vision seemed to continue indefinitely; but at last he waked and it was clear day. He rose with a bewildered feeling, and went to little Hart's room. The child lay asleep, her round face tangled in her brown curls, and one plump, tanned arm stretched over her eyes. She waked at his step, and broke out into her customary sweet asseveration, "Brother Frank, I love you!"

Dismissing the child, he pondered on his first experiment. It had succeeded, surely, in so far as he had given something like a direction to his nightly thought. He could not doubt that it was the picture of Mont Saint Michel which had transported him to the steep hillside. That day he spent in the most restless anxiety to see if the dream would come again. Writing down all that he could remember of the previous night's vision, he studied again the photograph that had so touched his fancy, and then he closed his eyes. Again he found himself—at some time between night and morning—on the high hillside, with the clouds around him. But this time the vapors lifted, and he could see that the hill stretched for an immeasurable distance on each side, always at the same steep slope. Everywhere it was covered with human beings,—men, women, and children,—all trying to pursue various semblances of occupation; but all clinging to the short grass. Sometimes he thought—but this was not positive—that he saw one of them lose his hold and glide downwards. For this he cared strangely little; but he waked feverish, excited, trembling. At last his effort had succeeded: he had, by an effort of will, formed a connection between two dreams.

He came down to breakfast exhilarated and eager. What triumph of mind, what ranges of imagination equalled those now opening before him! As an outlet for his delight, he gave up the day to little Hart, always ready to monopolize. With her he visited the cows in the barn, the heifers in the pasture; heard their names, their traits, and—with much vagueness of arithmetic—their ages. She explained to him that Brindle was cross, and Mabel roguish; and that she had put her arm around little Pet's neck. Animals are to children something almost as near as human beings, because they have those attributes of humanity which children chiefly prize,—instinct and affection. Then Hart had the horses to exhibit, the pigs, a few sheep, and a whole poultry-yard of chickens. She was already initiated into the art and mystery of looking for hen's eggs, and indeed already trotted about after Cyrus Gerry, a little acolyte at the altar of farming. "She likes to play at it," said Cyrus, "same as my boys do: but just call it work, and—there! I don't blame 'em. The fact is," he added apologetically, "neither me nor my boys like to be kep' always at the same dull roundelay o' choppin' wood and doin' chores."

It was quite true that Cyrus Gerry and his boys, like many a New England farm household, had certain tastes and aptitudes that sadly interfered with their outdoor work. One son played the organ in the neighboring city, another was teaching himself the violin, and the third filled the barn with half-finished models of machinery. Cyrus himself read over and over again, in the winter evenings, his one favorite book,—a translation of Lamartine's "History of the Girondists," —pronounced habitually Guyrondists; and he found in its pages a pithy illustration for every event that could befall his chosen hero, Humanity. Most of his warnings were taken from the career of Robespierre, and his high and heroic examples from Vergniaud; while these characters lost nothing in vigor by being habitually quoted as "Robyspierry," and "Virginnyord."

In the service of his little sister, Ayrault explored that day many an old barn and shed; while she took thrilling leaps from the haymow or sat with the three gray kittens in her lap. Together they decked the parlors with gay masses of mountain laurel, or with the first-found red lilies, or with white water-lilies, from the pond. To the child, life was full of incident on that lonely farm. One day it was a young wood-

chuck caught in a trap, and destined to be petted;
another day, the fearful assassination of a whole brood
of young chickens by a culprit owl; the next, a startling
downfall of a whole nest of swallows in the chimney.
On this particular day she chattered steadily, and
Ayrault enjoyed it. But that night he lost utterly the
new-found control of his dream, and waked in irritation with himself and the world.

He spent the next day alone. It cost Hart a few tears
to lose her new-found playmate, but a tame pigeon
consoled her. That night Ayrault pondered long over
his memoranda of previous dreaming, and over the
photograph with which he had begun the spell, and
was rewarded by a renewal of his visions; but this time
wavering and uncertain. Sometimes he was again on
the bare hillside, clutching at the soft grass; then the
scene shifted to some castle, whose high battlements
he was climbing; then he found himself among the
Alps, treading some narrow path between rock and
glacier, with the tinkling herd of young goats crowding
round him for comradeship and impeding his progress;
again, he was following the steep course of some dried
brook among the Scottish Highlands, or pausing to
count the deserted hearthstones of a vanished people.
Always at short intervals he reverted to the grassy hill;
it seemed the foundation of his visions, the rest were
like dreams within dreams. At last a heavier sleep
came on, featureless and purposeless, till he waked
unrefreshed.

On the following night he grasped his dream once
more. Again he found himself on the precipitous slope,
this time looking off through clear air upon that line of
detached mountain peaks, Wachusett, Monadnock,
Mossilauke, which make the southern outposts of New
England hills. In the valley lay pellucid lakes, set in
summer beauty,—while he clung to his perilous hold.
Presently there came a change; the mountains sank
away softly beneath him, and the grassy slope remained a plain. The men and women, his former
companions, had risen from their reclining postures

and were variously busy; some of them even looked at him, but there was nothing said. Great spaces of time appeared to pass: suns rose and set. Sometimes one of the crowd would throw down his implements of labor, turn his face to the westward, walk swiftly away, and disappear. Yet some one else would take his place, so that the throng never perceptibly diminished. Ayrault began to feel rather unimportant in all this gathering, and the sensation was not agreeable.

On the succeeding night the hillside vanished, never to recur; but the vast plain remained, and the people. Over the wide landscape the sunbeams shed passing smiles of light, now here, now there. Where these shone for a moment, faces looked joyous, and Ayrault found, with surprise, that he could control the distribution of light and shade. This pleased him; it lifted him into conscious importance. There was, however, a singular want of all human relation in the tie between himself and all these people. He felt as if he had called them into being, which indeed he had; and could annihilate them at pleasure, which perhaps could not be so easily done. Meanwhile, there was a certain hardness in his state of mind toward them; indeed, why should a dreamer feel patience or charity or mercy toward those who exist but in his mind? Ayrault at any rate felt none; the sole thing which disturbed him was that they sometimes grew a little dim, as if they might vanish and leave him unaccompanied. When this happened, he drew with conscious volition a gleam of light over them, and thereby refreshed their life. They enhanced his weight in the universe: he would no more have parted with them than a Highland chief with his clansmen.

For several nights after this he did not dream. Little Hart became ill and his mind was preoccupied. He had to send for physicians, to give medicine, to be up with the child at night. The interruption vexed him; and he was also pained to find that there seemed to be a slight barrier between himself and her. Yet he was rigorously faithful to his duties as nurse; he even liked to hold her hand, to soothe her pain, to watch her sweet, patient face. Like Coleridge in misanthropic mood, he saw, not felt, how beautiful she was. Then, with the rapidity of childish convalescence, she grew well again; and he found with joy that he could resume the thread of his dream-life.

Again he was on his boundless plain, with his circle of silent allies around him. Suddenly they all vanished, and there rose before him, as if built out of the atmosphere, a vast building, which he entered. It included all structures in one,—legislative halls where men were assembled by hundreds, waiting for him; libraries, where all the books belonged to him, and whole alcoves were filled with his own publications; galleries of art, where he had painted many of the pictures, and selected the rest. Doors and corridors led to private apartments; lines of obsequious servants stood for him to pass. There seemed no other proprietor, no guests; all was for him; all flattered his individual greatness. Suddenly it occurred to him that he was painfully alone. Then he began to pass eagerly from hall to hall, seeking an equal companion, but in vain. Wherever he went, there was a trace of some one just vanished,—a book laid down, a curtain still waving. Once he fairly came, he thought, upon the object of his pursuit; all retreat was cut off, and he found himself face to face with a mirror that reflected back to him only his own features. They had never looked to him less attractive.

Ayrault's control of his visions became plainly more complete with practice, at least as to their early stages. He could lie down to sleep with almost a perfect certainty that he should begin where he left off. Beyond this, alas! he was powerless. Night after night he was in the same palace, but always differently occupied, and always pursuing, with unabated energy, some new vocation. Sometimes the books were at his command, and he grappled with whole alcoves; sometimes he ruled a listening senate in the halls of legislation; but the peculiarity was that there were always menials and subordinates about him, never an equal. One night, in looking over these obsequious crowds, he made a startling discovery. They either had originally, or were acquiring, a strange resemblance to one another, and to some person whom he had somewhere seen. All the next day, in his waking hours, this thought haunted him. The next night it flashed upon him that the person whom they all so closely resembled, with a likeness that now amounted to absolute identity, was himself.

From the moment of this discovery, these figures multiplied; they assumed a mocking, taunting, defiant aspect. The thought was almost more than he could bear, that there was around him a whole world of innumerable and uncontrollable beings, every one of whom was Francis Ayrault. As if this were not sufficient, they all began visibly to duplicate themselves before his eyes. The confusion was terrific. Figures divided themselves into twins, laughing at each other, jeering, running races, measuring heights, actually playing leap-frog with one another. Worst of all, each one of these had as much apparent claim to his personality as he himself possessed. He could no more retain his individual hold upon his consciousness than the infusorial animalcule in a drop of water can know to which of its subdivided parts the original individuality attaches. It became insufferable, and by a mighty effort he waked.

The next day, after breakfast, old Susan sought an interview with Ayrault, and taxed him roundly with neglect of little Hart's condition. Since her former illness she never had been quite the same; she was growing pale and thin. As her brother no longer played with her, she only moped about with her kitten, and talked to herself. It touched Ayrault's heart. He took pains to be with the child that day, carried her for a long drive, and went to see her guinea-hen's eggs. That night he kept her up later than usual, instead of hurrying her off as had become his wont; he really found himself shrinking from the dream-world he had with such effort created. The most timid and shy person can hardly hesitate more about venturing among a crowd of strangers than Francis Ayrault recoiled, that evening, from the thought of this mob of intrusive persons, every one of whom reflected his own image. Gladly would he have undone the past, and swept them all away forever. But the shrinking was all on one side: the moment he sank to sleep, they all crowded upon him, laughing, frolicking, claiming detestable intimacy. No one among strangers ever longed for a friendly face, as he, among these intolerable duplicates, longed for the sight of a stranger. It was worse yet when the images grew smaller and smaller, until they had shrunk to a pin's length. He found himself trying with all his strength of will to keep them at their ampler size, with only the effect that they presently became no larger than the heads of pins. Yet his own individuality was still so distributed among them that it could not be distinguished from them; but he found himself merged in this crowd of little creatures an eighth of an inch long.

As the days went on old Susan kept repeating her warnings about Hart, and finally proposed to take her into her own room. "She does not get sound sleep, sir; she complains of her dreams." "Of what dreams?" said Ayrault. "Oh, about you, sir," was the reply, "she sees you very often, and a great many people who look just like you." Ayrault sank back in his chair terrified. Was it not enough that his own life was hopelessly haunted by a turbulent kingdom of his own creating? but must the malign influence extend also to this innocent child? He watched Hart the next morning at breakfast—she looked pale and had circles under her eyes, and glanced at him timidly; her eager endearments were all gone. A terrible temptation crossed Ayrault's mind for a moment, to employ this unspoiled nature in the perilous path of experiments on which he had entered. It vanished from him as soon as it had presented itself. He would tread his course alone, and send the child away, rather than risk any transmitted peril for her young life. It may be that her dreams had only an accidental resemblance to his; at any rate she was sent away on a visit, and they were soon forgotten.

After the child had gone, a feeling of deep sadness fell on Ayrault. By night he was tangled in the meshes of a dream-life that had become a nightmare; by day there was now nothing to arouse him. The child's insatiable affection, her ardent ebullitions, were absent. Cyrus Gerry's watchful and speculative mind grew suspicious and critical.

"I shouldn't wonder," he said to his wife, "if there was gettin' to be altogether too much dreamin'. There was Robyspierry, he was what you might call a dreamer. But that Virginnyord he was much nigher my idee of an American citizen."

"Got somethin' on his mind, think likely?" said the slow and placid Mrs. Gerry, who seldom had much upon hers.

"Dunno as I know," responded Cyrus. "But there, what if he has? As I look at it, humanity, a-ploddin' over this planet, meets with consid'able many left-handed things. And the best way I know of is to summons up courage and put right through 'em."

Cyrus's conceptions of humanity might, however, rise to such touches of Wandering-Jew comprehensiveness as this, and yet not reach Ayrault, who went his way lonelier than ever.

Having long since fallen out of the way of action, or at best grown satisfied to imagine enterprises and leave others to execute them, he now, more than ever, drifted on from day to day. There had been a strike at the neighboring manufacturing village, and there was to be a public meeting, at which he was besought, as a person not identified with either party, to be present, and throw his influence for peace. It touched him, and he meant to attend. He even thought of a few things, which, if said, might do good; then forgot the day of the meeting, and rode ten miles in another direction. Again, when at the little post-office one day, he was asked by the postmaster to translate several letters in

the French language, addressed to that official, and
coming from an unknown village in Canada. They
proved to contain anxious inquiries as to the whereabouts of a pretty young French girl, whom Ayrault
had occasionally met driving about in what seemed
doubtful company. His sympathy was thoroughly
aroused by the anxiety of the poor parents, from whom
the letters came. He answered them himself, promis-
ing to interfere in behalf of the girl; delayed, day by
day, to fulfil the promise; and when he at last looked
for her she was not to be found. Yet, while his power
of efficient action waned, his dream-power increased.
His little people were busier about him than ever,
though he controlled them less and less. He was Gulliver
bound and fettered by Lilliputians.

But a more stirring appeal was on its way to him.
The storm of the civil war began to roll among the
hills; regiments were recruited, camps were formed.
The excitement reached the benumbed energies of
Ayrault. Never, indeed, had he felt such a thrill. The
old Huguenot pulse beat strongly within him. For days,
and even nights, these thoughts possessed his mind,
and his dreams utterly vanished. Then there was a lull
in the excitement; recruiting stopped, and his nightly
habit of confusing visions set in again with dreary
monotony. Then there was a fresh call for troops. An
old friend of Ayrault's came to a neighboring village,
and held a noon-day meeting in one of the churches to
recruit a company. Ayrault listened with absorbed interest to the rousing appeal, and, when recruits were
called for, was the first to rise. It turned out that the
matter could not be at once consummated, as the
proper papers were not there. Other young men from
the neighborhood followed Ayrault's example, and it
was arranged that they should all go to the city for
regular enlistment the next day. All that afternoon
was spent in preparations, and in talking with other
eager volunteers, who seemed to look to Ayrault as
their head. It was understood, they told him, that he
would probably be an officer in the company. He felt

himself a changed being; he was as if floating in air, and ready to swim off to some new planet. What had he now to do with that pale dreamer who had nourished his absurd imaginings until he had barely escaped being controlled by them? When they crossed his mind it was only to make him thank God for his escape. He flung wide the windows of his chamber. He hated the very sight of the scene where his proud vision had been fulfilled, and he had been Monarch of Dreams. No matter: he was now free, and the spell was broken. Life, action, duty, honor, a redeemed nation, lay before him; all entanglements were cut away.

That evening there went a summons through the little village that opened the door of every house. A young man galloped out from the city, waking the echoes of the hills with his somewhat untutored bugle-notes, as he dashed along. Riding from house to house of those who had pledged themselves, he told the news. There had been a great defeat; reinforcements had been summoned instantly; and the half-organized regiment, undrilled, unarmed, not even uniformed, was ordered to proceed that night to the front, and replace in the forts round Washington other levies that were a shade less raw. Every man desiring to enlist must come instantly; yet, as before daybreak the regiment would pass by special train on the railway that led through the village, those in that vicinity might join it at the station, and have still a few hours at home. They were hurried hours for Ayrault, and toward midnight he threw himself on his bed for a moment's repose, having left strict orders for his awakening. He gave not one thought to his world of visions; had he done so, it would have only been to rejoice that he had eluded them forever.

Let a man at any moment attempt his best, and his life will still be at least half made up of the accumulated results of past action. Never had Ayrault seemed so absolutely safe from the gathered crowd of his own delusions: never had they come upon him with a power so terrific. Again he was in those stately halls which his imagination had so laboriously built up: again the mob of unreal beings came around him, each more himself than he was. Ayrault was beset, encircled, overwhelmed; he was in a manner lost in the crowd of himself. If any confused thought of his projected army life entered his dream, it utterly subordinated itself; or merely helped to emphasize the vastness and strengthen the sway of that phantom army to which he had given himself, and of which he was already the pledged recruit.

In the midst of this tumultuous dreaming, came confused sounds from without. There was the rolling of railway wheels, the scream of locomotive engines, the beating of drums, the cheers of men, the report and glare of fireworks. Mingled with all, there came the repeated sound of knocking at his own door, which he had locked, from mere force of habit, ere he lay down. The sounds seemed only to rouse into new tumult the figures of his dream. These suddenly began to increase steadily in size, even as they had before diminished; and the waxing was more fearful than the waning. From being Gulliver among the Lilliputians, Ayrault was Gulliver in Brobdingnag. Each image of himself, before diminutive, became colossal: they blocked his path; he actually could not find himself, could not tell which was he that should arouse himself, in their vast and endless self-multiplication. He became vaguely conscious, amidst the bewilderment, that the shouts in the village were subsiding, the illuminations growing dark; and the train with its young soldiers was again in motion, throbbing and resounding among the hills, and bearing the lost opportunity of his life away—away—away.

THE CIRCLE OF ZERO

by Stanley G. Weinbaum

CHAPTER 1

Try for Eternity

If there were a mountain a thousand miles high and every thousand years a bird flew over it, just brushing the peak with the tip of its wing, in the course of inconceivable eons the mountain would be worn away. Yet all those ages would not be one second to the length of eternity.

I don't know what philosophical mind penned the foregoing, but the words keep recurring to me since last I saw old Aurore de Neant, erstwhile professor of psychology at Tulane. When, back in '24, I took that course in Morbid Psychology from him, I think the only reason for taking it at all was that I needed an eleven o'clock on Tuesdays and Thursdays to round out a lazy program.

I was gay Jack Anders, twenty-two years old, and the reason seemed sufficient. At least, I'm sure that dark and lovely Yvonne de Neant had nothing to do with it. She was but a slim child of sixteen.

Old de Neant liked me, Lord knows why, for I was a poor enough student. Perhaps it was because I never, to his knowledge, punned on his name. Aurore de Neant translates to Dawn of Nothingness, you see;

you can imagine what students did to such a name. "Rising Zero—Empty Morning"—those were two of the milder soubriquets.

That was in '24. Five years later I was a bond salesman in New York and Professor Aurore de Neant was fired. I learned about it when he called me up. I had drifted quite out of touch with University days.

He was a thrifty sort. He had saved a comfortable sum, and had moved to New York and that's when I started seeing Yvonne again, now darkly beautiful as a Tanagra figurine. I was doing pretty well and was piling up a surplus against the day when Yvonne and I . . .

At least that was the situation in August, 1929. In October of the same year I was as clean as a gnawed bone and old de Neant had but little more meat. I was young and could afford to laugh—he was old and he turned bitter. Indeed, Yvonne and I did little enough laughing when we thought of our own future—but we didn't brood like the professor.

I remember the evening he broached the subject of the Circle of Zero. It was a rainy, blustering fall night and his beard waggled in the dim lamplight like a wisp of gray mist. Yvonne and I had been staying in evenings of late. Shows cost money and I felt that she appreciated my talking to her father, and—after all—he retired early.

She was sitting on the davenport at his side when he suddenly stabbed a gnarled finger at me and snapped, "Happiness depends on money!"

I was startled. "Well, it helps," I agreed.

His pale blue eyes glittered. "We must recover ours!" he rasped.

"How?"

"I know how. Yes, I know how," he grinned thinly. "They think I'm mad. *You* think I'm mad. Even Yvonne thinks so."

The girl said softly, reproachfully, "Father!"

"But I'm not," he continued. "You and Yvonne and all the fools holding chairs at universities—yes! But not I."

"I will be all right, if conditions don't get better soon," I murmured. I was used to the old man's outbursts.

"They will be better for us," he said, calming. "Money! We will do anything for money, won't we, Anders?"

"Anything honest."

"Yes, anything honest. Time is honest, isn't it? An honest cheat, because it takes everything human and turns it into dust." He peered at my puzzled face. "I will explain," he said, "how we can cheat time."

"Cheat—"

"Yes. Listen, Jack. Have you ever stood in a strange place and felt a sense of having been there before? Have you ever taken a trip and sensed that sometime, somehow, you had done exactly the same thing—when you know you hadn't?"

"Of course. Everyone has. A memory of the present, Bergson calls it."

"Bergson is a fool! Philosophy without science. Listen to me." He leaned forward. "Did you ever hear of the Law of Chance?"

I laughed. "My business is stocks and bonds. I *ought* to know of it."

"Ah," he said, "but not enough of it. Suppose I have a barrel with a million trillion white grains of sand in it and one black grain. You stand and draw single grains, one after the other, look at each one and throw it back into the barrel. What are the odds against drawing the black grain?"

"A million trillion to one, on each draw."

"And if you draw half of the million trillion grains?"

"Then the odds are even."

"So!" he said. "In other words, if you draw long enough, even though you return each grain to the barrel and draw again, some day you will draw the black one—*if you try long enough!*"

"Yes," I said.

* * *

He half smiled.

"Suppose now you tried for eternity?"

"Eh?"

"Don't you see, Jack? In eternity the Law of Chance functions perfectly. In eternity, sooner or later, every possible combination of things and events must happen. *Must* happen, *if* it's a possible combination. I say, therefore, that in eternity, *whatever can happen, will happen!*" His blue eyes blazed in pale fire.

I was a trifle dazed. "I guess you're right," I muttered.

"Right! Of course I'm right. Mathematics is infallible. Now do you see the conclusion?"

"Why—that sooner or later everything will happen."

"Bah! It is true that there is eternity in the future; we cannot imagine time ending. But Flammarion, before he died, pointed out that there is also an eternity in the past. Since in eternity everything possible must happen, it follows that everything *must already have happened!*"

I gasped. "Wait a minute! I don't see—"

"Stupidity!" he hissed. "It is but to say with Einstein that not only space is curved, but time. To say that, after untold eons of millennia, the same things repeat themselves because they must! The Law of Chance says they must, given time enough. The past and the future are the same thing, because everything that will happen must already have happened. Can't you follow so simple a chain of logic?"

"Why—yes. But where does it lead?"

"To our money! To our money!"

"What?"

"Listen. Do not interrupt. In the past all possible combinations of atoms and circumstances must have occurred." He paused then stabbed that bony finger of his at me. "Jack Anders, *you* are a possible combination of atoms and circumstances! Possible because you exist at this moment!"

"You mean—that *I* have happened before?"

"How apt you are! Yes, you have happened before and will again."

"Transmigration!" I gulped. "That's unscientific."

"Indeed?" He frowned as if in effort to gather his thoughts. "The poet Robert Burns was buried under an apple tree. When, years after his death, he was to be removed to rest among the great men of Westminster Abbey, do you know what they found? Do you know?"

"I'm sorry, but I don't."

"They found a root! A root with a bulge for a head, branch roots for arms and legs and little rootlets for fingers and toes. The apple tree had eaten Bobby Burns—but who had eaten the apples?"

"Who—what?"

"Exactly. Who and what? The substance that had been Burns was in the bodies of Scotch countrymen and children, in the bodies of caterpillars who had eaten the leaves and become butterflies and been eaten by birds, in the wood of the tree. Where is Bobby Burns? Transmigration, I tell you! Isn't that transmigration?"

"Yes—but not what you meant about me. His body may be living, but in a thousand different forms."

"Ah! And when some day, eons and eternities in the future, the Laws of Chance form another nebula that will cool to another sun and another earth, is there not the same chance that those scattered atoms may reassemble another Bobby Burns?"

"But what a chance! Trillions and trillions to one!"

"But eternity, Jack! In eternity that one chance out of all those trillions must happen—*must* happen!"

I was floored. I stared at Yvonne's pale and lovely features, then at the glistening old eyes of Aurore de Neant.

"You win," I said with a long sigh. "But what of it? This is still nineteen twenty-nine, and our money's still sunk in a very sick securities market."

"*Money!*" he groaned. "Don't you see? That memory we started from—that sense of having done a thing before—that's a memory out of the infinitely remote future. If only—if only one could remember clearly!

But I have a way." His voice rose sudddenly to a shrill scream. "Yes, I have a way!"

Wild eyes glared at me. I said, "A way to remember our former incarnations?" One had to humour the old professor. "To remember—the future?"

"Yes! Reincarnation!" His voice crackled wildly. "*Re-in-carnatione*, which is Latin for 'by the thing in the carnation,' but it wasn't a carnation—it was an apple tree. The carnation is *dianthus carophyllus*, which proved that the Hottentots plant carnations on the graves of their ancestors, whence the expression 'nipped in the bud.' If carnations grow on apple trees—"

"Father!" cut in Yvonne sharply. "You're tired!" Her voice softened. "Come. You're going to bed."

"Yes," he cackled. "To a bed of carnations."

CHAPTER II

Memory of Things Past

Some evenings later Aurore de Neant reverted to the same topic. He was clear enough as to where he had left off.

"So in this millennially dead past," he began suddenly, "there was a year nineteen twenty-nine and two fools named Anders and de Neant, who invested their money in what are sarcastically called securities. There was a clown's panic, and their money vanished." He leered fantastically at me.

"Wouldn't it be nice if they could remember what happened in, say, the months from December, nineteen twenty-nine, to June, nineteen thirty—next year?" His voice was suddenly whining. "They could get their money back then!"

I humoured him. "If they could remember."

"They can!" he blazed. "They can!"

"How?"

His voice dropped to a confidential softness. "Hypnotism! You studied Morbid Psychology under me, didn't you, Jack? Yes—I remember."

"But, hypnotism!" I objected. "Every psychiatrist uses that in his treatments and no one has remembered a previous incarnation or anything like it."

"No. They're fools, these doctors and psychiatrists. Listen—do you remember the three stages of the hypnotic state as you learned them?"

"Yes. Somnambulism, lethargy, catalepsy."

"Right. In the first the subject speaks, answers questions. In the second he sleeps deeply. In the third, catalepsy, he is rigid, stiff, so that he can be laid across two chairs, sat on—all that nonsense."

"I remember. What of it?"

He grinned bleakly. "In the first stage the subject remembers everything that ever happened during his life. His subconscious mind is dominant and that never forgets. Correct?"

"So we were taught."

He leaned tensely forward. "In the second stage, lethargy, my theory is that he remembers everything that happened in his other lives! He remembers the future!"

"Huh? Why doesn't someone do it, then?"

"He remembers while he sleeps. He forgets when he wakes. That's why. But I believe that with proper training he can learn to remember."

"And you're going to try?"

"Not I. I know too little of finance. I wouldn't know how to interpret my memories."

"Who, then?"

"You!" He jabbed that long finger against me.

I was thoroughly startled. "Me? Oh, no! Not a chance of it!"

"Jack," he said querulously, "didn't you study hypnotism in my course? Didn't you learn how harmless it is? You know what tommy-rot the idea is of one mind dominating another. You know the subject really hypnotizes himself, that no one can hypnotize an unwilling person. Then what are you afraid of?"

"I—well," I didn't know what to answer.

"I'm not afraid," I said grimly. "I just don't like it."

"You're afraid!"

"I'm not!"

"You are!" He was growing excited.

It was at that moment that Yvonne's footsteps sounded in the hall. His eyes glittered. He looked at me with a sinister hint of cunning.

"I dislike cowards," he whispered. His voice rose. "So does Yvonne!"

The girl entered, perceiving his excitement. "Oh!" she frowned. "Why do you have to take these theories so to heart, father?"

"Theories?" he screeched. "Yes! I have a theory that when you walk you stand still and the sidewalk moves back. No—then the sidewalk moves back. No—then the sidewalk would split if two people walked toward each other—or maybe it's elastic. Of course it's elastic! That's why the last mile is the longest. It's been stretched!"

Yvonne got him to bed.

Well, he talked me into it. I don't know how much was due to my own credulity and how much to Yvonne's solemn dark eyes. I half-believed the professor by the time he'd spent another evening in argument but I think the clincher was his veiled threat to forbid Yvonne my company. She'd have obeyed him if it killed her. She was from New Orleans too, you see, and of Creole blood.

I won't describe that troublesome course of training. One has to develop the hypnotic habit. It's like any other habit, and must be formed slowly. Contrary to the popular opinion morons and people of low intelligence can't ever do it. It takes real concentration—the whole knack of it is the ability to concentrate one's attention—and I don't mean the hypnotist, either.

I mean the subject. The hypnotist hasn't a thing to do with it except to furnish the necessary suggestion by murmuring, "Sleep—sleep—sleep—sleep . . ." And even that isn't necessary once you learn the trick of it.

I spent half-an-hour or more nearly every evening,

learning that trick. It was tedious and a dozen times I became thoroughly disgusted and swore to have no more to do with the farce. But always, after the half-hour's humouring of de Neant, there was Yvonne, and boredom vanished. As a sort of reward, I suppose, the old man took to leaving us alone. And we used our time, I'll wager, to better purpose than he used his.

But I began to learn, little by little. Came a time, after three weeks of tedium, when I was able to cast myself into a light somnambulistic state. I remember how the glitter of the cheap stone in Professor de Neant's ring grew until it filled the world and how his voice, mechanically dull, murmured like the waves in my ears. I remember everything that transpired during those minutes, even his query, "Are you sleeping?" and my automatic reply, "Yes."

By the end of November we had mastered the second state of lethargy and then—I don't know why, but a sort of enthusiasm for the madness took hold of me. Business was at a standstill. I grew tired of facing customers to whom I had sold bonds at a par that were now worth fifty or less and trying to explain why. After a while I began to drop in on the professor during the afternoon and we went through the insane routine again and again.

Yvonne comprehended only a part of the bizarre scheme. She was never in the room during our half-hour trials and knew only vaguely that we were involved in some sort of experiment which was to restore our lost money. I don't suppose she had much faith in it but she always indulged her father.

It was early in December that I began to remember things. Dim and formless things at first—sensations that utterly eluded the rigidities of words. I tried to express them to de Neant but it was hopeless.

"A circular feeling," I'd say. "No—not exactly—a sense of spiral—not that, either. Roundness—I can't recall it now. It slips away."

He was jubilant. "It comes!" he whispered, grey

beard awaggle and pale eyes glittering. "You begin to remember!"

"But what good is a memory like that?"

"Wait! It will come clearer. Of course not all your memories will be of the sort we can use. They will be scattered. Through all the multifold eternities of the past-future circle you can't have been always Jack Anders, securities salesman.

"There will be fragmentary memories, recollections of times when your personality was partially existent, when the Laws of Chance had assembled a being who was not quite Jack Anders, in some period of the infinite worlds that must have risen and died in the span of eternities.

"But somewhere, too, the same atoms, the same conditions, must have made *you*. You're the black grain among the trillions of white grains and, with all eternity to draw in from, you must have been drawn before—many, many times."

"Do you suppose," I asked suddenly, "that anyone exists twice on the same earth? Reincarnation in the sense of the Hindus?"

He laughed scornfully. "The age of the earth is somewhere between a thousand million and three thousand million years. What proportion of eternity is that?"

"Why—no proportion at all. Zero."

"Exactly. And zero represents the chance of the same atoms combining to form the same person twice in one cycle of a planet. But I have shown that trillions, or trillions of trillions of years ago, there *must* have been another earth, another Jack Anders, and"—his voice took on that whining note—"another crash that ruined Jack Anders and old de Neant. That is the time you must remember out of lethargy."

"Catalepsy!" I said. "What would one remember in that?"

"God knows."

"What a mad scheme!" I said suddenly. "What a crazy pair of fools we are!" The adjectives were a mistake.

"Mad? Crazy?" His voice became a screech. "Old de Neant is mad, eh? Old Dawn of Nothingness is crazy! You think time doesn't go in a circle, don't you? Do you know what a circle represents? I'll tell you!

"A circle is the mathematical symbol for zero! Time is zero—time is a circle. I have a theory that the hands of a clock are really the noses, because they're on the clock's face, and since time is a circle they go round and round and round . . ."

Yvonne slipped quietly into the room and patted her father's furrowed forehead. She must have been listening.

CHAPTER III

Nightmare or Truth?

"Look here," I said at a later time to de Neant. "If the past and future are the same thing, then the future's as unchangeable as the past. How, then, can we expect to change it by recovering our money?"

"Change it?" he snorted. "How do you know we're changing it? How do you know that this same thing wasn't done by that Jack Anders and de Neant back on the other side of eternity? I say it *was!*"

I subsided, and the weird business went on. My memories—if they were memories—were becoming clearer now. Often and often I saw things out of my own immediate past of twenty-seven years, though of course de Neant assured me that these were visions from the past of that other self on the far side of time.

I saw other things too, incidents that I couldn't place in my experience, though I couldn't be quite sure they didn't belong there. I might have forgotten, you see, since they were of no particular importance. I recounted everything dutifully to the old man immediately upon awakening and sometimes that was difficult—like trying to find words for a half-remembered dream.

There were other memories as well—bizarre, outlandish dreams that had little parallel in human history. These were always vague and sometimes very horrible and only their inchoate and formless character kept them from being utterly nerve-racking and terrifying.

At one time, I recall, I was gazing through a little crystalline window into a red fog through which moved indescribable faces—not human, not even associable with anything I had ever seen. On another occasion I was wandering, clad in furs, across a cold grey desert and at my side was a woman who was not quite Yvonne.

I remember calling her Pyroniva, and knowing that the name meant "Snowy-fire." And here and there in the air about us floated fungoid things, bobbing around like potatoes in a water-bucket. And once we stood very quiet while a menacing form that was only remotely like the small fungi droned purposefully far overhead, toward some unknown objective.

At still another time I was peering, fascinated, into a spinning pool of mercury, watching an image therein of two wild winged figures playing in a roseate glade—not at all human in form but transcendently beautiful, bright and iridescent.

I a felt a strange kinship between these two creatures and myself and Yvonne but I had no inkling of what they were, nor upon what world, nor at what time in eternity, nor even of what nature was the room that held the spinning pool that pictured them.

Old Aurore de Neant listened carefully to the wild word-pictures I drew.

"Fascinating!" he muttered. "Glimpses of an infinitely distant future caught from a ten-fold infinitely remote past. These things you describe are not earthly; it means that somewhere, sometime, men are actually to burst the prison of space and visit other worlds. Some day . . ."

"If these glimpses aren't simply nightmares," I said.

"They're not nightmares," he snapped, "but they might as well be for all the value they are to us." I could see him struggle to calm himself. "Our money is still gone. We must try, keep trying for years, for centuries, until we get the black grain of sand, because black sand is a sign of gold-bearing ore . . ." He paused. "What am I talking about?" he said querulously.

Well, we kept trying. Interspersed with the wild, all but indescribable visions came others almost rational. The thing became a fascinating game. I was neglecting my business—though that was small loss—to chase dreams with old Professor Aurore de Neant.

I spent evenings, afternoons and finally mornings, too, living in the slumber of the lethargic state or telling the old man what fantastic things I had dreamed —or, as he said, remembered. Reality became dim to me. I was living in an outlandish world of fancy and only the dark, tragic eyes of Yvonne tugged at me, pulled me back into the daylight world of sanity.

I have mentioned more nearly rational visions. I recall one—a city—but what a city! Sky-piercing, white and beautiful and the people of it were grave with the wisdom of gods, pale and lovely people, but solemn, wistful, sad. There was the aura of brilliance and wickedness that hovers about all great cities, that was born, I suppose, in Babylon and will remain until great cities are no more.

But that was something else, something intangible. I don't know exactly what to call it but perhaps the word decadence is as close as any word we have. As I stood at the base of a colossal structure there was the whir of quiet machinery but it seemed to me, nevertheless, that the city was dying.

It might have been the moss that grew green on the north walls of the buildings. It might have been the grass that pierced here and there through the cracks of the marble pavements. Or it might have been only the grave and sad demeanor of the pale inhabitants. There was something that hinted of a doomed city and a dying race.

A strange thing happened when I tried to describe this particular memory to old de Neant. I stumbled

over the details, of course—these visions from the
unplumbed depths of eternity were curiously hard to
fix between the rigid walls of words. They tended to
grow vague, to elude the waking memory. Thus, in
this description I had forgotten the name of the city.

"It was called," I said hesitatingly, "Termis or
Termoplia, or . . ."

"Termopolis!" cried de Neant impatiently. "City of
the End!"

I stared amazed. "That's it! But how did you know?"
In the sleep of lethargy, I was sure, one never speaks.

A queer, cunning look flashed in his pale eyes. "I
knew," he muttered. "I knew." He would say no
more.

But I think I saw that city once again. It was when I
wandered over a brown and treeless plain, not like the
cold gray desert but apparently an arid and barren
region of the earth. Dim on the western horizon was
the circle of a great cool reddish sun. It had always
been there, I remembered, and knew with some other
part of my mind that the vast brake of the tides had at
last slowed the earth's rotation to a stop, that day and
night no longer chased each other around the planet.

The air was biting cold and my companions and
I—there were half a dozen of us—moved in a huddled
group as if to lend each other warmth from our half-
naked bodies. We were all of us thin-legged, skinny
creatures with oddly deep chests and enormous, luminous eyes, and the one nearest me was again a woman
who had something of Yvonne in her but very little.
And I was not quite Jack Anders, either. But some
remote fragment of me survived in that barbaric brain.

Beyond a hill was the surge of an oily sea. We crept
circling about the mound and suddenly I perceived
that sometime in the infinite past that hill had been a
city. A few Gargantuan blocks of stone lay crumbling
on it and one lonely fragment of a ruined wall rose
gauntly to four or five times a man's height. It was at
this spectral remnant that the leader of our miserable

crew gestured then spoke in sombre tones—not English words but I understood.

"The Gods," he said—"the Gods who piled stones upon stones are dead and harm us not who pass the place of their dwelling."

I knew what that was meant to be. It was an incantation, a ritual—to protect us from the spirits that lurked among the ruins—the ruins, I believe, of a city built by our own ancestors thousands of generations before.

As we passed the wall I looked back at a flicker of movement and saw something hideously like a black rubber doormat flop itself around the angle of the wall. I drew closer to the woman beside me and we crept on down to the sea for water—yes, water, for with the cessation of the planet's rotation rainfall had vanished also, and all life huddled near the edge of the undying sea and learned to drink its bitter brine.

I didn't glance again at the hill which had been Termopolis, the City of the End. But I knew that some chance-born fragment of Jack Anders had been—or will be (what difference, if time is a circle?)—witness of an age close to the day of humanity's doom.

It was early in December that I had the first memory of something that might have been suggestive of success. It was a simple and very sweet memory, just Yvonne and I in a garden that I knew was the inner grounds on one of New Orleans' old homes—one of those built in the Continental fashion about a court.

We sat on a stone bench beneath the oleanders and I slipped my arm very tenderly about her and murmured, "Are you happy, Yvonne?"

She looked at me with those tragic eyes of hers and smiled, and then answered, "As happy as I have ever been."

And I kissed her.

That was all, but it was important. It was vastly important because it was definitely not a memory out of my own personal past. You see, I had never sat

beside Yvonne in a garden sweet with oleanders in the
Old Town of New Orleans and I had never kissed her
until we met in New York.

Aurore de Neant was elated when I described this
vision.

"You see!" he gloated. "There is evidence. You
have remembered the future! Not your own future, of
course, but that of another ghostly Jack Anders, who
died trillions and quadrillions of years ago."

"But it doesn't help us, does it?" I asked.

"Oh, it will come now! You wait. The thing we
want will come."

And it did, within a week. This memory was curiously bright and clear, and familiar in every detail. I
remember the day. It was the eighth of December,
1929, and I had wandered aimlessly about in search of
business during the morning. In the grip of that fasci-
nation I mentioned I drifted to de Neant's apartment
after lunch. Yvonne left us to ourselves, as was her
custom, and we began.

This was, as I said, a sharply outlined memory—or
dream. I was leaning over my desk in the company's
office, that too-seldom visited office. One of the other
salesmen—Summers was his name—was leaning over
my shoulder.

We were engaged in the quite customary pastime of
scanning the final market reports in the evening paper.
The print stood out, clear as reality itself. I glanced
without surprise at the dateline. It was Thursday, April
27th, 1930—almost five months in the future!

Not that I realised that during the vision, of course.
The day was merely the present to me. I was simply
looking over the list of the day's trading. Figures—
familiar names. Telephone 210½—US Steel—161; Paramount, 68½.

I jabbed a finger at Steel. "I bought that at 72," I
said over my shoulder to Summers. "I sold out everything today. Every stock I own. I'm getting out before
there's a secondary crash."

"Lucky stiff!" he murmured. "Buy at the December

lows and sell out now! Wish I'd had money to do it."
He paused, "What you gonna do? Stay with the
company?"

"No, I've enough to live on. I'm going to stick it in
Governments and paid-up insurance and live on the
income. I've had enough of gambling."

"You lucky stiff!" he said again. "I'm sick of the
Street too. Staying in New York?"

"For a while. Just till I get my stuff invested properly; Yvonne and I are going to New Orleans for the
winter." I paused. "She's had a tough time of it. I'm
glad we're where we are."

"Who wouldn't be?" asked Summers, and then again,
"You lucky stiff!"

De Neant was frantically excited when I described
this to him.

"That's it!" he screamed. "We buy! We buy tomorrow! We sell on the twenty-seventh of April and then—
New Orleans!"

Of course I was nearly equally enthusiastic. "By
heaven!" I said. "It's worth the risk! We'll do it!" And
then a sudden hopeless thought. "Do it? Do it with
what? I have less than a hundred dollars to my name.
And you . . ."

The old man groaned. "I have nothing," he said in
abrupt gloom. "Only the annuity we live on. One
can't borrow on that." Again a gleam of hope. "The
banks. We'll borrow from them!"

I had to laugh, although it was a bitter laugh. "What
bank would lend us money on a story like this? They
wouldn't lend Rockefeller himself money to play this
sick market, not without security. We're sunk, that's
all."

I looked at his pale, worried eyes. "Sunk," he echoed
dully. Then again that wild gleam. "*Not* sunk!" he
yelled. "How can we be? We *did* do it! You remembered our doing it! We must have found the way!"

I gazed speechless. Suddenly a queer, mad thought
flashed over me. This other Jack Anders, this ghost of
quadrillions of centuries past—or future—he too must

be watching, or had watched, or yet would watch, me—the Jack Anders of this cycle of eternity.

He must be watching as anxiously as I to discover the means. Each of us watching the other—neither of us knowing the answer. The blind leading the blind! I laughed at the irony.

But old de Neant was not laughing. The strangest expression I have ever seen in a man's eyes was in his as he repeated very softly, "We must have found the way because it *was* done. At least you and Yvonne found the way."

"Then all of us must," I answered sourly.

"Yes. Oh, yes. Listen to me, Jack. I am an old man, old Aurore de Neant. I am old Dawn of Nothingness and my mind is cracking. Don't shake your head!" he snapped. "I am not mad. I am simply misunderstood. None of you understand.

"Why, I have a theory that trees, grass and people do not grow taller at all. They grow by pushing the earth away from them, which is why you keep hearing that the earth is getting smaller every day. But you don't understand—Yvonne doesn't understand."

The girl must have been listening. Without my seeing her, she had slipped into the room and put her arms gently about her father's shoulders, while she gazed across at me with anxious eyes.

CHAPTER IV

The Bitter Fruit

There was one more vision, irrelevant in a way, yet vitally important in another way. It was the next evening. An early December snowfall was dropping its silent white beyond the windows and the ill-heated apartment of the de Neants was draughty and chill.

I saw Yvonne shiver as she greeted me and again as she left the room. I noticed that old de Neant followed her to the door with his thin arms about her and that he returned with very worried eyes.

"She is New Orleans born," he murmured. "This dreadful Arctic climate will destroy her. We must find a way at once."

That vision was a sombre one. I stood on a cold, wet, snowy ground—just myself and Yvonne and one who stood beside an open grave. Behind us stretched rows of crosses and white tomb stones, but in our corner the place was ragged, untended, unconsecrated. The priest was saying, "And these are things that only God understands."

I slipped a comforting arm about Yvonne. She raised her dark, tragic eyes and whispered, "It was yesterday, Jack—just yesterday—that he said to me, 'Next winter you shall spend in New Orleans, Yvonne.' Just yesterday!"

I tried a wretched smile, but I could only stare mournfully at her forlorn face, watching a tear that rolled slowly down her right cheek, hung glistening there a moment, then was joined by another to splash unregarded on the black bosom of her dress.

That was all but how could I describe that vision to old de Neant? I tried to evade. He kept insisting.

"There wasn't any hint of the way," I told him. Useless—at last I had to tell anyway.

He was very silent for a full minute. "Jack," he said finally, "do you know when I said that to her about New Orleans? This morning when we watched the snow. This morning!"

I didn't know what to do. Suddenly this whole concept of remembering the future seemed mad, insane. In all my memories there had been not a single spark of real proof, not a single hint of prophecy.

So I did nothing at all but simply gazed silently as old Aurore de Neant walked out of the room. And when, two hours later, while Yvonne and I talked, he finished writing a certain letter and then shot himself through the heart—why, that proved nothing either.

It was the following day that Yvonne and I, his only mourners, followed old Dawn of Nothingness to his suicide's grave. I stood beside her and tried as best I could to console her, and roused myself from a dark reverie to hear her words.

"It was yesterday, Jack—just yesterday—that he said to me, 'Next winter you shall spend in New Orleans, Yvonne.' Just yesterday!"

I watched the tear that rolled slowly down her right cheek hung glistening there a moment, then was joined by another to splash on the black bosom of her dress.

But it was later, during the evening, that the most ironic revelation of all occurred. I was gloomily blaming myself for the weakness of indulging old de Neant in the mad experiment that had led, in a way, to his death.

It was as if Yvonne read my thoughts, for she said suddenly:

"He was breaking, Jack. His mind was going. I heard all those strange things he kept murmuring to you."

"What?"

"I listened, of course, behind the door there. I never left him alone. I heard him whisper the queerest things—faces in a red fog, words about a cold grey desert, the name Pyroniva, the word Termopolis. He leaned over you as you sat with closed eyes and he whispered, whispered all the time."

Irony of ironies! It was old de Neant's mad mind that had suggested the visions! He had described them to me as I sat in the sleep of lethargy!

Later we found the letter he had written and again I was deeply moved. The old man had carried a little insurance. Just a week before he had borrowed on one of the policies to pay the premiums on it and the others. But the letter—well, he had made *me* beneficiary of half the amount! And the instructions were—

"You, Jack Anders, will take both your money and Yvonne's and carry out the plan as you know I wish."

Lunacy! De Neant had found the way to provide the money but—I couldn't gamble Yvonne's last dollar on the scheme of a disordered mind.

"What will we do?" I asked her. "Of course the money's all yours. I won't touch it."

"Mine?" she echoed. "Why, no. We'll do as he wished. Do you think I'd not respect his last request?"

Well, we did. I took those miserable few thousands and spread them around in that sick December market. You remember what happened, how during the spring the prices skyrocketed as if they were heading back toward 1929, when actually the depression was just gathering breath.

I rode that market like a circus performer. I took profits and pyramided them back and, on April 27th, with our money multiplied fifty times, I sold out and watched the market slide back.

Coincidence? Very likely. After all, Aurore de Neant's mind was clear enough most of the time. Other economists predicted that spring rise. Perhaps he foresaw it too. Perhaps he staged this whole affair just to trick us into the gamble, one which we'd never have dared risk otherwise. And then when he saw we were going to fail from lack of money he took the only means he had of providing it.

Perhaps. That's the rational explanation, and yet— that vision of ruined Termopolis keeps haunting me. I see again the grey cold desert of the floating fungi. I wonder often about the immutable Law of Chance and about a ghostly Jack Anders somewhere beyond eternity.

For perhaps he does—did—will exist. Otherwise, how to explain that final vision? What of Yvonne's words beside her father's grave? Could he have foreseen those words and whispered them to me? Possibly. But what, then, of those two tears that hung glistening, merged and dropped from her cheeks?

What of them?

THE SOFT PREDICAMENT

by *Brian W. Aldiss*

> "Calculate thyself within, seek not thyself in
> the Moon, but in thine own Orb or Microcosmical
> Circumference. Let celestial aspects admonish
> and advise, not conclude and determine thy ways."
> Sir Thomas Browne: *Christian Morals*

I. JUPITER

With increasing familiarity, he saw that the slow writhings were not inconsequential movement but ponderous and deliberate gesture.

Ian Ezard was no longer aware of himself. The
panorama entirely absorbed him.

What had been at first a meaningless blur had resolved into an array of lights, gently drifting. The
lights now took on pattern, became luminous wings or
phosphorescent backbones or incandescent limbs. As
they passed, the labored working of those pinions
ceased to look random and assumed every appearance
of deliberation—of plan—of consciousness! Nor was
the stew in which the patterns moved a chaos any
longer; as Ezard's senses adjusted to the scene, he
became aware of an environment as much governed
by its own laws as the environment into which he had
been born.

With the decline of his first terror and horror, he

could observe more acutely. He saw that the organisms of light moved over and among—what would you call them? Bulwarks? Fortifications? Cloud formations? They were no more clearly defined than sandbanks shrouded in fog; but he was haunted by a feeling of intricate detail slightly beyond his retinal powers of resolution, as if he were gazing at flotillas of baroque cathedrals, sunk just too deep below translucent seas.

He thought with unexpected kinship of Lowell, the astronomer, catching imaginary glimpses of Martian canals—but his own vantage point was much the more privileged.

The scale of the grand gay solemn procession parading before his vision gave him trouble. He caught himself trying to interpret the unknown in terms of the known. These organisms reminded him of the starry skeletons of Terrestrial cities by night, glimpsed from the stratosphere, or of clusters of diatoms floating in a drop of water. It was hard to remember that the living geometries he was scanning were each the size of a large island—perhaps a couple of hundred miles across.

Terror still lurked. Ezard knew he had only to adjust the infrared scanners to look miles deeper down into Jupiter's atmosphere and find—life?—images?—of a different kind. To date, the Jupiter Expedition had resolved six levels of life-images, each level separated from the others almost as markedly as sea was separated from air, by pressure gradients that entailed different chemical compositions.

Layer on layer, down they went, stirring slowly, right down far beyond detection into the sludgy heart of the protosun! Were all layers full of at least the traces and chimeras of life?

"It's like peering down into the human mind!" Ian Ezard exclaimed; perhaps he thought of the mind of Jerry Wharton, his mixed-up brother-in-law. Vast pressures, vast darknesses, terrible wisdoms, age-long electric storms—the parallel between Jupiter's atmospheric depths and the mind was too disconcerting. He sat up and pushed the viewing helmet back on its swivel.

The observation room closed in on him again, unchanging, wearily familiar.

"My god!" he said, feebly wiping his face. "My god!" And after a moment, "By Jove!" in honor of the monstrous protosun riding like a whale beneath their ship. Sweat ran from him.

"It's a spectacle right enough," Captain Dudintsev said, handing him a towel. "And each of the six layers we have surveyed is over one hundred times the area of Earth. We are recording most of it on tape. Some of the findings are being relayed back to Earth now."

"They'll flip!"

"Life on Jupiter—what else can you call it but life? This is going to hit Russia and America and the whole of Westciv harder than any scientific discovery since reproduction!"

Looking at his wristputer, Ezard noted that he had been under the viewer for eighty-six minutes. "Oh, it's consciousness there right enough. It stands all our thinking upside down. Not only does Jupiter contain most of the inorganic material of the system, the sun apart—it contains almost all the life as well. Swarming, superabundant life. . . . Not an amoeba smaller than Long Island. . . . It makes Earth just a rocky outpost on a far shore. That's a big idea to adjust to!"

"The White World will adjust, as we adjusted to Darwinism. We always do adjust."

"And who cares about the Black World. . . ."

Dudintsev laughed. "What about your sister's husband that you're always complaining about? He'd care!"

"Oh, yes, he'd care. Jerry'd like to see the other half of the globe wiped out entirely."

"Well, he's surely not the only one."

With his head still full of baffling luminescent gestures, Ezard went forward to shower.

II. LUNA

Near the deep midnight in Rainbow Bay City. Standing under Main dome at the top of one of the viewtowers. The universe out there before us, close to the panes; stars like flaming fat, distorted by the dome's curvature, Earth like a chilled fingernail clipping. Chief Dream-Technician Wace and I talking sporadically, killing time until we went back on duty to what my daughter Ri calls "the big old black thing" over in Plato.

"Specialization—it's a wonderful thing, Jerry!" Wave said. "Here we are, part-way to Jupiter and I don't even know where in the sky to look for it! The exterior world has never been my province."

He was a neat little dry man, in his mid-thirties and already wizened. His province was the infinitely complex state of being of sleep. I had gained a lot of my interest in psychology from Johnnie Wace. Like him, I would not have been standing where I was were it not for the CUFL project, on which we were both working. And that big old black thing would not have been established inconveniently on the Moon had not the elusive hypnoid states between waking and sleeping which we were investigating been most easily sustained in the light-gravity condition of Luna.

I gave up the search for Jupiter. I knew where it was no more than Wace did. Besides, slight condensation was hatching drops off the aluminum bars overhead; the drafts of the dome brought the drops down slantingly at us. Tension was returning to me as the time to go on shift drew near—tension we were not allowed to blunt with drink. Soon I would be plugged in between life and death, letting CUFL suck up my psyche. As we turned away, I looked outside at an auxiliary dome under which cactus grew in the fertile Lunar soil, sheltered only slightly from external rigors.

"That's the way we keep pushing on, Johnnie," I said, indicating the cacti. "We're always extending the margins of experience—now the Trans-Jupiter Expedition has discovered that life exists out there. Where does the West get its dynamism from, while the rest of the world—the Third World—still sits on its haunches?"

Wace gave me an odd look.

"I know, I'm on my old hobbyhorse! You tell me, Johnnie, you're a clever man, how is it that in an age of progress half the globe won't progress?"

"Jerry, I don't feel about the Blacks as you do. You're such an essential part of CUFL because your basic symbols are confused."

He noticed that the remark angered me. Yet I saw the truth as I stated it. Westciv, comprising most of the Northern Hemisphere and little else bar Australia, was a big armed camp, guarding enormously long frontiers with the stagnating Black or Third World, and occasionally making a quick raid into South America or Africa to quell threatening power build-ups. All the time that we were trying to move forward, the rest of the overcrowded world was dragging us back.

"You know my views, Johnnie—they may be unpopular but I've never tried to hide them." I told him, letting my expression grow dark. "I'd wipe the slate of the useless Third World clean and begin over, if I had my way. What have we got to lose? No confusion in my symbols there, is there?"

"Once a soldier, always a soldier. . . ." He said no more until we were entering the elevator. Then he added, in his quiet way, "We can all of us be mistaken, Jerry. We now know that the freshly-charted upsilon-areas of the brain make no distinction between waking reality and dream. They deal only with altering time-scales, and form the gateway to the unconscious. My personal theory is that Western man, with his haste for progress, may have somehow closed that gate and lost touch with something that is basic to his psychic well-being."

"Meaning the Blacks are still in touch?"

"Don't sneer! The history of the West is nothing to be particularly proud of. You know that our CUFL project is in trouble and may be closed down. Sure, we progress astonishingly on the material plane, we have stations orbiting the Sun and inner planets and Jupiter—yet we remain at odds with ourselves. CUFL is intended to be to the psyche what the computer is to knowledge, yet it consistently rejects our data. The fault is not in the machine. Draw your own conclusions."

I shrugged. "Let's get on shift!"

We reached the surface and climbed out, walking in the direction of the tube where a shuttle for Plato would be ready. The big old black thing would be sitting waiting by the crater terminus and, under the care of Johnnie Wace's team, I and the other feeds would be plugged in. Sometimes I felt lost in the whole tenuous world that Wace found so congenial, and in all the clever talk about what was dream, what was reality—though I used it myself sometimes, in self-defense.

As we made for the subway, the curve of the dome distorted the cacti beyond. Frail though they were, great arms of prickly pear grew and extended and seemed to wrap themselves around the dome, before being washed out by floods or reflected electroluminescence. Until the problem of cutting down glare at night was beaten, tempers in Main Dome would stay edgy.

In the subway, still partly unfinished, Wace and I moved past the parade of fire-fighting equipment and emergency suits and climbed into the train. The rest of the team were already in their seats, chattering eagerly about the ambiguous states of mind that CUFL encouraged; they greeted Johnnie eagerly, and he joined in their conversation. I longed to be back with my family—such as it was—or playing a quiet game of chess with Ted Greaves, simple old soldier Ted Greaves. Maybe I should have stayed a simple old soldier myself, helping to quell riots in the overcrowded lanes of Eastern Seaboard, or cutting a quick swathe through Brazil.

"I didn't mean to rub you up the wrong way, Jerry,"

Wace said as the doors closed. His little face wrinkled with concern.

"Forget it. I jumped at you. These days, life's too complex."

"That from you, the apostle of progress!"

"It's no good talking. . . . Look, we've found life on Jupiter. That's great. I'm really glad, glad for Ezard out there, glad for everyone. But what are we going to do about it? Where does it get us? We haven't even licked the problem of life on Earth yet!"

"We will," he said.

We began to roll into the dark tunnel.

III. RI

One of the many complications of life on Earth was the dreams of my daughter. They beguiled me greatly: so much that I believe they often became entangled with my fantasies as I lay relaxed on Wace's couch under the encephalometers and the rest of the CUFL gear. But they worried me even as they enchanted me. The child is so persistently friendly that I don't always have time for her; but her dreams are a different matter.

In the way that Ri told them, the dreams had a peculiar lucidity. Perhaps they were scenes from a world I wanted to be in, a toy world—a simplified world that hardly seemed to contain other people.

Ri was the fruit of my third-decade marriage. My fourth-decade wife, Natalie, also liked to hear Ri's prattle; but Natalie is a patient woman, both with Ri and me; more with Ri, maybe, since she likes to show me her temper.

A certain quality to Ri's dreams made Natalie and me keep them private to ourselves. We never mentioned them to our friends, almost as if they were little shared guilty secrets. Nor did I ever speak of them to my buddies sweating on the CUFL project, or to Wace or the mind-wizards in the Lunar Psyche Lab. For that matter, Natalie and I avoided discussing them between

211 THE SOFT PREDICAMENT

ourselves, partly because we sensed Ri's own reverence for her nocturnal images.

Then my whole pleasure at the child's dreams was turned into disquiet by a casual remark that Ted Greaves dropped.

This is how it came about.

I had returned from Luna on the leave-shuttle only the previous day, more exhausted than usual. The hops between Kennedy and Eastern and Eastern and Eurocen were becoming more crowded than ever, despite the extra jumbos operating; the news of the discovery of life on Jupiter—even the enormous telecasts of my brother-in-law's face burning over every Westciv city—seemed to have stirred up the ants' heap considerably. What people thought they could do about it was beyond computation, but Wall Street was registering a tidal wave of optimism.

So with one thing and another, I arrived home exhausted. Ri was asleep. Yes, still wetting her bed, Natalie admitted. I took a sauna and fell asleep in my wife's arms. The world turned. Next thing I knew, it was morning and I was roused by Ri's approach to our bedside.

Small girls of three have a ponderous tread; they weigh as much as baby elephants. I can walk across our bedroom floor without making a sound, but this tot sets up vibrations.

"I thought you were still on the Moon feeding the Clective Unctious, Daddy," she said. The "Clective Unctious" is her inspired mispronunciation of the Collective Unconscious; wisely, she makes no attempt at all at the Free-Living tail of CUFL.

"The Unctious has given me a week's leave, Ri. Now let me sleep! Go and read your book!"

I watched her through one half open eye. She put her head on one side and smiled at me, scratching her behind.

"Then that big old black thing is a lot clevererer and kinder than I thought it was."

From her side of the bed, Natalie laughed. "Why, that's the whole idea of the Clective Unctious, Ri—to be kinder and wiser than one person can imagine."

"I can imagine *lots* of kindness," she said. She was not to be weaned of her picture of the Unctious as a big black thing.

Climbing onto the bed, she began to heave herself between Natalie and me. She had brought along a big plastic talkie-picture-book of traditional design tucked under one arm. As she rolled over me, she swung the book and a corner of it caught me painfully on the cheek. I yelled.

"You clumsy little horror! Get off me!"

"Daddy, I didn't mean to do it, really! It was an acciment!"

"I don't care what it was! Get out! Go on! Move! Go back to your own bed!"

I tugged at her arm and dragged her across me. She burst into tears.

Natalie sat up angrily. "For god's sake, leave the kid alone! You're always bullying her!"

"You keep quiet—she didn't catch you in the eye! And she's peed her bed again, the dirty little tyke!"

That was how that row started. I'm ashamed to relate how it went on. There were the tears from the child and tears from Natalie. Only after breakfast did everyone simmer down. Oh, I can be fairly objective now in this confession, and record my failings and what other people thought of me. Believe me, if it isn't art, it's therapy!

It's strange to recall now how often we used to quarrel over breakfast. . . . Yet that was one of the calmest rooms, with the crimson carpet spread over the floor-tiles, and the white walls and dark Italian furniture. We had old-fashioned two-dimensional oil painting, nonmobile, on the walls, and no holoscreen. In one corner, half-hidden behind a vase of flowers from the courtyard, stood Jannick, our robot house-maid; but Natalie, preferring not to use her, kept her switched off. Jannick was off on this occasion. Peace reigned. Yet we quarreled.

As Natalie and I were drinking a last cup of coffee, Ri trotted around to me and said, "Would you like to hear my dream now, Daddy, if you're really not savage anymore?"

I pulled her onto my knee. "Let's hear it then, if we must. Was it the one about warm pools of water again?"

She shook her head in a dignified manner.

"This dream came around three in the morning," she said. "I know what the time was because a huge black bird like a starving crow came and pecked at my window as if it wanted to get in and wake us all up."

"That was all a part of the dream, then. There aren't any crows in this stretch of Italy."

"Perhaps you're right, because the house was sort of dirtier than it really is. . . . So I sat up and immediately I began dreaming I was fat and heavy and carrying a big fat heavy talkie-book up the hill. It was a much bigger book than any I got here. I could hardly breathe because there was hardly any air up the hillside. It was a very *plain* sort of dream."

"And what happened in it?"

"Nothing."

"Nothing at all?"

"Nothing except just one thing. Do you know what? I saw there was one of those new Japanese cars rushing down the hill toward me—you know, the kind where the body's inside the wheel and the big wheel goes all around the body."

"She must mean the Toyota Monocar," Natalie said.

"Yes, that's right, Natalie, the Toyta Moggacar. It was like a big flaming wheel and it rolled right past me and went out."

"Out where?"

"I don't know. Where do things go out to? I didn't even know where it came from! In my dream I was puzzled about that, so I looked all around and by the roadside there was a big drop. It just went down and down! And it was guarded by eight posts protecting it, little round white posts like teeth, and the Moggacar must have come from there."

Natalie and I sat over the table thinking about the dream after Ri had slipped out into the courtyard to play; she had some flame- and apricot-colored finches in cages which she loved.

I was on her small imaginary hillside, where the air was thin and the colors pale, and the isolated figure of the child stood clutching its volume and watched the car go past like a flame. A sun-symbol, the wheel on which Ixion was crucified, image of our civilization maybe, Tantric sign of sympathetic fires. . . . All those things, and the first unmanned stations now orbiting the sun—one of the great achievements of Westciv, and itself a symbol awakening great smoldering responses in man. Was that response reverberating through the psyches of all small children, changing them, charging them further along the trajectory the White World follows? What would the news from Jupiter bring on? What sort of role would Uncle Ian, the life-finder, play in the primitive theaters of Ri's mind?

I asked the questions of myself only idly. I enjoyed popping the big questions, on the principle that if they were big enough they were sufficient in themselves and did not require answers. Answers never worried me in those days. I was no thinker. My job in Plato concerned feelings, and for that they paid me. Answers were for Johnnie Wace and his cronies.

"We'd better be moving," Natalie said, collecting my coffee cup. "Since you've got a free day, make the most of it. You're on frontier duty with Greaves again tomorrow."

"I know that without being reminded, thanks."

"I wasn't really reminding you—just stating a fact."

As she passed me to go into the kitchen, I said, "I know this house is archaic—just a peasant's home. But if I hadn't volunteered for irregular frontier service during my off-duty spells, we wouldn't be here. We'd be stuck in Eastern or some other enormous city-complex, such as the one you spent your miserable childhood in. Then you'd complain even more!"

She continued into the kitchen with the cups and plates. It was true the house had been built for and by peasants, or little better; its stone walks, a meter thick, kept out the heat of summer; and the brief chill of winter when it rolled around. Natalie was silent and then she said, so quietly that I could scarcely hear her where I sat in the living room, "I was not complaining, Jerry, not daring to complain. . . ."

I marched in to her. She was standing by the sink, more or less as I imagined her, her dark wings of hair drawn into place by a rubber band at the nape of her neck. I loved her, but she could make me mad!

"What's that meant to mean—'not daring to complain'?"

"Please don't quarrel with me, Jerry. I can't take much more."

"Was I quarreling? I thought I was simply asking you what you meant by what you said!"

"Please don't get worked up!" She came and stood against me, putting her arms around my waist and looking up at me. I stiffened myself and would not return her gaze. "I mean no harm, Jerry. It's terrible the way we row just like everyone else—I know you're upset!"

"Of course I'm upset! Who wouldn't be upset at the state of the world? Your marvelous brother and his buddies have discovered life on Jupiter! Does that affect us? *My* project, CUFL, that will have to close down unless we start getting results. Then there's all the disturbance in the universities—I don't know what the younger generation thinks it's doing! Unless we're strong, the Thirdies are going to invade and take over—"

She was growing annoyed herself now. "Oh yes, that's really why we came to live down here in the back of beyond, isn't it?—Just so that you could get an occasional crack at the enemy. It wasn't for any care about where I might want to live."

"Unlike some people, I care about doing my duty by my country!"

She broke away from me. "It's not part of your duty to be incessantly beastly to Ri and me, is it? Is it? You don't care about us one bit!"

It was an old tune she played.

"Don't start bringing that up again, woman! If I didn't care, why did I buy you that robot standing idle in the next room? You never use it, you prefer to hire a fat old woman to come in instead! I should have saved my money! And you have the brass nerve to talk about not caring!"

Her eyes were wild now. She looked glorious standing there.

"You don't care! You don't care! You hurt your poor little daughter, you neglect me! You're always off to the Moon, or at the frontier, or else here bullying us. Even your stupid friend Ted Greaves has more sense than you! You hate us! You hate everyone!"

Running forward, I grabbed her arm and shook her.

"You're always making a noise. Not much longer till the end of the decade and then I'm rid of you! I can't wait!"

I strode through the house and slammed out of the door into the street. Thank the stars it was frontier duty the next day! People greeted me but I ignored them. The sun was already high in the South Italian sky; I sweated as I walked, and rejoiced in the discomfort.

It was not true that I bullied them. Natalie might have suffered as a child, but so had I! There had been a war in progress then, the first of the Westciv-Third wars, although we had not thought of it in quite those terms at the time, before the Cap-Com treaty. I had been drafted, at an age when others were cutting a figure in universities. I had been scared, I had suffered, been hungry, been wounded, been lost in the jungle for a couple of days before the chopper patrol picked me up. And I'd killed off a few Thirdies. Even Natalie would not claim I had *enjoyed* doing that. It was all over long ago. Yet it was still with me. In my mind, it never grew fainter. The Earth revolved; the lights on that old stage never went dim.

Now I was among the hills above our village. I sat under the shade of an olive tree and looked back. It's strange how you find yourself thinking things that have nothing to do with your daily life.

It was no use getting upset over a husband-wife quarrel. Natalie was OK; just a little hasty-tempered. My watch said close to ten o'clock. Ted Greaves would be turning up at the house for a game of chess before long. I would sit where I was for a moment, breathe deep, and then stroll back. Act naturally. There was nothing to be afraid of.

IV. GREAVES

Ted Greaves arrived at the house at about ten-fifty. He was a tall fair-haired man, dogged by ill-luck most of his military career and somewhat soured toward society. He enjoyed playing the role of bluff soldier. After many years in the service, he was now Exile Officer commanding our sector of the southern frontier between Westciv and the Blacks. As such, he would be my superior tomorrow, when I went on duty. Today, we were just buddies and I got the chess board out.

"I feel too much like a pawn myself to play well today," he said, as we settled down by the window. "Spent all the last twenty-four hours in the office filling in photoforms. We're sinking under forms! The famine situation in North Africa is now reinforced by a cholera epidemic."

"The Third's problems are nothing to do with us!"

"Unfortunately we're more connected than appears on the surface. The authorities are afraid that the cholera won't respect frontiers. We've got to let some refugees through tomorrow, and they could be carriers. An emergency isolation ward is being set up. It's Westciv's fault—we should have given aid to Africa from the start."

On the Rainbow-Kennedy flight, I had bought a can of bourbon at a duty-free price. Greaves and I broached it now. But he was in a dark mood, and was soon launched on an old topic of his, the responsibility of the States for the White-Black confrontation. I did not accept his diagnosis for one minute, and he knew I didn't; but that did not stop him rambling on about the evils of our consumer society, and how it was all based on jealousy, and the shame of the Negro Solution—though how we could have avoided the Solution, he did not say. Since we had been mere children at the time of the Solution, I could not see why he needed to feel guilt about it. In any case, I believed that the colored races of Third were undeveloped because they lacked the intellect and moral fiber of Westciv, their hated Pinkyland.

So I let Greaves give vent to his feelings over the iced bourbon while I gazed out through the window to our inner courtyard.

The central stone path, flanked by a colonnade on which bougainvillea rioted, led to a little statue of Diana, executed in Carrara marble, standing against the far wall. All the walls of the courtyard were plastered in yellow. On the left-hand side, Ri's collection of finches chirped and flitted in their cages. In the beds, orange and lemon trees grew. Above the far wall, the mountains of Calabria rose.

I never tired of the peace of that view. But what chiefly drew my eyes was the sight of Natalie in her simple green dress. I had loved her in many forms, I thought, and at the end of the decade it would not come too hard to exchange her for another—better anyhow than being stuck with one woman a life long, as under the old system—but either I was growing older or there was something particular about Natalie. She was playing with Ri and talking to the Calabrian servant. I couldn't hear a word they said, though the windows were open to let in warmth and fragrance; only the murmur of their voices reached me.

Yes, she had to be exchanged. You had to let things go. That was what kept the world revolving. Planned obsolescence as a social dynamic, in human relationships as in consumer goods. When Ri was ten, she would have to go to the appropriate Integration Center, to learn to become a functioning member of society—just as my other daughter, Melisande, had left the year before, on her tenth birthday.

Melisande, who wept so much at the parting . . . a sad indication of how much she needed integration. We were all required to make sacrifices; otherwise the standard of living would go down. Partings one grew hardened to. I scarcely thought of Melisande nowadays.

And when I'd first known Natalie. Natalie Ezard. That was before the integration laws. "Space travel nourishes our deepest and most bizarre wishes." Against mental states of maximum alertness float extravagant hypnoid states which color the outer darkness crimson and jade, and make unshapely things march to the very margins of the eye. Maybe it is because at the very heart of the richness of metal-bound space travel lies sensory deprivation. For all its promise of renaissance, vacuum-flight is life's death, and only the completely schizoid are immune to its terrors. I was never happy, even on the Kennedy-Rainbow trip.

Between planets, our most outré desires become fecund. Space travel nourishes our deepest and most bizarre wishes. "Awful things can happen!" Natalie had cried, in our early days, flinging herself into my returning arms. And while I was away, Westciv passed its integration laws, separating parents from children, bestowing on ten-year-olds the honorable orphanage of the state, to be trained as citizens.

It all took place again before the backdrop of our sunlit courtyard, where Natalie Wharton now stood. She was thinner and sharper than she had been once, her hair less black. Some day, we would have to take the offensive and wipe out every single Black in the Black-and-White World. To my mind, only the fear of what neutral China might do had prevented us taking such a necessary step already.

"You see how old it is out there!" Ted Greaves said, misreading my gaze as he gestured into the court-yard. "Look at that damned vine, that statue! Apart from lovely little Natalie and your daughter, there's not a thing that hasn't been in place for a couple of hundred years. Over in the States, it's all new, new, everything has to be the latest. As soon as roots begin forming, we tear them up and start over. The result—no touchstones! How long's this house been standing? Three centuries? In the States, it would have been swept away long ago. Here, loving care keeps it going, so that it's as good as new. Good as new! See how I'm victim of my own clichés! It's better than fucking new, it's as good as old!"

"You're a sentimentalist, Ted. It isn't things but other people that matter. People are old, worlds are old. The Russo-American ships now forging around the System are bringing home to us just how old we are, how familiar we are to ourselves. Our roots are in ourselves."

We enjoyed philosophizing, that's true.

He grunted and lit a flash-cigar. "That comes well from you, when you're building this Free-Living Collective Unconscious. Isn't that just another American project to externalize evil and prune our roots?"

"Certainly not! CUFL will be an emotions-bank, a computer if you like, which will store—not the fruits of the human intellect—but the fruits of the psyche. Now that there are too many people around and our lives have to be regimented, CUFL will restore us to the freedom of our imaginations."

"If it works!"

"Sure, if it works," I agreed. "As yet, we can get nothing out of our big old black thing but primitive archetypal patterns. It's a question of keeping on feeding it." I always spoke more cheerfully than I felt with Greaves: to counteract his vein of pessimism, I suppose.

He stood up and stared out of the window. "Well, I'm just a glorified soldier—and without much glory. I don't understand emotion banks. But maybe you overfed your big black thing and it is dying of over-nourishment, just like Westciv itself. Certain archetypal dreams—the human young get them, so why not your newborn machine? The young get them especially when they are going to die young."

Death was one of his grand themes: "The peace that passeth all standing," he called it once.

"What sort of dreams?" I asked, unthinking.

"To the nervous system, dream imagery is received just like sensory stimuli. There are prodromic dreams, dreams that foretell of death. We don't know what wakefulness is, do we, until we know what dreams are. Maybe the whole Black-White struggle is a super-dream, like a blackbird rapping on a windowpane."

Conversation springs hidden thoughts. I'd been listening, but more actively I'd wondered at the way he didn't answer questions quite directly, just as most people fail to. Someone told me that it was the effect of holovision, split attention. All this I was going through when he came up with the remark about blackbirds tapping on windows, and it brought to mind the start to Ri's latest dream, when she was unsure whether she woke or slept.

"What's that to do with dying?"

"Let's take a walk in the sun before it gets too stinking hot. Some children are too ethereal for life. Christ, Jerry, a kid's close to the primal state, to the original psychological world; they're the ones to come through with uncanny prognoses. If they aren't going to make it to maturity, their psyches know about it and have no drive to gear themselves onto the next stage of being."

"Let's go out in the sun," I said. I felt ill. The poinsettias were in flower, spreading their scarlet tongues. A lizard lay along a carob branch. That sun

disappearing down Ri's hill—death? And the eight
teeth or posts or what the hell they were, on the edge
of nothing—her years? The finches hopped from perch
to perch, restless in their captivity.

V. SICILY

Almost before daybreak next morning, I was flying
over Calabria and the toe of Italy. Military installa-
tions glittered below. This was one of the southern
points of Europe which marked the frontier between
the two worlds. It was manned by task forces of Ameri-
cans, Europeans, and Russians. I had left before Ri
woke. Natalie, with her wings of dark hair, had risen
to wave me good-bye. Good-bye, it was always good-
bye. And what was the meaning of the big black book
Ri had been carrying in her dream? It couldn't be
true.

The Straits of Messina flashed below our wingless
fuselage. Air, water, earth, fire, the original elements.
The fifth, space, had been waiting. God alone knew
what it did in the hearts and minds of man, what
aboriginal reaction was in process. Maybe once we
finished off the Thirdies, the Clective Unctious would
give us time to sort things out. There was never time
to sort things out. Even the finches in their long im-
prisonment never had enough time. And the bird at
her window? Which side of the window was in, which
out?

We were coming down toward Sicily, toward its tan
mountains. I could see Greaves's head and shoulders
in the driver's seat.

Sicily was semineutral ground. White and Black
World met in its eroded valleys. My breakfast had
been half a grapefruit, culled fresh from the garden,
and a cup of bitter black coffee. Voluntary regulation
of intake. The other side of the looming frontier,
starvation would have made my snack seem a fine
repast.

Somewhere south, a last glimpse of sea and the

smudged distant smoke of Malta, still burning after ten years. Then up came Etna and the stunned interior, and we settled for a landing.

This barren land looked like machine-land itself. Sicily—the northern, Westciv half—had as big a payload of robots on it as the Moon itself. All worked in mindless unison in case the lesser breeds in the southern half did anything desperate. I grabbed up my gas-cannon and climbed out into the heat as a flight of steps snapped itself into position.

Side by side, Greaves and I jumped into proffered pogo-armor and bounded off across the field in thirty-foot kangaroo-steps.

The White boundary was marked by saucers standing on poles at ten-meter intervals; between saucers, the force barrier shimmered, carrying its flair for hallucination right up into the sky.

The Black World had its boundary too. It stood beyond our force field—stood, I say! It lurched across Sicily, a ragged wall of stone. Much of the stone came from dismembered towns and villages and churches. Every now and again, a native would steal some of the stone back, in order to build his family a hovel to live in. Indignant Black officials would demolish the hovel and restore the stone. They should have worried! I could have pogoed over their wall with ease!

And a wall of eight posts. . . .

We strode across the crowded field to the forward gate. Sunlight and gravity. We were massive men, nine feet high or more; boots two feet high; over our heads, umbrella-helmets over a foot high. Our megavoices could carry over a land-mile. We might have been evil machine-men from the ragged dreams of Blacks. At the forward gate, we entered in and shed the armor in magnetized recesses.

Up in the tower, Greaves took over from the auto-controls and opened his link with Palermo and the comsats high overhead. I checked with Immigration and Isolation to see that they were functioning.

From here, we could look well into the hated enemy territory, over the tops of their wooden towers, into the miserable stone villages, from which hordes of people were already emerging, although fifty minutes had yet to elapse before we lowered the force-screens to let any of them through. Beyond the crowds, the mountains crumbling into their thwarted valleys, fly-specked with bushes. No fit habitation. If we took over the island—as I always held we should—we would raise desalination-plants on the coast, import topsoil and fertilizer and the new plus-crops, and make the whole place flow with riches in five years. With the present status quo, the next five would bring nothing but starvation and religion; that was all they had there. A massive cholera epidemic, with deaths counted in hundreds of thousands, was raging through Africa already, after moving westward from Calcutta, its traditional capital.

"The bastards!" I said. "One day, there will be a law all over the world forbidding people to live like vermin!"

"And a law forbidding people to make capital out of it," Greaves said. His remark meant nothing to me. I guessed it had something to do with his cranky theory that Westciv profited by the poor world's poverty by raising import tariffs against it. Greaves did not explain, nor did I ask him to.

At the auxiliary control panel, I sent out an invisible scanner to watch one of the enemy villages. Although it might register on the antiquated radar screens of the Blacks, they could only rave at the breach of international regulations without ever being able to intercept it.

The eye hovered over a group of shacks and adjusted its focus. Three-dimensionally, the holograph of hatred traveled toward me in the cube.

Against doorways, up on balconies decked with ragged flowers, along alleys, stood groups of Blacks. They would be Arabs, refugee Maltese, branded Sicilians, renegades from the White camp; ethnic groups were indistinguishable beneath dirt and tan and old non-synthetic clothes. I centered on a swarthy young woman standing in a tavern doorway with one hand on a small boy's shoulder. As Natalie stood in the courtyard under the poinsettias, what had I thought to myself? That once we might have propagated love between ourselves?

Before the world had grown too difficult, there had been a sure way of multiplying and sharing love. We would have bred and raised children for the sensuous reward of having them, of helping them grow up sane and strong. From their bowels also, health would have radiated.

But the Thirdies coveted Westciv's riches without accepting its disciplines. They bred. Indiscriminately and prodigally. The world was too full of children and people, just as the emptiness of space was stuffed with lurid dreams. Only the weak and helpless and starved could cast children onto the world unregulated. Their weak and helpless and starved progeny clogged the graves and wombs of the world. That laughing dark girl on my screen deserved only the bursting seed of cannonfire.

"Call that scanner back, Jerry!" Greaves said, coming toward me.

"What's that?"

"Call your scanner back."

"I'm giving the Wogs the once-over."

"Call it back in, I told you. As long as no emergency's in force, you are contravening regulations."

"Who cares!"

"I care," he said. He looked very nasty. "I care, and I'm Exile Officer."

As I guided the eye back in, I said, "You were rough all yesterday too. You played a bum game of chess. What's got into you?"

But as soon as I had asked the question, I could answer it myself. He was a bag of nerves because he must have had word that his son was coming back from the wastes of the Third World.

"You're on the hook about your anarchist son Pete, aren't you?"

It was then he flung himself at me.

In the dark tavern, Pete Greaves was buying his friends one last round of drinks. He had been almost three weeks in the seedy little town, waiting for the day the frontier opened; in that time, he had got to know just about everyone in the place. All of them—not just Max Spineri who had traveled all the way from Alexandria with him—swore eternal friendship on this parting day.

"And a plague on King Cholera!" Pete said, lifting his glass.

"Better get back to the West before King Cholera visits Sicily!" a mule-driver said.

The drink was strong. Pete felt moved to make a short speech.

"I came here a stupid prig, full of all the propaganda of the West," he said. "I'm going back with open eyes. I've become a man in my year in Africa and Sicily, and back home I shall apply what I've learned."

"Here's your home now, Pete," Antonio the Barman said. "Don't go back to Pinkyland or you'll become a machine like the others there. We're your friends—stay with your friends!" But Pete noticed the crafty old devil shortchanged him.

"I've got to go back, Antonio—Max will tell you. I want to stir people up, make them listen to the truth. There's got to be change, got to be, even if we wreck the whole present setup to get it. All over Pinkyland, take my word, there are thousands—millions—of men and girls my age who hate the way things are run."

"It's the same as here!" a peasant laughed.

"Sure, but in the West, it's different. The young are tired of the pretense that we have some say in government, tired of bureaucracy, tired of a technocracy that simply reinforces the powers of the politicians. Who cares about finding life on Jupiter when life here just gets lousier!"

He saw—it had never ceased to amaze him all his time in Blackyland—that they were cool to such talk. He was on their side, as he kept telling them. Yet at best their attitude to the Whites was ambivalent: a mixture of envy and contempt for nations that they saw as slaves to consumer goods and machines.

He tried again, telling them about Student Power and the Underground, but Max interrupted him. "You have to go soon, Pete. We know how you feel. Take it easy—your people find it so hard to take it easy. Look, I've got a parting gift for you. . . ."

Drawing Pete back into a corner, he produced a gun and thrust it into his friend's hand. Examining it, Pete saw it was an ancient British Enfield revolver, well-maintained. "I can't accept this, Max!"

"Yes, you can! It's not from me but from the Organization. To help you in your revolution. It's loaded with six bullets! You'll have to hide it, because they will search you when you cross the frontier."

He clasped Max's hand. "Every bullet will count, Max!"

He trembled. Perhaps it was mainly fear of himself.

When he was far from that heat and flies and dust and his ragged unwashed friends, he would hold this present brave image of himself, and draw courage from it.

He moved out into the sun, to where Roberta Arneri stood watching the convoy assembling for the short drive to the frontier gate. He took her hand.

"You know why I have to go, Roberta?"

"You go for lots of reasons."

It was true enough. He stared into the harsh sunlight and tried to remember. Though hatred stood between the two worlds, there were areas of weakness where they relied on each other. Beneath the hatred were ambiguities almost like love. Though a state of war existed, some trade continued. And the young could not be pent in. Every year, young Whites—

"anarchists" to their seniors—slipped over the frontier with ambulances and medical supplies. And the supplies were paid for by their seniors. It was conscience money. Or hate money. A token, a symbol—nobody knew for what, though it was felt to be important, as a dream is felt to be important even when it is not comprehended.

Now he was going back. Antonio could be right. He would probably never return to the Third World; his own world would most likely make him into a machine.

But he had to bear witness. He was sixteen years old.

"Life without plumbing, life with a half full belly," he had to go home and say. "It has a savor to it. It's a positive quality. It doesn't make you less a human being. There's no particular virtue in being white of skin and fat of gut and crapping into a nice china bowl every time the laxatives take hold."

He wondered how convincing he could make it sound, back in the immense hygienic warrens of Westciv—particularly when he still longed in his inner heart for all the conveniences and privileges, and a shower every morning before a sit-down breakfast. It had all been fun, but enough was enough. More than enough, when you remembered what the plague was doing.

"You go to see again your father," Roberta diagnosed.

"Maybe. In America, we are trying to sever the ties of family. After you get through with religion you destroy the sacredness of the family. It encourages people to move to other planets, to go where they're told."

He was ashamed of saying it—and yet half proud.

"That's why you all are so nervous and want to go to war all the time. You don't get enough kisses as little kids, eh?"

"Oh, we're all one-man isolation units! Life isn't as bad as you think, up there among the wheels of progress, Roberta," he said bitterly. He kissed her, and her lips tasted of garlic.

Max slapped him on his shoulder.

"Cut all that out, fellow—you're going home! Get aboard!"

Pete climbed onto the donkey cart with another anarchist White who had recently sailed across to the island from Tunisia. Pete had arrived in the mysterious Third World driving a truck full of supplies. The truck had been stolen in Nubia, when he was down with malaria and dysentery. He was going back empty-handed. But the palms of those hands were soft no longer.

He shook Max's hand now. They looked at each other wordlessly as the cart driver goaded his animal into movement. There was affection there, yes—undying in its way, for Max was also a would-be extremist; but there was also the implacable two-way enmity that sprang up willy-nilly between Haves and Have-nots. An enmity stronger than men, incurable by men. They both dropped their gaze.

Hiding his embarrassment, Pete looked about him. In his days of waiting, the village had become absolutely familiar, from the church at one end of the broken-down bursts of cactus in between. He had savored too the pace of life here, geared to the slowest and most stupid, so that the slowest and most stupid could survive. Over the frontier, time passed in overdrive.

Across the drab stones, the hooves of the donkey made little noise. Other carts were moving forward, with dogs following, keeping close to the walls. There was a feeling—desperate and exhilarating—that they were leaving the shelter of history, and heading toward where the powerhouse of the world began.

Pete waved to Max and Roberta and the others, and squinted toward the fortifications of his own sector. The frontier stood distant but clear in the pale air. As he looked, he saw a giant comic-terror figure, twice as high as a grown man, man-plus-machine, bound across the plain toward him. Bellowing with an obscene anger as it charged, the monster appeared to burn in the sun.

It came toward him like a flaming wheel rushing down a steep hill, all-devouring.

VI. EGO

Ted Greaves was my friend of long standing. I don't know why he flung himself on me in hatred just because I taunted him about his son. For that matter, I don't know why anger suddenly blazed up in me as it did.

My last spell on CUFL had left me in relatively poor shape, but fury lent me strength. I ducked away from his first blow and chopped him hard below the heart. As he doubled forward, grunting with pain, I struck him again, this time on the jaw. He brought his right fist up and grazed my chin, but by then I was hitting him again and again. He went down.

These fits had come over me before, but not for many years. When I was aware of myself again, I was jumping into the pogo-armor, with only the vaguest recollections of what I had done to Greaves. I could recall I had let the force barrier down.

I went leaping forward toward the hated land. I could hear the gyros straining, hear my voice bellowing before me like a spinnaker.

"You killed my daughter! You killed my daughter! You shan't get in! You shan't even look in!"

I didn't know what I was about.

There were animals scattering. I overturned a cart. I was almost at the first village.

It felt as if I were running at a hundred miles an hour. Yet when the shot rang out, I stopped at once. How beautiful the hills were if one's eyes never opened and closed again. Pigeons wheeling white above tawdry roofs. People immobile. One day they would be ours, and we would take over the whole world. The whole world shook with the noise of my falling armament, and dust spinning like the fury of galaxies.

Better pain than our eternal soft predicament. . . .

I was looking at a pale-faced boy on a cart, he was

staggering off the cart, the cart was going from him. People were shouting and fluttering everywhere like rags. My gaze was fixed only on him. His eyes were only on me. He had a smoking revolver in his hand.

Wonderingly, I wondered how I knew he was an American. An American who had seized Ted Greaves's face and tugged it from inside until all the wrinkles were gone from it and it looked obscenely young again. My executioner wore a mask.

A gyro labored by my head as if choked with blood. I could only look up at that mask. Something had to be said to it as it came nearer.

"It's like a Western. . . ." Trying to laugh?

Death came down from the Black hills till only his stolen eyes were left, like wounds in the universe.

They disappeared.

When the drugs revived me from my hypnoid trance, I was still plugged to CUFL, along with the eleven other members of my shift, the other slaves of the Clective Unctious.

To the medicos bending over me, I said, "I died again."

They nodded. They had been watching the monitor screens.

"Take it easy," one of them said. As my eyes pulled into focus, I saw it was Wace.

I was used to instructions. I worked at taking it easy. I was still in the front line, where individuality fought with the old nameless tribal consciousness. "I died again," I groaned.

"Relax, Jerry," Wace said. "It was just a hypnoid dream like you always get."

"But I died again. Why do I always have to die?"

Tommy Wace. His first name was Tommy. Data got mislaid.

Distantly, he tried to administer comfort and express compassion on his dried-up face. "Dreams are mythologies, part-individual, part-universal. Both de-programming dreams and prognostic-type dreams are natural functions of the self-regulating psychic system. There's nothing unnatural about dreaming of dying."

"But I died again. . . . And I was split into two people. . . ."

"The perfect defense in a split world. A form of adaptation."

You could never convey personal agony to these people, although they had watched it all on the monitors. Wearily, I passed a hand over my face. My chin felt like cactus.

"So much self-hatred, Tommy. . . . Where does it all come from?"

"Johnnie. At least you're working it out of your system. Now, here's something to drink."

I sat up. "CUFL will have to close down, Johnnie," I said. I hardly knew what I said. I was back in the real world, in the abrasive lunar laboratory under Plato—and sudddenly I saw that I could distinguish true from false.

For years and years—*I'd been mistaken!*

I had been externalizing my self-hatred. The dream showed me that I feared to become whole again in case becoming whole destroyed me.

Gasping, I pushed Wace's drink aside. I was seeing visions. The White World had shed religion. Shed religion, you shed other hope-structures; family life disintegrates. You are launched to the greater structure of science. That was the Westciv way. We had made an ugly start but we were going ahead. There was no going back. The rest of the world had to follow. No—had to be led. Not shunned, but bullied. Led. Revelation!

Part of our soft predicament is that we can never entirely grasp what the predicament is.

"Johnnie, I don't always have to die," I said. "It's my mistake, our mistake!" I found I was weeping and couldn't stop. Something was dissolving. "The Black-and-White are one, not two! We are fighting ourselves. I was fighting myself. Plug me back in again!"

"End of shift," Wace said, advancing the drink again.

"You've done more than your stint. Let's get you into Psych Lab for a checkup and then you're due for leave back on Earth."

"But do you see—" I gave up and accepted his beastly drink.

Natalie, Ri . . . I too have my troubled dreams, little darling. . . .

My bed is wetted and my mattress soaked with blood.

John Wace got one of the nurses to help me to my feet. Once I was moving, I could get to Psych Lab under my own power.

"You're doing fine, Jerry!" Wace called. "Next time you're back on Luna, I'll have Jupiter pinpointed for you!"

Doing fine!—I'd only just had all my strongest and most emotionally-held opinions switched through one hundred and eighty degrees!

In the Psych Lab, I was so full of tension that I couldn't let them talk. "You know what it's like, moving indistinguishably from hypnoid to dream state— like sinking down through layers of cloud. I began by reliving my last rest period with Natalie and Ri. It all came back true and sweet, without distortion, from the reservoirs of memory! Distortion only set in when I recollected landing in Sicily. What happened in reality was that Ted Greaves and I let his son back through frontier with the other White anarchists. I found the revolver he was trying to smuggle in—he had tucked it into his boot-top.

"That revolver was the symbol that triggered my nightmare. Our lives revolve through different aspects like the phases of the Moon. I identified entirely with Pete. And at his age, I too was a revolutionary, I too wanted to change the world, I too would have wished to kill my present self!"

"At Pete Greaves's age, you were fighting *for* Westciv, not against it, Wharton," one of the psychiatrists reminded me.

"Yes," I said. "I was in Asia, and handy with a gun.

I carved up a whole gang of Thirdies. That was about the time when the Russians threw in their lot with us." I didn't want to go on. I could see it all clearly. They didn't need a true confession.

"The guilt you felt in Asia was natural enough," the psychiatrist said. "To suppress it was equally natural—suppressed guilt causes most of the mental and physical sickness in the country. Since then, it has gone stale and turned to hate."

"I'll try to be a good boy in the future," I said, smiling and mock-meek. At the time, the ramifications of my remark were not apparent to me, as they were to the psychiatrist.

"You've graduated, Wharton," he said. "You're due a vacation on Earth right now."

VII. CLECTIVE

The globe, in its endless revolution, was carrying us into shade. In the courtyard, the line of the sun was high up our wall. Natalie had set a mosquito-coil burning; its fragrance came to us where we sat at the table with our beers. We bought the mosquito-coils in the local village store; they were smuggled in from the Third World, and had "Made in Cairo" stamped on the packet.

Ri was busy at one end of the courtyard with a couple of earthenware pots. She played quietly, aware that it was after her bedtime. Ted Greaves and Pete sat with us, drinking beer and smoking. Pete had not spoken a word since they arrived. At that time I could make no contact with him. Did not care to. The ice flows were still melting and smashing.

As Natalie brought out another jar and set it on the rough wood table, Greaves told her, "We're going to have a hero on our hands if your brother flies over to see you when he gets back from Jupiter. Do you think he'll show up here?"

"Sure to! Ian hates Eastern Seaboard as much as most people."

"Sounds like he found Jupiter as crowded as Eastern Seaboard!"

"We'll have the Clective Unctious working by the time he arrives," I said.

"I thought you were predicting it would close down?" Greaves said.

"That was when it was choked with hate."

"You're joking! How do you choke a machine with hate?"

"Input equals output. CUFL is a reactive store—you feed in hate, so you get out hate."

"Same applies to human beings and human groups," Pete Greaves broke in, rubbing his thumbnail along the grain of the table.

I looked at him. I couldn't feel sweet about him. He was right in what he said but I couldn't agree with him. He had killed me—though it was me masquerading as him—though it had been a hypnoid illusion.

I forced myself to say, "It's a paradox how a man can hate people he doesn't know and hasn't even seen. You can easily hate people you know—people like yourself."

Pete made no answer and wouldn't look up.

"It would be a tragedy if we started hating these creatures on Jupiter just because they are there."

I said it challengingly, but he merely shrugged. Natalie sipped her beer and watched me.

I asked him, "Do you think some of your wild friends from over the frontier would come along and feed their archetypes into CUFL? Think they could stand the pace and the journey?"

Both he and his father stared at me as if they had been struck.

Before the kid spoke, I knew I had got through to him. He would not have to go quietly schizoid. He would talk to Natalie and me eventually, and we would hear of his travels at firsthand. Just a few defensive layers had to come down first. Mine and his.

"You have to be joking!" he said.

Suddenly, I laughed. Everyone thought I was joking. Depending on your definition of a joke, I felt I had at last ceased joking after many a year. I turned suddenly from the table, to hide a burning of my eyes.

Taking Natalie by the arm, I said, "Come on, we must get Ri to bed. She thinks we've forgotten about her."

As we walked down the path, Natalie said, "Was your suggestion serious?"

"I think I can work it. I'll speak to Wace. Things have to change. CUFL is unbalanced." The finches fluttered in their cages. The line of sun was over the wall now. All was shadow among our orange trees, and the first bat was flying. I loomed over Ri before she noticed me. Startled, she stared up at me and burst into tears. Many things had to change.

I picked her up in my arms and kissed her cheeks.

Many things had to change. The human condition remained enduringly the same, but many things had to change.

Even the long nights on Earth were only local manifestations of the sun's eternal daylight. Even the different generations of man had archetypes in common, their slow writhings not merely inconsequential movement but ponderous and deliberate gesture.

So I carried her into the dim house to sleep.

HEARTSTOP

by George Alec Effinger

In the nearby towns, places like Indian Bog and Leeper, they still talk about "the Gremmage murders." In the town of Gremmage itself, though, they don't talk about them at all. Those murders happened a long time ago, and there are always new people and new things happening in Gremmage.

This is despite the fact that Gremmage has to be one of the most neglectable places in all of Pennsylvania, if not the country. There isn't even a good-sized shopping center to drive around in. When a man wants to teach his daughter how to park her Mustang, he has to take her five, ten miles away just to find the right kind of yellow lines. And that's today. It was even worse fifteen years ago.

Now there's an interstate highway that skirts the town; there's an exit, but it's diabolically placed, about thirty yards on the far side of an overpass, so you can't see it coming. Between the overpass and the exit there is a small green sign that says *Gremmage*, with an arrow. Of course, at interstate speeds, you have maybe a squint and a half from the time you leave the shade of the overpass until you're to the sign. If you read the thing, before you finish the two syllables and pointer you've passed the exit. And there's a bush growing up in front of the green sign, and it doesn't look like the highway people are going to do anything about trimming it. So either you know where you're going and look for the exit, or you get off completely by accident and stupidity. In either case, you deserve what you get.

But, again, that's *today*. Fifteen years ago, a traveler didn't even have that obscure green sign. A weary salesman could only stop along the narrow blacktop road and try to get information from a farmer. "Yeah," the farmer would say, "there's a town a ways from here, maybe seven or eight miles. I can never remember the name of it, though. You just go on here 'til you come to it." The farmer would pause, relishing the bewildered, unhappy look on the salesman's face. "You'll recognize the town," the farmer would say slowly. "There's a cannon on the square. These here farms don't have no cannons, nohow." The farmer wouldn't grin until the salesman had climbed back into his dusty car and driven off toward Gremmage.

At least the information was accurate. Fifteen years ago, Gremmage *was* about seven or eight miles from a lot of farms. And the salesman wouldn't have any trouble at all, once he located the town. Fifteen years ago, before the interstate, there weren't any motels, no Holidays Inn, no Qualities Court, no Howards Johnson. So the poor salesman would be little cheered by the sight of the meager row of shops along Ridge Street. Particularly if it was after six o'clock (three o'clock on Saturdays); then there wouldn't be a single store open, where he could even find out about hotel rooms. Except the diner, of course. Mrs. Perkins' diner was pretty dependable. So that's where the salesman ended up, out of desperation.

There was a slight haze of burnt grease in the diner, but otherwise it seemed like a pleasant enough place. Mrs. Perkins didn't have the time to bother much with decorations. The result was an establishment that was plain without being sterile. The atmosphere was purely hick town (no, not rural. Really and truly *hick*). The salesman, after too many hours on the road, found it nearly refreshing. Almost.

"Can I take your order, sir?" asked the waitress.

The salesman looked up tiredly. The girl was young, high school age, probably working part-time in the diner to earn money for movie magazines.

"Can I see a menu?" asked the salesman. The girl nodded and reached past the salesman to pull the menu from its place behind the napkin container. There was nothing listed on it that could set Mrs. Perkins' diner apart from any of several thousand like it anywhere in America. That was one of its charms. It was almost a reflex action for the salesman to order the baked meat loaf, mashed potatoes, green beans, and coffee. He always studied the menu, and he always ordered the same thing. His wife, back home in Stroudsburg, always ordered eggplant Parmesan. His son always ordered cheeseburgers. But there was some kind of exotic, wistful hope that someday someone would come up with something tremendously exciting on his menu. The salesman always wondered, if that were ever to happen, whether or not he'd order it.

Some minutes later, the waitress brought the meat loaf dinner. The salesman muttered a thank you. The waitress did not go away. She stood by his booth; the salesman wondered what he had done wrong. "You're new in town, aren't you?" she asked.

He just looked at her. He didn't say anything.

"The reason I say that, I know just about everybody in Gremmage," she said. "It's not that big of a town."

"No," said the salesman, chewing his food slowly, "no, it's not."

"Are you from New York?" she asked.

"Stroudsburg."

"Oh." She fidgeted nervously. The salesman was sure that she was going to ask him for something. She was pretty enough, he guessed, in a way that would be immature whatever her age. Her hair was a dull carrot color, tied into two short braids. Her face was so lacking in memorable features as to be indescribable. She spoke in a low, husky voice which the salesman found vaguely unpleasant. "Do you have business here in Gremmage?" she asked.

"No, none at all. I was just seeing the sights." The girl stared for a moment, then laughed. The salesman smiled. "I was wondering, though," he said, "if there was a hotel around here. I don't feel much like driving any more tonight."

"No," said the waitress. "No hotels. But if you go over to Aunt Rozji's, she'll probably have a guest room vacant. She usually does."

"Is she your aunt?"

The waitress shook her head. "We all call her that. She's old enough to be *anybody's* aunt."

"All right," said the salesman, "I'll try that. Can you give me directions? Maybe I can drop you somewhere."

"No, that's okay," said the girl. "Thank you. I don't get off here for a while yet. But if you want to wait a few minutes, Old Man Durfee comes in every night about now. He could take you over there. Aunt Rozji doesn't like to rent her rooms to just anyone, you see. But if Old Man Durfee took you over there, and if you told her that I sent you, why, I guess it would be all right."

"Old Man Durfee, huh?"

"Yes," said the waitress. "Why don't you have a piece of pie while you're waiting?"

"A piece of pie, then," said the salesman, sighing. "While I'm waiting for Old Man Durfee. Who'll take me to Aunt Rozji. This is a very folksy town you have here."

The waitress smiled. "Thank you. It's not very big, though."

"No," he muttered, "it's not very big." She went back behind the counter and brought him a piece of apple pie and some more coffee.

"Do you want your check now, Mr., uh, Mr.—"

"Newby," said the salesman. "My name's Newby."

"Well," said the waitress, "my name's Lauren. Do you want anything else?"

"Like Bacall, right?" asked Newby.

"Sort of," she said. "Only my last name's Kromberger." She put the check down by his plate and went away again, this time disappearing into the kitchen. Newby ate his dessert slowly, wondering if he could leave the diner and drive off without looking like a fool. He had gone through a complex set of arrangements with the girl; he would be too embarrassed now to tell her just to forget the whole thing. He sneered at his own idiocy. He would never see Lauren Kromberger again. What possible difference could it make, what she thought of him? He ought to pay his check and leave without a word. But, truthfully, he didn't feel like driving any more. He might as well wait for this Old Man Durfee. Anyway, Newby was getting curious about him.

The salesman had finished his pie and was just taking the last lukewarm gulp of coffee when the door swung open. An incredibly broken-down man came into the diner. Newby had no doubt this was Old Man Durfee, he who would be Newby's guide through the shaded, crickety roads of Gremmage to the mysterious rooming house of Aunt Rozji. If the old man were any indication, Newby thought, maybe the weary traveler would be better advised to toss a brick through a plate-glass window and accept a night's lodging from the county.

Old Man Durfee was probably not all that old. To Newby, he seemed to be in his early fifties. His hair was long, hanging in greasy curls behind his ears and over his collar. The man's face was lined deeply, and the growth of stubble and the cracked, swollen lips gave him an appearance which was at the same time both repellent and pitiable. His eyes were nearly closed by the heavy pouches which limited them, and he gazed at Newby briefly through red, watery slits. He wore a faded plaid shirt and a pair of ancient corduroy trousers, which were much too short for him. He had no socks, and his sharp, filthy ankles hung between the torn cuffs of the pants and his decaying slippers. He carried a dirty blue towel. He looked at Newby again and mumbled something; then he took a seat at the counter. After a few seconds he stood and shuffled slowly to one of the booths. Newby watched him without emotion. Old Man Durfee sat in the booth, then rose one more time and moved around to the opposite seat.

"You know," said Newby, "if you sit in that other booth behind you, and I go to the counter, and you come here, we'll have mate in three moves."

"I couldn't find the right place," said Old Man Durfee.

"A lot of us have that trouble," said Newby.

"I have a regular place. I come in every night, and sit in the same place. Sometimes I forget which it is, though."

"Well, good night," said Newby, getting up to go. Just then, Lauren the waitress returned.

"Do you play chess?" she asked. "I heard you speaking just now."

"Yeah," said Newby. "I carry a little magnetic board with me when I travel. There's nothing else to do." For some reason, Lauren giggled. Newby shrugged and headed for the door. "I'd like to play," said Old Man Durfee. Newby stopped suddenly, halfway to the door. The drunk's voice had been loud, clear, and authoritative. "I used to be pretty good."

"I have to go," said Newby, not turning around.

"You had time for the pie," said Lauren. "You can stay for a game. Old Man Durfee just lives to play chess. I wish *I* knew how. Besides, he's going to take you over to Aunt Rozji's, isn't he?"

The salesman turned around and went back to his booth. "Okay," he said. "I suppose the fates are conspiring against me."

Lauren frowned slightly. "You don't have to, if you don't want to," she said. "I just think it would be nice."

"Daviolsokoff *vs*. Drean," said Old Man Durfee. "Copenhagen, 1926. Remember the second game? The Forgotten Rook. A real masterpiece."

"Were you there?" asked Newby.

Old Man Durfee stared for a moment, his red eyes narrowing even more. He coughed, and the wet, thick sound disgusted Newby. "No," said the drunk. "I read about it. I just read about it, that's all."

"What difference does it make?" asked Lauren.

"I just want to know what I'm up against," said Newby. "I've heard about chess hustlers before, you know. I know how you small town types are always gunning for people like me."

"We don't get many people like you," said Old Man Durfee.

"This town isn't so big," said Lauren.

"No, it's not," said Newby. "I wish it was. Then we could all go bowling or something."

"They have bowling hustlers, too," said Lauren. The salesman just nodded.

"I just like to read about chess," said Old Man Durfee. "I don't get to play very often. I read, though. I've read just about every word on chess there is in town."

"It's not a very big town," said Newby sarcastically.

"No, it's not," said Lauren.

There was an uncomfortable silence. Newby toyed with the dishes and objects on the table top. He was very aware of a low mechanical humming from the kitchen, and of a flickering tube in the fluorescent lights. "Well," he thought, "I'll just get up, say goodbye, and duck out. This is infantile. It's turning into a scene from *Marty*, for Pete's sake." He didn't leave, though. A minute later, the door of the diner opened again, and an old woman came in.

"Aunt Rozji!" cried Lauren. "What an incredible coincidence!"

Newby just snorted and turned to observe the woman. She was very old. Her steps were tiny and so obviously painful that Newby wondered why she didn't spend her days on a cranked-up hospital bed. She was thin, gaunt; cracked leather shrunken on a frame of spun glass; mere purposeless tufts of white hair; erratic motions so bizarre that gestures could not be distinguished from involuntary spasms; a complex bed of wrinkles and lines that led the observer's eye away from hers—Newby knew that he might never learn the color of her irises; a black dress that drooped between knee and ankle, decorated with pink and green floral specks, and a pair of huge, square, black shoes. She moved slowly, bent over, squeezed closer to the moist earth every hour. She wouldn't die for a while, though; like a battered wreck of a car, she wouldn't be worth trading in. While she could perform the slightest function in the world, she would be kept around.

"We were just talking about you, dear," said Old Man Durfee, rising from the booth and helping her to take a seat.

"Were you?" she said. Her voice was cracked, as dry as the old drunk's was saturated. She spoke in a heavy European accent, some strange Slavic influence. "I was thinking about you, too. I came down."

"She doesn't come in very often," said Lauren to Newby. "She's a little frail to be making the walk from her house."

"I'm amazed that she came at all," said Newby.

"And surprised that she arrived just as we finished speaking of her, eh?" said Old Man Durfee. The drunk didn't wait for Newby's reaction. He turned back to Aunt Rozji. "This young man plays chess, dear."

"Chess?" said Aunt Rozji, turning to peer around the corner of her booth. "You play chess? Then you came to the right place. Young Durfee plays chess. Did he tell you?"

"Yes," said Newby, sighing, realizing that the final nail had been driven in place, the last brick cemented to wall him up for the night in Gremmage.

"He needs a place to stay tonight," said Lauren. "We've already set up a game for him with Old Man Durfee, but he has to be back on the road in the morning. I thought maybe you could rent him a guest room for the night."

"Rent?" said Aunt Rozji. "*Shueblik*, if he wants to play Young Durfee, I won't ask him to pay."

"That's very kind," said Newby. "But I'd be happy to."

"No, no, no," said Aunt Rozji. "You give me happiness by playing Young Durfee. It has been such a long time."

"I'm glad I drove through, then," said the salesman. "It sounds like you haven't had a chess-playing stranger in quite a while."

"That's true," said Lauren. "But the other travelers find something else to do."

"Gremmage has a lot to offer," said Old Man Durfee.

"For such a small town," said Lauren.

"No," said Aunt Rozji, "it's not a very big town. But it tailors itself, you will find. It fills your needs. Tonight, it is chess. Young Lauren, find us the board."

The waitress bent down behind the counter for a few seconds. Newby sipped some of the stale water from the glass by his dishes. He heard a rattling of silverware and the heavy sliding of bottles. He wondered what sort of an opponent Old Man Durfee would be. He didn't especially care.

"I found it!" said Lauren. She waved a flimsy cardboard chessboard, with squares colored black and orange. It had been a long time since Newby had seen a chessboard with orange squares.

"The pieces?" asked Aunt Rozji.

"They're here, too," said Lauren. She held up a grease-stained paper sack.

"Fine," said Old Man Durfee.

"Fine," said Newby. "Should you go get Mrs. Perkins? Maybe she'll want to watch this battle of the century."

"No," said Lauren. "She has to get ready for breakfast in the morning. She's a busy little bee."

"I wonder what she does for fun around here," said Newby idly.

"She takes mambo lessons," said the waitress. "Over at the Y." Newby winced.

"Well, then," said Old Man Durfee, as Lauren opened the cheap board on the counter and everyone else took seats, "I think you should have white."

"Thank you," said Newby.

"Not at all," said the drunk. "I do have the home court advantage, so to speak."

"We're all rooting for Young Durfee," said Aunt Rozji. "It's nothing against you, you understand."

"Sure," said Newby. "He's the hometown boy." Old Man Durfee snickered.

The two men wordlessly arranged their pieces. Newby just wanted to get the game over with as quickly as possible, drive Aunt Rozji back to her house, get a good night's sleep, and flee the entire town at first light. This was not his idea of the most entertaining way of spending an evening.

"Your move?" asked Old Man Durfee.

Newby exhaled heavily, reached out, and moved his pawn to Queen Four.

"Ah, the Queen's Gambit, an excellent choice," said the drunk. "A conservative opening. The king-side openings lead to more spectacular games. You've taken the opportunity of seizing the center of the board, a good strategic idea, backing up your threat with immediate protection from your queen. You are trying to tempt me into surrendering a defensive position in exchange for the pawn which you shall move to Queen's Bishop Four. Shall I take it? Let us see!" The old man moved his own pawn to Queen Four, and smiled at Newby.

"Playing with Old Man Durfee is fun," said Lauren. "He knows so much about the game. I can learn a lot just from watching."

Newby only nodded. The drunk was a little strange; the salesman wondered just how much about chess Old Man Durfee really knew. Newby decided to move off the usual opening routines. He posted his knight at King's Bishop Three.

"Wonderful, wonderful," cried Old Man Durfee. "You see, Aunt Rozji, you see, Miss Kromberger, how his knight defends the original pawn move, while itself strains forward to the attack. A most practical move, and one I entirely expected. The pawn allurement I spoke of will no doubt have to be postponed through this development. I can find no fault with Mr. Newby's play. I shall make it myself." Old Man Durfee moved his knight to King's Bishop Three.

"An axis of symmetry forms through the middle of the board," whispered Lauren.

"Are you afraid, Young Durfee?" asked Aunt Rozji. "Is that why you mimic each of your opponent's moves? That cannot be wise. Do not forget that he has the advantage of the first play."

"Then watch," said Old Man Durfee, laughing gently.

"For Pete's sake," thought Newby. Without hesitation, he moved a pawn to King Three.

"Good God, man!" cried the drunk. "What have you done?"

"I've moved," said Newby.

"Yes," said Old Man Durfee, "but are you sure?"

"Is something wrong?" asked Lauren.

"Terribly," said the drunk. "Our friend has blundered badly. He has as good as lost the game, here on the third move."

"Perhaps you should allow him to retract his move," said Aunt Rozji mildly.

"All right, then," said Old Man Durfee.

Newby smiled. "Can I have a Coke?" he asked. Lauren nodded and went to fetch it. "My move will stand," he said. The drunk shrugged.

"I can see that Mr. Newby has bottled up one of his bishops," said Aunt Rozji. "That can't be a good idea."

"No, it isn't," said Old Man Durfee. "Besides, he has moved a pawn instead of developing a piece. That will hurt him later on." He moved his own pawn to King Three.

"Now, why in heaven's name did you do that, too?" asked Lauren.

The drunk made a funny expression. "Charity," he said. Aunt Rozji laughed.

Newby still said nothing. He was making the preparatory moves of the Colle system, and apparently the drunk didn't recognize them. Old Man Durfee would be in for a surprise. Newby quickly made his next play, bishop to Queen Three.

"All right, I suppose," said Old Man Durfee. "Now watch. I move a pawn to Queen's Bishop Four. See how it opens up my pieces? That's very important. Your men are all hemmed in."

"What did you say your name was?" asked Aunt Rozji.

"Newby," said the salesman.

"Where did you say you were from?"

"Stroudsburg." Newby moved a pawn to Queen's Bishop Three.

Old Man Durfee jumped to his feet and began wildly pacing about the diner. Newby wondered how such a dissipated, wornout person as had entered the place could have become so animated. "I give up!" shouted the drunk. "I try to help him a little. I don't take advantage of his stupidity. But does he learn? No. Does he do anything about the idiocy of his position? No. All right, Newby. You asked for it." Old Man Durfee sat down again. He considered the board for a minute, then made his play, the other knight to Bishop Three.

"Oho," said Lauren. "Things are beginning to pile up there in the middle."

"Ah, Young Newby," said Aunt Rozji, "that lead pawn of yours is attracting a lot of attention."

"And it's not even such a big piece," said Lauren.

"No," said Newby, "no, it's not." He took his queen's knight and put it in front of his queen, at Queen Two.

"That's stupid," said Aunt Rozji. "I hope you don't mind me speaking frankly. You are not a fit opponent."

"I won't say anything," said Old Man Durfee. Newby smiled coldly. The drunk played his bishop to King Two.

"I castle king-side," said Newby.

"It doesn't take much skill to do that," said Old Man Durfee scornfully. "Observe how easily I remove your one threatening piece." He moved his pawn at Bishop Four ahead one square, attacking Newby's bishop.

"I retreat," said Newby. He moved the bishop back a square, until it stood in front of the other, unmoved bishop.

"When is somebody going to kill another piece?" asked Lauren.

"Wait," said Aunt Rozji. "All in good time."

"Pawn to Queen's Knight Four," said the drunk. "Notice now how I open up the bishop, and threaten with an advance of my queen-side pawns."

"I see," said Newby. He moved the pawn at King Three ahead to King Four. He swung around on the stool. This was the key move in the old system he was playing. Now, at last, Old Man Durfee must be seeing the trouble he was in. All the restrained force of the white position was now set loose. It was a simple, deceptive line of play, and one very familiar to experts in the 1920s and '30s. But it had lost favor since then; Newby had guessed correctly that Old Man Durfee lacked the sophistication to understand this line of attack.

"Ah, well," said the drunk. He gazed up at Newby, his eyes suddenly bleary again, his voice thick and barely intelligible. "I don' know, now. Lemme see."

"Something wrong, Young Durfee?" asked Aunt Rozji.

"I don' know, now." The drunk shook out his filthy blue towel and folded it up again.

"You can't let that pawn move forward again," said Lauren. "It would chase your knight away, cost you a turn, and ruin your center position."

"You don't have much choice," said Aunt Rozji.

"Right, right, I know," said Old Man Durfee. "Okay, you bastard, I'll take the pawn. I still don't see what it'll get you." He took the pawn with the queen's pawn.

"Ah," said Lauren, sighing, "first blood!"

Newby recaptured the pawn with the knight from Queen Two. At once, Newby's pieces commanded the center of the board. His position, previously cramped and unpromising, was now obviously superior to black's.

"I castle," said Old Man Durfee.

"Are you worried now?" asked Lauren.

"*Everybody* castles," said the drunk with some irritation.

"Don't worry, Young Durfee, we won't abandon you," said Aunt Rozji.

"Queen to King Two," said Newby.

"Don't rush," said Old Man Durfee. "We have all night." The drunk studied the board. "All right, now. Cautiously. You have me, if I let you get away with it. I see your plan. Is it not as follows: your knight takes mine, I take back with my bishop, then you move your queen forward to King Four? You'll checkmate me on the next move, taking my rook pawn with your queen. If I rush to do something about that threat, you win the isolated knight on the other side of the board. That's what you're after, isn't it? I protect that knight, ruining your scheme. I move bishop to Knight Two."

"Well done, Young Durfee!"

"We're with you," said Lauren.

"A partisan crowd," said Newby.

"We have to be," said Aunt Rozji.

"There's little enough else to do," said Lauren.

"All right," said Newby, "the knight at Bishop Three up to Knight Five."

"I have to save the pawn," said Old Man Durfee, looking around helplessly. He moved the threatened pawn forward to King's Rook Three.

"We understand," said Aunt Rozji.

"It's a cardinal rule, never to move those protective pawns in front of your king, unless you have to," said Lauren. "But, as you say, you'll lose it otherwise: knight takes knight, check. Bishop takes knight. Knight takes pawn. And you're also attacking that offensive knight, so I suppose it's the only move you have."

"How have you allowed yourself to get into this untenable defensive position?" asked Aunt Rozji.

"Knight takes knight," said Newby. "Check."

"He proceeds anyway," said Lauren, astounded.

"As do I," said Old Man Durfee. "Bishop takes knight."

"Queen to King Four," said Newby.

"It's as you foresaw," said Lauren. "If he slides his queen down, he'll have you mated on the next move. You saw it coming. Why didn't you plan a better defense?"

"My hands were tied," said Old Man Durfee. "I can only create an escape route." He moved the knight pawn to Knight Three.

"You're stalling," said Lauren.

"I think that's enough for tonight, don't you?" asked Aunt Rozji. Newby realized that for some time, her words had been spoken without a trace of accent. Now, though, she sounded like a recent immigrant from Czechoslovakia.

"If you say so," said Old Man Durfee.

"Why don't we play on?" asked Newby. "The end can't be too far away."

Lauren looked irritated. "I think we need an official referee here," she said. "How about Aunt Rozji?"

"She's not the most impartial judge I could ask for," said Newby.

"It's okay with me," said Old Man Durfee.

"I'll bet," said Newby. "All right. Aunt Rozji, you can be referee."

The old woman smiled, a narrow, quivering expression. "Good, good. We stop, then. Tomorrow morning, we finish."

"We finish fast," said Newby. "I have to be on the road early."

"Nine o'clock, here?" said Aunt Rozji. Lauren, Newby, and Old Man Durfee nodded.

"Can I drive you anywhere?" asked Newby.

"No," said Lauren. "My daddy comes to meet me."

"I'll find my own way," said Old Man Durfee. "Do you have maybe a quarter, though? I need another quarter for a pint of Thunderbird."

"Here," said Newby, giving the old drunk the money. Newby shook his head as Old Man Durfee shuffled out of the diner. The salesman took Aunt Rozji's arm and led her out to his car. The old woman said little as they drove to her house. The narrow, red brick-paved streets were dark; slender wells of light beamed down from streetlamps, but otherwise there was only the occasional floating yellow from a porch light or a distant pair of rat eyes on the back end of a car. Trees grew dense and tall. The air was warm and moist, and pleasant-smelling. Newby enjoyed the low thrumming sound of the tires on the street.

"Pull up here," said Aunt Rozji at last. "I suppose you'll want to get right to sleep."

"Yes, I guess so. I have a little work to do first, but I can look forward to another day of driving tomorrow."

"After your tournament is completed, of course."

Newby pulled out the ignition key and shrugged. "Oh, yeah. Sure," he said. They went slowly up the flagstone walk to the huge, dim house. The front door was open. They went inside; the salesman was given an impression of old furnishings, polished dark wood paneling, hundreds of china figurines, fat chairs and sofas, final boredom. He carried his suitcase up the stairway, at the top of which Aunt Rozji said he'd find his room and the bathroom. She was too old to climb the steps herself, and she apologized. Newby called down that the room was fine, said good night, and stretched out on the bed for a few minutes' rest. He was asleep instantly.

Newby dozed fitfully; he had planned to sort out the brightly colored cloth samples in his case before he went to sleep. The case rested at the foot of the bed. The salesman's legs were bent to avoid the samples which were stacked on the folded comforter, with the suitcase tight behind his knees. He was cramped and uncomfortable, but he had not meant to fall asleep. He had only removed his shirt and tie; he had not even slipped out of his shoes.

After a few minutes he began to dream. They were strange visions, dreams of a kind he had never had before. He was used to sleeping in a different bed every night, awakening in odd, unknown towns that he might never see again. It wasn't that he was isolated and alone that caused his dreams. It was something else.

For a time he dreamed of shapes, just meaningless shapes. Great, looming blocks, towering cylinders, stacks of rectangular solids in unattractive, olive greens and dark browns. Then the shapes began to be *located*, to find a setting. Spaces formed among them and remained constant. The shapes were on a large plain. The shapes became buildings, trees, parked automobiles. It was still dark, midnight, no light but the dream light of Newby's tired imagination.

Newby became part of his dream. Before, he had only viewed the nightmarish setting. Now he himself walked through it. The ominous shapes-become-buildings were vast, ancient houses, lined one after the other along a narrow, brick-paved street. Each house was set well back from the sidewalk. The front doors sparkled with crystal, rainbow flickers, gleams reflected from an unreal source. The windows on the first floor were invariably dark, shaded, inviolable. Windows on the second story were drawn up tight, also, but lamps were lit behind the drapes. Shadows whipped along the vertical folds of the curtains, as furtive strangers rushed about the interior rooms on secret errands. Newby walked past each house, examining every one as he strolled, feeling a peculiar sense of uneasiness. The insects chorused like massed rattlesnakes. A pair of nighthawks swooped the star-glittered sky. Newby was frightened by the moon.

"Hi." Immediately, with a shock of dream intensity, the scene became particular, real, a little more tangible and a little less lonely. The salesman looked down.

He saw a young girl, perhaps ten or eleven years old. She was wearing a white blouse, a plaid blazer from a parochial school, and a gray felt skirt with rustling crinolines beneath. There was a pink poodle cut out and fixed to the skirt. "Hi," she said again.

"Hello," said Newby.

"You know why I'm out so late?" she asked.

"No. Of course not."

"My name is Theresa Muldower."

"Why are you out so late," asked Newby.

"Because of the Russians." She looked up at Newby with a curious expression. "I hate the Russians, don't you?"

"Sure," said Newby.

"I hate the Russians so much, the only thing in the whole world I hate more is polio."

"Me too."

"My daddy's finishing up the fallout shelter tonight. We're going to have a party in it. Only he thought he'd have it done by now. I'm usually sent to bed at nine or ten. Ten on Fridays and Saturdays. But we're all waiting for him to finish the fallout shelter. Mom says she can just see how the Russians are going to H-bomb us all tonight, and we won't get to have our party. Daddy says it's okay with him, as long as the fallout shelter's finished. Do you have a fallout shelter?"

"Not yet," said Newby.

"You don't have much time," said Theresa. "You ought to get one. Before the Russians H-bomb us."

"If I built a fallout shelter," said Newby, "and if the Russians H-bombed us, I'd be all alone in there and I'd get polio."

"From a rusty nail."

"Yes," said Newby. "From a rusty nail."

They walked past some more houses. After a while a voice somewhere ahead of them called Theresa's name. "I have to go," she said.

"Is that your parents?"

"No," she said. "I don't know who it is." Newby watched her uninterestedly, as she skipped away ahead of him. Somewhere down the block, in a black tangle of shadows, he saw someone gesture to her. He stopped on the sidewalk and watched. The person held out its hand; Theresa took it. The street was lit by fire. Orange sparks first, then ribbons of flame spat outward from the girl's body. Newby didn't want to move, but in the dream he was suddenly right there, beside her, watching, saying nothing, doing nothing, watching Aunt Rozji and Old Man Durfee. The fiery light made gruesome, disgusting masks of their faces. They nodded silent greeting to him. Theresa looked wildly around her. She strained her arms toward Newby. The salesman could only observe. Fire spurted from her eyes and ears. Trickles of flame dribbled from her nostrils. She rolled on the ground in the pain of nightmares. When she tried to scream, only a fine gray ash came out of her mouth. She writhed. The flames from her eyes grew smaller. Her motions became convulsive, slowed, then stopped. Aunt Rozji and Old Man Durfee each took one of Newby's hands. The three stepped over the unmarked corpse of Theresa Muldower and walked along the cavernous street, beneath the arching trees, past the ramparts of houses.

"And you have come from the east?" said Aunt Rozji, in a hollow, distant voice.

"Yes," said Newby.

"Knowledge in the east," said Old Man Durfee.

"And you travel into the west?" said Aunt Rozji.

"Yes," said Newby.

"Death in the west," said Old Man Durfee.

"And you bring with you?" asked Aunt Rozji.

"Fear," said Old Man Durfee. "Pain. Desire for cleansing."

"Expiation," said Newby.

"There is no expiation short of death," said Old Man Durfee.

"And there is no death," said Aunt Rozji. "No death, no death, three times, as the figures of art, as the candles, the scepters, the chalked arribles, the incense, the passes of hand, the laden words, as all these are used up, death is forgotten. Without death, there is no redemption.''

"Without redemption," said Old Man Durfee, "there is fear."

"There is pain," said Aunt Rozji.

The two old people still held Newby's hands; with their free hands they touched his head. Throbbing agony grew in his temples. He could not breathe. His body began to sweat and shake. His chest was crippled with stabbing pains. His legs would not hold him. He fell. He awoke.

The suitcase had fallen on the floor; perhaps it was that noise that had roused Newby. Whatever it had been, he was grateful. He still felt his heart beating rapidly. His hands were moist with the dampness of terror. That child! He was afraid and repulsed to think that his own mind could invent such a hideous thing. He scooped up the cloth samples, intending to arrange them in their proper groups; instead, he quickly grew bored and shoved them all into the case. He undressed slowly, trying not to think about his nightmare. He went to the bathroom and brushed his teeth with the chlorophyll toothpaste his wife had bought. He remembered how much he hated to bring it with him. Everything in the world was being colored, scented, or flavored with chlorophyll these days. He didn't notice any difference. It was only an advertising fad. He hated to be conned by advertising. After his brief toilet, he returned to his room, pulled back the bed-spread, and went back to sleep. He had no more unusual dreams that night.

In the morning he was awakened by Aunt Rozji, calling up the stairs to him. "Good day, Young Newby," she said. "It is morning. Have you rested?"

"Yes," he said, rubbing his eyes regretfully. "More or less."

"Good, then," she said. "It is time to renew your combat."

"Oh, yes. I was trying to forget."

"That is very gracious of you," she said. "But do

not worry about besting our local champion. We are good sportsmen in Gremmage."

Newby dressed quickly and came downstairs with his suitcase. Aunt Rozji was ready to go. She told the salesman that breakfast could be taken at the diner. Together they went out to his car.

It wasn't there. From Aunt Rozji's porch, Newby could see the place along the tree lawn where he had left it. An empty space, now, between a black Studebaker and a red and white Dodge. He felt an anger growing, an ugly feeling, a sickness in his stomach. "My car's gone," he said through clenched teeth.

"Your car?" asked Aunt Rozji.

"It's gone, damn it."

"Are you sure you left it here?"

"You know damn well where I left it," he said. "You were with me."

"Perhaps someone took it by mistake," she said. Newby didn't answer. "Well, I suppose you ought to tell the police."

"You have police in this idiotic town?" he asked.

"Yes," she said. "Even towns as small as this sometimes have crime."

"So what do I do now?"

"You must walk with me to the diner. The police department won't be open for another forty-five minutes. We can have breakfast first. Perhaps the others will have something to suggest."

"What happens if you have an emergency after the police go home for the night?" asked Newby.

Aunt Rozji looked at him in surprise. "Why, we all chip in," she said. "We all work together. That is how we shall find your car." A while later they arrived at the diner on Ridge Street. Newby was out of breath, but the old woman seemed in good shape.

"Good morning," said Lauren cheerfully.

"Young Newby's car has been stolen," said Aunt Rozji.

"Stolen?" said Old Man Durfee, already studying

the final position of the chess game from the day before.

"You know," said Newby. "Unauthorized theft or something."

"I don't think I'm in as much difficulty as we believed last evening," said Old Man Durfee.

"That's certainly good news," said Lauren.

"I don't give a damn about that," said Newby. "I have work to do. I want my car."

"Sit down," said the waitress. "Have some coffee. Do you want a muffin? French toast?"

"Don't you have to go to school?" asked Newby.

"No," she said. "This isn't such a big town."

"It really isn't," said Old Man Durfee.

"Whose move is it?" asked Aunt Rozji. "I forget."

"Mine," said Old Man Durfee.

"No," said Newby, "I think it's mine. You moved that pawn to Knight Three."

"Yes," said Old Man Durfee, "you're right. I'm sorry. What's your move?"

"It's obvious," said Newby. "I'm going to call the cops and see if they've recovered my car. Then I'm going to leave this nuthouse as fast as I can."

"Can I move for you?" asked Lauren.

"You don't know how to play, remember?" said Newby. "Here. I'll take your king pawn with the knight. Now I'm attacking both your queen and the rook guarding your king."

"That's very true," said Old Man Durfee slowly.

" 'Don't be cruel, to a heart that's true,' " sang Lauren.

"Will you be quiet?" asked the drunk.

" 'Don't be cruel,' " she sang.

"All right," said Old Man Durfee, "before I take your knight, I wonder if you'd do something for me. I had these made up last night. Would you go through these two pages? It's sort of a little quiz. It won't take you very long. I think the results may surprise you. Maybe you ought to do it before you try talking with the police." The old man handed Newby two pages, covered with questions in blurry mimeograph ink.

"What is this?" asked the salesman.

"Here," said Lauren, "you can use my ballpoint."

Newby read the first multiple-choice question: *What is today's date?* The answers were *a) March 8, 1956; b) September 12, 1954; c) June 26, 1959; d) August 30, 1957.* Newby had some difficulty deciding which answer was appropriate. The trouble bothered him. He hesitated a few seconds, then checked *a*. The second question was: *What was yesterday's date?* The possibilities were *a) May 21, 1955; b) January 2, 1951; c) November 15, 1957; d) April 28, 1958.* More confused, he checked *c*. There were a few more questions in a similar mode, requiring him to decide what the date of a week from Friday would be, and so on. He did the best he could.

The second page asked questions of a more concrete nature. *Where are you? a) in a town in Colorado; b) in a suburb of Dallas; c) in a European nation that has not existed since the end of the First World War; d) in the garment district.* Newby checked *b*, hoping that it was the closest to the truth. He really wasn't certain. The next question asked him the same thing, and presented him with even more baffling choices. By the time he completed the two pages, he was very uncomfortable. He was beginning to feel a little unreal, a bit lightheaded, dreamlike.

"Do you feel like you've been pushed into a different world?" asked Lauren.

"Sort of," said Newby sadly. "What's going on?"

"You see," said Old Man Durfee with a kindly smile, "you really can't trust yourself any longer. You've lost a little of the real you. It's nothing important, but we thought you ought to know."

"It happens sometimes," said Aunt Rozji.

"You have to learn to relax," said Lauren. "Things that are important in a big town like Stroudsburg, just don't seem so vital here."

"This isn't such a big town," said Old Man Durfee.

"No," said Newby, "no, it's not."

"Now," said the drunk, "I suppose I have to take your other knight with the bishop pawn. I do so."

Newby glanced over the quiz sheets again. He wondered if he ought to change a few of his answers. *Who is President of the United States? a) Harry S. Truman; b) Everett Dirksen; c) Dwight David Eisenhower; d) John F. Kennedy.* He had originally checked Truman, but on second thought erased that and marked *c.* "I like Ike," he thought. "I really do." *Have the Russians orbited their first Sputnik yet?* That was *no. Have the quiz show scandals been exposed? No,* but interesting. Maybe it was *yes,* come to think about it. He decided to leave that question and come back to it. *What kind of a day was it?* Newby marked *A day like all days, filled with those events which alter and illuminate our time.*

"None of this makes any sense at all," he said.

"What difference does that make?" asked Aunt Rozji. "What has reality ever done for you?"

"Good morning, everybody," said a newcomer.

"Morning, Bob," said Lauren. The waitress turned to Newby. "This is Bob Latcher, the shoe repairman. Bob, this is Mr. Newby, a visitor to our town."

"Morning, Mr. Newby," said Latcher. "Sad to have you here today, of all days. Have you heard the news?"

"About Mr. Newby's car?" asked Old Man Durfee.

"No," said Latcher. "About that Muldower girl." Newby started, then struggled to catch his breath.

"Theresa?" asked Lauren. "What about her?"

"They found her near her house," said Latcher. "She was done in all peculiar. She was all burnt up from the inside. She looked fine on the outside, excepting that she was dead. But when they touched her, her body all collapsed, like a puffed-up popover. Just powdered into ashes."

"That's odd," said Lauren. Newby buried his head in his hands.

"Want breakfast, Bob?" asked the waitress.

"No," said Latcher, "I just came to in see if I could

find Larry Muldower. I wanted to tell him how sorry I was. About his daughter and all."

"He's probably in his new fallout shelter," said Newby in a strangled voice.

"Yeah, that's right," said Latcher. "Thanks." The man waved and left.

"Sad about the little girl, isn't it?" asked Old Man Durfee.

"It just goes to show you," said Aunt Rozji. "Some people just shouldn't go walking around late at night." She smiled at Newby.

" 'Like a puffed-up popover,' " said Lauren. "What a typically rural use of simile."

"Hick," said Newby, "not rural."

"I think we ought to try to make this chess match a little more interesting," said Aunt Rozji.

"I find it fascinating," said Newby.

"A little more interesting," said Old Man Durfee.

"Will you take a check?" asked Newby.

Aunt Rozji and the drunk laughed. "No," said the old woman, "I don't mean that way. The way I see it, Young Newby has mate in no more than seven moves. Now, don't look so glum, Young Durfee. We can't always emerge victorious. But I wonder if our handsome visitor would be interested in giving you another chance in this game. A sort of handicap."

"I don't think so," said Newby. "I just want to get going."

"If it's your car that you're so worried about," said Lauren, "you might as well take it easy. I suppose the police are going to be occupied all day with old Theresa Popover."

"Don't be cruel, Young Lauren," said Aunt Rozji.

"Are you going to play, or aren't you?" asked the drunk.

"He *has* to," said the old woman. Newby nodded. "Well, then. Here is what I say, in my capacity as omnipotent referee. From now on, every time you take an opponent's piece, your own piece that did the capturing will change to the type of the captured enemy. Including pawns. So if you take your opponent's queen with a pawn, you'll have two queens."

"That's ridiculous," said Newby. "You just can't change the rules of chess like that."

"*She* can," said Lauren. "You agreed to abide by her decisions."

"She's like the inscrutable forces of nature," said Old Man Durfee, evidently enjoying Newby's uneasiness.

The salesman shook his head, but said nothing more. He looked at the position of the chess pieces. Aunt Rozji was correct; as things stood, he could finish off Old Man Durfee in just a few more moves. But now the situation had been changed. In a legitimate game, the thing for him to do would be queen takes knight pawn, check. Newby chewed his lip. If he were to do that, under Aunt Rozji's arbitrary rule change, he would capture the pawn, but his queen would be demoted to that level. He would lose his most potent weapon. The entire strategy of his game would have to be altered. The thing to do, apparently, was work with the pawns, promoting them by successfully capturing higher-ranking enemy pieces. The more he looked at the board, the more confused he became. "All right," he said at last. "I don't even care any more."

"You ought to," said Lauren. "This is an important game."

"How is it important?" asked Newby.

"It's very symbolic," said Aunt Rozji.

"It's the forces of simple life here in rural America against the snares and wiles of corporate industry," said Old Man Durfee.

Newby stared at them. They smiled back. "Do I look like a shifty-eyed con man?"

"You *are* a salesman," said Aunt Rozji.

"You *are* from Stroudsburg," said Lauren.

"The big time," said Old Man Durfee.

Newby sighed. They were really out to get him. He laughed bitterly, and moved his queen bishop from its original square down to King's Rook Six, capturing the old drunk's pawn there.

"Why did you do that?" asked Lauren. "You lost your bishop, you know. It turned into a pawn, now."

"I know," said Newby. "Sometimes a pawn can be more useful than a piece. I'm going to beat you at your own game."

Aunt Rozji made a cackling sound. "I ought to warn you," she said, "I haven't decided yet whether I'll change the rule about normal pawn promotion. If you move that pawn ahead two squares, you may or may not get the queen you're after."

"I'll chance it," said Newby.

Old Man Durfee picked up the rook which guarded his castled king. "Here," he said. "This rook will stop you." He moved it forward a square, so that Newby's pawn couldn't advance without inviting capture.

Newby didn't hesitate. "I wasn't planning that at all," he said. He swept his queen down and captured the knight pawn. He turned the queen upside-down to indicate that it was now a pawn, standing on the square next to the bishop-turned-pawn of the previous move. Together the two pawns stared straight at the drunk's suddenly vulnerable king.

"The position isn't as bad as it looks," said Old Man Durfee.

"That's good," said Lauren. "It certainly looks bad."

"I've got this bishop tying him up," said the drunk.

Aunt Rozji stood up from her stool. "I think it's time we recessed for lunch."

"Lunch?" asked Newby. "It isn't even ten o'clock yet."

"Lunch," said the old woman. "I think Young Durfee could use the opportunity to study the game, and you might find it comforting to report the theft of your car. Perhaps the police have solved the untidy mystery of little Miss Popover's death. I think that I am in need of a nap, in any event. Young Lauren will stay here, guarding the game and making certain that no pieces are inadvertently moved."

"I surely will, Aunt Rozji," said the waitress.

Newby realized that argument was futile. He shrugged

and stood up. "What time should I come back?" he asked.

"Oh," said the old woman lazily, "perhaps three o'clock."

"She does like her naps," said Old Man Durfee.

The day was sunny and warm. Newby felt a shock of heat as he left the diner; rippling waves floated in the air above the black asphalt of Ridge Street. The temperature would get even higher by afternoon. Newby had no idea what to do for the next five hours. He supposed that he ought to walk into the center of town to the police department. After that, he could kill time browsing through the poor collection of stores. Get a haircut. Sit on the square and read magazines. Find the library. Maybe just get on a bus and leave.

The town was much like many others he had seen in the last four years, during which he had been a salesman for the Jennings Fabric Corporation. He knew without looking what sort of things would be in the windows of each shop: the faded cardboard signs of beautiful women with bright yellow poodle cuts in the beauty parlor, the brassy saxophones on stands in the display of the music store, the barbecue sets and the taped-up sign—*Tulip Sundae 35¢*—in the five and dime. It made him feel better, somehow. The odd assortment of people in the diner didn't seem to be typical. The impulse to run away grew; he could easily give up his car as lost, take the insurance money, buy another. The company would give him a week off without pay. His suitcase was in the diner, now, but he could tell them the samples had been in the trunk of the Packard. He might even be reimbursed for his personal things. "No," he thought, "I'm letting that dream spook me. I won't let myself be manipulated like this. I just have to settle down."

He strolled past the store windows, bored, still a little sleepy. He came to the police department, the last building before the square. He went up the granite steps and opened the door. There didn't seem to be anyone inside. He sat on a bench under an old framed photograph of Eisenhower, wearing his army uniform. Newby waited. A clock on one wall moved past ten-thirty. Then to eleven o'clock. Finally, a police officer appeared from the back of the building. He nodded to Newby.

"I want to report a stolen car," said the salesman.

"In a minute, buddy," said the policeman. "We have a real emergency today."

"The Muldower girl?"

The policeman stared at Newby for a moment. "Yeah," he said slowly. "What do you know about it?"

"Nothing. Just what this guy Latcher told me in the diner."

The other man nodded. "All right, then. Your car's going to have to wait."

Newby stood and stretched. "Do you know how she died?" he asked.

"Yeah," said the policeman. "The coroner said it was some kind of stroke. I ain't never seen nothing like that, though."

"It was magic," said Newby.

"You're nuts," said the other man.

"What time should I come in to check on the car?"

"We'll be tied up all day," said the officer. "Come in tomorrow morning." Newby nodded, but inside he was annoyed. Another night, another day in the town. He'd have to call his wife, have her get in touch with the Jennings people, have her send him some money.

The salesman left the police station and walked into the small parklike square. Narrow gravel paths ran straight as a surveyor's transit could make them, among huge elms and oaks, diagonally from northeast to southwest, from northwest to southeast. At the center, where the paths intersected, there was the promised cannon and a pyramid of cannon balls. The end of the cannon's barrel was stuffed with paper cups and broken glass. There was a drinking fountain next to it, with a step for little children to use. A tiny trickle of water ran from the rusty fixture. No amount of handle turning could make the trickle run harder. The fountain was impossible to drink from. It made Newby very thirsty.

Old Man Durfee walked toward him along a gravel path. The drunk didn't seem to notice Newby. The old man moved in wide, sweeping curves, stumbling, talking to himself. He still carried his filthy blue towel, looped through the binder's twine that served him as a belt. Old Man Durfee passed Newby by the drinking fountain and continued across the square. The salesman watched him; several yards away, the drunk left the path and walked toward a broad, shady tree. Aunt Rozji stepped out from behind it. The two grasped hands and sat down, slowly, painfully. Newby watched them curiously. The two old people chatted. The drunk no longer seemed as inebriated, the old woman no longer as decrepit.

After a few minutes a middle-aged homemaker passed by, pulling a two-wheeled shopping cart filled with bags of groceries. Aunt Rozji raised a hand and waved to the woman. Newby moved closer.

"Hello, Aunt Rozji," said the woman pleasantly.

"Good morning, Mrs. Siebern," said the old woman. "How are you today?"

"Healthy, thank God," said Mrs. Siebern. "The last couple of days I haven't been so well."

"But today you feel fine?" asked Old Man Durfee.

Mrs. Siebern scowled at the drunk. "Yes," she said, her tone more disapproving. She turned back to Aunt Rozji. "How is your sister these days?"

"Fine," said Aunt Rozji. "She doesn't complain, the dear. Onyuish is three years younger than I, you know. But she has such troubles with her back."

"Well," said Mrs. Siebern, "have a good day. I have to get home. Eddie bought one of those power lawn mowers and he stayed home from work just to tinker with it. I want to get back before he cuts off both of his feet." The woman turned her back to the old people sitting on the ground; Aunt Rozji gestured to Newby. The salesman was surprised that the old woman had been aware of his presence. Her motions indicated that she wanted Newby to engage Mrs. Siebern in conversation. He hurried to catch up to the woman.

"Excuse me," he said nervously. "I'm just passing through this town, and it looks like I'll have to stay here the night. I was wondering if you could tell me if there are any good hotels in the area?"

Mrs. Siebern shaded her eyes and looked at him for a few seconds. "Well," she said slowly, "Aunt Rozji has some nice rooms for travelers, but she's particular about her guests. You'd have to speak to her. Here, let me—" She turned around to introduce Newby to Aunt Rozji, but the old woman and the drunk had risen and moved one to each side of Mrs. Siebern. Now they took her arms and led her from the gravel path. Old Man Durfee looked back at Newby and winked. He signaled that the salesman should follow them. Newby did.

"Here," said Aunt Rozji, "let's sit here under this mighty oak, eh?"

"I really have to get back to my Eddie," said Mrs. Siebern.

"Oh, he's old enough to handle a grasscutter, dear," said Old Man Durfee.

"It's television's fault," said Aunt Rozji. "All the husbands on those comedy shows look so stupid. All except Robert Young, and he's just fatuous. Your husband will be all right."

"Take this, Newby," said Old Man Durfee, handing the salesman an ancient, leather-bound book. "Follow along. Read the part that's underlined."

"This oak, all like oaks, oak trees blended in universal commune," chanted Aunt Rozji. "Pillar of sacred wood, leaf-secret bower, shelter us, cloak us, hide us now."

"This oak, our strength," said Old Man Durfee. "This oak, our weapon, this oak, our souls."

"This oak, its roots to the very earth's heart delving," read Newby haltingly. "Now, its limbs, our hands, delve this woman's spirit fire."

Newby glanced up. Mrs. Siebern's face bore an expression of surprise; then her features slackened, twisted again, seemed to contort with utter agony. Like Theresa Muldower, she tried to shriek, tossing her head wildly, kicking and thrashing. Her voice was stopped; from her mouth came only a blue, cold mist. Her eyes turned white, her lids drooped and were sealed shut with ice. Her blood froze where it ran down her chin. Old Man Durfee and Aunt Rozji held the woman tightly as she shook in the last stages of her ice-death. Her skin was tinged blue, her muscles chiseled in hard ridges beneath. The two old people eased the corpse gently to the ground, but even so, Mrs. Siebern's frozen right foot snapped off with a gentle tinking sound. A blue-white powder lay about the stump, dusting the rich green grass with what had been flesh, bone, blood, all living.

"Quick now, Young Newby," said Aunt Rozji. "We must finish."

The salesman looked at the book. He had the next speech, too. "Weakness, weariness, done to an end," he said. "Misery is now no longer, as acorn's shell is by the oaken shaft blasted."

As in the dream of the night before, the drunk grasped one of Newby's arms, and the old woman took the other. They walked away from the corpse quickly, back the way Newby had come. When they arrived at the police station, he stopped. "I have to go in," he said. "I have to report my car."

"You've already done that," said Old Man Durfee. But neither of the old people tried to stop him. Newby ran up the steps and into the station. He woke up on the bench. The clock said it was almost two.

"Another dream," he thought. He was too unnerved, though, to do the proper thing; he didn't have any intention of walking through the square to see whether Mrs. Siebern really rested there, cold, dead, and blue. Instead, Newby headed back toward the diner.

He met Lauren on the way. "Hello," he said. "I

thought you were supposed to be guarding the chess pieces."

"Oh," she said, pouting, "I always get stuck with dumb jobs like that. Nobody would want to mess with the game, anyway. I wish one of these days they'd let me help in the bigger jobs."

"Like Theresa Muldower?" he asked. "Like Mrs. Siebern?"

"Mrs. Siebern?" said Lauren. "Well, they finally did it. I'm glad. Her husband teaches chemistry, you know. Gave me a C+ last year. You know, you look a lot like Howard Keel."

"Howard Keel?"

"He's my second-favorite actor."

Newby laughed. "I suppose I ought to be flattered. Who's first on the list?"

"James Dean, of course," she said. "I send him birthday cards and everything."

Newby took a deep breath. "He's dead, you know," he said finally.

Lauren shook her head. "I don't believe it. In New York, even Stroudsburg, you believe those things. Here you don't have to. It doesn't make any difference what happens here, and what happens out there doesn't have any effect on us. I can believe what I want. This isn't such a big town, you know."

"Yes, I know."

" 'Don't be cruel,' " she sang.

"We should be getting back soon," said Newby. "It's almost three."

"You're not going to let that old nosebleed wino and Madame Ooglepuss boss you around, are you?" asked Lauren.

Newby waved a hand. "I thought you were on their side."

"That was until I realized how much you look like Howard Keel. 'To a heart that's true.' "

"I always get Howard Keel mixed up with Phil Gatelin," he said.

"They're nothing alike," she said.

"And neither am I."

"I don't know what you're talking about," said Lauren. They pushed open the door to the diner and stepped into the frigid blast of the air conditioning. Newby was stunned to see another Lauren Kromberger still sitting on one of the stools by the counter.

"What's going on?" screamed Newby.

The Lauren at the counter looked up and gasped. She went behind the counter and came back with a broken bottle, which she waved at the first Lauren menacingly. "It's just part of your dream," said the Lauren with the bottle. "Sometimes you have to shake them off like this. They're like nightmare hangovers." The armed Lauren took a few steps toward the Lauren that stood next to Newby. The salesman watched, mystified. The girl he had come into the diner with shrugged and leered at him, then began to fade and waver. In a minute she was completely gone. The waitress put down the broken bottle and sighed. "Did they get somebody else?" she asked.

"Who?"

"I don't know," she said. "You were the one out there. I've just been sitting in here the whole time."

"I mean, did *who* get somebody else."

"Aunt Rozji and Old Man Durfee, of course. Wait a minute." She picked up the bottle and started moving toward Newby. "Maybe you're part of my dream." Newby didn't fade. Lauren smiled and sat down again, patting the stool next to hers. "Come on," she said. "They'll be back any minute."

"They *got* Mrs. Siebern," he said.

"Oh. That's all right, I guess."

"What importance does this chess game have?" he asked.

"None, really," she said. "I mean, it won't go into *Chess Review* or anything, if that's what you're asking. I doubt if anyone else in town will even find out who won. You won't have any trouble finding other people to play you. You're really very good, you know."

"I don't want other people to play," he said impatiently. "I just want to go home already."

"You'll have to learn how to relax," she said smiling. "You have a really neurotic thing about getting away."

"I've seen some strange things in the last day," he said.

"How do you know they're real?"

Newby was annoyed. "If they're not, then I must be pretty sick."

The waitress nodded. "That's right. But there's a good chance that what you've seen *is* real. In which case, you're certainly not reacting with the proper horror, the essential dismay."

"My emotions seem to have been blunted," said Newby. "I think it's Aunt Rozji's doing. If she can perform her hideous tricks, she can just as easily hypnotize me into not running into the street screaming. Besides, they're only dreams."

"Old Mr. Latcher didn't think Theresa Popover was a dream," said Lauren. "And wait until they find Mrs. Siebern on the square."

Newby looked at her closely. "I never told you that's where they got her."

Lauren smiled once more. "See? It may all be a dream. But if it's not, then you have to worry. Your emotional reactions have been dulled. You admitted that yourself. Psychiatrists call that 'planed-down affect,' in their peculiar jargon. That, coupled with the difficulty you had on the little quiz this morning, would indicate that you're well into advanced schizophrenia."

"Then I *am* imagining all this?" he asked, not especially concerned.

"No," she said. "You're schizophrenic only if all this is real."

"Never mind," he said. "Can I have a Coke?"

Lauren brought him the soft drink. He sipped it, trying to make sense of her words. What did he know about schizophrenia? Very little, actually. Just some things he'd picked up from watching television. *Medic.*

The business about the split personality. He thought his brother-in-law might be like that. But why would Newby's symptoms wait until just now, here, in the tiny village so far from anything, before they became noticeable? If he were going insane, how could he just calmly discuss the matter with the waitress? How did she know so much about what he was feeling?

How much of what had happened *had* been only dreams? Might he still be asleep?

He swallowed some more of the Coke and picked up one of the discarded chess pieces, his demoted bishop. It felt heavy in his hand, in a way that dream objects never do. "This is one sure way to get locked up," he thought. "All I have to do is ask a doctor if I'm just dreaming. They'll never see me in Stroudsburg again."

"Is there a phone I can use?" he asked.

"Over there," she said. "By the jukebox."

He went to the phone, fished some change from his pocket, and dialed the operator. He got the number of the Green & Greene Bus Company, and gave them a call.

"Good afternoon, Green & Greene," said the girl who answered. "Can we help you?"

"Yes," said Newby. "I was wondering if you could tell me if there's a bus from Gremmage to Harrisburg?"

"No, I'm afraid not," said the girl. "You'd have to get the bus to Oil City, change there for Pittsburgh, and change again for Harrisburg."

"Fine," said Newby. "When is the next Oil City bus?"

"Oh, I'm sorry," she said, her voice conveying true concern and pity. "You just missed it this morning. There won't be another one for a while. They only run once a week."

"I see," said Newby. "What do people do if they have to go somewhere?"

"They drive, mostly," said the girl. "That's why there aren't more buses. It all works out, don't you see?"

"Yeah," he said. Then he hung up. It had been a long-shot, anyway. He went back to the counter.

"Do you think you can beat Old Man Durfee?" asked Lauren.

"No," said Newby. "I don't think I want to."

"That's wise," she said. "There's a lot more to him than most people would suspect."

"Is he, uh, going steady with Aunt Rozji?"

Lauren giggled. "No," she said, "they're just good friends."

"She'd make 'December Bride' look like cradle-robbing."

"They do some of that, too," said Lauren. "Only in the wintertime, though. Propitiating the frost nixies, and all that."

"Hello, hello!" cried Old Man Durfee. Newby turned around to see the drunk holding the door open for Aunt Rozji.

"Hello," said Newby.

"Talking about us, were you?" asked the old woman, as she hobbled across the floor to the counter.

"More or less," said Lauren.

"I don't know anyone else in town to talk about," said Newby.

"Small men talk about people," said Old Man Durfee. "Medium men talk about things. Big men talk about *ideas*."

"Well, we were discussing some ideas, too," said Lauren.

"That's all right, child," said Aunt Rozji. "Don't let that old wetbrain bother you. He doesn't talk about *anything*."

Old Man Durfee took his place on the stool. "Well," he said, "might as well get going with this again. Whose move was it? Mine?"

"Yes," said Newby, "it's yours. Fire away."

"That was last night," said Aunt Rozji. "Today is a day for ice." Newby only nodded.

" 'The old hooty owl hooty-hoots to the dove,' " sang Lauren.

"Owls are birds of death to some folk," said Aunt Rozji, smiling. "And doves, well, you know. The soul, in some symbologies. So you have a specter of destruction tempting the immortal soul. It happens all the time."

" 'Tammy, Tammy, Tammy's in love,' " sang Lauren.

Old Man Durfee looked up. "Yes, that's the way it always starts," he said.

"Are you ready to move yet?" asked Newby.

" 'Hooty-hoot,' " said Lauren. "That's dumb."

"Hey, everybody," called a stranger.

"Hey, Ronnie," said Lauren. "That's Ronnie Glanowsky. He has a Shell station out on Logan Road."

"Hey," said Glanowsky, "have you heard about poor old Mrs. Siebern?"

"Aw, she wasn't so old," said Newby.

Glanowsky studied the salesman's face for a few seconds. "I don't believe we've met," he said.

"My name's Newby," said the salesman. "I'm just passing through."

"You know Mrs. Siebern?" asked Glanowsky.

"No," said Newby cautiously. "I was just being gallant."

Glanowsky shrugged. "Anyway, they found her lying in the square. She's dead. Just keeled right over." At the word "keel," Lauren jabbed Newby's arm; he looked at her, and she made a kissing sound. He blushed and turned away.

"What happened to her?" asked the drunk.

"They figure she had some kind of attack," said Glanowsky.

"Well, goodbye," said Aunt Rozji.

"Goodbye," said Glanowsky. He hurried out.

"Did he come in here just to tell us that?" asked Newby.

"Probably," said Old Man Durfee. "He does that a lot. Anyway, he knows we like to keep informed."

Newby shook his head. "I really thought it was all a dream."

"It was," said Aunt Rozji. "But that's no reason that it can't be real, too."

"Watch this," said Old Man Durfee. He removed Newby's queen pawn on the fourth rank and set down his knight. Then, according to Aunt Rozji's rule, he took the knight off the board and replaced it with a pawn.

"I don't understand," said Lauren.

"Well," said Old Man Durfee jovially, "I certainly won't explain it now."

"Another rule change!" cried Aunt Rozji. "Another rule change! This ought to liven up the match."

"I can hardly wait to hear," said the drunk.

"From now on," said the old woman slowly, "whenever you move a rook, the next piece on the rank or file along which the rook traveled will be 'destroyed.' That goes whether the victim piece is friend or foe. So be careful."

"How about kings?" asked Newby.

"Hmm," muttered Aunt Rozji. "You're right. Kings will be immune, but if there's a piece *beyond* the king, it will be taken off the board instead."

"Terrific," said Newby.

"It's your move," said the drunk.

"I move the rook pawn to Rook Seven," said Newby. "Check."

"I take the pawn with my rook," said Old Man Durfee.

"The rook becomes a pawn," said Lauren.

"That's right," said Newby. "What about the rook, though? Does it destroy anything on the line it just moved?"

"No, I don't think so," said Aunt Rozji. "That power stops at the end of the board. If this were a cylindrical board you were playing on, the ray would go all the way around and catch the other rook pawn."

"All right," said Newby. He was getting more and more annoyed; neither the game itself nor his opponent seemed to have much grounding in rationality. The referee served no purpose at all, other than to try to aid the drunken old man. The waitress winked at Newby every time he glanced at her. Now the pieces in the game were adopting odd powers. And every minute he felt more trapped.

"Why don't you just try to get away?" asked Lauren.

"I don't know," said Newby. "I honestly admit that I don't know."

"That's a sure sign of something," said Old Man Durfee. "You ought to be running scared by now. Maybe we're having more of an effect on you than you think."

"Maybe he has a crush on Young Lauren," said Aunt Rozji.

"It could be a real Liz-Eddie-Debbie case," said the waitress. "You could leave your plain but nice wife to have a mad affair with me. What does your wife do?"

Newby scowled. "She's what we call in Stroudsburg a 'homemaker.' "

"See?" said Lauren.

"No," said Newby.

"All right," said the girl. "I was only kidding, anyway. I don't have any interest in you at all. You don't even look like Howard Keel."

"What was all the flirting for, then?" he asked.

"Part of the scheme," she said. "To make you stay here. We needed someone to—"

"Easy, there, youngster," said Old Man Durfee. "You'd better watch your tongue, or you'll end up looking like a pail full of rising dough."

"I want to know what she means," said Newby.

"I guess it's all right to tell him," said Aunt Rozji. "We needed someone in town to look suspicious for us. We have dark deeds planned."

"More?" asked the salesman.

"What do you mean, 'more'?" asked Old Man Durfee. "We haven't done anything."

"Except the eleven-year-old popover and the middle-aged Wifesicle," said Newby.

"We didn't have anything to do with them," said the old woman. "We've been too busy planning our job. We're going to knock over the Shell station. Ronnie Glanowsky's in on it too. It's his station."

"All the rest has been my imagination?" asked Newby.

"Sure," said the old drunk.

"But now we can't use you," said Aunt Rozji. "Now that your car's been stolen, and you'll be around for a while. You'll be too well known. We wanted a stranger to pin the rap on. We like you too much for that."

"I'm glad," said Newby. "Can we knock off this game, then?"

"For now, I suppose," said Old Man Durfee. "We can finish it in the morning."

"Yeah," said Newby. "Sure."

Old Man Durfee waved to Newby; Aunt Rozji smiled, and wiggled her fingers to indicate that the salesman should run along. He did so gratefully. The chess game, for all intents and purposes, was over. That marked some kind of turning point in the day's events. It meant that, for good or evil, the old people had taken their fill of him. Was he now expendable, in a way Theresa Muldower and Mrs. Siebern had been? Could he expect to find an unnatural death, now that they had moved on to other projects?

"That's not true, what they say about the gas station," said Lauren. She startled Newby. He had thought that he was walking alone, down Ridge Street toward Aunt Rozji's house.

"I'm glad to hear it," he said. "Two falling-apart people like them are in no condition to heist a gas station."

"They know it too," said Lauren. "That's why they had Ronnie Glanowsky in on it. But he wanted too big of a cut, for one thing. And, besides, they couldn't get together on where they'd run for their getaway. The old man wanted Jamaica, and Aunt Rozji wanted swinging Acapulco."

"There's a basic difference in attitudes, there," said Newby.

"I suppose." They walked along a little more, neither having much to say. They turned down Aunt Rozji's street. "Why are you going back?" she asked.

"I don't know," said Newby. "I don't have anywhere else to go. I'll call the police in the morning. If they don't have my car, I'll try hitching out of town."

"Oh. Be careful."

"I'm usually careful," he said.

"You came into the diner, didn't you?"

"Yeah. That was a mistake. Look, do you think I'm in any danger from them? Now that my part is over with?"

Lauren grabbed his arm; they stopped beneath a peeling sycamore, and she looked up frightened. "Don't think your part is over," she whispered.

"What?" he said. She had spoken too low for him to understand.

"I said, you're still in it. In fact, your big moment is still coming up." She saw his anxious expression and smiled. "Don't be too worried, though. *You* won't be hurt." She waved and started walking back in the direction they had come.

"That sounded more like the dream Lauren," he thought. "The one the real Lauren chased away with the broken bottle. I like the dream better, I think." He went up the stairs to Aunt Rozji's front door. It wasn't locked, and he went inside.

"Hello," said a man in a dark suit. "You must be Mr. Newby."

"That's right," said the salesman warily.

"Well," said the man, "my name is Greg Rembrick. I'm a Young Christians' Outdoor Health leader here in town. Me and the YCOH teens were hoping that you'd play an active part in our monthly group session this afternoon. Aunt Rozji told me that she thought you'd be happy to oblige, but I can understand that this comes at awfully short notice. So if you'd like to back out, we can just get on with the meeting."

"You're holding a meeting here now?" asked Newby.

"Yes," said Rembrick, smiling. "Aunt Rozji has been so kind to us, ever since our community social center teen canteen burnt to the ground last year. A strange fire it was, too."

"The others?"

"Oh, they're all out now, gathering different sorts of local leaves for our scrapbook. They'll be back in, uh," he glanced at his watch, "about ten minutes."

"What sort of thing will I have to do?" asked Newby.

Rembrick indicated that they should sit. The salesman took a place on one of the old woman's sofas, facing the youth leader. "Nothing difficult," said Rembrick. "We just need to have an outside adult read a short speech during our devotional fellowship nondenominational brotherhood council prayer-circle union of love."

"I see," said Newby. "I guess that would be all right."

"Fine," said Rembrick, smiling and nodding eagerly. "Fine. Thank you very much. The teens will be so happy." The two men chatted briefly, and after a couple of minutes the younger members of the group began joining them. Not long afterward, Mr. Rembrick announced that everyone was present. He had them all stand in a circle with himself in the center. They joined hands and sang a hymn, then closed their eyes and bowed their heads, while he recited a short invocation.

"Just read those words now, if you please, Mr. Newby," said Rembrick.

"Those words?" asked the salesman. Newby saw the words written in the air in terrifying green flames. He heard no reply from the other man. Newby stood and walked slowly toward the fiery letters. He stopped a few feet from them, and began reading slowly. "As earth the father water holds," he said in a low voice, "so air may fire in its cool embrace retain. Here the yearning mind of man entails the pinnacle of knowledge, the pit of wisdom's horror." With a sudden flicker, the words changed. Newby glanced at Rembrick and the youth group; they had all fallen to their knees, their faces contorted in strange ecstasy. He continued.

"Let the vast wheeling of the universe transform their knotted bowels. Let the great sky drama of blazing suns blast their hearts, shrivel lungs and steal breath, poach brains in boiling blood. Let heaven's yawning emptiness draw up their sensibilities, let the pendant mass of all the spheres and orbs crush their bones to sacrificial powder." Newby read the last of the flickering words, and they disappeared. Rembrick and his young charges were quite still upon the carpet of the parlor, their faces stretched in the extremities of suffering. As he watched, they screamed soundlessly. A blackness escaped their mouths and cloaked their heads, a dark fog in which Newby thought he could see the stark, unwinking stars of night. The blackness quickly vanished, and the salesman knew they were all grotesquely dead.

Chimes rang. There was someone at Aunt Rozji's door. Newby panicked for a moment, then fought for control. He knew that the authorities had not been able to find any element of criminal activity in the deaths of the Muldower girl or Mrs. Siebern. What could anyone say about the corpses on Aunt Rozji's floor? It could only be some kind of poisoning. Perhaps it was something they had eaten together. Newby took a deep breath, then went to answer the door.

"Hi," said Lauren. "Are you done yet?"

Newby nodded. "Just finished up a few seconds before you rang. Now what?"

"What do you mean?" she said, walking past him into the parlor.

"Well, what do we do with the bodies?"

" '*We*'?"

"What do *I* do with the bodies?"

Lauren shook her head sadly. "Don't you learn *anything*? What happened to Miss Popover? What did they do with Mrs. Siebern? They just left them there. We'll just leave these here for the police to find."

"I don't know what I'd do without you," said Newby scornfully.

"Look, fella," she said angrily, "I'm really glad this

thing is wrapping up to a close. It hasn't been so much fun, you know. You're not the neatest guy around. I did it because I have to. I can think of better ways of spending a lifetime."

"Like what?"

"Like bombing around," she said. "Trying on gloves at Sears. Anything."

"You don't have any junior murderers' league or something?"

"The sarc remark," she said. "The emblem of the stunted intellect."

"I'm doing my best," said Newby.

"How do you feel that you've changed?" asked Lauren. "You are no longer able to state with any assurance what the correct date is. You are frequently unable to recall where you are, geographically speaking. Your emotions are not appropriate to the situation. You are rapidly exhibiting signs of sociopathic behavior. Have you detected any further deviation in your outlook since this afternoon?"

"I don't know," he said.

"Well, I think you may soon discover that you are no longer able to discern right from wrong. How do you feel about what you just did to Mr. Rembrick and the kids?"

"Nothing," said Newby. "I don't feel anything at all."

"Do you think you would have felt nothing, say, a week ago?"

"I can't say," he muttered. He stared at the misshapen bodies. He still didn't feel anything.

"With Miss Popover, you were merely a witness. With Mrs. Siebern, you helped out. Here, you were on your own. Aunt Rozji and Old Man Durfee have managed to destroy the very last shred of your old self, without your even guessing what was happening. You don't know when you are, where you are, now you don't even know what or who you are. You've become a complete nonbeing, a blank, ready to be stamped with the first identity that is chosen for you."

"That's ridiculous," said Newby.

Lauren smiled; the expression frightened the salesman. "Do you know what?" she asked. "If Old Man Durfee gave you his quiz again, right now, you wouldn't even know how to hold the pencil."

"Sure, I would."

"You show typical ambivalent notions, common in even mild cases of schizophrenia. Sometimes you want to run away, but you never do. Sometimes you defend those two old monsters, but you know you hate them."

"What about you?" asked Newby.

"Do you mean, how do I feel about them?" she said. "Or how do you feel about me?"

"I don't know."

"Of course you don't. You're not supposed to. That's the whole point. You've been worn down."

Newby collapsed on a sofa. He rubbed his eyes. He felt nothing. He was not afraid. He was not disgusted. He was not at all anxious to leave. He knew that it would be a tremendous effort to plan anything. "What happens now?" he asked.

"More of the same, I'm afraid," said Old Man Durfee. Newby looked up; the drunk and the old woman had come in.

"Why do you always seem to appear while I'm sitting with my eyes closed?" he asked.

"Why do you always seem to have your eyes closed when we arrive?" asked Aunt Rozji, busily examining the bodies on her floor. "Young Lauren, would you be so kind as to call the police?" Newby laughed.

"Are you amused, Newby?" asked Old Man Durfee.

"No," said the salesman. "It just seems like you're going to try to use me as a scapegoat now."

"That's an idea," said Aunt Rozji, raising an eyebrow.

" 'Hooty-hoot,' " said Lauren. " 'The old owl of doom hooty-hoots to the dove.' " She dialed the phone and spoke to the police officer who answered.

"Ask them about my car," said Newby.

"I have some interesting statistics," said Old Man

Durfee. "I took the trouble of digging these up this afternoon. It seems that for every hundred thousand persons in the United States, there are some two hundred ninety people with schizophrenia in one form or another. Of course, 'schizophrenia' takes in a large number of different disorders. But of those nearly three hundred suffering souls, only half are being treated. That leaves another hundred fifty maniacs per hundred thousand running around loose."

"Should I turn myself in?" asked Newby skeptically.

"You already have," said Aunt Rozji. "We'll take care of you."

"You already have," said Newby to himself.

"If you went into a hospital," said Lauren, hanging up the telephone, "you'd probably be locked up for quite a while."

"Thirteen years is the average," said the drunk.

"Thirteen years," said Aunt Rozji gently. "Just think of it."

"Some murderers get out in less time," said Newby.

"We don't like to talk about that," said the old man.

Aunt Rozji sat down next to Newby, and took his hands in hers. Her old skin was rough, with sharp, hard points of callus that stabbed Newby's fingers. He felt a general anxiety, without specific cause. He wanted to stay and find a secure home, or go and discover his lost identity, or something; he wasn't sure. It was the uncertainty, rather than the unusual events and the piling up of dead persons that upset him. "You may well be the victim of simple schizophrenia," said the old woman. "It has taken these somewhat bizarre happenings to point it out to you. You thought you were well-adjusted and normal. It must be quite a blow to your stability to find out that you're not."

"What happened to your accent?" he asked. "What happened to Old Man Durfee's drunken wino ways?"

"Most simple schizophrenics never realize they're ill," said Aunt Rozji. "They seem to be merely a bit antisocial. They become vagrants, like Young Durfee, although his case is quite a bit different. Perhaps your brain will turn even stranger, leading to hebephrenia, characterized by inappropriate foolishness and giggling, or, at other times, unexplained weeping. What about hallucinations? Have you been troubled by them?"

"So far, they've been rather nice," said Newby. "I haven't actually been convinced that I've *had* hallucinations, you see. I'm more or less taking the word of Lauren for that."

"She ought to know," said Old Man Durfee. "She's been a hallucination often enough herself."

"Thank God you're not paranoid," said the old woman. "You're not catatonic, either. You've a lot to be thankful for."

"I am," said Newby.

The chimes rang again. Lauren answered the door; it was the police. They came in and stood around the corpses on the carpet. Newby was surprised by their reaction. Many of the police officers gasped in horror, or ran back outside, sickened. The salesman had thought that a policeman would see many such sights in the course of his career. He was amazed that they would be so affected.

"Who found these individuals?" asked a sergeant.

"He did," said Old Man Durfee, pointing to Newby.

The sergeant nodded. "I suppose they couldn't go undiscovered for very long," he said. "This isn't such a big town."

"No, it isn't," said Old Man Durfee.

"There doesn't seem to be any indication of foul play," said the sergeant. "I won't have to question you, in that case. But the final word will have to come from the coroner."

"In just a few seconds," said a small, gray man who was busily prodding the dead bodies. "Ah. Their bones are shattered from within, as though they fell from an enormous height. But there are no outward signs at all. A most curious case."

"There have been a number of them of late," said the sergeant with a rueful smile.

"I judge that they all died from some manner of apoplexy," said the coroner.

"All?" asked Aunt Rozji. "At the same time? What a strange coincidence."

"There have been quite a few of those, too," said Old Man Durfee.

"Well," said the sergeant, "I want to thank you people for your help. We'll have somebody come by in the morning to collect these jokers. I'll just ask that you not move any of the individuals here in the meantime. We'll want to get plaster molds and things like that. Clues. You understand."

"Certainly," said Old Man Durfee. The sergeant waved and followed the coroner to the door. After the police had gone, Lauren turned to Aunt Rozji.

"Why do they need clues, if they all died of apoplexy?" she asked.

"To help find a cure for apoplexy, I guess," said Aunt Rozji. "The police department has become much more scientifically minded since I was a girl."

"Now we can relax," said the old drunk.

There was an immediate hush in the dim house. In the sudden silence, Newby wondered what he had been listening to in the minutes previously: clocks in the parlor ticking, electric hum of kitchen appliances, wood creaking in the humid heat, restless tapping of fingers and shoes, noise from the street, neighbors mowing lawns, airplanes, all these sounds died together. It was perfectly still, a waiting moment, an interval, a preparation.

"Ah," said Aunt Rozji, "you will be happy to learn that everything that concerns you is now in its absolute final stage."

"That cheers me up considerably," said Newby.

"I took the liberty of ending our little contest," said Old Man Durfee. "With Aunt Rozji's help, of course." The drunk smiled roguishly at her, and the old woman laughed.

"May I inquire as to the results?" asked Newby.

"I won," said Old Man Durfee. "The enmity between us is ended. Aunt Rozji took over your moves and, with the aid of a few more spontaneous alterations of the rules, I was able to checkmate your harried king in splendid style."

"Well," said Newby, somewhat bored, "let me congratulate you. How was this marvelous stratagem wrought?"

"First of all," said Aunt Rozji, "I added a condition that no piece could be moved unless the nearest pawn of the same color could make a congruent move at the same time, legally. So each player would then be moving two pieces per turn, his desired piece, plus the nearest pawn."

"As you can imagine," said Old Man Durfee, "this cuts down somewhat on the number of available moves each player has to choose from. As it developed, I was better able to visualize the situation."

"Better than Aunt Rozji, at least," said Newby.

"Well, we all agreed to bow to her judgments. Then, finally, I was given the weapon to break your position. Aunt Rozji declared that the queen was to be given a new power. She called it the 'H-bomb capability.' "

Lauren laughed. "For an immigrant, she certainly has a way with words," she said.

Old Man Durfee gave the girl a disapproving look. "In any event," he said, "at any one time during the game, the queen could be placed on *any* vacant square on the board. All pieces, friend and foe alike, on the eight adjacent squares are considered 'destroyed,' and removed from the game, except the kings. You can see what terrible havoc this piece can wreak on any well-defended position. And, you may recall, you no longer had your queen. Well, given this instrument, it was no great trouble to bring your tattered army to its knees."

"It doesn't sound like you have much to be proud of," said Newby. "It didn't end up to be much like chess."

"The rules are always arbitrary," said Aunt Rozji. "It's just that you're used to them being arbitrary the same way each time."

"I'm sorry," said Newby.

"That's all right," said Old Man Durfee.

"Well," said Aunt Rozji, standing and stretching her thin, spotted arms, "let's get going, Young Newby. Your epiphany awaits."

"What?" said Newby. "I thought it was all over. You said yourself that I was pretty much depersonalized. How can a diluted being like me have an epiphany?"

"You'll see," said Lauren, tugging at Newby's hand. "Come on." The four people walked to the door and out onto the porch. It was getting cooler outside, although the humidity was still uncomfortable. A fresh breeze brushed through the dense leaves around Aunt Rozji's house.

"Where are we going?" asked Newby. "Back to the diner?"

"You'll see," said Lauren.

"The diner's played its part," said Old Man Durfee. "It doesn't make any real difference *where* we go now. Just start walking."

Aunt Rozji took the salesman's arm. With a shock, Newby waited for Old Man Durfee to take the other; that was how it began, both for Theresa Popover and Mrs. Siebern. Greg Rembrick and the YCOH teens had all joined hand before Newby had killed them. He was relieved to see that the old drunk had fallen back to speak softly with Lauren. He turned his attention to the doddering woman at his side.

"I wonder if you've noticed this interesting fact," she said. "After each of the introductory interludes, you seemed to awaken as from a nap. The episodes seemed to you like dreams. To a large extent they were. To that same extent, you are now."

"This is a dream?" asked Newby, not sure what she meant.

"Well, partly so," she said. "Can you think of any

difference between the affair of the Young Christian Outdoor Health group and the earlier encounters?"

"Well," said Newby slowly, "I was on my own with the last one. I didn't see you or Old Man Durfee until the whole thing was over. In fact, I saw Lauren before you came in."

"That's true. And you ought to be congratulated. You handled the matter with precision, taste, and dispatch. But now you're such a formless person. It is indeed a great waste. You have little effect on the world, you know."

Newby laughed sadly. "When have I ever had any effect?"

"That's just it," said Aunt Rozji. "We're trying to change that for you."

"I appreciate it."

"Now, think again," she said. "What other differences can you find?"

"I give up," said Newby.

"Well, you've never roused from the Young Christian Outdoor Health dream. Everything's continued in an unbroken line since then."

"Yes," cried Newby, "that's true! I knew there was something wrong."

Aunt Rozji stopped on the sidewalk and stroked the salesman's arm. "Because we love you, Young Newby," she said, "and because Young Durfee conquered you at chess, we're going to help you. It is in our power to leave you as you are, a breathing cipher. We have done it before. But we have taken a special interest in you. We will push you that final step."

It was very dark. Newby couldn't decide whether night had swiftly fallen, or if the blackness were some artificial trick of his dream. A round yellow moon hung in the sky, huge, far too big, as if it were resting on the horizon instead of staring down from the summit of the sky. Newby glanced at the moon and felt an unpleasant chill. The cold yellow light seeped through his eyes into his veins. He had to look away.

He heard the ragged scraws of the evening's birds, as they fought over insects. He heard the cicadas shrilling at him. There was no way that he could interpret their warning. He walked on. Aunt Rozji and Old Man Durfee were silent. Lauren was humming "Volare." Newby walked past the sealed houses, each flashing tiny lights from the crystal faces mounted in windows and doors. The houses presented no threat tonight, though. Newby could sense that they were merely curious observers. The solitary figures that glided within them were almost as powerless as he. They watched, but they could be of no help, either. The great buildings seemed to roll past, one by one. Newby was aware that he was walking down a steep, shaded hill. The street was no longer paved with red brick, but instead was covered with a black material imbedded with diamond points of light. The minute beams from the blacktop tried to communicate, but he would not understand.

He looked back at the houses, his only and impotent allies. They were gone. They had become massive abstract shapes, black solids blocking sharp-edged swaths of the night sky. He walked past towering cubes and rectangular pyramids. The moon's light colored them unpleasant shades of dark yellow-green. The trees were gone too. The insects and birds were gone. All sound was gone. Lauren and the old people were gone.

Newby moved through a flat landscape; the ground was hard beneath his feet, level, without rock or curb or root. The vast shapes dwindled in number as he passed, until at last he could see only one, far ahead of him on the moonlit plain. He hurried toward it. It was the only clue to where he was, how he might get out, who he might be. He ran, and he seemed to run for hours, but the black bulk in the distance did not come closer. After a time, the moon settled below the horizon, leaving Newby to the pale light of the stars. The monstrous shape became a black patch on the black shade of night. He ran, and he was amazed that he did not grow tired.

When at last he reached the gigantic green-black thing he saw that it was not a smooth façade, as the other shapes had been. Bits of starlight caught in grooves and pits on the object's face. Although the block rose hundreds of feet above his head, all the peculiar hollows were within easy reach. Newby stretched his hand out and felt one of the markings; his fingers traced a letter *A*. He explored further; all of the carvings proved to be letters. He could not read the entire inscription at once. He had to search out its meaning, letter by letter, word by word. He raised himself up and deciphered the first word. "This," he said aloud. The next word. "World," he said. He was able to read them more quickly. "This world," he said, "this island of stone. This trimmed and dressed block of marbled mud. This hanging ball in space, this single monument to me. I am alone. I, this block of stone. I, this captive world. I read these words. I become these words. I become this mighty pedestal of stone, whose function is to give form to these words. I become this reckless celestial sphere, whose function alone is to support this mighty pedestal of stone. I am here, alone, and my function is to read these words." Newby paused, his voice becoming hoarse. He looked back at the letter he had already traced. Their indentations into the rock had filled with a spectral lumination. He could easily read them, now; the words yet ahead, though, were still hidden in the darkness.

He continued. "If any doubt my existence, let him doubt himself. If any question my purpose, let him question himself." Newby felt suddenly afraid. His throat felt dry, his blood rushed, roaring, in his ears. He could not stop. "As the words, the rock, the world careen through the empty night, let him who reads these words shake within himself, like a long-dead leaf rattles withered in the winter storm." Newby felt his mind coming loose, his personality falling from its anchored place in the intangible secret place of his soul. There were no more words. Newby stepped back and stared at the steady radiation that outlined the letters. He took a few more paces away from the immense stone thing; he turned and saw himself still standing by the rock face, his hands plunged to the wrists in the cold white flames.

"Hey!" cried Newby. He wanted to run. He wanted to escape, back across the plain, through the jumbled mountains of stone, until they became houses again; he wanted to run toward the single mighty tower and his silent image. He did neither. He stood and watched, as the other Newby fell to his knees and began to pray. The other Newby worshiped the terrible pillar of stone, and the glowing letters carved in its side. The other Newby shrieked incoherent words; he waved his arms slowly above his head, then folded his hands in a submissive attitude of adoration. "Don't put your hands together!" shouted Newby, horrified. It was too late. The other Newby jerked violently, as though he were pulled about by invisible wires. The man's skin seemed to shatter and flake away. Newby stared as his double began to crumble, bits of formerly vibrant flesh falling to the ground and degenerating to powder. A gust of wind puffed the dust, all that remained of the other Newby, away in a misty cloud of gray.

"Good God, what's going on?" said Newby, his eyes filling with tears.

"You've molted yourself," said the voice of Aunt Rozji. "You've left your dream self, like an insect abandons its dead, husky skin."

Newby turned to find her. The empty plain was gone. The towers of stone were gone. He was back in Aunt Rozji's parlor. "I don't understand," he said.

"That's a very good sign," said Old Man Durfee. "If you *did* understand, we'd have more of a job to do. You're one of us, now, in a way. You're a real Gremmager. You're ready to find a job here, find a place to live, a new wife, perhaps. You're ready to help us whenever another stranger comes to visit."

"We'll let you know if we ever need you," said Aunt Rozji.

"You're not schizo, anymore," said Lauren, walking over to hug him. "'You're just, well, *plain*. You don't have to worry about anything ever again."

"Good," he said.

"It's not everyone that can kill his own dream self," said Old Man Durfee. "Some of us don't even have one."

"Don't be pompous, Young Durfee," said the old woman. She turned again to Newby. 'You're completely assimilated now. You're very lucky. This town is very selective about whom it chooses."

"It can afford to be," said Old Man Durfee.

"Because it's not such a big town," said Lauren.

"Hooty-hoot," said Newby. "Hooty-hoot."

THE DETECTIVE OF DREAMS

by Gene Wolfe

I was writing in my office in the rue Madeleine when
Andrée, my secretary, announced the arrival of Herr
D____. I rose, put away my correspondence, and offered him my hand. He was, I should say, just short of
fifty, had the high, clear complexion characteristic of
those who in youth (now unhappily past for both of
us) have found more pleasure in the company of horses
and dogs and the excitement of the chase than in the
bottles and bordels of city life, and wore a beard and
mustache of the style popularized by the late emperor.
Accepting my invitation to a chair, he showed me his
papers.

"You see," he said, "I am accustomed to acting as
the representative of my government. In this matter I
hold no such position, and it is possible that I feel a
trifle lost."

"Many people who come here feel lost," I said.
"But it is my boast that I find most of them again.
Your problem, I take it, is purely a private matter?"

"Not at all. It is a public matter in the truest sense
of the words."

"Yet none of the documents before me—admirably
stamped, sealed, and beribboned though they are—
indicates that you are other than a private gentleman
traveling abroad. And you say you do not represent
your government. What am I to think? What is this
matter?"

"I act in the public interest," Herr D___ told me. "My fortune is not great, but I can assure you that in the event of your success you will be well recompensed; although you are to take it that I alone am your principal, yet there are substantial resources available to me."

"Perhaps it would be best if you described the problem to me?"

"You are not averse to travel?"

"No."

"Very well then," he said, and so saying launched into one of the most astonishing relations—no, *the* most astonishing relation—I have ever been privileged to hear. Even I, who had at first hand the account of the man who found Paulette Renan with the quince seed still lodged in her throat; who had received Captain Brotte's testimony concerning his finds amid the antarctic ice; who had heard the history of the woman called Joan O'Neil, who lived for two years behind a painting of herself in the Louvre, from her own lips—even I sat like a child while this man spoke.

When he fell silent, I said, "Herr D___, after all you have told me, I would accept this mission though there were not a *sou* to be made from it. Perhaps once in a lifetime one comes across a case that must be pursued for its own sake; I think I have found mine."

He leaned forward and grasped my hand with a warmth of feeling that was, I believe, very foreign to his usual nature. "Find and destroy the Dream-Master," he said, "and you shall sit upon a chair of gold, if that is your wish, and eat from a table of gold as well. When will you come to our country?"

"Tomorrow morning," I said. "There are one or two arrangements I must make here before I go."

"I am returning tonight. You may call upon me at any time, and I will apprise you of new developments." He handed me a card. "I am always to be found at this address—if not I, then one who is to be trusted, acting in my behalf."

"I understand."

"This should be sufficient for your initial expenses. You may call on me should you require more." The cheque he gave me as he turned to leave represented a comfortable fortune.

I waited until he was nearly out the door before saying, "I thank you, Herr Baron." To his credit, he did not turn; but I had the satisfaction of seeing a flush red rising above the precise white line of his collar before the door closed.

Andrée entered as soon as he had left. "Who was that man? When you spoke to him—just as he was stepping out of your office—he looked as if you had struck him with a whip."

"He will recover," I told her. "He is the Baron H____, of the secret police of K____. D____ was his mother's name. He assumed that because his own desk is a few hundred kilometers from mine, and because he does not permit his likeness to appear in the daily papers, I would not know him; but it was necessary, both for the sake of his opinion of me and my own of myself, that he should discover that I am not so easily deceived. When he recovers from his initial irritation, he will retire tonight with greater confidence in the abilities I will devote to the mission he has entrusted to me."

"It is typical of you, monsieur," Andrée said kindly, "that you are concerned that your clients sleep well."

Her pretty cheek tempted me, and I pinched it. "I am concerned," I replied; "but the Baron will not sleep well."

My train roared out of Paris through meadows sweet with wild flowers, to penetrate mountain passes in which the danger of avalanches was only just past. The glitter of rushing water, sprung from on high, was everywhere; and when the express slowed to climb a grade, the song of water was everywhere, too, water running and shouting down the gray rocks of the Alps. I fell asleep that night with the descant of that icy purity sounding through the plainsong of the rails, and I woke in the station of L____, the old capital of J____, now a province of K____.

I engaged a porter to convey my trunk to the hotel where I had made reservations by telegraph the day before, and amused myself for a few hours by strolling about the city. Here I found the Middle Ages might almost be said to have remained rather than lingered. The city wall was complete on three sides, with its merloned towers in repair; and the cobbled streets surely dated from a period when wheeled traffic of any kind was scarce. As for the buildings—Puss in Boots and his friends must have loved them dearly; there were bulging walls and little panes of bull's-eye glass, and overhanging upper floors one above another until the structures seemed unbalanced as tops. Upon one grey old pile with narrow windows and massive doors, I found a plaque informing me that though it had been first built as a church, it had been successively a prison, a customhouse, a private home, and a school. I investigated further, and discovered it was now an arcade, having been divided, I should think at about the time of the first Louis, into a multitude of dank little stalls. Since it was, as it happened, one of the addresses mentioned by Baron H____, I went in.

Gas flared everywhere, yet the interior could not have been said to be well lit—each jet was sullen and secretive, as if the proprietor in whose cubicle it was located wished it to light none but his own wares. These cubicles were in no order; nor could I find any directory or guide to lead me to the one I sought. A few customers, who seemed to have visited the place for years, so that they understood where everything was, drifted from one display to the next. When they arrived at each, the proprietor came out, silent (so it seemed to me) as a specter, ready to answer questions or accept a payment; but I never heard a question asked, or saw any money tendered—the customer would finger the edge of a kitchen knife, or hold a garment up to her own shoulders, or turn the pages of some moldering book; and then put the thing down again, and go away.

At last, when I had tired of peeping into alcoves lined with booths still gloomier than the ones on the main concourse outside, I stopped at a leather merchant's and asked the man to direct me to Fräulein A___.

"I do not know her," he said.

"I am told on good authority that her business is conducted in this building, and that she buys and sells antiques."

"We have several antique dealers here. Herr M___"

"I am searching for a young woman. Has your Herr M___ a niece or a cousin?"

"—handles chairs and chests, largely. Herr O___, near the guildhall—"

"It is within this building."

"—stocks pictures, mostly. A few mirrors. What is it you wish to buy?"

At this point we were interrupted, mercifully, by a woman from the next booth. "He wants Fräulein A___. Out of here, and to your left; past the wigmaker's, then right to the stationer's, then left again. She sells old lace."

I found the place at last, and sitting at the very back of her booth Fräulein A___ herself, a pretty, slender, timid-looking young woman. Her merchandise was spread on two tables; I pretended to examine it and found that it was not old lace she sold but old clothing, much of it trimmed with lace. After a few moments she rose and came out to talk to me, saying, "If you could tell me what you require? . . ." She was taller than I had anticipated, and her flaxen hair would have been very attractive if it were ever released from the tight braids coiled round her head.

"I am only looking. Many of these are beautiful—are they expensive?"

"Not for what you get. The one you are holding is only fifty marks."

"That seems like a great deal."

"They are the fine dresses of long ago—for visiting, or going to the ball. The dresses of wealthy women of aristocratic taste. All are like new; I will not handle anything else. Look at the seams in that one you hold, the tiny stitches all done by hand. Those were the work of dressmakers who created only four or five in a year, and worked twelve and fourteen hours a day, sewing at the first light, and continuing under the lamp, past midnight."

I said, "I see that you have been crying, Fräulein. Their lives were indeed miserable, though no doubt there are people today who suffer equally."

"No doubt there are," the young woman said. "I, however, am not one of them." And she turned away so that I should not see her tears.

"I was informed otherwise."

She whirled about to face me. "You know him? Oh, tell him I am not a wealthy woman, but I will pay whatever I can. Do you really know him?"

"No." I shook my head. "I was informed by your own police."

She stared at me. "But you are an outlander. So is he, I think."

"Ah, we progress. Is there another chair in the rear of your booth? Your police are not above going outside your own country for help, you see, and we should have a little talk."

"They are not our police," the young woman said bitterly, "but I will talk to you. The truth is that I would sooner talk to you, though you are French. You will not tell them that?"

I assured her that I would not; we borrowed a chair from the flower stall across the corridor, and she poured forth her story.

"My father died when I was very small. My mother opened this booth to earn our living—old dresses that had belonged to her own mother were the core of her original stock. She died two years ago, and since that time I have taken charge of our business and used it to support myself. Most of my sales are to collectors and theatrical companies. I do not make a great deal of money, but I do not require a great deal, and I have managed to save some. I live alone at Number 877 _____strasse; it is an old house divided into six apartments, and mine is the gable apartment."

"You are young and charming," I said, "and you tell me you have a little money saved. I am surprised you are not married."

"Many others have said the same thing."

"And what did you tell them, Fräulein?"

"To take care of their own affairs. They have called me a manhater—Frau G____, who has the confections in the next corridor but two, called me that because I would not receive her son. The truth is that I do not care for people of either sex, young or old. If I want to live by myself and keep my own things to myself, is not it my right to do so?"

"I am sure it is; but undoubtedly it has occurred to you that this person you fear so much may be a rejected suitor who is taking his revenge on you."

"But how could he enter and control my dreams?"

"I do not know, Fräulein. It is you who say that he does these things."

"I should remember him, I think, if he had ever called on me. As it is, I am quite certain I have seen him somewhere, but I cannot recall where. Still . . ."

"Perhaps you had better describe your dream to me. You have the same one again and again, as I understand it?"

"Yes. It is like this. I am walking down a dark road. I am both frightened and pleasurably excited, if you know what I mean. Sometimes I walk for a long time, sometimes for what seems to be only a few moments. I think there is moonlight, and once or twice I have noticed stars. Anyway, there is a high, dark hedge, or perhaps a wall, on my right. There are fields to the left, I believe. Eventually I reach a gate of iron bars, standing open—it's not a large gate for wagons or carriages, but a small one, so narrow I can hardly get through. Have you read the writings of Dr. Freud of

Vienna? One of the women here mentioned once that he had written concerning dreams, and so I got them from the library, and if I were a man I am sure he would say that entering that gate meant sexual commerce. Do you think I might have unnatural leanings?" Her voice had dropped to a whisper.

"Have you ever felt such desires?"

"Oh, no. Quite the reverse."

"Then I doubt it very much," I said. "Go on with your dream. How do you feel as you pass through the gate?"

"As I did when walking down the road, but more so—more frightened, and yet happy and excited. Triumphant, in a way."

"Go on."

"I am in the garden now. There are fountains playing, and nightingales singing in the willows. The air smells of lilies, and a cherry tree in blossom looks like a giantess in her bridal gown. I walk on a straight, smooth path; I think it must be paved with marble chips, because it is white in the moonlight. Ahead of me is the *Schloss*—a great building. There is music coming from inside."

"What sort of music?"

"Magnificent—joyous, if you know what I am trying to say, but not the tinklings of a theater orchestra. A great symphony. I have never been to the opera at Bayreuth; but I think it must be like that—yet a happy, quick tune."

She paused, and for an instant her smile recovered the remembered music. "There are pillars, and a grand entrance, with broad steps. I run up—I am so happy to be there—and throw open the door. It is brightly lit inside; a wave of golden light, almost like a wave from the ocean, strikes me. The room is a great hall, with a high ceiling. A long table is set in the middle and there are hundreds of people seated at it, but one place, the one nearest me, is empty. I cross to it and sit down; there are beautiful golden loaves on the table, and bowls of honey with roses floating at their centers, and crystal carafes of wine, and many other good things I cannot remember when I awake. Everyone is eating and drinking and talking, and I begin to eat too."

I said, "It is only a dream, Fräulein. There is no reason to weep."

"I dream this each night—I have dreamed so every night for months."

"Go on."

"Then he comes. I am sure he is the one who is causing me to dream like this because I can see his face clearly, and remember it when the dream is over. Sometimes it is very vivid for an hour or more after I wake—so vivid that I have only to close my eyes to see it before me."

"I will ask you to describe him in detail later. For the present, continue with your dream."

"He is tall, and robed like a king, and there is a strange crown on his head. He stands beside me, and though he says nothing, I know that the etiquette of the place demands that I rise and face him. I do this. Sometimes I am sucking my fingers as I get up from his table."

"He owns the dream palace, then."

"Yes, I am sure of that. It is his castle, his home; he is my host. I stand and face him, and I am conscious of wanting very much to please him, but not knowing what it is I should do."

"That must be painful."

"It is. But as I stand there, I become aware of how I am clothed, and—"

"How are you clothed?"

"As you see me now. In a plain, dark dress—the dress I wear here at the arcade. But the others—all up and down the hall, all up and down the table—are wearing the dresses I sell here. These dresses." She held one up for me to see, a beautiful creation of many layers of lace, with buttons of polished jet. "I know then that I cannot remain; but the king signals to the others, and they seize me and push me toward the door."

"You are humiliated then?"

"Yes, but the worst thing is that I am aware that he knows that I could never drive myself to leave, and he wishes to spare me the struggle. But outside—some terrible beast has entered the garden. I smell it—like the hyena cage at the *Tiergarten*—as the door opens. And then I wake up."

"It is a harrowing dream."

"You have seen the dresses I sell. Would you credit it that for weeks I slept in one, and then another, and then another of them?"

"You reaped no benefit from that?"

"No. In the dream I was clad as now. For a time I wore the dresses always—even here to the stall, and when I bought food at the market. But it did no good."

"Have you tried sleeping somewhere else?"

"With my cousin who lives on the other side of the city. That made no difference. I am certain that this man I see is a real man. He is in my dream, and the cause of it; but he is not sleeping."

"Yet you have never seen him when you are awake?"

She paused, and I saw her bite at her full lower lip. "I am certain I have."

"Ah!"

"But I cannot remember when. Yet I am sure I have seen him—that I have passed him in the street."

"Think! Does his face associate itself in your mind with some particular section of the city?"

She shook her head.

When I left her at last, it was with a description of the Dream-Master less precise than I had hoped, though still detailed. It tallied in almost all respects with the one given me by Baron H____; but that proved nothing, since the baron's description might have been based largely on Fräulein A____'s.

*   *   *

The bank of Herr R——was a private one, as all the greatest banks in Europe are. It was located in what had once been the town house of some noble family (their arms, overgrown now with ivy, were still visible above the door) and bore no identification other than a small brass plate engraved with the names of Herr R—— and his partners. Within, the atmosphere was more dignified—even if, perhaps, less tasteful—than it could possibly have been in the noble family's time. Dark pictures in gilded frames lined the walls, and the clerks sat at inlaid tables upon chairs upholstered in tapestry. When I asked for Herr R——, I was told that it would be impossible to see him that afternoon; I sent in a note with a sidelong allusion to "unquiet dreams," and within five minutes I was ushered into a luxurious office that must once have been the bedroom of the head of the household.

Herr R——was a large man—tall, and heavier (I thought) than his physician was likely to have approved. He appeared to be about fifty; there was strength in his wide, fleshy face; his high forehead and capacious cranium suggested intellect; and his small, dark eyes, forever flickering as they took in the appearance of my person, the expression of my face, and the position of my hands and feet, ingenuity.

No pretense was apt to be of service with such a man, and I told him flatly that I had come as the emissary of Baron H——, that I knew what troubled him, and that if he would cooperate with me I would help him if I could.

"I know you, monsieur," he said, "by reputation. A business with which I am associated employed you three years ago in the matter of a certain mummy." He named the firm. "I should have thought of you myself."

"I did not know that you were connected with them."

"I am not, when you leave this room. I do not know what reward Baron H—— has offered you should you apprehend the man who is oppressing me, but I will give you, in addition to that, a sum equal to that you were paid for the mummy. You should be able to retire to the south then, should you choose, with the rent of a dozen villas."

"I do not choose," I told him, "and I could have retired long before. But what you just said interests me. You are certain that your persecutor is a living man?"

"I know men." Herr R___ leaned back in his chair and stared at the painted ceiling. "As a boy I sold stuffed cabbage-leaf rolls in the street—did you know that? My mother cooked them over wood she collected herself where buildings were being demolished, and I sold them from a little cart for her. I lived to see her with half a score of footmen and the finest house in Lindau. I never went to school; I learned to add and subtract in the streets—when I must multiply and divide I have my clerk do it. But I learned men. Do you think that now, after forty years of practice, I could be deceived by a phantom? No, he is a man—let me confess it, a stronger man than I—a man of flesh and blood and brain, a man I have seen somewhere, sometime, here in this city—and more than once."

"Describe him."

"As tall as I. Younger—perhaps thirty or thirty-five. A brown, forked beard, so long." (He held his hand about fifteen centimeters beneath his chin.) "Brown hair. His hair is not yet grey, but I think it may be thinning a little at the temples."

"Don't you remember?"

"In my dream he wears a garland of roses—I cannot be sure."

"Is there anything else? Any scars or identifying marks?"

Herr R___ nodded. "He has hurt his hand. In my dream, when he holds out his hand for the money, I see blood in it—it is his own, you understand, as though a recent injury had reopened and was beginning to bleed again. His hands are long and slender—like a pianist's."

"Perhaps you had better tell me your dream."

"Of course." He paused, and his face clouded, as though to recount the dream were to return to it. "I am in a great house. I am a person of importance there, almost as though I were the owner; yet I am not the owner—"

"Wait," I interrupted. "Does this house have a banquet hall? Has it a pillared portico, and is it set in a garden?"

For a moment Herr R____'s eyes widened. "Have you also had such dreams?"

"No," I said. "It is only that I think I have heard of this house before. Please continue."

"There are many servants—some work in the fields beyond the garden. I give instructions to them—the details differ each night, you understand. Sometimes I am concerned with the kitchen, sometimes with the livestock, sometimes with the draining of a field. We grow wheat, principally, it seems; but there is a vineyard too, and a kitchen garden. And of course the house itself must be cleaned and swept and kept in repair. There is no wife; the owner's mother lives with us, I think, but she does not much concern herself with the housekeeping—that is up to me. To tell the truth, I have never actually seen her, though I have the feeling that she is there."

"Does this house resemble the one you bought for your own mother in Lindau?"

"Only as one large house must resemble another."

"I see. Proceed."

"For a long time each night I continue like that, giving orders, and sometimes going over the accounts. Then a servant, usually it is a maid, arrives to tell me that the owner wishes to speak to me. I stand before a mirror—I can see myself there as plainly as I see you now—and arrange my clothing. The maid brings rose-scented water and a cloth, and I wipe my face; then I go in to him.

"He is always in one of the upper rooms, seated at a table with his own account book spread before him. There is an open window behind him, and through it I can see the top of a cherry tree in bloom. For a long time—oh, I suppose ten minutes—I stand before him while he turns over the pages of his ledger."

"You appear somewhat at a loss, Herr R____ —not a common condition for you, I believe. What happens then?"

"He says, 'You owe . . .' " Herr____ paused. "That is the problem, monsieur, I can never recall the amount. But it is a large sum. He says, 'And I must require that you make payment at once.'

"I do not have the amount, and I tell him so. He says, 'Then you must leave my employment.' I fall to my knees at this and beg that he will retain me, pointing out that if he dismisses me I will have lost my source of income, and will never be able to make payment. I do not enjoy telling you this, but I weep. Sometimes I beat the floor with my fists."

"Continue. Is the Dream-Master moved by your pleading?"

"No. He again demands that I pay the entire sum. Several times I have told him that I am a wealthy man in this world, and that if only he would permit me to make payment in its currency, I would do so immediately."

"That is interesting—most of us lack your presence of mind in our nightmares. What does he say then?"

"Usually he tells me not to be a fool. But once he said, 'That is a dream—you must know it by now. You cannot expect to pay a real debt with the currency of sleep.' He holds out his hand for the money as he speaks to me. It is then that I see the blood in his palm."

"You are afraid of him?"

"Oh, very much so. I understand that he has the most complete power over me. I weep, and at last I throw myself at his feet—with my head under the table, if you can credit it, crying like an infant.

"Then he stands and pulls me erect, and says, 'You would never be able to pay all you owe, and you are a false and dishonest servant. But your debt is forgiven, forever.' And as I watch, he tears a leaf from his account book and hands it to me."

"Your dream has a happy conclusion, then."

"No. It is not yet over. I thrust the paper into the front of my shirt and go out, wiping my face on my sleeve. I am conscious that if any of the other servants should see me, they will know at once what has happened. I hurry to reach my own counting room; there is a brazier there, and I wish to burn the page from the owner's book."

"I see."

"But just outside the door of my own room, I meet another servant—an upper-servant like myself, I think, since he is well dressed. As it happens, this man owes me a considerable sum of money, and to conceal from him what I have just endured, I demand that he pay at once." Herr R___ rose from his chair and began to pace the room, looking sometimes at the painted scenes on the walls, sometimes at the Turkish carpet at his feet. "I have had reason to demand money like that often, you understand. Here in this room.

"The man falls to his knees, weeping and begging for additional time; but I reach down, like this, and seize him by the throat."

"And then?"

"And then the door of my counting room opens. But it is not my counting room with my desk and the charcoal brazier, but the owner's own room. He is standing in the doorway, and behind him I can see the open window, and the blossoms of the cherry tree."

"What does he say to you?"

"Nothing. He says nothing to me. I release the other man's throat, and he slinks away."

"You awaken then?"

"How can I explain it? Yes, I wake up. But first we stand there; and while we do I am conscious of . . . certain sounds."

"If it is too painful for you, you need not say more."

Herr R___ drew a silk handkerchief from his pocket and wiped his face. "How can I explain?" he said again. "When I hear those sounds, I am aware that the owner possesses certain other servants, who have never been under my direction. It is as though I have always known this, but had no reason to think of it before."

"I understand."

"They are quartered in another part of the house—in the vaults beneath the wine cellar, I think sometimes. I have never seen them, but I know—then—that they are hideous, vile and cruel; I know too that he thinks me but little better than they, and that as he permits me to serve him, so he allows them to serve him also. I stand—we stand—and listen to them coming through the house. At last a door at the end of the hall begins to swing open. There is a hand like the paw of some filthy reptile on the latch."

"Is that the end of the dream?"

"Yes." Herr R___ threw himself into his chair again, mopping his face.

"You have this experience each night?"

"It differs," he said slowly, "in some details."

"You have told me that the orders you give the under-servants vary."

"There is another difference. When the dreams began, I woke when the hinges of the door at the passage-end creaked. Each night now the dream endures a moment longer. Perhaps a tenth of a second. Now I see the arm of the creature who opens that door, nearly to the elbow."

I took the address of his home, which he was glad enough to give me, and leaving the bank made my way to my hotel.

When I had eaten my roll and drunk my coffee the next morning, I went to the place indicated by the card given me by Baron H___, and in a few minutes was sitting with him in a room as bare as those tents from which armies in the field are cast into battle. "You are ready to begin the case this morning?" he asked.

"On the contrary. I have already begun; indeed, I am about to enter a new phase of my investigation. You would not have come to me if your Dream-Master were not torturing someone other than the people whose names you gave me. I wish to know the identity of that person, and to interrogate him."

"I told you that there were many other reports. I—"

"Provided me with a list. They are all of the petite bourgeoisie, when they are not persons still less important. I believed at first that it might be because of the urgings of Herr R____ that you engaged me; but when I had time to reflect on what I know of your methods, I realized that you would have demanded that he provide my fee had that been the case. So you are sheltering someone of greater importance, and I wish to speak to him."

"The Countess—" Baron H____ began.

"Ah!"

"The Countess herself has expressed some desire that you should be presented to her. The Count opposes it."

"We are speaking, I take it, of the governor of this province?"

The Baron nodded. "Of Count von V____. He is responsible, you understand, only to the Queen Regent herself."

"Very well. I wish to hear the Countess, and she wishes to talk with me. I assure you, Baron, that we will meet; the only question is whether it will be under your auspices."

The Countess, to whom I was introduced that afternoon, was a woman in her early twenties, deep-breasted and somber-haired, with skin like milk, and great dark eyes welling with fear and (I thought) pity, set in a perfect oval face.

"I am glad you have come, monsieur. For seven weeks now our good Baron H____ has sought this man for me, but he has not found him."

"If I had known my presence here would please you, Countess, I would have come long ago, whatever the obstacles. You then, like the others, are certain it is a real man we seek?"

"I seldom go out, monsieur. My husband feels we are in constant danger of assassination."

"I believe he is correct."

"But on state occasions we sometimes ride in a glass coach to the *Rathaus*. There are uhlans all around us to protect us then. I am certain that—before the dreams began—I saw the face of this man in the crowd."

"Very well. Now tell me your dream."

"I am here, at home—"

"In this palace, where we sit now?"

She nodded.

"That is a new feature, then. Continue, please."

"There is to be an execution. In the garden." A fleeting smile crossed the Countess's lovely face. "I need not tell you that that is not where the executions are held; but it does not seem strange to me when I dream.

"I have been away, I think, and have only just heard of what is to take place. I rush into the garden. The man Baron H____ calls the Dream-Master is there, tied to the trunk of the big cherry tree; a squad of soldiers faces him, holding their rifles; their officer stands beside them with his saber drawn, and my husband is watching from a pace or two away. I call out for them to stop, and my husband turns to look at me. I say: 'You must not do it, Karl. You must not kill this man.' But I see by his expression that he believes that I am only a foolish, tender-hearted child. Karl is . . . several years older than I."

"I am aware of it."

"The Dream-Master turns his head to look at me. People tell me that my eyes are large—do you think them large, monsieur?"

"Very large, and very beautiful."

"In my dream, quite suddenly, his eyes seem far, far larger than mine, and far more beautiful; and in them

I see reflected the figure of my husband. Please listen carefully now, because what I am going to say is very important, though it makes very little sense, I am afraid."

"Anything may happen in a dream, Countess."

"When I see my husband reflected in this man's eyes, I know—I cannot say how—that it is this reflection, and not the man who stands near me, who is the real Karl. The man I have thought real is only a reflection of that reflection. Do you follow what I say?"

I nodded. "I believe so."

"I plead again: 'Do not kill him. Nothing good can come of it. . . .' My husband nods to the officer, the soldiers raise their rifles, and . . . and . . .'"

"You wake. Would you like my handkerchief, Countess? It is of coarse weave; but it is clean, and much larger than your own."

"Karl is right—I am only a foolish little girl. No, monsieur, I do not wake—not yet. The soldiers fire. The Dream-Master falls forward, though his bonds hold him to the tree. And Karl flies to bloody rags beside me."

On my way back to my hotel, I purchased a map of the city; and when I reached my room I laid it flat on the table there. There could be no question of the route of the Countess's glass coach—straight down the Hauptstrasse, the only street in the city wide enough to take a carriage surrounded by cavalrymen. The most probable route by which Herr R____ might go from his house to his bank coincided with the Hauptstrasse for several blocks. The path Fräulein A____ would travel from her flat to the arcade crossed the Hauptstrasse at a point contained by that interval. I needed to know no more.

Very early the next morning I took up my post at the intersection. If my man were still alive after the fusillade Count von V____ fired at him each night, it seemed certain that he would appear at this spot within a few days, and I am hardened to waiting. I smoked cigarettes while I watched the citizens of I____ walk up and down before me. When an hour had passed, I bought a newspaper from a vendor, and stole a few glances at its pages when foot traffic was light.

Gradually I became aware that I was watched—we boast of reason, but there are senses over which reason holds no authority. I did not know where my watcher was, yet I felt his gaze on me, whichever way I turned. So, I thought, you know me, my friend. Will I too dream now? What has attracted your attention to a mere foreigner, a stranger, waiting for who-knows-what at this corner? Have you been talking to Fräulein A____? Or to someone who has spoken with her?

Without appearing to do so, I looked up and down both streets in search of another lounger like myself. There was no one—not a drowsing grandfather, not a woman or a child, not even a dog. Certainly no tall man with a forked beard and piercing eyes. The windows then—I studied them all, looking for some movement in a dark room behind a seemingly innocent opening. Nothing.

Only the buildings behind me remained. I crossed to the opposite side of the Hauptstrasse and looked once more. Then I laughed.

They must have thought me mad, all those dour burghers, for I fairly doubled over, spitting my cigarette to the sidewalk and clasping my hands to my waist for fear my belt would burst. The presumption, the impudence, the brazen insolence of the fellow! The stupidity, the wonderful stupidity of myself, who had not recognized his old stories! For the remainder of my life now, I could accept any case with pleasure, pursue the most inept criminal with zest, knowing that there was always a chance he might outwit such an idiot as I.

For the Dream-Master had set up His own picture, and full-length and in the most gorgeous colors, in His window. Choking and spluttering I saluted it, and then, still filled with laughter, I crossed the street once more and went inside, where I knew I would find Him. A man awaited me there—not the one I sought, but one who understood Whom it was I had come for, and knew as well as I that His capture was beyond any thief-taker's power. I knelt, and there, though not to the satisfaction I suppose of Baron H____, Fräulein A____, Herr R____, and the Count and Countess von V____, I destroyed the Dream-Master as He has been sacrificed so often, devouring His white, wheaten flesh that we might all possess life without end.

Dear people, dream on.

JADE BLUE

by Edward Bryant

"And this," said Timnath Obregon, "is the device I have invented to edit time."

The quartet of blurred and faded ladies from the Craterside Park Circle of Aesthetes made appreciative sounds; the whisper of a dry wind riffling the plates of a long-out-of-print art folio.

"Time itself."

"Fascinating, yes."

"Quite."

The fourth lady said nothing, but pursed wrinkled lips. She fixed the inventor in a coquettish gaze. Obregon averted his eyes. How, he wondered, did he deserve to be appreciated in this fashion? He had begun to wish the ladies would leave him to his laboratory.

"Dear Mr. Obregon," said the hitherto silent one. "You have no idea how much we appreciate the opportunity to visit your laboratory. This district of Cinnabar was growing tedious. It is so refreshing to encounter an eminent personality such as yourself."

Obregon's smile was strained. "I thank you, but my fame may be highly transitory."

Four faces were enraptured.

"My APE—" The inventor took a cue from the concert of rising eyebrows. "Ah, that's my none-too-clever acronym for the artificial probability enhancer. My device seems on the brink of being invented

314

simultaneously—or worse, first—by a competitor at the Tancarae Institute. One Dr. Sebastian Le Goff."

"Then this machine is not yet, um, fully invented?"

"Not fully developed. No, I'm afraid not." Obregon thought he heard one of the ladies *tsking*, an action he had previously believed only a literary invention. "But it's very, very close to completion," he hastened to say. "Here, let me show you. I can't offer a full demonstration, of course, but—" He smiled winningly.

Obregon seated himself before the floor-to-ceiling crystal pillar which was the APE. He placed his hands on a brushed-metal console. "These are the controls. The keyboard is for the programming of probability changes." He stabbed the panel with an index finger; the crystal pillar glowed fluorescent orange. "The device is powdered inductively by the vortical time streams which converge in the center of Cinnabar." His finger darted again and the pillar resumed it transparency. "For now I'm afraid that's all I can show you."

"Very pretty, though."

"I think blue would be so much more attractive."

"I found the most cunning sapphire curtain material yesterday."

"Tea would be marvelous, Mr. Obregon."

"Please, ladies. Call me Timnath." The inventor walked to a tangle of plastic tubing on an antiseptic counter. "I'm an habitual tea drinker, so I installed this instant brewing apparatus." He slid a white panel aside and removed five delicate double-handled cups. "The blend for today is black dragon pekoe. Satisfactory with everyone?"

Nodding of heads; brittle rustle of dying leaves.

"Cream and sugar?"

The tall one: "Goat cream, please."

The short one: "Two sugars, please."

The most indistinct one: "Nothing, thank you."

The flirtatious one: "Mother's milk, if you would."

Obregon punched out the correct combinations on the teamaker's panel and rotated the cups under the spigot.

From behind him one of the ladies said, "Timnath, what will you do with your machine?"

Obregon hesitated. "I'm not sure, really. I've always rather liked the way things are. But I've invented a way of changing them. Maybe it's a matter of curiousity."

Then he turned and distributed the tea. They sat and sipped and talked of science and the arts.

"I firmly believe," said the inventor, "that science *is* an art."

"Yes," said the flirtatious lady. "I gather that you pay little attention to either the practical or commercial applications of technology." She smiled at him from behind steepled fingers.

"Quite so. Many at the Institute call me a dilettante."

The tall lady said, "I believe it's time to go. Timnath, we thank you for allowing us to impose. It has been a pleasure." She dashed her teacup to the tile floor. Her companions followed suit.

Startled by their abruptness, Obregon almost forgot to smash his own nearly empty cup. He stood politely as the ladies filed past him to the door. Their postures were strangely alike; each in her brown dress reminded him of the resurrectronic cassowaries he admired at the Natural History Club.

"A pleasure," repeated the tall lady.

"Quite." (The short one.)

Exit the flirt. "Perhaps I'll be seeing you again soon?" Her gaze lingered and Obregon looked aside, mumbling some pleasantry.

The fourth lady, the one whose features had not seemed to jell, paused in the doorway. She folded her arms so that the hands tucked into her armpits. She jumped up and down, flapping her truncated limbs. "Scraw! Scraw!" The soft door whuffed shut.

Taken aback, Obregon felt the need for another cup of tea and he sat down. On the table a small black cylinder stood on end. It could have been a tube of lip-salve. Apparently it had been forgotten by one of his guests. Curious, he picked it up. It was very light.

He unscrewed one end; the cylinder was empty. Obregon raised the object to his nose. There was the distinct acrid tang of silver iodide emulsion.

"It appears," said Obregon softly, "to be an empty film cannister."

A child's scream in a child's night. A purring, enfolding comfort. A loneliness of nightmares and the waking world and the indistinct borderland. A feline reassurance.

"Don't cry, baby. I'll hold you close and rock you."

George buried his face in the soft blue fur which blotted his tears. "Jade Blue, I love you."

"I know," said the catmother softly. "I love you too. Now sleep."

"I can't," George said. "They'll find me again." His voice rose in pitch and his body moved restlessly; he clutched at Jade Blue's warm flank. "They'll find me in the shadows, and some will hold me down, and the one will reach for—"

"Dreams," said Jade Blue. "They can't hurt you." Feeling inside her the lie. Her fingerpads caressed the boy's head and drew it close again.

"I'm afraid." George's voice was distantly hysterical.

The governess guided the boy's head. "Drink now." His lips found the rough nipple and sucked instinctively. Her milk soothed, gently narcotic, and he swallowed slowly. "Jade Blue," the whisper was nearly inaudible. "I love you." The boy's body began to relax.

Jade Blue rocked him slowly, carefully wiping away the thin trickle of milk from one corner of his mouth, then lay down and cuddled the boy against her. After a time she also slept.

And awoke, night-wary. She was alone. With an angry snarl, quickly clipped off, she struggled from the bed. Jade Blue extended all her senses and caught a subtle scent of fear, a soft rub of something limp on flagstones, the quick flash of shadow on shadow.

A black, vaguely anthropomorphic shape moved in the darkness of the doorway. There were words, but they were so soft as to seem exhaled rather than spoken: "Forget it, pussy." A mouth gaped and grinned. "He's ours, cat."

Jade Blue screamed and leaped with claws outthrust. The shadow figure did not move; it squeaked and giggled as the catmother tore it apart. Great portions of shadowstuff, light as ash, flew about the room. The mocking laughter faded.

She paused in the doorway, flanks heaving, sucking in breath. Her wide, pupilless eyes strained to interpret the available light. Sharp-pointed ears tilted forward. The enormous house, very quiet; except—

Jade Blue padded swiftly down the hall, easily threading the irregular masses of inert sculpture. She ran silently, but in her mind:

Stupid cat! That shadow was a decoy, a diversion.
    Foolish woman! The boy is my trust.
Find him. If anything has happened to him, I will
    be punished.
    If anything has happened to him, I shall kill
    myself.
A sound. The game room.
    They couldn't have taken him far.
That bitch Merreile! I could tear out her throat.
    How could she do it to him?
Close now. Quietly.

The double doors of the game room stood ajar. Jade Blue slipped between their baroquely carved edges. The room was large and echoing with the paraphernalia of childhood: glaze-eyed hobbyhorses, infinite shelves of half-assembled model kits, ranks of books and tapes and dot-cases, balls, mallets, frayed creatures spilling stuffing, instruments of torture, gaming boards, and an infrared spectrometer. The catmother moved carefully through George's labyrinth of memories.

In a cleared space in the far end she found him. George lay on his back, spread-eagled, straining weakly against intangible fetters. Around him flocked the moving shadows, dark succubus-shapes. One of them crouched low over the boy and brushed shadow lips around flesh.

George's mouth moved and he mewed weakly, like a kitten. He raised his head and stared past the shadows at Jade Blue.

The catmother resisted her first berserker reaction. Instead she stepped quickly to the near wall and found the lighting panel. She pressed a square, and dim illumination glowed from the walls; pressed harder and the light brightened, then seared. Proper shadows vanished. The moving shadow creatures raveled like poorly woven fabric and were gone. Jade Blue felt an ache beginning in her retinas and dimmed the light to a bearable level.

On the floor George was semiconscious. Jade Blue picked him up easily. His eyes were open, their movements rapid and random, but he was seeing nothing. Jade Blue cradled the boy close and walked down the long hallways to their bedroom.

George was dreamless the remainder of the long night. Once, closer to wakening, he stirred and lightly touched Jade Blue's breasts. "Kitty, kitty," he said. "Nice kitty." Friendlier shadows closed about them both until morning.

When George awoke he felt a coarse grade of sand abrade the inside of his eyelids. He rubbed with his fists, but the sensation lingered. His mouth was dry. George experimentally licked the roof of his mouth; it felt like textured plastic. There was no taste. He stretched, winced, joints aching. The syndrome was familiar; it was the residue of bad dreams.

"I'm hungry." He reclined against crumpled blue satin. A seed of querulousness, "I'm hungry." Still no response. "Jade Blue?" He was hungry, and a bit lonely. The two conditions were complementary in George, and both omnipresent.

George swung his legs off the bed. "Cold!" He drew

on the pair of plush slippers; then, otherwise naked, he walked into the hall.

Sculptures in various stages of awakening nodded at George as he passed. The stylization of David yawned and scratched its crotch. "Morning, George."

"Good morning, David."

The replica of a Third Cycle odalisque ignored him as usual.

"Bitch," George mumbled.

"Mommy's boy," mocked the statue of Victory Rampant.

George ignored her and hurried past.

The abstract Pranksters Group tried to cheer him up, but failed miserably.

"Just shut up," said George. "All of you."

Eventually the sculptures were left behind and George walked down a paneled hallway.

The hall finally described a klein turn, twisted in upon itself, and exited into the laboratory of Timnath Obregon.

Luminous pearl walls funneled him toward the half-open door. George saw a quick swirl of lab smock. He was suddenly conscious of the silence of his steps. He knew he should announce himself. But then he overheard the dialogue:

"If his parents would come home, that might help." The voice was husky, the vowels drawn out. Jade Blue.

"Not a chance," said Obregon's tenor. "They're too close to City Center by now. I couldn't even begin to count the subjective years before they'll be back."

George waited outside the doorway and listened.

Jade Blue's voice complained. "Well, couldn't they have found a better time for a second honeymoon? Or third, or fourth, or whatever."

A verbal shrug. "They are, after all, researchers with a curious bent. And the wonders which lie closer to the center of Cinnabar are legendary. I can't blame them for their excursion. They *had* lived in this family group a rather long time."

"Oh shit, you idiot human! You're rationalizing."

"Not entirely. George's mother and father are sentients. They have a right to their own life."

"They also have responsibilities." Pause. "Merreile. That fathersucking little—"

"They couldn't have known when they hired her, Jade Blue. Her, um, peculiarities didn't become apparent until she had been George's governess for several months. Even then, no one knew the ultimate results."

"No one knew! No one cared, you mean."

"That's a bit harsh, Jade—"

"Listen, you pale imitation of an open mind. Can't you see? They're the most selfish people alive. They want to take nothing from themselves, give nothing to their son."

Silence for a few seconds.

Jade Blue again: "You're a kind man, but so damned obtuse!"

"I'm quite fond of George," said the inventor.

"And I also. I love him as one of my own. It's too bad his own parents don't."

In the hallway George was caught in an ambivalence of emotion. He missed his parents horribly. But he also loved Jade Blue. So he began to cry.

Obregon tinkered with a worms' warren of platinum filaments.

Jade Blue paced the interior of the laboratory and wished she could switch her vestigial tail.

George finished his milk and licked the last cookie crumb from his palm.

A large raven flapped lazily through a window in the far end of the lab. "Scraw! Scraw!"

"Ha!" The inventor snapped his fingers and glistening panes slid into place; the doors shut; the room was sealed. Apparently confused, the raven fluttered in a tight circle, screaming in hoarse echoes.

"Jade, get the boy down!" Obregon reached under the APE's console and came up with a cocked and loaded crossbow. The bird saw the weapon, snap-rolled into a turn and dive, darted for the closest window. It struck the pane and rebounded.

George let Jade Blue pull him down under one of the lab tables.

Wings beat furiously as the raven caromed off a wall, attempting evasive action. Obregon coolly aimed the crossbow and squeezed the trigger. The short square-headed quarrel passed completely through the raven and embedded itself in the ceiling. The bird, wings frozen in mid-flap, cartwheeled through the air and struck the floor at Obregon's feet. Stray black feathers autumnleafed to the floor.

The inventor gingerly toed the body; no movement. "Fool. Such underestimation." He turned to Jade Blue and his nephew, who were extracting themselves from beneath the table. "Perhaps I'm less distracted than you charge."

The catmother licked delicately at her rumpled blue fur. "Care to explain all this?"

Obregon picked up the body of the raven with the air of a man lifting a package of particularly fulsome garbage. "Simulacrum," he said. "A construct. If I dissected it properly I'd discover a quite sophisticated surveillance and recording system." He caught Jade Blue's unblinking green eyes. "It's a spy, you see." He dropped the carcass into the disposer, where it vanished in a golden flare and the transitory odor of well-done meat.

"It was big," said George.

"Good observation. Wingspread of at least two meters. That's larger than any natural raven."

"Who," asked Jade Blue, "is spying?"

"A competitor, fellow named Le Goff, a man of no certain ethics and fewer scruples. A day ago he brought his spies here to check the progress of my new invention. It was all done very clumsily so that I'd notice. Le Goff is worse than a mere thief. He mocks me." Obregon gestured toward the artificial probability enhancer.

"It's *that* he wishes to complete before I do."

"A crystal pillar?" said Jade Blue. "How marvelous."

"Quiet, cat. My machine can edit time. I will be able to alter the present by modifying the past."

"Is that all it does?"

Obregon seemed disgusted. "In my own home I don't need mockery."

"Sorry. You sounded pompous."

The inventor forced a laugh. "I suppose so. It's Le Goff who has driven me to that. All I've ever wanted was to be left in peace to work my theories. Now I feel I'm being forced into some sort of confrontation."

"And competition?"

Obregon nodded. "Just why, I don't know. I worked with Le Goff for years at the Institute. He was always a man of obscure motives."

"You're a good shot," said George.

Obregon self-consciously set the crossbow on the console. "It's a hobby. I'd only practiced with stationary targets before."

"Can I try it?"

"I think you're probably too small. It takes a great deal of strength to cock the bow."

"I'm not too small to pull the trigger."

"No," said Obregon. "You're not." He smiled. "After lunch we'll go out to the range. I'll let you shoot."

"Can I shoot a bird?"

"No, not a live one. I'll have some simulacrae made up."

"Timnath," said Jade Blue. "I don't suppose— No, probably not."

"What."

"Your machine. It can't change dreams."

Mother, Father, help me I don't want the dreams any more. Just the warm black that's all. Mother? Father? Why did you go when will you come back? You leave me left me make me hurt.

Uncle Timnath, get them bring them back. Tell them I hurt I need. Make them love me.

Jade Blue, rock me hold me love me bring them back now. No no don't touch me there you're like

Merreile I don't want more bad dreams don't hurt
don't—

And Merreile would come into his bedroom
each evening to take him from his toys and prepare him for bed. She would undress him slowly
and slip the nightshirt over his head, then sit
cross-legged at the foot of the bed while he lay
back against the pillow.

"A story before sleeping? Of course, my love.
Shall I tell again of the vampires?

"Do you remember my last telling, love? No?
Perhaps I caused you to forget." And she would
smile, showing the bands of scarlet cartilage where
most people had teeth.

"Once upon a time, there was a little boy,
much like you, who lived in an enormous old
house. He was alone there, except for his parents
and his loving governess.

"Oh, quite true that there were vampires hiding
in the attic, but they weren't much like living
creatures at all. They seldom ventured from the
attic and the boy was never allowed to go there.
His parents had forbidden him, despite the fact
that the attic was filled with all manner of interesting and enjoyable things.

"The boy's curiosity grew and grew until one
night he slipped out of his room and quietly climbed
the stairs to the attic. At the top of the flight he
paused, remembering his parents' warning. Then
he recalled what he had heard about the strange
treasures that lay within. He knew that warnings
come from dull people and should be ignored.
That barriers are made to be crossed. And then
he opened the attic dor.

"Inside were rows of tables stacked high with
every sort of game and toy imaginable. Between
were smaller tables laden with candy and cakes
and pitchers of delicious drink. The boy was never
happier.

"At that moment the vampires came out to play. They looked much like you and me, except that they were black and very quiet and just as thin as shadows.

"They crowded around the boy and whispered to him to come join their games.

"They loved the boy very much, because people came so seldom to the attic to visit. They were very honest (for folk so thin cannot hold lies) and the boy knew how silly his parents' warnings had been. Then they went off to the magic lands in the far end of the attic and played for hours and hours.

"What games, darling? I will show you."

And then Merreile would switch off the light and reach for him.

No, it can't change dreams, Timnath had said, musing. Then, looking through the catmother's eyes as though jade were glass, he said, *Give me time; I must think on it.*

They sat and talked in the blue bedroom.

"Did you ever have children like me?" George hugged his drawn-up knees.

"Not like you."

"I mean, were they kittens, or more like babies?"

"Both if you like. Neither." Her voice was neutral.

"You're not playing fair. Answer me." The child's voice was ancient, petulant from long practice.

"What do you want to know?"

George's fists beat a rapid tattoo on his knees. "Your children, what were they like? I want to know what happened to them."

Silence for a while. Small wrinkles under Jade Blue's lip, as though she held something bitter in her mouth. "They were never like anything."

"I don't understand."

"Because they *weren't*. They came from Terminex the computer. They lived in him and died in him; he placed the bright images in my brain."

George sat straighter; this was better than a bedtime story. "But why?"

"I'm the perfect governess. My maternal instincts are augmented. I've hostages in my mind." Each word was perfectly cut with gemstone edges.

Petulance softened to a child's compassion. "It makes you very sad."

"Sometimes."

"When I'm sad I cry."

"I don't," said Jade Blue. "I can't cry."

"I'll be your son," said George.

The hall of diurnal statues was still. Jade Blue prowled the shadows, seeking the slight sounds and odors and temperature differentials. The encroaching minutes frustrated and made her frantic. The many nights of sleepless watch—and the eventual betrayal by her body. Again she looked for a lost child.

Not in the game room this time; the hobbyhorses grinned vacantly.

Nor in the twenty gray parlors where George's ancestors kept an embalmed and silent vigil from their wall niches.

Nor in the attic, dusty and spiderwebbed.

Not in the dining hall, arboretum, kitchens, aquatorium, library, observatory, family rooms, or linen closets.

Not—Jade Blue ran down the oak hallway and the minute sings vindicated her caprice. She ran faster and when she hurled herself into the corner which kleined into the approach to Timnath Obregon's laboratory, her stomach turned queasily.

The door slid open at a touch. The lab was dimly illuminated by the distorted yellow lights of Cinnabar. Several things occurred at once:

—In front of her, a startled figure looked up from the console of Obregon's APE. A reeled measuring tape dropped and clattered on tile.

—Across the lab a group of capering shadow figures stopped the act they were committing on George's prone body and looked toward the door.

—A screeching bird-shape flapped down from the dark ceiling and struck at Jade Blue's eyes.

The catmother ducked and felt claws cut harmless runnels through fur. She rolled onto her back and lashed out, her own claws extended. She snagged something heavy that screamed and buffeted her face with feathered wings. She knew she could kill it.

Until the booted foot came down on her throat and Jade Blue looked up past the still-struggling bird-thing at whoever had been examining Obregon's invention. "Sorry," said the man, and pressed harder.

"George!" Her voice was shrill, strangled. "Help." And then the boot was too heavy to let by any words at all. The darkness thickened intolerably.

The pressure stopped. Jade Blue could not see, but—painfully—she could again breathe. She could hear, but she didn't know what the noises were. There were bright lights and Timnath's concerned face, and arms lifting her from the floor. There was warm tea and honey poured into a saucer. George was hugging her and his tears put salt in the tea.

Jade Blue rubbed her throat gingerly and sat up; she realized she was on a white lab table. On the floor a little way from the table was an ugly mixture of feathers and wet red flesh. Something almost unrecognizable as a man took a ragged breath.

"Sebastian," said Timnath, kneeling beside the body. "My dear friend." He was crying.

"Scraw!" said the dying man; and died.

"Did you kill him?" said Jade Blue, her voice hoarse.

"No, the shadows did."

"How?"

"Unpleasantly." Timnath snapped his fingers twice and the glittering labrats scuttled out from the walls to clean up the mess.

"Are you all right?" George stood very close to his governess. He was shivering. "I tried to help you."

"I think you did help me. We're all alive."

"He did, and we are," said Timnath. "For once, George's creations were an aid rather than a hindrance."

"I still want you to do something with your machine," said Jade Blue.

Timnath looked sadly down at the body of Sebastian Le Goff. "We have time."

Time progressed helically, and one day Timnath pronounced his invention ready. He called George and Jade Blue to the laboratory. "Ready?" he said, pressing the button which would turn on the machine.

"I don't know," said George, half hiding behind Jade Blue. "I'm not sure what's happening."

"It will help him," said Jade Blue. "Do it."

"He may be lost to you," said Timnath.

George whimpered. "No."

"I love him enough," said the governess. "Do it."

The crystal pillar glowed bright orange. A fine hum cycled up beyond the auditory range. Timnath tapped on the keyboard: GEORGE'S DREAMS OF THE SHADOW VAMPIRES ARE AS NEVER WERE. MERREILE NEVER EXISTED. GEORGE IS OPTIMALLY HAPPY.

The inventor paused, then stabbed a special button: REVISE.

The crystal pillar glowed bright orange. A fine hum cycled up beyond the auditory range. Timnath tapped on the keyboard: GEORGE'S DREAMS OF THE SHADOW VAMPIRES ARE AS NEVER WERE. MERREILE NEVER EXISTED. GEORGE IS REASONABLY HAPPY.

Timnath considered then pushed another button: ACTIVATE: "That's it," he said.

"Something's leaving us," Jade Blue whispered.

They heard a scuff of footsteps in the outer hall. Two people walking. There was the clearing of a throat, a parental cough.

"Who's there?" said Jade Blue, knowing.

SOMETHING WILD IS LOOSE

by Robert Silverberg

~~~~~~~~~~~~~~~~~~~~~~~~

The Vsiir got aboard the Earthbound ship by accident.
It had absolutely no plans for taking a holiday on a
wet, grimy planet like Earth. But it was in its metamorphic phase, undergoing the period of undisciplined
change that began as winter came on, and it had
shifted so far up-spectrum that Earthborn eyes couldn't
see it. Oh, a really skilled observer might notice a
slippery little purple flicker once in a while, a kind of
snore, as the Vsiir momentarily dropped down out of
the ultraviolet; but he'd have to know where to look,
and when. The crewman who was responsible for putting the Vsiir on the ship never even considered the
possibility that there might be something invisible sleeping atop one of the crates of cargo being hoisted into
the ship's hold. He simply went down the row, slapping a floater-node on each crate and sending it glid-
ing up the gravity wall toward the open hatch. The
fifth crate to go inside was the one on which the Vsiir
had decided to take its nap. The spaceman didn't
know that he had inadvertently given an alien organism a free ride to Earth. The Vsiir didn't know it,
either, until the hatch was sealed and an oxygen-nitrogen
atmosphere began to hiss from the vents. The Vsiir
did not happen to breathe those gases, but, because it
was in its time of metamorphosis, it was able to adapt
itself quickly and nicely to the sour, prickly vapors
seeping into its metabolic cells. The next step was to

fashion a set of full-spectrum scanners and learn some-thing about its surroundings. Within a few minutes, the Vsiir was aware—

—that it was in a large, dark place that held a great many boxes containing various mineral and vegetable products of its world, mainly branches of the greenfire tree but also some other things of no comprehensible value to a Vsiir—

—that a double wall of curved metal enclosed this place—

—that just beyond this wall was a null-atmosphere zone, such as is found between one planet and another—

—that this entire closed system was undergoing acceleration—

—that this therefore was a spaceship, heading rap-idly away from the world of Vsiirs and in fact already some ten planetary diameters distant, with the gap growing alarmingly moment by moment—

—that it would be impossible, even for a Vsiir in metamorphosis, to escape from the spaceship at this point—

—and that, unless it could persuade the crew of the ship to halt and go back, it would be com-pelled to undertake a long and dreary voyage to a strange and probably loathsome world, where life would at best be highly inconvenient, and might present great dangers. It would find itself cut off painfully from the rhythm of its own civilization. It would miss the Festival of Changing. It would miss the Holy Eclipse. It would not be able to take part in next spring's Rising of the Sea. It would suffer in a thousand ways.

There were six human beings aboard the ship. Ex-tending its perceptors, the Vsiir tried to reach their minds. Though humans had been coming to its planet for many years, it had never bothered making contact with them before; but it had never been in this much trouble before, either. It sent a foggy tendril of thought, roving the corridors, looking for traces of human intel-ligence. Here? A glow of electrical activity within a sphere of bone: a mind, a mind! A busy mind. But surrounded by a wall, apparently; the Vsiir rammed up against it and was thrust back. That was startling and disturbing. What kind of beings were these, whose minds were closed to ordinary contact? The Vsiir went on, hunting through the ship. Another mind: again closed. Another. Another. The Vsiir felt panic rising. Its mantle fluttered; its energy radiations dropped far down into the visible spectrum, then shot nervously toward much shorter waves. Even its physical form experienced a series of quick involuntary metamorphoses, to the Vsiir's intense embarrassment. It did not get control of its body until it had passed from spherical to cubical to chaotic, and had become a gridwork of fibrous threads held together only by a pulsing strand of ego. Fiercely it forced itself back to the spherical form and resumed its search of the ship, dismally realizing that by this time its native world was half a stellar unit away. It was without hope now, but it continued to probe the minds of the crew, if only for the sake of thoroughness. Even if it made contact, though, how could it communicate the nature of its plight, and even if it communicated, why would the humans be disposed to help it? Yet it went on through the ship. And—

Here: an open mind. No wall at all. A miracle! The Vsiir rushed into close contact, overcome with joy and surprise, pouring out its predicament. *Please listen. Unfortunate nonhuman organism accidentally transported into this vessel during loading of cargo. Metabolically and psychologically unsuited for prolonged life on Earth. Begs pardon for inconvenience, wishes prompt return to home planet recently left, regrets disturbance in shipping schedule but hopes that this large favor will not prove impossible to grant. Do you comprehend my sending? Unfortunate nonhuman organism accidentally transported—*

Lieutenant Falkirk had drawn the first sleep-shift after floatoff. It was only fair; Falkirk had knocked him-

self out processing the cargo during the loading stage,
slapping the floater-nodes on every crate and feeding
the transmit manifests to the computer. Now that the
ship was spaceborne he could grab some rest while the
other crewmen were handling the floatoff chores. So he
settled down for six hours in the cradle as soon as they
were on their way. Below him, the ship's six gravity-
drinkers spun on their axes, gobbling inertia and pushing up the acceleration, and the ship floated Earthward
at a velocity that would reach the galactic level before
Falkirk woke. He drifted into drowsiness. A good trip:
enough greenfire bark in the hold to see Earth through
a dozen fits of the molecule plague, and plenty of other
potential medicinals besides, along with a load of interesting mineral samples, and—Falkirk slept. For half an
hour he enjoyed sweet slumber, his mind disengaged,
his body loose.

Until a dark dream bubbled through his skull.

Deep purple sunlight, hot and somber. Something
slippery tickling the edges of his brain. He lies on a
broad white slab in a scorched desert. Unable to move.
Getting harder to breathe. The gravity—a terrible pull,
bending and breaking him, ripping his bones apart.
Hooded figures moving around him, pointing, laughing, exchanging blurred comments in an unknown language. His skin melting and taking on a new texture:
porcupine quills sprouting inside his flesh and forcing
their way upward, poking out through every pore. Points
of fire all over him. A thin scarlet hand, withered
fingers like crab claws, hovering in front of his face.
Scratching. Scratching. Scratching. His blood running
among the quills, thick and sluggish. He shivers, struggling to sit up—lifts a hand, leaving pieces of quivering
flesh stuck to the slab—sits up—

Wakes, trembling, screaming.

Falkirk's shout still sounded in his own ears as his
eyes adjusted to the light. Lieutenant Commander
Rodriguez was holding his shoulders and shaking him.

"You all right?"

Falkirk tried to reply. Words wouldn't come. Hallucinatory shock, he realized, as part of his mind attempted to convince the other part that the dream was over. He was trained to handle crises; he ran through a quick disciplinary countdown and calmed himself, though he was still badly shaken. "Nightmare," he said hoarsely. "A beauty. Never had a dream with that kind of intensity before."

Rodriguez relaxed. Obviously he couldn't get very upset over a mere nightmare. "You want a pill?"

Falkirk shook his head. "I'll manage, thanks."

But the impact of the dream lingered. It was more than an hour before he got back to sleep, and then he fell into a light, restless doze, as if his mind were on guard against a return of those chilling fantasies. Fifty minutes before his programmed wake-up time, he was awakened by a ghastly shriek from the far side of the cabin.

Lieutenant Commander Rodriguez was having a nightmare.

When the ship made floatdown on Earth a month later it was, of course, put through the usual decontamination procedures before anyone or anything aboard it was allowed out of the starport. The outer hull got squirted with sealants designed to trap and smother any microorganism that might have hitchhiked from another world; the crewmen emerged through the safety pouch and went straight into a quarantine chamber without being exposed to the air; the ship's atmosphere was cycled into withdrawal chambers, where it underwent a thorough purification, and the entire interior of the vessel received a six-phase sterilization, beginning with fifteen minutes of hard vacuum and ending with an hour of neutron bombardment.

These procedures caused a certain degree of inconvenience for the Vsiir. It was already at the low end of its energy phase, due mainly to the repeated discouragements it had suffered in its attempts to communicate with the six humans. Now it was forced to adapt to a variety of unpleasant environments with no chance to rest between changes. Even the most adaptable of organisms can get tired. By the time the starport's decontamination team was ready to certify that the ship was wholly free of alien life-forms, the Vsiir was very, very tired indeed.

The oxygen-nitrogen atmosphere entered the hold once more. The Vsiir found it quite welcome, at least in contrast to all that had just been thrown at it. The hatch was open; stevedores were muscling the cargo crates into position to be floated across the field to the handling dome. The Vsiir took advantage of this moment to extrude some legs and scramble out of the ship. It found itself on a broad concrete apron, rimmed by massive buildings. A yellow sun was shining in a blue sky; infrared was bouncing all over the place, but the Vsiir speedily made arrangements to deflect the excess. It also compensated immediately for the tinge of ugly hydrocarbons in the atmosphere, for the frightening noise level, and for the leaden feeling of homesickness that suddenly threatened its organic stability at the first sight of this unfamiliar, disheartening world. How to get home again? How to make contact, even? The Vsiir sensed nothing but closed minds—sealed like seeds in their shells. True, from time to time the minds of these humans opened, but even then they seemed unwilling to let the Vsiir's message get through.

Perhaps it would be different here. Perhaps those six were poor communicators, for some reason, and there would be more receptive minds available in this place. Perhaps. Perhaps. Close to despair, the Vsiir hurried across the field and slipped into the first building in which it sensed open minds. There were hundreds of humans in it, occupying many levels, and the open minds were widely scattered. The Vsiir located the nearest one and, worriedly, earnestly, hopefully, touched the tip of its mind to the human's. *Please listen. I mean no harm. Am nonhuman organism arrived on your planet through unhappy circumstances, wishing only quick going back to own world—*

*　　　*　　　*

The cardiac wing of Long Island Starport Hospital was on the ground floor, in the rear, where the patients could be given floater therapy without upsetting the gravitational ratios of the rest of the building. As always, the hospital was full—people were always coming in sick off starliners, and most of them were hospitalized right at the starport for their own safety—and the cardiac wing had more than its share. At the moment it held a dozen infarcts awaiting implant, nine postimplant recupes, five coronaries in emergency stasis, three ventricle-regrowth projects, an aortal patch job, and nine or ten assorted other cases. Most of the patients were floating, to keep down the gravitational strain on their damaged tissues—all but the regrowth people, who were under full Earthnorm gravity so that their new hearts would come in with the proper resilience and one of the lowest mortality rates in the hemisphere.

Losing two patients the same morning was a shock to the entire staff.

At 0917 the monitor flashed the red light for Mrs. Maldonado, 87, postimplant and thus far doing fine. She had developed acute endocarditis coming back from a tour of the Jupiter system; at her age there wasn't enough vitality to sustain her through the slow business of growing a new heart with a genetic prod, but they'd given her a synthetic implant and for two weeks it had worked quite well. Suddenly, though, the hospital's control center was getting a load of grim telemetry from Mrs. Maldonado's bed: valve action zero, blood pressure zero, respiration zero, pulse zero, everything zero, zero, zero. The EEG tape showed a violent lurch—as though she had received some abrupt and intense shock—followed by a minute or two of irregular action, followed by termination of brain activity. Long before any hospital personnel had reached her bedside, automatic revival equipment, both chemical and electrical, had gone to work on the patient, but she was beyond reach: a massive cerebral hemorrhage, coming totally without warning, had done irreversible damage.

At 0928 came the second loss: Mr. Guinness, 51, three days past surgery for a coronary embolism. The same series of events. A severe jolt to the nervous system, an immediate and fatal physiological response. Resuscitation procedures negative. No one on the staff had any plausible explanation for Mr. Guinness' death. Like Mrs. Maldonado, he had been sleeping peacefully, all vital signs good, until the moment of the fatal seizure.

"As though someone had come up and yelled *boo* in their ears," one doctor muttered, puzzling over the charts. He pointed to the wild EEG track. "Or as if they'd had unbearably vivid nightmares and couldn't take the sensory overload. But no one was making noise in the ward. And nightmares aren't contagious."

Dr. Peter Mookherji, resident in neuropathology, was beginning his morning rounds on the hospital's sixth level when the soft voice of his annunciator, taped behind his left ear, asked him to report to the quarantine building immediately. Dr. Mookherji scowled. "Can't it wait? This is my busiest time of day, and—"

"You are asked to come at once."

"Look, I've got a girl in a coma here, due for her teletherapy session in fifteen minutes, and she's counting on seeing me. I'm her only link to the world. If I'm not there when—"

"You are asked to come at once, Dr. Mookherji."

"Why do the quarantine people need a neuropathologist in such a hurry? Let me take care of the girl, at least, and in forty-five minutes they can have me."

"Dr. Mookherji—"

It didn't pay to argue with a machine. Mookherji forced his temper down. Short tempers ran in his family, along with a fondness for torrid curries and a talent for telepathy. Glowering, he grabbed a data terminal, identified himself, and told the hospital's control center to reprogram his entire morning schedule. "Build in a half-hour postponement somehow," he snapped. "I can't help it—see for yourself. I've been requisitioned by the quarantine staff." The computer was thoughtful enough to have a rollerbuggy waiting for him when he emerged from the hospital. It whisked him across the starport to the quarantine building in three minutes, but he was still angry when he got there. The scanner at the door ticked off his badge and one of the control center's innumerable voice-outputs told him solemnly, "You are expected in Room 403, Dr. Mookherji."

Room 403 turned out to be a two-sector interrogation office. The rear sector of the room was part of the building's central quarantine core, and the front sector belonged to the public-access part of the building, with a thick glass wall in between. Six haggard-looking spacemen were slouched on sofas behind the wall, and three members of the starport's quarantine staff paced about in the front. Mookherji's irritation ebbed when he saw that one of the quarantine men was an old medical-school friend, Lee Nakadai. The slender Japanese was a year older than Mookherji—29 to 28; they met for lunch occasionally at the starport commissary, and they had double-dated a pair of Filipina twins earlier in the year, but the pressure of work had kept them apart for months. Nakadai got down to business quickly now: "Pete, have you ever heard of an epidemic of nightmares?"

"Eh?"

Indicating the men behind the quarantine wall, Nakadai said, "These fellows came in a couple of hours ago from Norton's Star. Brought back a cargo of greenfire bark. Physically they check out to five decimal places, and I'd release them except for one funny thing. They're all in a bad state of nervous exhaustion, which they say is the result of having had practically no sleep during their whole month-long return trip. And the reason for that is that they were having nightmares—every one of them—real mind-wrecking dreams, whenever they tried to sleep. It sounded so peculiar that I thought we'd better run a neuropath checkup, in case they've picked up some kind of cerebral infection."

Mookherji frowned. "For this you get me out of my ward on emergency requisition, Lee?"

"Talk to them," Nakadai said. "Maybe it'll scare you a little."

Mookherji glanced at the spacemen. "All right," he said. "What about these nightmares?"

A tall, bony-looking officer who introduced himself as Lieutenant Falkirk said, "I was the first victim— right after floatoff. I almost flipped. It was like, well, something touching my mind, filling it with weird thoughts. And everything absolutely real while it was going on—I thought I was choking, I thought my body was changing into something alien, I felt my blood running out my pores—" Falkirk shrugged. "Like any sort of bad dream, I guess, only ten times as vivid. Fifty times. A few hours later Lieutenant Commander Rodriguez had the same kind of dream. Different images, same effect. And then, one by one, as the others took their sleep-shifts, they started to wake up screaming. Two of us ended up spending three weeks on happy-pills. We're pretty stable men, doctor—we're trained to take almost anything. But I think a civilian would have cracked up for good with dreams like those. Not so much the images as the intensity, the realness of them."

"And these dreams recurred, throughout the voyage?" Mookherji asked.

"Every shift. It got so we were afraid to doze off, because we knew the devils would start crawling through our heads when we did. Or we'd put ourselves real down on sleeper-tabs. And even so we'd have the dreams, with our minds doped to a level where you wouldn't imagine dreams would happen. A plague of nightmares, doctor. An epidemic."

"When was the last episode?"

"The final sleep-shift before floatdown."

"You haven't gone to sleep, any of you, since leaving ship?"

"No," Falkirk said.

One of the other spacemen said, "Maybe he didn't make it clear to you, doctor. These were killer dreams.

They were mind-crackers. We were lucky to get home sane. If we did."

Mookherji drummed his fingertips together, rummaging through his experience for some parallel case. He couldn't find any. He knew of mass hallucinations, plenty of them, episodes in which whole mobs had persuaded themselves they had seen gods, demons, miracles, the dead walking, fiery symbols in the sky. But a series of hallucinations coming in sequence, shift after shift, to an entire crew of tough, pragmatic spacemen? It didn't make sense.

Nakadai said, "Pete, the men had a guess about what might have done it to them. Just a wild idea, but maybe—"

"What is it?"

Falkirk laughed uneasily. "Actually, it's pretty fantastic, doctor."

"Go ahead."

"Well, that something from the planet came aboard the ship with us. Something, well, telepathic. Which fiddled around with our minds whenever we went to sleep. What we felt as nightmares was maybe this thing inside our heads."

"Possibly it rode all the way back to Earth with us," another spaceman said. "It could still be aboard the ship. Or loose in the city by now."

"The Invisible Nightmare Menace?" Mookherji said, with a faint smile. "I doubt that I can buy that."

"There *are* telepathic creatures," Falkirk pointed out.

"I know," Mookherji said sharply. "I happen to be one myself."

"I'm sorry, doctor, if—"

"But that doesn't lead me to look for telepaths under every bush. I'm not ruling out your alien menace, mind you. But I think it's a lot more likely that you picked up some kind of inflammation of the brain out there. A virus disease, a type of encephalitis that shows itself in the form of chronic hallucinations." The spacemen looked troubled. Obviously they would rather be victims of an unknown monster preying on them from outside than of an unknown virus lodged in their brains. Mookherji went on, "I'm not saying that's what it is, either. I'm just tossing around hypotheses. We'll know more after we've run some tests." Checking his watch, he said to Nakadai, "Lee, there's not much more I can find out right now, and I've got to get back to my patients. I want these fellows plugged in for the full series of neuropsychological checkouts. Have the outputs relayed to my office as they come in. Run the tests in staggered series and start letting the men go to sleep, two at a time, after each series—I'll send over a technician to help you rig the telemetry. I want to be notified immediately if there's any nightmare experience."

"Right."

"And get them to sign telepathy releases. I'll give them a preliminary mind-probe this evening after I've had a chance to study the clinical findings. Maintain absolute quarantine, of course. This thing might just be infectious. Play it very safe."

Nakadai nodded. Mookherji flashed a professional smile at the six somber spacemen and went out, brooding. A nightmare virus? Or a mind-meddling alien organism that no one can see? He wasn't sure which notion he liked less. Probably, though, there was some prosaic and unstartling explanation for that month of bad dreams—contaminated food supplies, or something funny in the atmosphere recycler. A simple, mundane explanation.

Probably.

The first time it happened, the Vsiir was not sure what had actually taken place. It had touched a human mind; there had been an immediate vehement reaction; the Vsiir had pulled back, alarmed by the surging fury of the response, and then, a moment later, had been unable to locate the mind at all. Possibly it was some defense mechanism, the Vsiir thought, by which the humans guarded their minds against intruders. But that seemed unlikely since the human's minds were quite effectively guarded most of the time anyway. Aboard the ship, whenever the Vsiir had managed to slip past the walls that shielded the minds of the crewmen, it had always encountered a great deal of turbulence—plainly these humans did not enjoy mental contact with a Vsiir—but never this complete shutdown, this total cutoff of signal. Puzzled, the Vsiir tried again, reaching toward an open mind situated not far from where the one that had vanished had been. *Kindly attention, a moment of consideration for confused other-worldly individual, victim of unhappy circumstances, who—*

Again the violent response: a sudden tremendous flare of mental energy, a churning blaze of fear and pain and shock. And again, moments later, complete silence, as though the human had retreated behind an impermeable barrier. *Where are you? Where did you go?* The Vsiir, troubled, took the risk of creating an optical receptor that worked in the visible spectrum—and that therefore would itself be visible to humans—and surveyed the scene. It saw a human on a bed, completely surrounded by intricate machinery. Colored lights were flashing. Other humans, looking agitated, were rushing toward the bed. The human on the bed lay quite still, not even moving when a metal arm descended and jabbed a long bright needle into his chest.

Suddenly the Vsiir understood.

The two humans must have experienced termination of existence!

Hastily the Vsiir dissolved its visible-spectrum receptor and retreated to a sheltered corner to consider what had happened. *Datum:* two humans had died. *Datum:* each had undergone termination immediately after receiving a mental transmission from the Vsiir. *Problem:* had the mental transmission brought about the terminations?

The possibility that the Vsiir might have destroyed two lives was shocking and appalling, and such a chill went through its body that it shrank into a tight, hard ball, with all thought-processes snarled. It needed several minutes to return to a fully functional state. If its attempts at communicating with these humans produced such terrible effects, the Vsiir realized, then its prospects of finding help on this planet were slim. How could it dare risk trying to contact other humans, if—

A comforting thought surfaced. The Vsiir realized that it was jumping to a hasty conclusion on the basis of sketchy evidence, while overlooking some powerful arguments against that conclusion. All during the voyage to this world the Vsiir had been making contact with humans, the six crewmen, and none of *them* had terminated. That was ample evidence that humans could withstand contact with a Vsiir mind. Therefore contact alone could not have caused these two deaths.

Possibly it was only coincidental that the Vsiir had approached two humans in succession that were on the verge of termination. Was this the place where humans were brought when their time of termination was near? Would the terminations have happened even if the Vsiir had not tried to make contact? Was the attempt at contact just enough of a drain on dwindling energies to push the two over the edge into termination? The Vsiir did not know. It was uncomfortably conscious of how many important facts it lacked. Only one thing was certain: its time was running short. If it did not find help soon, metabolic decay was going to set in, followed by metamorphic rigidity, followed by a fatal loss in adaptability, followed by . . . termination.

The Vsiir had no choice. Continuing its quest for contact with a human was its only hope of survival. Cautiously, timidly, the Vsiir again began to send out its probes, looking for a properly receptive mind. This one was walled. So was this. And all these: no entrance, no entrance! The Vsiir wondered if the barriers these humans possessed were designed merely to keep out intruding nonhuman consciousnesses, or actually shielded each human against mental contact of all kinds, including contact with other humans. If any human-to-human contact existed, the Vsiir had not detected it, either in this building or aboard the spaceship. What a strange race!

Perhaps it would be best to try a different level of this building. The Vsiir flowed easily under a closed door and up a service staircase to a higher floor. Once more it sent forth its probes. A closed mind here. And here. And here. And then a receptive one. The Vsiir prepared to send its message. For safety's sake it stepped down the power of its transmission, letting a mere wisp of thought curl forth. *Do you hear? Stranded extraterrestrial being is calling. Seeks aid. Wishes—*

From the human came a sharp, stinging displeasure-response, wordless but unmistakably hostile. The Vsiir at once withdrew. It waited, terrified, fearing that it had caused another termination. No: the human mind continued to function, although it was no longer open, but now surrounded by the sort of barrier humans normally wore. Drooping, dejected, the Vsiir crept away. Failure, again. Not even a moment of meaningful mind-to-mind contact. Was there no way to reach these people? Dismally, the Vsiir resumed its search for a receptive mind. What else could it do?

The visit to the quarantine building had taken forty minutes out of Dr. Mookherji's morning schedule. That bothered him. He couldn't blame the quarantine people for getting upset over the six spacemen's tale of chronic hallucinations, but he didn't think the situation, mysterious as it was, was grave enough to warrant calling him in on an emergency basis. Whatever was troubling the spacemen would eventually come to light; meanwhile they were safely isolated from the rest of the starport. Nakadai should have run more tests before asking him. And he resented having to steal time from his patients.

But as he began his belated morning rounds, Mookherji calmed himself with a deliberate effort: it wouldn't do him or his patients any good if he visited them while still loaded with tensions and irritations. He was sup-

posed to be a healer, not a spreader of anxieties. He
spent a moment going through a deescalation routine,
and by the time he entered the first patient's room—
that of Satina Ransom—he was convincingly relaxed
and amiable.

Satina lay on her left side, eyes closed, a slender girl
of sixteen with a fragile-looking face and long, soft
straw-colored hair. A spidery network of monitoring
systems surrounded her. She had been unconscious for
fourteen months, twelve of them here in the starport's
neuropathology ward and the last six under Mookherji's
care. As a holiday treat, her parents had taken her to
one of the resorts on Titan during the best season for
viewing Saturn's rings; with great difficulty they succeeded in booking reservations at Galileo Dome, and
were there on the grim day when a violent Titanquake
ruptured the dome and exposed a thousand tourists to
the icy moon's poisonous methane atmosphere. Satina
was one of the lucky ones: she got no more than a
couple of whiffs of the stuff before a dome guide with
whom she'd been talking managed to slap a breathing
mask over her face. She survived. Her mother, father,
and younger brother didn't. But she had never regained consciousness after collapsing at the moment of
the disaster. Months of examination on Earth had
shown that her brief methane inhalation hadn't caused
any major brain damage; organically there seemed to
be nothing wrong with her, but she refused to wake
up. A shock reaction, Mookherji believed: she would
rather go on dreaming forever than return to the living
nightmare that consciousness had become. He had
been able to reach her mind telepathically, but so far
he had been unable to cleanse her of the trauma of
that catastrophe and bring her back to the waking
world.

Now he prepared to make contact. There was nothing easy or automatic about his telepathy; "reading"
minds was strenuous work for him, as difficult and as
taxing as running a cross-country race or memorizing a
lengthy part in *Hamlet*. Despite the fears of laymen,

he had no way of scanning anyone's intimate thoughts with a casual glance. To enter another mind, he had to go through an elaborate procedure of warming up and reaching out, and even so it was a slow business to tune in on somebody's "wavelength," with little coherent information coming across until the ninth or tenth attempt. The gift had been in the Mookherji family for at least a dozen generations, helped along by shrewdly planned marriages designed to conserve the precious gene; he was more adept than any of his ancestors, yet it might take another century or two of Mookherjis to produce a really potent telepath. At least he was able to make good use of such talent for mind-contact as he had. He knew that many members of his family in earlier times had been forced to hide their gift from those about them, back in India, lest they be classed with vampires and werewolves and cast out of society.

Gently he placed his dark hand on Satina's pale wrist. Physical contact was necessary to attain the mental linkage. He concentrated on reaching her. After months of teletherapy, her mind was sensitized to his; he was able to skip the intermediate steps, and, once he was warmed up, could plunge straight into her troubled soul. His eyes were closed. He saw a swirl of pearly-gray fog before him: Satina's mind. He thrust himself into it, entering easily. Up from the depths of her spirit swam a question mark.

—*Who is it? Doctor?*

—*Me, yes. How are you today, Satina?*

—*Fine. Just fine.*

—*Been sleeping well?*

—*It's so peaceful here, doctor.*

—*Yes. Yes, I imagine it is. But you ought to see how it is here. A wonderful summer day. The sun in the blue sky. Everything in bloom. A perfect day for swimming, eh? Wouldn't you like a swim?* He puts all the force of his concentration into images of swimming: a cold mountain stream, a deep pool at the base of a creamy waterfall, the sudden delightful shock of diving in, the crystal flow tingling against her warm skin, the

laughter of her friends, the splashing, the swift powerful strokes carrying her to the far shore—

—*I'd rather stay where I am*, she tells him.

—*Maybe you'd like to go floating instead?* He summons the sensations of free flight: a floater-node fas-
tened to her belt, lifting her serenely to an altitude of
a hundred feet, and off she goes, drifting over fields
and valleys, her friends beside her, her body totally
relaxed, weightless, soaring on the updrafts, rising until the ground is a checkerboard of brown and green,
looking down on the tiny houses and the comical cars,
now crossing a shimmering silvery lake, now hovering
over a dark, somber forest of thick-packed spruce,
now simply lying on her back, legs crossed, hands
clasped behind her head, the sunlight on her cheeks,
three hundred feet of nothingness underneath her—

But Satina doesn't take his bait. She prefers to stay
where she is. The temptations of floating are not strong
enough.

Mookherji does not have enough energy left to try a
third attempt at luring her out of her coma. Instead he
shifts to a purely medical function and tries to probe
for the source of the trauma that has cut her off from
the world. The fright, no doubt; and the terrible crack
in the dome, spelling the end to all security; and the
sight of her parents and brother dying before her eyes;
and the swampy reek of Titan's atmosphere hitting her
nostrils—all of those things, no doubt. But people
have rebounded from worse calamities. Why does she
insist on withdrawing from life? Why not come to
terms with the dreadful past, and accept existence
again?

She fights him. Her defenses are fierce; she does not
want him meddling with her mind. All of their sessions
have ended this way: Satina clinging to her retreat,
Satina blocking any shot at knocking her free of her
self-imposed prison. He has gone on hoping that one
day she will lower her guard. But this is not to be the
day. Wearily, he pulls back from the core of her mind
and talks to her on a shallower level.

—*You ought to be getting back to school, Satina.*

—*Not yet. It's been such a short vacation!*

—*Do you know how long?*

—*About three weeks, isn't it?*

—*Fourteen months so far,* he tells her.

—*That's impossible. We just went away to Titan a little while ago—the week before Christmas, wasn't it, and—*

—*Satina, how old are you?*

—*I'll be fifteen in April.*

—*Wrong,* he tells her. *That April's been here and gone, and so has the next one. You were sixteen two months ago. Sixteen, Satina.*

—*That can't be true, doctor. A girl's birthday is something special, don't you know that? My parents are going to give me a big party. All my friends invited. And a nine-piece robot orchestra with synthesizers. And I know that that hasn't happened yet, so how can I be sixteen?*

His reservoir of strength is almost drained. His mental signal is weak. He cannot find the energy to tell her that she is blocking reality again, that her parents are dead, that time is passing while she lies here, that it is too late for a Sweet Sixteen party.

—*Well talk about it . . . another time, Satina. I'll . . . see . . . you . . . again . . . tomorrow . . . Tomorrow . . . morning . . .*

—*Don't go so soon, doctor!* But he can no longer hold the contact, and lets it break.

Releasing her, Mookherji stood up, shaking his head. A shame, he thought. A damned shame. He went out of the room on trembling legs and paused a moment in the hall, propping himself against a closed door and mopping his sweaty forehead. He was getting nowhere with Satina. After the initial encouraging period of contact, he had failed entirely to lessen the intensity of her coma. She had settled quite comfortably into her delusive world of withdrawal, and, telepathy or no, he could find no way to blast her loose.

He took a deep breath. Fighting back a growing

mood of bleak discouragement, he went toward the next patient's room.

The operation was going smoothly. The dozen third-year medical students occupied the observation deck of the surgical gallery on the starport hospital's third floor, studying Dr. Hammond's expert technique by direct viewing and by simultaneous microamplified relay to their individual desk-screens. The patient, a brain-tumor victim in his late sixties, was visible only as a head and shoulders protruding from a life-support chamber. His scalp had been shaved; blue lines and dark red dots were painted on it to indicate the inner contours of the skull, as previously determined by short-range sonar bounces; the surgeon had finished the job of positioning the lasers that would excise the tumor. The hard part was over. Nothing remained except to bring the lasers to full power and send their fierce, precise bolts of light slicing into the patient's brain. Cranial surgery of this kind was entirely bloodless; there was no need to cut through skin and bone to expose the tumor, for the beams of the lasers, calibrated to a millionth of a millimeter, would penetrate through minute openings and, playing on the tumor from different sides, destroy the malignant growth without harming a bit of the surrounding healthy brain tissue. Planning was everything in an operation like this. Once the exact outlines of the tumor were determined, and the surgical lasers were mounted at the correct angles, any intern could finish the job.

For Dr. Hammond it was a routine procedure. He had performed a hundred operations of this kind in the past year alone. He gave the signal; the warning light glowed on the laser rack; the students in the gallery leaned forth expectantly—

And, just as the lasers' glittering fire leaped toward the operating table, the face of the anesthetized patient contorted weirdly, as though some terrifying dream had come drifting up out of the caverns of the man's drugged mind. His nostrils flared; his lips drew back;

his eyes opened wide; he seemed to be trying to scream; he moved convulsively, twisting his head to one side. The lasers bit deep into the patient's left temple, far from the indicated zone of the tumor. The right side of his face began to sag, all muscles paralyzed. The medical students looked at each other in bewilderment. Dr. Hammond, stunned, retained enough presence of mind to kill the lasers with a quick swipe of his hand. Then, gripping the operating table with both hands in his agitation, he peered at the dials and meters that told him the details of the botched operation. The tumor remained intact; a vast sector of the patient's brain had been devastated. "Impossible," Hammond muttered. What could goad a patient under anesthesia into jumping around like that? "Impossible. Impossible." He strode to the end of the table and checked the readings on the life-support chamber. The question now was not whether the brain tumor would be successfully removed; the immediate question was whether the patient was going to survive.

By four that afternoon Mookherji had finished most of his chores. He had seen every patient; he had brought his progress charts up to date; he had fed a prognosis digest to the master computer that was the starport hospital's control center; he had found time for a gulped lunch. Ordinarily, now, he could take the next four hours off, going back to his spartan room in the residents' building at the edge of the starport complex for a nap, or dropping in at the recreation center to have a couple rounds of floater-tennis, or looking in at the latest cube-show, or whatever. His next round of patient-visiting didn't begin until eight in the evening. But he couldn't relax: there was that business of the quarantined spacemen to worry about. Nakadai had been sending test outputs over since two o'clock, and now they were stacked deep in Mookherji's data terminal. Nothing had carried an *urgent* flag, so Mookherji had simply let the reports pile up; but now he felt he ought to have a look. He tapped the keys of the terminal, requesting printouts, and Nakadai's outputs began to slide from the slot.

Mookherji ruffled through the yellow sheets. Reflexes, synapse charge, degree of neural ionization, endocrine balances, visual response, respiratory and circulatory, cerebral molecular exchange, sensory percepts, EEG both enhanced and minimated . . . No, nothing unusual here. It was plain from the tests that the six men who had been to Norton's Star were badly in need of a vacation—frayed nerves, blurred reflexes—but there was no indication of anything more serious than chronic loss of sleep. He couldn't detect signs of brain lesions, infection, nerve damage, or other organic disabilities.

Why the nightmares, then?

He tapped out the phone number of Nakadai's office. "Quarantine," a crisp voice said almost at once, and moments later Nakadai's lean, tawny face appeared on the screen. "Hello, Pete. I was just going to call you."

Mookherji said, "I didn't finish up until a little while ago. But I've been through the outputs you sent over. Lee, there's nothing here."

"As I thought."

"What about the men? You were supposed to call me if any of them went into nightmares."

"None of them have," Nakadai said. "Falkirk and Rodriguez have been sleeping since eleven. Like lambs. Schmidt and Carroll were allowed to conk out at half past one. Webster and Schiavone hit the cots at three. All six are still snoring away, sleeping like they haven't slept in years. I've got them loaded with equipment and everything's reading perfectly normal. You want me to shunt the data to you?"

"Why bother? If they aren't hallucinating, what'll I learn?"

"Does that mean you plan to skip the mind-probes tonight?"

"I don't know," Mookherji said, shrugging. "I suspect there's no point in it, but let's leave that part open. I'll be finishing my evening rounds about eleven, and if there's some reason to get into the heads of those spacemen then, I will." He frowned. "But look—didn't they say that each one of them went into the nightmares on *every single sleep-shift?*"

"Right."

"And here they are, sleeping outside the ship for the first time since the nightmares started, and none of them having any trouble at all. And no sign of possible hallucinogenic brain lesions. You know something, Lee? I'm starting to come around to a very silly hypothesis that those men proposed this morning."

"That the hallucinations were caused by some unseen alien being?" Nakadai asked.

"Something like that. Lee, what's the status of the ship they came in on?"

"It's been through all the routine purification checks, and now it's sitting in an isolation vector until we have some idea of what's going on."

"Would I be able to get aboard it?" Mookherji asked.

"I suppose so, yes, but—why—?"

"On the wild shot that something external caused those nightmares, and that that something may still be aboard the ship. And perhaps a low-level telepath like myself will be able to detect its presence. Can you set up clearance fast?"

"Within ten minutes," Nakadai said. "I'll pick you up."

Nakadai came by shortly in a rollerbuggy. As they headed out toward the landing field, he handed Mookherji a crumpled spacesuit and told him to put it on.

"What for?"

"You may want to breathe inside the ship. Right now it's full of vacuum—we decided it wasn't safe to leave it under atmosphere. Also it's still loaded with radiation from the decontamination process. Okay?"

Mookherji struggled into the suit.

They reached the ship: a standard interstellar null-gravity-drive job, looking small and lonely in its corner of the field. A robot cordon kept it under isolation, but, tipped off by the control center, the robots let the two doctors pass. Nakadai remained outside; Mookherji crawled into the safety pouch and, after the hatch had gone through its admission cycle, entered the ship. He moved cautiously from cabin to cabin, like a man walking in a forest that was said to have a jaguar in every tree. While looking about, he brought himself as quickly as possible up to full telepathic receptivity, and, wide open, awaited telepathic contact with anything that might be lurking in the ship.

—*Go on. Do your worst.*

Complete silence on all mental wavelengths. Mookherji prowled everywhere: the cargo hold, the crew cabins, the drive compartments. Everything empty, everything still. Surely he would have been able to detect the presence of a telepathic creature in here, no matter how alien; if it was capable of reaching the mind of a sleeping spaceman, it should be able to reach the mind of a waking telepath as well. After fifteen minutes he left the ship, satisfied.

"Nothing, there," he told Nakadai. "We're still nowhere."

The Vsiir was growing desperate. It had been roaming this building all day; judging by the quality of the solar radiation coming through the windows, night was beginning to fall now. And, though there were open minds on every level of the structure, the Vsiir had had no luck in making contact. At least there had been no more terminations. But it was the same story here as on the ship: whenever the Vsiir touched a human mind, the reaction was so negative as to make communication impossible. And yet the Vsiir went on and on and on, to mind after mind, unable to believe that this whole planet did not hold a single human to whom it could tell its story. It hoped it was not doing severe damage to these minds it was approaching; but it had its own fate to consider.

Perhaps this mind would be the one. The Vsiir started once more to tell its tale—

Half past nine at night. Dr. Peter Mookherji, bloodshot, tense, hauled himself through his neuropathological responsibilities. The ward was full: a schizoid collapse, a catatonic freeze, Satina in her coma, half a dozen routine hysterias, a couple of paralysis cases, an aphasic, and plenty more, enough to keep him going for sixteen hours a day and strain his telepathic powers, not to mention his conventional medical skills, to their limits. Some day the ordeal of residency would be over; some day he'd be quit of this hospital, and would set up private practice on some sweet tropical isle, and commute to Bombay on weekends to see his family, and spend his holidays on planets of distant stars, like any prosperous medical specialist . . . Some day. He tried to banish such lavish fantasies from his mind. If you're going to look forward to anything, he told himself, look forward to midnight. To sleep. Beautiful, beautiful sleep. And then in the morning it all begins again, Satina and the coma, the schizoid, the catatonic, the aphasic . . .

As he stepped into the hall, going from patient to patient, his annunciator said, "Dr. Mookherji, please report at once to Dr. Bailey's office."

Bailey? The head of the neuropathology department, still hitting the desk this late. What now? But of course there was no ignoring such a summons. Mookherji notified the control center that he had been called off his rounds, and made his way quickly down the corridor to the frosted-glass door marked SAMUEL F. BAILEY, M.D.

He found at least half the neuropath staff there already: four of the other senior residents, most of the interns, even a few of the high-level doctors. Bailey, a puffy-faced, sandy-haired, fiftyish man of formidable professional standing, was thumbing a sheaf of outputs and scowling. He gave Mookherji a faint nod by way of greeting. They were not on the best of terms; Bai-

ley, somewhat old-school in his attitudes, had not made
a good adjustment to the advent of telepathy as a tool
in the treatment of mental disturbance. "As I was just
saying," Bailey began, "these reports have been accu-
mulating all day, and they've all been dumped on me,
God knows why. Listen: two cardiac patients under
sedation undergo sudden violent shocks, described by
one doctor as sensory overloads. One reacts with cardiac arrest, the other with cerebral hemorrhage. Both
die. A patient being treated for endocrine restabilization
develops a runaway adrenalin flow while asleep, and
gets a six-month setback. A patient undergoing brain
surgery starts lurching around on the operating table,
despite adequate anesthesia, and gets badly carved up
by the lasers. Et cetera. Serious problems like this all
over the hospital today. Computer check of general
EEG patterns shows that fourteen patients, other than
those mentioned, have experienced exceptionally severe episodes of nightmare in the last eleven hours,
nearly all of them of such impact that the patient has
sustained some degree of psychic damage and often
actual physiological harm. Control center reports no
case histories of previous epidemics of bad dreams. No
reason to suspect a widespread dietary imbalance or
similar cause for the outbreak. Nevertheless, sleeping
patients are continuing to suffer, and those whose
condition is particularly critical may be exposed to
grave risks. Effective immediately, sedation of critical
patients has been interrupted where feasible, and sleep
schedules of other patients have been rearranged, but
this is obviously not an expedient that is going to do
much good if this outbreak continues into tomorrow."
Bailey paused, glanced around the room, let his gaze
rest on Mookherji. "Control center has offered one
hypothesis: that a psychopathic individual with strong
telepathic powers is at large in the hospital, preying on
sleeping patients and transmitting images to them that
take the form of horrifying nightmares. Mookherji,
what do you make of that idea?"

Mookherji said, "It's perfectly feasible, I suppose,

although I can't imagine why any telepath would want to go around distributing nightmares. But has control center correlated any of this with the business over at the quarantine building?"

Bailey stared at his output slips. "What business is that?"

"Six spacemen who came in early this morning, reporting that they'd all suffered chronic nightmares on their voyage homeward. Dr. Lee Nakadai's been testing them; he called me in as a consultant, but I couldn't discover anything useful. I imagine there are some late reports from Nakadai in my office, but—"

Bailey said, "Control center seems only to be concerned about events in the hospital, not in the starport complex as a whole. And if your six spacemen had their nightmares during their voyage, there's no chance that their symptoms are going to find their way onto—"

"That's just it!" Mookherji cut in. "They had their nightmares in space. But they've been asleep since morning, and Nakadai says they're resting peacefully. Meanwhile an outbreak of hallucinations has started over here. Which means that whatever was bothering them during their voyage has somehow got loose in the hospital today—some sort of entity capable of stirring up such ghastly dreams that they bring veteran spacemen to the edge of nervous breakdowns and can seriously injure or even kill someone in poor health." He realized that Bailey was looking at him strangely, and that Bailey was not the only one. In a more restrained tone, Mookherji said, "I'm sorry if this sounds fantastic to you. I've been checking it out all day, so I've had some time to get used to the concept. And things began to fit together for me just now. I'm not saying that my idea is necessarily correct. I'm simply saying that it's a reasonable notion, that it links up with the spaceman's own idea of what was bothering them, that it corresponds to the shape of the situation—and that it deserves a decent investigation, if we're going to stop this stuff before we lose some more patients."

"All right, doctor," Bailey said. "How do you propose to conduct the investigation?"

Mookherji was shaken by that. He had been on the go all day; he was ready to fold. Here was Bailey abruptly putting him in charge of this snark-hunt, without even asking! But he saw there was no way to refuse. He was the only telepath on the staff. And, if the supposed creature really was at large in the hospital, how could it be tracked except by a telepath?

Fighting back his fatigue, Mookherji said rigidly, "Well, I'd want a chart of all the nightmare cases, to begin with, a chart showing the location of each victim and the approximate time of onset of hallucination—"

They would be preparing for the Festival of Changing, now, the grand climax of the winter. Thousands of Vsiirs in the metamorphic phase would be on their way toward the Valley of Sand, toward that great natural amphitheater where the holiest rituals were performed. By now the firstcomers would already have taken up their positions, facing the west, waiting for the sunrise. Gradually the rows would fill as Vsiirs came in from every part of the planet, until the golden valley was thick with them, Vsiirs that constantly shifted their energy levels, dimensional extensions, and inner resonances, shuttling gloriously through the final joyous moments of the season of metamorphosis, competing with one another in a gentle way to display the great variety of form, the most dynamic cycle of physical changes—and, when the first red rays of the sun crept past the Needle, the celebrants would grow even more frenzied, dancing and leaping and transforming themselves with total abandon, purging themselves of the winter's flamboyance as the season of stability swept across the world. And finally, in the full blaze of sunlight, they would turn to one another in renewed kinship, embracing, and—

The Vsiir tried not to think about it. But it was hard to repress that sense of loss, that pang of nostalgia. The pain grew more intense with every moment. No imaginable miracle would get the Vsiir home in time for the Festival of Changing, it knew, and yet it could not really believe that such a calamity had befallen it.

Trying to touch minds with humans was useless. Perhaps if it assumed a form visible to them, and let itself be noticed, and *then* tried to open verbal communication—

But the Vsiir was so small, and these humans were so large. The dangers were great. The Vsiir, clinging to a wall and carefully keeping its wavelength well beyond the ultraviolet, weighed one risk against another, and, for the moment, did nothing.

"All right," Mookherji said foggily, a little before midnight. "I think we've got the trail clear now." He sat before a wall-sized screen on which the control center had thrown a three-dimensional schematic plan of the hospital. Bright red dots marked the place of each nightmare incident, yellow dashes the probable path of the unseen alien creature. "It came in the side way, probably, straight off the ship, and went into the cardiac wing first. Mrs. Maldonado's bed here, Mr. Guinness' over here, eh? Then it went up to the second level, coming around to the front wing and impinging on the minds of patients here and here and here between ten and eleven in the morning. There were no reported episodes of hallucination in the next hour and ten minutes, but then came that nasty business in the third-level surgical gallery, and after that—" Mookherji's aching eyes closed a moment; it seemed to him that he could still see the red dots and yellow dashes. He forced himself to go on, tracing the rest of the intruder's route for his audience of doctors and hospital security personnel. At last he said, "That's it. I figure that the thing must be somewhere between the fifth and eighth levels by now. It's moving much more slowly than it did this morning, possibly running out of energy. What we have to do is keep the hospital's wings tightly sealed to prevent its free movement, if that can be done, and attempt to narrow down the number of places where it might be found."

One of the security men said, a little belligerently, "Doctor, just how are we supposed to find an invisible entity?"

Mookherji struggled to keep impatience out of his voice. "The visible spectrum isn't the only sort of electromagnetic energy in the universe. If this thing is alive, it's got to be radiating *somewhere* along the line. You've got a master computer with a million sensory pickups mounted all over the hospital. Can't you have the sensors scan for a point-source of infrared or ultra-violet moving through a room? Or even X-rays, for God's sake: we don't know where the radiation's likely to be. Maybe it's a gamma emitter, even. Look, something wild is loose in this building, and we can't see it, but the computer can. Make it search."

Dr. Bailey said, "Perhaps the energy we ought to be trying to trace it by is, ah, telepathic energy, doctor."

Mookherji shrugged. "As far as anybody knows, telepathic impulses propagate somewhere outside the electromagnetic spectrum. But of course you're right that I might be able to pick up some kind of output, and I intend to make a floor-by-floor search as soon as this briefing session is over." He turned toward Nakadai. "Lee, what's the word from your quarantined spacemen?"

"All six went through eight-hour sleep periods today without any sign of a nightmare episode: there was some dreaming, but all of it normal. In the past couple of hours I've had them on the phone talking with some of the patients who had the nightmares, and everybody agrees that the kind of dreams people have been having here today are the same in tone, texture, and general level of horror as the ones the men had aboard the ship. Images of bodily destruction and alien landscapes, accompanied by an overwhelming, almost intolerable, feeling of isolation, loneliness, separation from one's own kind."

"Which would fit the hypothesis of an alien being as

the cause," said Martinson of the psychology staff. "If it's wandering around trying to communicate with us, trying to tell us it doesn't want to be here, say, and it's communications reach human minds only in the form of frightful nightmares—"

"Why does it communicate only with sleeping people?" an intern asked.

"Perhaps those are the only ones it can reach. Maybe a mind that's awake isn't receptive," Martinson suggested.

"Seems to me," a security man said, "that we're making a whole lot of guesses based on no evidence at all. You're all sitting around talking about an invisible telepathic thing that breathes nightmares in people's ears, and it might just as easily be a virus that attacks the brain, or something in yesterday's food, or—"

Mookherji said, "The ideas you're offering now have already been examined and discarded. We're working on this line of inquiry now because it seems to hold together, fantastic though it sounds, and because it's all we have. If you'll excuse me, I'd like to start checking the building for telepathic output, now." He went out, pressing his hands to his throbbing temples.

Satina Ransom stirred, stretched, subsided. She looked up and saw the dazzling blaze of Saturn's rings overhead, glowing through the hotel's domed roof. She had never seen anything more beautiful in her life. This close to them, only about 750,000 miles out, she could clearly make out the different zones of the rings, each revolving about Saturn at its own speed, with the blackness of space visible through the open places. And Saturn itself, gleaming in the heavens, so bright, so huge—

What was that rumbling sound? Thunder? Not here, not on Titan. Again: louder. And the ground swaying. A crack in the dome! Oh, no, no, no, feel the air rushing out, look at that cold greenish mist pouring in—people falling down all over the place—what's happening, what's happening, what's happening? Saturn seems to be falling toward us. That taste in my mouth—oh—oh—oh—

Satina screamed. And screamed. And went on screaming as she slipped down into darkness, and pulled the soft blanket of unconsciousness over her, and shivered, and gave thanks for finding a safe place to hide.

Mookherji had plodded through the whole building accompanied by three security men and a couple of interns. He had seen whole sectors of the hospital that he didn't know existed. He had toured basements and sub-basements and sub-sub-basements; he had been through laboratories and computer rooms and wards and exercise chambers. He had kept himself in a state of complete telepathic receptivity throughout the trek, but he had detected nothing, not even a flicker of mental current anywhere. Somehow that came as no surprise to him. Now, with dawn near, he wanted nothing more than sixteen hours or so of sleep. Even with nightmares. He was tired beyond all comprehension of the meaning of tiredness.

Yet something wild was loose, still, and the nightmares still were going on. Three incidents, ninety minutes apart, had occurred during the night: two patients on the fifth level and one on the sixth had awakened in states of terror. It had been possible to calm them quickly, and apparently no lasting harm had been done; but now the stranger was close to Mookherji's neuropathology ward, and he didn't like the thought of exposing a bunch of mentally unstable patients to that kind of stimulus. By this time, the control center had reprogrammed all patient-monitoring systems to watch for the early stages of nightmare—hormone changes, EEG tremors, respiration rate rise, and so forth—in the hope of awakening a victim before the full impact could be felt. Even so, Mookherji wanted to see that thing caught and out of the hospital before it got to any of his own people.

But how?

As he trudged back to his sixth-level office, he considered some of the ideas people had tossed around in that midnight briefing session. *Wandering around trying to communicate with us*, Martinson had said. *Its communications reach human minds only in the form of frightful nightmares. Maybe a mind that's awake isn't receptive.* Even the mind of a human telepath, it seemed, wasn't receptive while awake. Mookherji wondered if he should go to sleep and hope the alien would reach him, and then try to deal with it, lead it into a trap of some kind—but no. He wasn't that different from other people. If he slept, and the alien did open contact, he'd simply have a hell of a nightmare and wake up, and nothing gained. That wasn't the answer. Suppose, though, he managed to make contact with the alien through the mind of a nightmare victim—someone he could use as a kind of telepathic loudspeaker—someone who wasn't likely to wake up while the dream was going on—

Satina.

Perhaps. Perhaps. Of course, he'd have to make sure the girl was shielded from possible harm. She had enough horrors running free in her head as it was. But if he lent her his strength, drained off the poison of the nightmare, took the impact himself via their telepathic link, and was able to stand the strain and still speak to the alien mind—that might just work. Might.

He went to her room. He clasped her hand between his.

—*Satina?*

—*Morning so soon, doctor?*

—*It's still early, Satina. But things are a little unusual here today. We need your help. You don't have to if you don't want to, but I think you can be of great value to us, and maybe even to yourself. Listen to me very carefully, and think it over before you say yes or no—*

God help me if I'm wrong, Mookherji thought, far below the level of telepathic transmission.

Chilled, alone, growing groggy with dismay and hopelessness, the Vsiir had made no attempts at contact for several hours now. What was the use? The results were always the same when it touched a human mind; it was exhausting itself and apparently bothering the humans, to no purpose. Now the sun had risen. The Vsiir contemplated slipping out of the building and exposing itself to the yellow solar radiation while dropping all defenses; it would be a quick death, an end to all this misery and longing. It was folly to dream of seeing the home planet again. And—

What was that?

A call. Clear, intelligible, unmistakable. *Come to me.* An open mind somewhere on this level, speaking neither the human language nor the Vsiir language, but using the wordless, universally comprehensible communion that occurs when mind speaks directly to mind. *Come to me. Tell me everything. How can I help you?*

In its excitement the Vsiir slid up and down the spectrum, emitting a blast of infrared, a jagged blurt of ultraviolet, a lively blaze of visible light, before getting control. Quickly it took a fix on the direction of the call. Not far away: down this corridor, under this door, through this passage. *Come to me.* Yes. Yes. Extending its mind-probes ahead of it, groping for contact with the beckoning mind, the Vsiir hastened forward.

Mookherji, his mind locked to Satina's, felt the sudden crashing shock of the nightmare moving in, and even at second remove the effect was stunning in its power. He perceived a clicking sensation of mind touching mind. And then, into Satina's receptive spirit, there poured—

A wall higher than Everest. Satina trying to climb it, scrambling up a smooth white face, digging fingertips into minute crevices. Slipping back one yard for every two gained. Below, a roiling pit, flames shooting up, foul gases rising, monsters with needle-sharp fangs waiting for her to fall. The wall grows taller. The air is so thin—she can barely breathe, her eyes are dimming, a greasy hand is squeezing her heart, she can feel her veins pulling free of her flesh like wires coming out of a broken plaster ceiling, and the gravitational pull is growing constantly—pain, her lungs crumbling, her face sagging hideously—a river of terror surging through her skull—

—*None of it is real, Satina. They're just illusions. None of it is really happening.*

—*Yes,* she says, *yes, I know,* but still she resonates with fright, her muscles jerking at random, her face flushed and sweating, her eyes fluttering beneath the lids. The dream continues. How much more can she stand?

—*Give it to me,* he tells her. *Give me the dream!*

She does not understand. No matter. Mookherji knows how to do it. He is so tired that fatigue is unimportant; somewhere in the realm beyond collapse he finds unexpected strength, and reaches into her numbed soul, and pulls the hallucinations forth as though they were cobwebs. They engulf him. No longer does he experience them indirectly; now all the phantoms are loose in his skull, and, even as he feels Satina relax, he braces himself against the onslaught of unreality that he has summoned into himself. And he copes. He drains the excess of irrationality out of her and winds it about his consciousness, and adapts, learning to live with the appalling flood of images. He and Satina share what is coming forth. Together they can bear the burden; he carries more of it than she does, but she does her part, and now neither of them is overwhelmed by the parade of bogeys. They can laugh at the dream monsters; they can even admire them for being so richly fantastic. That beast with a hundred heads, that bundle of living copper wires, that pit of dragons, that coiling mass of spiky teeth—who can fear what does not exist?

Over the clatter of bizarre images Mookherji sends a coherent thought, pushing it through Satina's mind to the alien.

—*Can you turn off the nightmares?*

—*No,* something replies. *They are in you, not in me.*

I only provide the liberating stimulus. You generate the images.

—All right. Who are you, and what do you want here?

—*I am a Vsiir.*

—A what?

—*Native life-form of the planet where you collect the greenfire branches. Through my own carelessness I was transported to your planet.* Accompanying the message is an overriding impulse of sadness, a mixture of pathos, self-pity, discomfort, exhaustion. Above this the nightmares still flow, but they are insignificant now. The Vsiir says, *I wish only to be sent home. I did not want to come here.*

And this is our alien monster? Mookherji thinks. This is our fearsome nightmare-spreading beast from the stars?

—Why do you spread hallucinations?

—*This was not my intention. I was merely trying to make mental contact. Some defect in the human receptive system, perhaps—I do not know. I do not know. I am so tired, though. Can you help me?*

—*We'll send you home, yes,* Mookherji promises. *Where are you? Can you show yourself to me? Let me know how to find you, and I'll notify the starport authorities, and they'll arrange for your passage home on the first ship out.*

Hesitation. Silence. Contact wavers and perhaps breaks.

—*Well?* Mookherji says, after a moment. *What's happening? Where are you?*

From the Vsiir an uneasy response:

—*How can I trust you? Perhaps you merely wish to destroy me. If I reveal myself—*

Mookherji bites his lip in sudden fury. His reserve of strength is almost gone; he can barely sustain the contact at all. And if he now has to find some way of persuading a suspicious alien to surrender itself, he may run out of steam before he can settle things. The situation calls for desperate measures.

—Listen, Vsiir. I'm not strong enough to talk much longer, and neither is this girl I'm using. I invite you into my head. I'll drop all defenses if you can look at who I am, look hard, and decide for yourself whether you can trust me. After that it's up to you. I can help you get home, but only if you produce yourself right away.

He opens his mind wide. He stands mentally naked. The Vsiir rushes into Mookherji's brain.

A hand touched Mookherji's shoulder. He snapped awake instantly, blinking, trying to get his bearings. Lee Nakadai stood above him. They were in—where? —Satina Ransom's room. The pale light of early morning was coming through the widow; he must have dozed only a minute or so. His head was splitting.

"We've been looking all over for you, Pete," Nakadai said.

"It's all right now," Mookherji murmured. "It's all all right." He shook his head to clear it. He remembered things. Yes. On the floor, next to Satina's bed, squatted something about the size of a frog, but very different in shape, color, and texture from any frog Mookherji had ever seen. He showed it to Nakadai. "That's the Vsiir," Mookherji said. "The alien terror. Satina and I made friends with it. We talked it into showing itself. Listen, it isn't happy here, so will you get hold of a starport official fast, and explain that we've got an organism here that has to be shipped back to Norton's Star at once, and—"

Satina said, "Are you Dr. Mookherji?"

"That's right. I suppose I should have introduced myself when—*you're awake?*"

"It's morning, isn't it?" The girl sat up, grinning. "You're younger than I thought you were. And so serious-looking. And I *love* that color of skin. I—"

"You're awake?"

"I had a bad dream," she said, "Or maybe a bad dream within a bad dream—I don't know. Whatever it was, it was pretty awful but I felt so much better when it went away—I just felt that if I slept any longer I was going to miss a lot of good things, that I had to get up and see what was happening in the world—do you understand any of this, doctor?"

Mookherji realized his knees were shaking. "Shock therapy," he muttered. "We blasted her loose from the coma—without even knowing what we were doing." He moved toward the bed. "Listen, Satina. I've been up for about a million years, and I'm ready to burn out from overload. And I've got a thousand things to talk about with you, only not now. Is that okay? Not now. I'll send Dr. Bailey in—he's my boss—and after I've had some sleep I'll come back and we'll go over everything together, okay? Say, five, six this evening. All right?"

"Well, of course, all right," Satina said, with a twinkling smile. "If you feel you really have to run off, just when I've—sure. Go. Go. You look awfully tired, doctor."

Mookherji blew her a kiss. Then, taking Nakadai by the elbow, he headed for the door. When he was outside he said. "Get the Vsiir over to your quarantine place pronto and try to put it in an atmosphere it finds comfortable. And arrange for its trip home. And I guess you can let your six spacemen out. I'll go talk to Bailey—and then I'm going to drop."

Nakadai nodded. "You get some rest, Pete. I'll handle things."

Mookherji shuffled slowly down the hall toward Dr. Bailey's office, thinking of the smile on Satina's face, thinking of the sad little Vsiir, thinking of nightmares—

"Pleasant dreams, Pete," Nakadai called.

THE VISITOR

by Poul Anderson

As we drove up between lawns and trees, Ferrier warned me, "Don't be shocked at his appearance."

"You haven't told me anything about him," I answered, "Not to mention."

"For good reason," Ferrier said. "This can never be a properly controlled experiment, but we can at least try to keep down the wild variables." He drummed fingers on the steering wheel. "I'll say this much. He's an important man in his field, investment counseling and brokerage."

"Oh, you mean he's a partner in— Why, I've done some business with them myself. But I never met him."

"He doesn't see clientele. Or very many people ever. He works the research end. Mail, telephone, teletype, and reads a lot."

"Why aren't we meeting in his office?"

"I'm not ready to explain that." Ferrier parked the car and we left it.

The hospital stood well out of town. It was a tall clean block of glass and metal which somehow fitted the Ohio countryside rolling away on every side, green, green, and green, here and there a white-sided house, red-sided barn, blue-blooming flax field, motley of cattle, to break the corn and woodlots, fence lines and toning telephone wires. A warm wind soughed through

367

birches and flickered their leaves; it bore scents of a rose bed where bees querned.

Leading me up the stairs to the main entrance, Ferrier said, "Why, there he is." A man in a worn and outdated brown suit waited for us at the top of the flight.

No doubt I failed to hide my reaction, but no doubt he was used to it, for his handclasp was ordinary. I couldn't read his face. Surgeons must have expended a great deal of time and skill, but they could only tame the gashes and fill in the holes, not restore an absolute ruin. That scar tissue would never move in human fashion. His hair did, a thin flutter of gray in the breeze; and so did his eyes, which were blue behind glasses. I thought they looked trapped, those eyes, but it could be only a fancy of mine.

When Ferrier had introduced me, the scarred man said, "I've arranged for a room where we can talk." He saw a bit of surprise on me and his tone flattened. "I'm pretty well known here." His glance went to Ferrier. "You haven't told me what this is all about, Carl. But"—his voice dropped—"considering the place—"

The tension in my friend had hardened to sternness. "Please let me handle this my way," he said.

When we entered, the receptionist smiled at our guide. The interior was cool, dim, carbolic. Down a hall I glimpsed somebody carrying flowers. We took an elevator to the uppermost floor.

There were the offices, one of which we borrowed. Ferrier sat down behind the desk, the scarred man and I took chairs confronting him. Though steel filing cabinets enclosed us, a window at Ferrier's back stood open for summer to blow in. From this level I overlooked the old highway, nowadays a mere picturesque side road. Occasional cars flung sunlight at me.

Ferrier became busy with pipe and tobacco. I shifted about. The scarred man waited. He had surely had experience in waiting.

"Well," Ferrier began. "I apologize to both you

gentlemen. This mysteriousness. I hope that when you have the facts, you'll agree it was necessary. You see, I don't want to predispose your judgments or . . . or imaginations. We're dealing with an extraordinarily subtle matter."

He forced a chuckle. "Or maybe with nothing. I give no promises, not even to myself. Parapsychological phenomena at best are"—he paused to search—"fugitive."

"I know you've made a hobby of them," the scarred man said. "I don't know much more."

Ferrier scowled. He got his pipe going before he replied: "I wouldn't call it a hobby. Can serious research only be done for an organization? I'm convinced there's a, well, a reality involved. But solid data are damnably hard to come by." He nodded at me. "If my friend here hadn't happened to be in on one of my projects, his whole experience might as well never have been. It'd have seemed like just another dream."

A strangeness walked along my spine. "Probably that's all it was," I said low. "Is."

The not-face turned toward me, the eyes inquired; then suddenly hands gripped tight the arms of the chair, as they do when the doctor warns he must give pain. I didn't know why. It made my voice awkward:

"I don't claim sensitivity, I can't read minds or guess Rhine cards, nothing of that sort works for me. Still, I do often have pretty detailed and, uh, coherent dreams. Carl's talked me into describing them on a tape recorder, first thing when I wake up, before I forget them. He's trying to check on Dunne's theory that dreams can foretell the future." Now I must attempt a joke. "No such luck, so far, or I'd be rich. However, when he learned about one I had a few nights ago—"

The scarred man shuddered. "And you happened to know *me*, Carl," broke from him.

The lines deepened around Ferrier's mouth. "Go

on," he directed me, "tell your story, quick," and
cannonaded smoke.

I sought from them both to the serenity beyond
these walls, and I also spoke fast:

"Well, you see, I'd been alone at home for several
days. My wife had taken our kid on a visit to her
mother. I won't deny, Carl's hooked me on this ESP.
I'm not a true believer, but I agree with him the
evidence justifies looking further, and into curious
places, too. So I was in bed, reading myself sleepy
with . . . Berdyaev, to be exact, because I'd been
reading Lenau earlier, and he's wild, sad, crazy, you
may know he died insane; nothing to go to sleep on.
Did he linger anyhow, at the bottom of my mind?"

I was in a formlessness which writhed. Nor had it
color, or heat or cold. Through it went a steady sound,
whether a whine or drone I cannot be sure. Unreason-
ably sorrowful, I walked, though there was nothing
under my feet, no forward or backward, no purpose in
travel except that I could not weep.

The monsters did when they came. Their eyes melted
and ran down the blobby heads in slow tears, while
matter bubbled from within to renew that stare. They
flopped as they floated, having no bones. They wavered around me and their lips made gibbering motions.

I was not afraid of attack, but a horror dragged
through me of being forever followed by them and
their misery. For now I knew that the nature of hell
lies in that it goes on. I slogged, and they circled and
rippled and sobbed, while the single noise was that
which dwelt in the nothing, and time was not because
none of this could change.

Time was reborn in a voice and a splash of light.
Both were small. She was barely six years old, I guessed,
my daughter's age. Brown hair in pigtails tied by red
bows, and a staunch way of walking, also reminded
me of Alice. She was more slender (elven, I thought)
and more neat than my child—starched white flowerbud-
patterned dress, white socks, shiny shoes, no trace of

dirt on knees or tip-tilted face. But the giant teddy bear she held, arms straining around it, was comfortably shabby.

I thought I saw ghosts of road and tree behind her, but could not be certain. The mourning was still upon me.

She stopped. Her own eyes widened and widened. They were the color of earliest dusk. The monsters roiled. Then: "Mister!" she cried. The tone was thin but sweet. It cut straight across the hum of emptiness. "Oh, Mister!"

The tumorous beings mouthed at her. They did not wish to leave me, who carried some of their woe. She dropped the bear and pointed. "Go 'way!" I heard. "Scat!" They shivered backward, resurged, clustered close. "Go 'way, I want!" She stamped her foot, but silence responded and I felt a defiance of the monsters. "All right," she said grimly. "Edward, you make them go."

The bear got up on his hind legs and stumped toward me. He was only a teddy, the fur on him worn off in patches by much hugging, a rip in his stomach carefully mended. I never imagined he was alive the way the girl and I were; she just sent him. Nevertheless he had taken a great hammer, which he swung in a fingerless paw, and became the hero who rescues people.

The monsters flapped stickily about. They didn't dare make a stand. As the bear drew close, they trailed off sullenly crying. The sound left us too. We stood in an honest hush and a fog full of sunglow.

"Mister, Mister, Mister!" The girl came running, her arms out wide. I hunkered down to catch her. She struck me in a tumult and joy exploded. We embraced till I lifted her on high, made to drop her, caught her again, over and over, while her laughter chimed.

Finally, breathless, I let her down. She gathered the bear under an elbow, which caused his feet to drag. Her free hand clung to mine. "I'm so glad you're here," she said. "Thank you, thank you. Can you stay?"

"I don't know," I answered. "Are you all by yourself?"

"'Yes. 'Cept for Edward and—" Her words died out. At the time I supposed she had the monsters in mind and didn't care to speak of them.

"What's your name, dear?"

"Judy."

"You know, I have a little girl at home, a lot like you. Her name's Alice."

Judy stood mute for a while and a while. At last she whispered, "Could she come play?"

My throat wouldn't let me answer.

Yet Judy was not too dashed. "Well," she said. "I didn't 'spect you, and you came." Happiness rekindled in her and caught in me. Could my presence be so overwhelmingly enough? Now I felt at peace, as though every one of the rat-fears which ride in each of us had fled me. "Come on to my house," she added, a shy invitation, a royal command.

We walked. Edward bumped along after us. The mist vanished and we were on a lane between low hedges. Elsewhere reached hills, their green a palette for the emerald or silver of coppices. Cows grazed, horses galloped, across miles. Closer, birds flitted and sparkled, a robin redbreast, a chickadee, a mockingbird who poured brook-trills from a branch, a hummingbird bejeweled among bumblebees in a surge of honeysuckle. The air was vivid with odors, growth, fragrance, the friendly smell of the beasts. Overhead lifted an enormous blue where clouds wandered.

This wasn't my country. The colors were too intense, crayon-brilliant, and a person could drown in the scents. Birds, bees, butterflies, dragonflies somehow seemed gigantic, while cattle and horses were somehow unreachably far off, forever cropping or galloping. The clouds made real castles and sailing ships. Yet there was rightness as well as brightness. I felt— maybe not at home, but very welcome.

Oh, infinitely welcome.

Judy chattered, no, caroled. "I'll show you my garden an' my books an', an' the whole house. Even where Hoo Boy lives. Would you push me in the swing? I only can pump myself. I pretend Edward is pushing me, an' he says, 'High, high, up in the sky, Judy fly, I wonder why,' like Daddy would, but it's only pretend, like when I play with my dolls or my Noah's ark animals an' make them talk. Would you play with me?" Wistfulness crossed her. "I'm not so good at making up ad—adventures for them. Can you?" She turned merry again and skipped a few steps. "We'll have dinner in the living room if you make a fire. I'm not s'posed to make fire, I remember Daddy said, 'cept I can use the stove. I'll cook us dinner. Do you like tea? We have lots of different kinds. You look, an' tell me what kind you want. I'll make biscuits an' we'll put butter an' maple syrup on them like Grandmother does. An' we'll sit in front of the fire an' tell stories, okay?" And on and on.

The lane was now a street, shaded by big old elms; but it was empty save for the dappling of the sunlight, and the houses had a flatness about them, as if nothing lay behind their fronts. Wind mumbled in leaves. We reached a gate in a picket fence, which creaked when Judy opened it.

The lawn beyond was quite real, aside from improbably tall hollyhocks and bright roses and pansies along the edges. So was this single house. I saw where paint had peeled and curtains faded, the least bit, as will happen to any building. (Its neighbors stood flawless.) A leftover from the turn of the century, it rambled in scale-shaped shingles, bays, turrets, and gingerbread. The porch was a cool cavern that resounded beneath our feet. A brass knocker bore the grinning face of a gnome.

Judy pointed to it. "I call him Billy Bungalow because he goes bung when he comes down low," she said. "Do you want to use him? Daddy always did, an' made him go a lot louder than I can. Please. He's waited such a long time." I have too, she didn't add.

I rattled the metal satisfactorily. She clapped her hands in glee. My ears were more aware of stillness behind the little noise. "Do you really live alone, brighteyes?" I asked.

"Sort of," she answered, abruptly going solemn.

"Not even a pet?"

"We had a cat, we called her Elizabeth, but she died an' . . . we was going to get another."

I lifted my brows. "We?"

"Daddy an' Mommy an' me. C'mon inside!" She hastened to twist the doorknob.

We found an entry where a Tiffany window threw rainbows onto hardwood flooring. Hat rack and umbrella stand flanked a coat closet, opposite a grandfather clock which broke into triumphant booms on our arrival: for the hour instantly was six o'clock of a summer's evening. Ahead of us swept a staircase; right and left, doorways gave on a parlor converted to a sewing room, and on a living room where I glimpsed a fine stone fireplace. Corridors went high-ceilinged beyond them.

"Such a big house for one small girl," I said. "Didn't you mention, uh, Hoo Boy?"

Both arms hugged Edward close to her. I could barely hear: "He's 'maginary. They all are."

It never occurred to me to inquire further. It doesn't in dreams.

"But *you're* here, Mister!" Judy cried, and the house was no longer hollow.

She clattered down the hall ahead of me, up the stairs, through chamber after chamber, basement, attic, a tiny space she had found beneath the witch-hat roof of a turret and assigned to Hoo Boy; she must show me everything. The place was bright and cheerful, didn't even echo much as we went around. The furniture was meant for comfort. Down in the basement stood shelves of jelly her mother had put up and a workshop for her father. She showed me a half-finished toy sailboat he had been making for her. Her personal room bulged with the usual possessions of a child, including books I remembered well from years gone. (The library had a large collection too, but shadowy, a part of that home which I cannot catalog.) Good pictures hung on the walls. She had taken the liberty of pinning clippings almost everywhere, cut from the stacks of magazines which a household will accumulate. They mostly showed animals or children.

In the living room I noticed a cabinet-model radiophonograph, though no television set. "Do you ever use that?" I asked.

She shook her head. "No, nothing comes out of it anymore. I sing for myself a lot." She put Edward on the sofa. "You stay an' be the lord of the manor," she ordered him. "I will be the lady making dinner, an' Mister will be the faithful knight bringing firewood." She went timid. "Will you, please, Mister?"

"Sounds great to me," I smiled, and saw her wriggle for delight.

"Quick!" She grabbed me anew and we ran back into the kitchen. Our footfalls applauded.

The larder was well stocked. Judy showed me her teas and asked my preference. I confessed I hadn't heard of several kinds; evidently her parents were connoisseurs. "So'm I," Judy said after I explained that word. "Then I'll pick. An' you tell me, me an' Edward, a story while we eat, okay?"

"Fair enough," I agreed.

She opened a door. Steps led down to the backyard. Unlike the closely trimmed front, this was a wilderness of assorted toys, her swing, and fever-gaudy flowers. I had to laugh. "You do your own gardening, do you?"

She nodded. "I'm not very expert. But Mother promised I could have a garden here." She pointed to a shed at the far end of the grounds. "The firewood's in that. I got to get busy." However firm her tone, the fingers trembled which squeezed mine. "I'm so happy," she whispered.

I closed the door behind me and picked a route

among her blossoms. Windows stood wide to a mild air full of sunset, and I heard her start singing.

> "The little red pony ran over the hill
> And galloped and galloped away—"

The horses in those meadows came back to me, and suddenly I stood alone, somewhere, while one of them who was my Alice fled from me for always; and I could not call out to her.

After a time, walking became possible again. But I wouldn't enter the shed at once; I hadn't the guts, when Judy's song had ended, leaving me here by myself. Instead, I brushed on past it for a look at whatever might lie behind for my comfort.

That was the same countryside as before, but long-shadowed under the falling sun and most quiet. A blackbird sat on a blackberry tangle, watched me and made pecking motions. From the yard, straight southward through the land, ran a yellow brick road.

I stepped onto it and took a few strides. In this light the pavement was the hue of molten gold, strong under my feet; here was the kind of highway which draws you ahead one more mile to see what's over the next hill, so you may forget the pony that galloped. After all, don't yellow brick roads lead to Oz?

"Mister!" screamed at my back. "No, stop, stop!"

I turned around. Judy stood at the border. She shuddered inside the pretty dress as she reached toward me. Her face was stretched quite out shape. "Not yonder, Mister!"

Of course I made haste. When we were safely in the yard, I held her close while the dread went out of her in a burst of tears. Stroking her hair and murmuring, at last I dared ask, "But where does it go?"

She jammed her head into the curve of my shoulder and gripped me. "T-t-to Grandmother's."

"Why, is that bad? You're making us biscuits like hers, remember?"

"We can't *ever* go there," Judy gasped. Her hands on my neck were cold.

"Well, now, well, now." Disengaging, while still squatted to be at her height, I clasped her shoulder and chucked her chin and assured her the world was fine; look what a lovely evening, and we'd soon dine with Edward, but first I'd better build our fire, so could she help me bring in the wood? Secretly through me went another song I know, Swedish, the meaning of it:

"Children are a mysterious folk, and they live in a wholly strange world—"

Before long she was glad once more. As we left, I cast a final glance down the highway, and then caught a breath of what she felt: less horror than unending loss and grief, somewhere on that horizon. It made me be extra jocular while we took armloads of fuel to the living room.

Thereafter Judy trotted between me and the kitchen, attending to her duties. She left predictable chaos, heaped dishes, scorched pan, strewn flour, smeared butter and syrup and Lord knows what else. I forbore to raise the subject of cleanup. No doubt we'd tackle that tomorrow. I didn't mind.

Later we sat cross-legged under the sofa where Edward presided, ate our biscuits and drank our tea with plenty of milk, and laughed a great deal. Judy had humor. She told me of a Fourth of July celebration she had been at, where there were so many people "I bet just their toes weighed a hundred pounds." That led to a picnic which had been rained out, and—she must have listened to adult talk—she insisted that in any properly regulated universe, Samuel Gompers would have invented rubber boots. The flames whirled red, yellow, blue, and talked back to the ticking, booming clock; shadows played tag across walls; outside stood a night of gigantic stars.

"Tell me another story," she demanded and snuggled into my lap, the calculating minx. Borrowing from what I had done for Alice, I spun a long yarn about a girl named Judy, who lived in the forest with her friends Edward T. Bear and Billy Bungalow and Hoo Boy, until they built a candy-striped balloon and departed on all sorts of explorations; and her twilight-colored eyes got wider and wider.

They drooped at last, though. "I think we'd better turn in," I suggested. "We can carry on in the morning."

She nodded. "Yesterday they said today was tomorrow," she observed, "but today they know better."

I expected that after those fireside hours the electrics would be harsh to us; but they weren't. We went upstairs, Judy on my right shoulder, Edward on my left. She guided me to a guest room, pattered off, and brought back a set of pajamas. "Daddy wouldn't mind," she said.

"Would you like me to tuck you in?" I asked.

"Oh—" For a moment she radiated. Then the seriousness came upon her. She put finger to chin, frowning, before she shook her head. "No, thanks. I don't think you're s'posed for that."

"All right." My privilege is to see Alice to her bed; but each family has its own tradition. Judy must have sensed my disappointment, because she touched me and smiled at me, and when I stopped she caught me and breathed,

"You're really real, Mister. I love you," and ran down the hall.

My room resembled the others, well and unpretentiously furnished. The wallpaper showed willows and lakes and Chinese castles which I had seen in the clouds. Gauzy white curtains, aflutter in easy airs, veiled away those lantern-big stars. Above the bed Judy had pinned a picture of a galloping pony.

I thought of a trip to the bathroom, but felt no need. Besides, I might disturb my hostess; I had no doubt she brushed her teeth, being such a generally dutiful person. Did she say prayers too? In spite of Alice, I don't really understand little girls, any more than I understand how a mortal could write *Jesu Joy of Man's Desiring*. Boys are different; it's true about

the slugs and snails and puppy dogs' tails. I've been
there and I know.

I got into the pajamas, lay down in the bed and the
breeze, turned off the light, and was quickly asleep.

Sometimes we remember a night's sleep. I spent this
one being happy about tomorrow.

Maybe that was why I woke early, in a clear, shad-
owless gray, cool as the air. The curtains rippled and
blew, but there was no sound whatsoever.

Or . . . a rustle? I lay half awake, eyes half open
and peace behind them. Someone moved about. She
was very tall, I knew, and she was tidying the house. I
did not try, then, to look upon her. In my drowsiness,
she might as well have been the wind.

After she had finished in this chamber, I came fully
to myself, and saw how bureau and chair and the
bulge of blankets that my feet made were strangers in
the dusk which runs before the sun. I swung legs
across bedside, felt hardwood under my soles. My
lungs drank odors of grass. Oh, Judy will snooze for
hours yet, I thought, but I'll go peek in at her before I
pop downstairs and start a surprise breakfast.

When dressed, I followed the hallway to her room.
Its door wasn't shut. Beyond, I spied a window full of
daybreak.

I stopped. A woman was singing.

She didn't use real words. You often don't, over a
small bed. She sang well-worn nonsense,

> "Cloddledy loldy boldy boo,
> Cloddledy lol-dy bol-dy boo-oo,"

to the tenderest melody I have ever heard. I think that
tune was what drew me on helpless, till I stood in the
entrance.

And she stood above Judy. I couldn't truly see her:
a blue shadow, maybe? Judy was as clear to me as she
is this minute, curled in a prim nightgown, one arm
under her cheek (how long the lashes and stray brown

hair), the other around Edward, while on a shelf over-head, Noah's animals kept watch.

The presence grew aware of me.

She turned and straightened, taller than heaven. Why have you looked? she asked me in boundless gentleness. Now you must go, and never come back.

No, I begged. Please.

When even I may do no more than this, she sighed, you cannot stay or ever return, who looked beyond the Edge.

I covered my eyes.

I'm sorry, she said; and I believe she touched my head as she passed from us.

Judy awakened. "Mister—" She lifted her arms, wanting me to come and be hugged, but I didn't dare.

"I have to leave, sweetheart," I told her.

She bolted to her feet. "No, no, no," she said, not loud at all.

"I wish I could stay awhile," I answered. "Can you guess how much I wish it?"

Then she knew. "You . . . were awful kind . . . to come see me," she got out.

She went to me with the same resolute gait as when first we met, and took my hand, and we walked down-stairs together and forth into the morning.

"Will you say hello to your daughter from me?" she requested once.

"Sure," I said. Hell, yes. Only how?

We went along the flat and empty street, toward the sun. Where a blackbird perched on an elm bough, and the leaves made darkness beneath, she halted. "Good-bye, you good Mister," she said.

She would have kissed me had I had the courage. "Will you remember me, Judy?"

"I'll play with my remembering of you. Always." She snapped after air; but her head was held bravely. "Thanks again. I do love you."

So she let me go, and I left her. A single time I turned around to wave. She waved back, where she stood under the sky all by herself.

*   *   *

The scarred man was crying. He wasn't skilled in it; he barked and hiccoughed.

Surgically, Ferrier addressed him. "The description of the house corresponds to your former home. Am I correct?"

The hideous head jerked a nod.

"And you're entirely unfamiliar with the place," Ferrier declared to me. "It's in a different town from yours."

"Right," I said. "I'd no reason before today to suppose I'd had anything more than a dream." Anger flickered. "Well, God damn your scientific caution, now I want some explanations."

"I can't give you those," Ferrier admitted. "Not when I've no idea how the phenomenon works. You're welcome to what few facts I have."

The scarred man toiled toward a measure of calm. "I, I, I apologize for the scene," he stuttered. "A blow, you realize. Or a hope?" His gaze ransacked me.

"Do you think we should go see her?" Ferrier suggested.

For reply, the scarred man led us out. We were silent in corridor and elevator. When we emerged on the third floor, the hospital smell struck hard. He regained more control over himself as we passed among rubber-tired nurses and views of occupied beds. But his gesture was rickety that, at last, beckoned us through a certain doorway.

Beyond lay several patients and a near-total hush. Abruptly I understood why he, important in the world, went ill-clad. Hospitals don't come cheap.

His voice grated: "Telepathy, or what? The brain isn't gone; not a flat EEG. Could you—" That went as far as he was able.

"No," I said, while my fingers struggled with each other. "It must have been a fluke. And since, I'm forbidden."

We had stopped at a cluster of machinery. "Tell hi

what happened," Ferrier said without any tone whatsoever.

The scarred man looked past us. His words came steady if a bit shrill. "We were on a trip, my wife and daughter and me. First we meant to visit my mother-in-law in Kentucky."

"You were southbound, then," I foreknew. "On a yellow brick road." They still have that kind, here and there in our part of the country.

"A drunk driver hit our car," he said. "My wife was killed. I became what you see. Judy—" He chopped a hand toward the long white form beneath us. "That was nineteen years ago," he ended.

DAW

A feline lovers' fantasy come true ...

CATFANTASTIC!

☐ **CATFANTASTIC** (UE2355—$3.95)
edited by Andre Norton and Martin H. Greenberg

A unique collection of fantastical cat tales, some set in the distant future on as yet unknown worlds, some set in our own world but not quite our dimension, some recounting what happens when beings from the ancient past and creatures out of myth collide with modern-day felines.

☐ **CATFANTASTIC II** (UE2461—$4.50)
edited by Andre Norton & Martin H. Greenberg

From the editors who created the bestselling CATFANTASTIC—here is an all-new collection of fantasy's most original cat tales! So join some of the most memorable cats ever on this journey into the feline world, with legends of mighty warriors and wizards ... and a host of other wonderful cats sure to make any cat lover's fantasies come true.

☐ **TAILCHASER'S SONG** (UE2374—$4.95)
by Tad Williams

This best-selling feline fantasy epic tells the adventures of Fritti Tailchaser, a young ginger cat who sets out, with boundless enthusiasm, on a dangerous quest which leads him into the underground realm of an evil cat-god—a nightmare world from which only his own resources can deliver him.

DAW

Don't Miss These Exciting DAW Anthologies

ANNUAL WORLD'S BEST SF
Donald A. Wollheim, editor
- [ ] 1990 Annual   UE2424—$4.50

ISAAC ASIMOV PRESENTS THE GREAT SF STORIES
Isaac Asimov & Martin H. Greenberg, editors
- [ ] Series 18 (1956)   UE2289—$4.50
- [ ] Series 19 (1957)   UE2326—$4.50
- [ ] Series 20 (1958)   UE2405—$4.95
- [ ] Series 21 (1959)   UE2428—$4.95
- [ ] Series 22 (1960)   UE2465—$4.50

SWORD AND SORCERESS
Marion Zimmer Bradley, editor
- [ ] Book I   UE2359—$3.95
- [ ] Book II   UE2360—$3.95
- [ ] Book III   UE2302—$3.95
- [ ] Book IV   UE2412—$4.50
- [ ] Book V   UE2288—$3.95
- [ ] Book VI   UE2423—$4.50
- [ ] Book VII   UE2457—$4.50

THE YEAR'S BEST HORROR STORIES
Karl Edward Wagner, editor
- [ ] Series XVII   UE2381—$3.95
- [ ] Series XVIII   UE2446—$4.95

PENGUIN USA
P.O. Box 999, Bergenfield, New Jersey 07621

Please send me the DAW BOOKS I have checked above. I am enclosing $_____
(check or money order—no currency or C.O.D.'s). Please include the list price plus
$1.00 per order to cover handling costs. Prices and numbers are subject to change
without notice. (Prices slightly higher in Canada.)

Name _____

Address _____

City _____ State _____ Zip _____
Please allow 4-6 weeks for delivery.